ONE LITTLE LIE

WHITNEY BARBETTI

To Talon, for believing in me when I couldn't believe in myself

&

To Whitney B the First for going above and beyond, always

"But he who dares not grasp the thorn
  Should never crave the rose."

— ANNE BRONTË

THREE YEARS AGO

HOLLIS

IT STARTED WITH A NOTE.

"Adam. I loved your speech."

No name. No identifying markers besides those five words. Well, unless you counted the hastily drawn rose, and the petals that I had doodled under them. I wasn't an artist, that was for sure. I held that sticky note in my pocket for a long time, eventually transferring it to reside behind the mirror in my locker. I didn't actually have the courage to slip it into his locker until our shared class on Fairy Tales, Folk Tales, and Their Adaptations had long been over.

We were firmly in the second semester of our senior year, schedules packed with last-minute credits and classes that would look good on our final transcripts. I wanted to wait so that he wouldn't remember who was in that class with him. Not that I was particularly memorable, one way or another.

And the note itself was unremarkable, without context. But I knew what it'd taken for him to stand in front of a class full of jocks who were failing a class on fairy tales, to lay out his speech on the symbolism of the rose in *Beauty and the Beast*—the Disney version. "Roses ordinarily bloom slowly, taking their time to reveal their beauty."

If I was a fanciful person—and let's just say I was—I ached to be compared to a rose. Not because they were beautiful, but because they made you wait to witness that beauty. His entire speech had captivated me, but if I was being honest, Adam Oliver had fascinated me long before he stood in front of our class and spoke eloquently and beautifully about my favorite Disney movie.

We were eighteen, so my girlish crush and fascination with fairy tales were probably pathetic to some. Like the entire group of jocks, who laughed at him when the rest of us—the handful who had actually paid attention—clapped. The same guys who hadn't prepared their speeches and would ultimately fail the class laughed at Adam Oliver.

Though he'd held his head high as he returned to his seat, there had been a certain kind of defeat in Adam's eyes, a defeat that made my heart pinch. I had angled my chair away from the jocks who'd laughed and the circle of people I normally aligned myself with, most of whom had all but ignored Adam's speech. I wasn't sure which was worse: being ignored or being laughed at.

Which brought us to the day I decided to finally suck it up and slip the note into his locker. I had a free period that morning, which meant I would be able to slip it into his locker undetected after the bell rang. As casually as possible, I slid my hand under my locker mirror and pulled the note out, staring at it for a moment. There was a big party that weekend, at Seth McCauley's house, to celebrate the start of Spring Break. I didn't know if Adam would go, but I suspected he might. As the end of senior year approached, I felt compelled to stop being such a wuss. So I flipped the note over and wrote, "See you at Seth's this weekend." It kind of killed the brief part of the front of the sticky note, but I hoped that in putting it out there, I would actually suck it up and say hi to the guy I had crushed on for a pathetically long time.

"What's up, toots?" Tori asked, practically slamming into my locker door from the other side. I shoved the note under a textbook and turned to her. I confided in Tori a lot, but when it came to this—I just didn't feel like sharing.

"Nothing. Getting ready for my free period."

Tori opened my locker door, looking at her reflection in the mirror. "Oh, another thrilling hour in the library."

"There are a lot of good books in there," I said defensively.

Tori slid a tube of something shiny out of her purse and held it to me. When I shook my head, she shrugged and began applying it to her lips. "I bet there are. But I don't have a free period. I would get too bored. Probably wind up in trouble."

She wasn't wrong. Though academically gifted, Tori had never really outgrown her boy crazy phase. "Who is it this week?" I asked.

"Keane is looking hotttt," she said in a hushed voice.

"Haven't you—"

"Yes," she said, reading my mind. "Been there, hit that." She made a pucker with her lips and turned to me. "But there are only so many guys to choose from. Besides, it will be nice to see him this weekend."

"At Seth's?" I asked. I swallowed and tried not to sound too eager when I asked, "Is he going?" Keane was Adam's best friend. If Keane was going, that meant Adam would too.

"I'll make sure he goes." She tapped out a few words on her phone before putting it away. "What about you? Gonna go?"

I thought of the note, and stared at the textbook it rested under. "Yeah, I think so."

"Wanna pick me up?" She pulled out her phone and I heard it buzz in her hand.

I started to reply, but she waved her phone at me with a grin. "Keane will pick us up at my house."

I glanced sideways down the hall, where Adam's locker was. People milled about, but he wasn't there yet. "Okay," I told her, already feeling a nip of anxiety at the thought of riding with Keane—and potentially Adam too.

"I gotta head to class," Tori said, tugging one of my braids gently. "See you at lunch. Subway?"

I nodded, smiling at her, and waited until she was out of sight before pulling the note out again. The hallway was clearing as people rushed to their next classes, but I could take my time. My parents hadn't originally gone for having a break in my schedule until they realized that I would have more time to dedicate specifically to my studies. Plus, since it was a period in the middle of the morning, it wasn't like I could sleep in or leave school early.

I fingered the corners of the sticky note, debating if I wanted to do this. There was nothing about the note that said, WRITTEN BY HOLLIS VINKE, but I felt the nerves all the same. It wasn't like he even knew I existed, much less my specific handwriting.

The hallway was empty, save for a few stragglers whose backpacks were being filled and emptied. I thought of Adam's face, the shine that had gone out in his eyes upon being ridiculed. There'd been no question that he'd put his heart into that speech, that he'd spoken about something he'd actually believed. He was a musician—just another one of the band geeks in the eyes of every 'popular' clique in school, but that speech had shown passion. I had been too cowardly to say anything in class, and though the note was anonymous, I hoped it'd mean something to him.

So I slipped down the hallway, keeping my eyes on the

textbook in my hands, and paused just outside his locker. After a look in both directions, I pushed it in the crack of his locker and hurried to the library.

"You're not wearing that," Tori said when I showed up to her house on Saturday. "Are you?"

I looked down at my black jeans and blue tank. "What's wrong with it?"

"Well, since you're such a smarty pants, I'll just say that if I were to grade your outfit, it'd get a solid B."

"B for blue?"

"B for boring. Come on, Hols. I'll give you something out of my closet."

To some, Tori was no pushover. I liked to think of her as an indomitable force. She was confident, poised when need be, and she faced fear like it didn't exist. Basically, she was the opposite of me.

"Here," she said, shoving a slip of olive-colored lace at me.

"This looks like lingerie," I said, holding it up in two fingers. It was a tank top, made of some kind of satiny fabric, with matching lace around the low neckline. The straps were two strips of barely-there fabric.

"Put it on, tuck the front into your jeans. It'll look great with your tan."

I looked at her doubtfully and she crossed her arms over her chest, giving me an impatient look.

"I mean, if you want to wear your boring old tank top, that's cool."

I eyed the tank top I was wearing, noting that while it was clean and wrinkle-free, it lacked anything to make it even a little bit exciting. The lace-trimmed tank top, on the other hand, was far outside of my comfort zone. And wasn't that what I was going for, anyway? I had slipped a note all but inviting Adam to look for me at the party that night—which was so far out of my comfort zone that it was practically in another dimension. Probably the same dimension where I wore clothes like Tori's.

"Can you help me with my hair?" I asked her as I swapped tanks. My everyday ponytail, while sleek, made me look more like a mom than a senior in high school.

"That was my next suggestion." Tori's eyes gleamed as she led me into her bathroom.

Thirty minutes later, Keane texted Tori that he had arrived. I felt sweat break out immediately along my hairline, and when Tori snagged my hand to tug me along with her, I nearly slipped from her grasp from the sweat that prickled my palms.

I mean, maybe I was overreacting. Maybe Adam wouldn't even be riding with Keane. Maybe I had more time to acquire a bit more courage.

But that hope was shot down as soon as we stepped outside, seeing Adam in the passenger seat of the ride. And, judging by the flat look in his eyes as he observed us, he wasn't exactly thrilled we were joining him.

When the passenger door opened and Adam stepped out, I could only stare as he came to standing. He was a solid six inches taller than me, wearing all black and a scowl that was more than a little intimidating. "Hey, Tori!" Keane called enthusiastically as he leaned over and patted the now-empty front passenger seat. "Hey, Hollis. You okay to sit in the back with Adam?"

I eyed Adam, who was eyeing me.

"Su-sure." I sounded anything but sure. Adam was standing in front of the backseat door eyeing me for a minute, as Tori climbed up front where Keane was. I heard them giggle, but my focus was on Adam. He didn't look me up and down, but the look he gave me directly in the eyes told me he didn't like me. Which meant bringing up that note was probably ill-advised.

He was tall and lanky. Maybe a little on the thin side, but he had a presence that was commanding regardless. His tanned arms had little blips of tattoo ink, but his arms crossed over his chest like he was hiding them from my perusal. He had a broad, sharp jawline and a mouth that belonged to someone in a magazine spread. His dark eyes and dark, straight eyebrows only added to that effect. His entire look could be defined as: *musician, dark and brooding.*

And those eyes. They looked at me like he *knew* me. Which unsettled me, because we'd barely spoken a handful of words in the last ten years of going to schools in the same town. But as he held my gaze, I realized it was the first time we'd ever made meaningful eye contact. And *this* was how he was looking at me.

I tried not to let my uneasiness with him show, but the way he looked at me was making my neck heat, and pretty soon that heat would climb into my face and I would resemble a tomato.

"Adam, stop being a dick," Keane said and Adam stepped aside, gesturing for me to get into the backseat. But *why* was he being a dick? Why did he so clearly not like me?

A voice in my head told me he'd figured out I was the author of the note and took it as me mocking him. I had to tamp down on that runaway anxiety train before I blurted out that it had been a sincere and genuine gesture. Adam slid into the car beside me so I was sitting directly behind Keane.

"Have you been to Seth's parents' house?" Keane asked, looking in the rear-view mirror at me.

"Uh, no," I said. I didn't get out much.

"It's cool, right on the lake. We're going to take the boat out."

"Oh?" I asked, fanning my face. It *wasn't* hot outside. But being in such close proximity with Adam was making it feel like a sauna. "Can you turn on the air conditioning?" I asked, and felt three pairs of eyes look at me. Which, naturally, did nothing to lessen the anxiety I was experiencing.

Be cool, I told myself repeatedly. *This is fine.* "It's warm in here," I said.

"No, it's not," Adam said flatly. He was wearing scuffed black boots, black jeans, and a tight black tee. On his lap was a light jacket, black like the rest of his ensemble. And he was still staring at me. I summoned whatever dregs of courage I had and faced him.

"You don't have hair." I nodded to his buzzed head and then felt the cool blast of A/C toss my hair in front of my face. He couldn't argue with that.

He turned away first, eyes firmly focused outside the window as Keane took off toward Amber Lake. Keane and Tori were talking quietly—well, too quiet for me to hear over the roar of the stereo—which left me alone to stare outside the window on my side of the car. Not for the first time, I wondered why I thought I could go to the party and be someone other than who I was.

"Is that true?" Tori asked, turning in her seat so she faced us, not realizing we couldn't hear what she and Keane had been saying.

"Is what true?" Adam asked.

"The note?" Tori asked.

So, Adam knew it was from me.

My stomach sank and no level of air conditioning could fix the sweat that was surely dampening my hairline. *He told Keane?*

"Yeah," Adam said, and turned to Keane. "Why do you have to tell everyone everything, man?"

"I hardly think I am *everyone*, Adam," Tori said. She turned to me, her eyes lit up. "Adam has a secret admirer."

I let go of a breath as discreetly as possible. He didn't know. I was safe. Thank God, because whatever illusion I had that tonight would be the night I would reveal my secret crush on him was most certainly squashed the moment he first glared at me. "Oh?" was all I managed.

8

"It's nothing," Adam said, waving it off. It was clear he didn't want to talk about it, and I wondered if I did the wrong thing by giving it to him. I rubbed my sweaty palms on the knees of my jeans as Tori plowed on.

"Who do you think it is?"

Adam turned so slowly to face her and the contempt on his face would be obvious even if she wasn't wearing her contact lenses. "If I knew, it wouldn't be secret, would it?"

But Tori wasn't intimidated. "Well, what did it say? We can do a process of elimination."

Oh, no. Oh, no. Oh, no. While Tori didn't know I was the author of the note, she knew I was in that class with him. If Adam gave the context of the note, if he told her it had to be someone from that class, she would *know*. She knew I had a crush on him. Her eyes swung to me, questioning. I shook my head as casually as possible. I couldn't tell her it was me. No way.

"He won't say what it said," Keane butted in. "Just that there was a cartoon on it."

That seemed to satisfy Tori because she gave me an imperceptible nod—one that said, *Oh, it wasn't you.*

Like I said before, drawing was not a strong suit of mine. "Ah," she said aloud. "Who's an artist?"

"Beats me," Keane said.

"It doesn't matter," Adam said curtly. "Can we not talk about it?" He gave Keane a pointed look. And that line effectively muted the rest of the car ride to the party.

"Beer?" Tori asked as she pulled me through throngs of bodies half-heartedly dancing to music that could be barely heard above their voices.

I scrunched up my nose and shook my head. "Wine coolers?"

She shrugged and pulled me further into the kitchen, to the large double-wide fridge at the end of the room. She knew her way around the house, even as it was crowded with the population of our senior class. I guess when you were a frequent guest at parties like this one, you got pretty familiar with the layout.

It was my first time at a high school party, my first time at the home of a boy when I wasn't in the company of my parents. Despite being surrounded by people who were in my daily classes, I only knew maybe a handful of people at the party.

Tori pushed an ice cold glass bottle into my hands, then popped the top of the wine cooler like it was second nature to her. I envied her a little. Well, not her. But her experience. Her confidence. She had it in droves. All I had to offer was a mumbled, self-conscious thanks before I took my first sip of alcohol.

It was too sweet. That was what I thought at first, grimacing around the swallow. I was used to the artificial sweeteners of my favorite diet sodas that something as innocent as sugar-laden juice felt...heavy. This felt like sipping straight sugar. Tori, on the other hand, had downed half of hers as she smiled and waved at someone over my shoulder. I turned around, my gaze colliding with Adam Oliver. It was the first time since we got to the party that we'd seen each other—which meant it was the second time we'd made meaningful contact and ... yup, he still hated me. I looked him over for a reprieve from the staring contest that I would lose anyway, spying the beer in his hands as he lifted it. Which meant I was once again making eye contact with him.

He eyed the glass bottle in my hand and the side of his mouth quirked up in what I might almost take as a smile before his attention turned to Keane.

"We made out last night," Tori whispered, her breath hot on my ear. "Keane, I mean. It was *hot*."

I turned, smiling and took another sip of the liquid sugar. "That's why you ignored my texts last night?"

"Yeah, sorry. After the lacrosse game, under the bleachers. He's a great kisser." She said that not to brag, but as if in offering. "If you're looking…" she added. The infatuation with Keane was already losing its spark.

I laughed. Like Keane would give me a second glance, especially when I stood beside Tori. "I'm not." I braved another sip, but that one made my stomach turn and I knew I needed to give up the bottle sooner than later. Gross. "Losing interest already?" Asking it was pointless, but it kept her talking which kept my eyes from drifting to Adam.

"I mean, I'm not looking for a boyfriend, you know?" she said, and I believed her. "I just wanted to kiss someone. You know how it happens sometimes."

But I didn't, and she knew it. "Sure."

She laughed, drawing the attention of a few people from our class around us. Sweat prickled my brow, partly from the oppressive heat of so many bodies around us but mostly from the unwanted attention. I had tagged along with Tori to this party hoping she could pull me out of my shell a little, show me some fun before I spent the rest of the weekend buried in a book.

"Adam though," Tori said. She sucked in her bottom lip as she glanced over at Adam and Keane and my head turned, staring at them with her. Thankfully, Adam was no longer trying to murder me with his eyes, his attention having turned solely to Keane. Surely, Tori couldn't mean she wanted to make out with Adam, too?

"Relax, Hols." She laughed, clapping me on the back. "I know he's yours."

I bristled. "He's not mine."

"Okay, not in the physical sense but in the romantic sense." She tapped my forehead. "At least in here, he's yours. I'm not going near him with a ten foot pole." She drained her wine cooler and set it on the surface closest to her. "But it sounded like you had competition in the car." She raised an eyebrow.

"Here." I handed her my wine cooler, wanting to change the topic before the subject of the note was discussed in depth. "This is too sweet for me."

"Thought so. We should get you something else."

But I was already reconsidering the whole partying thing altogether. This wasn't my scene. I couldn't be blasé about partying like Tori could. She was the girl everyone talked to, and the girl who talked to everyone. She was better than most people, but didn't think of herself that way. So when people mistook her forwardness or self-confidence as arrogance, I was quick to correct them. Tori knew who she was. She knew what she wanted. Both combined made her years beyond most of us.

She met my eyes. "Well then, come on."

"Huh?" But I had barely said it before she was tugging me along once again, but this time in the direction of Keane and Adam. "Wait," I said, pulling back.

She whipped her head toward me. "Let's go talk to them," she said, placing emphasis on *them* because what she meant was *You should talk to Adam.* But this wasn't some sappy teen movie where the girl finally gained the courage to talk to the guy she'd swooned over from afar. Yes, I swooned over Adam. But he hated me.

"What happened to not going near him with a ten-foot pole?" I asked, both of us in a tug of war, my arm as the rope.

"Okay, I'll bring you to him and then I'll pull Keane away for some more lip service."

I groaned and used up all my strength to yank her toward me. "No way, Tori. No. Way. You cannot abandon me."

Her eyes glittered mischievously, but dulled when she saw the fear in mine. "Okay, fine, we'll just makeout in front of you so you'll have no choice but to open your mouth and actually say something to Adam."

"I can't just do that."

"What?" She laughed. "Talk? Sure you can. It's easy."

"Tori." My stomach churned and I pressed my free hand to it. "You saw how he looked at me. I can't talk to him while you're making out with Keane. I'm not you."

"Hey, he looked at me the same way as you. That's just who he is." She shrugged. "He's like a human-sized ball of steel wool. Abrasive as fuck. You just gotta talk to him. Once he gets to know you, he'll chill out." She put an arm around me. "Hollis, you are smart and funny and you work harder than anyone I know. He's gotta work for it if he deserves even a shot at talking with you. But let's try, anyway."

It was hard to see myself the way Tori saw me. Adam was practically mythical for me, someone I had admired from afar but had never had the guts to talk to. Adam was musical and a deep thinker and also he looked at you like he was looking through you, finding out your contents and determining if you were worthy. And he'd clearly made up his mind about me before tonight's party. I wasn't convinced that Adam would ever see the things Tori saw in me. "You can't abandon me," I made her promise. "Seriously, you can't."

"I won't. Only if I see an opening, okay?"

I groaned. "No. No way."

"Hollis." She put a hand on my shoulder and leaned down so our foreheads touched. "We are seniors. In two months, we're graduating. This is your chance to finally talk to the one guy you've ever had a lasting crush on."

"Ugh," I said on a sigh.

"Ugh all you want to me. But if I see an opening for you and Adam to get to actually have a conversation, I'm out of there." She held up her pinky. After a moment's hesitation, I looped my pinky with hers and let her pull me back through the throng of people to where Adam and Keane stood, just off the side of the dining room, near the door that led out to a deck. The door was open, letting a cool breeze ruffle my hair. When he turned, he looked at me with the eyes of someone judging me, deeming me to be someone I probably was not.

Why, of all the guys in the room, did he make me feel compelled to prove myself? He hadn't asked me to prove myself with words, but his eyes spoke more than his lips ever could. "Hey guys," Tori said, bumping playfully into Keane. His cheeks pinked and he glanced sideways at Adam before smiling more fully at her.

"Tori. See your taste in booze hasn't improved."

Tori laughed and rested her head on his shoulder, looking more natural than I could ever hope to feel in this environment. "Don't judge, mister Rocky Mountain spring water." She clinked bottles with him. "Sure there's any alcohol in that?"

"Ha-ha," Keane said and wrapped a free arm around her. Turning to me he said, "You look uncomfortable, Hollis. You okay?"

My cheeks warmed and I hated, ferociously, that I was so terribly transparent. "This is my first time at a party," I admitted, feeling pathetic.

"Really?" Keane asked incredulously. "You're a party virgin."

Well, there was zero doubt that my cheeks were solidly red then. "Pretty much."

At that admission, Adam's eyes slanted to mine and then to my empty hand, the hard line between his eyes smoothed out. "Where's your drink?" he asked.

I could hardly believe he was talking to me. He had initiated it. And there wasn't a lick of hostility in his voice, for once. He'd asked me a question and my tongue sat, thick like lead in my mouth.

"I got her one of these." Tori held up the wine cooler I had given her. "But they're too sweet."

"Ah." Adam looked back at me, gaze cutting right through me. "I don't much care for them either." After a moment's consideration, he reached his beer toward me, a question in his dark eyes.

I blinked so that my stare wasn't awkward or trancelike. "Your beer?"

"Do you want a beer?"

I stared at it for a moment, indecisive. I knew, thanks to many after school programs, not to take a drink from someone I didn't fully trust, but surely, since he had been drinking from the same bottle, I would be fine.

Tori elbowed me subtly in the ribs, so I reached for the beer, my pinky brushing over Adam's thumb as I took it from him. "Just a sip," I told Adam, hoping the sip would wash away the heat climbing my face. In the dim lighting of the dining room, his eyes looked blacker, but not cold. Instead, his gaze felt warm. If I was someone else, someone naturally romantic like my friend Navy, I might idealize the way he looked at me with beautiful words and feeling. The best I could come up with, to describe the way he looked at me, was as if I was the only person in front of him, the only person he wanted to look at, in the entire room.

But I wasn't idealistic even with my romantic tendencies. I knew romance was for books, for fiction.

I tipped the beer back and let it coat my tongue before bringing it back down. The taste, while somewhat unpleasant, didn't churn my stomach like the wine cooler had. The bubbles reminded me of my favorite soda, and the cool the beer left on my tongue made me wish for another sip.

But instead, I handed it back to Adam. He waited a second longer than I expected him to, and his pinky laid over the top of mine when he grasped the bottle. His eyes, the entire time, never left mine. Maybe it was my imagination, but he seemed calmer since the car ride. "Better?" he asked.

The beer hadn't done much to lighten my leaden tongue so I simply nodded. I *wanted* to talk to Adam. And I knew that having a little bit of booze might lower my inhibitions but it also might prevent me from remembering the way he looked at me, the way the light from the backyard made him glow like some kind of fallen angel.

Wow, I thought. The romance book I stayed up late to finish last night had infected my brain. Adam was no fallen angel. He was just a guy I had lusted after for the last handful of years, or so. And if for one night—or just this moment—his eyes were on mine, that didn't mean he was suddenly into me, too. I only needed to remember the way he'd glared at me outside of Tori's house to humble me.

"I'll get you a beer," Tori offered, nudging me again but less discreetly than before. I nodded, but regretted it immediately because seconds later, Tori and Keane were retreating back into the kitchen, their bodies disappearing among the others. Leaving Adam and me alone.

Adam was still staring at me, unnerving me in the quiet way he was good at. "Think they'll start dating?" he asked me.

I was so lost in staring at him that it took a minute for it to click what he was asking me. "Tori and Keane?"

He took my dumbly-spoken words to mean it was ridiculous. Which, it was, but my words were slow because I had barely been able to drag my attention away from him to think about anything else. "Yeah, you're right. Tori is too flighty."

"She's not flighty," I said, almost too defensively. When Adam arched one dark brow, I elaborated. "She's smart. She knows that high school isn't forever and indulging in serious relationships in a temporary environment will most certainly end in disaster."

The side of his mouth lifted as if I had said something that was funny. "Right," he said. "Flighty."

"That's not flighty," I argued. I checked the tone of my voice, not wanting to actually *argue* argue. Especially since he was finally starting to warm up to me. "She isn't going to make promises she can't keep. I guess I think of flighty as her leading Keane on, and I don't think she will."

His smile dropped away and he looked thoughtful for a moment. "Okay, you're right."

Why did that simple little statement light up like a tentative firework inside of me?

"So what about you?" he asked.

Again, I stared dumbly at him. "I'm not interested in Keane."

The smile appeared fully this time, sinking a delicious little dimple in his cheek. I was dumb struck. Adam was actually smiling at me. "I didn't think you were. Rather, I was wondering if you shared her opinion. About relationships."

This conversation was making me feel stupid. Not that it was Adam's fault—it was mine, for not being able to look at him and think clearly. "Uh…" I said. "I don't think I've given it much thought." And I hadn't. Not only because my life was ruled by the pressures of my parents, but also because it had never been an option for me—to think about dating seriously. "I'm not someone who dates."

"Are you asexual?"

"No," I said, but it sounded unconvincing. "I'm just busy."

"Because of your dad."

Bitterness rose from my throat, but he didn't deserve it. Not because he was right—which he was—but because it was a natural conclusion. My father's company employed many of the parents whose kids were at that party, which was probably why I sat like the odd man out from social events. I didn't want people to look at me and see my dad; his name or his clout or his power. But that's what happened. People looked at me like I was the police, like I had the power to tattle on them, to have it get back to their parents. The truth was that I didn't tell my father anything about people from school, and wouldn't have. When I caught Jacob Coleman smoking a joint in his car after school, he looked at me in fear but my dad never knew, so his parents never heard it from me. But being the daughter to someone of power meant you had very little power yourself in the way of making and keeping friendships.

When Jacob was eventually caught by his parents, he'd eyed me disdainfully every time we passed each other in the hallway, believing that it made more sense that I had tattled than that his parents would smell his cheap pot on his clothes and figure it out themselves.

Rumors got around about me, and though I pretended to be unaffected, I wasn't. It bothered me that I wasn't invited to parties, that I was always a tag-along. But at the same time, the ability to be a homebody was a relief. There were no social pressures in being a homebody.

"My parents do keep me busy," I hedged. I couldn't seem to figure out what to do with my hands, which wanted to fidget someway. In truth, I was dying for some caffeine, but the house was fully stocked with booze and not more innocent beverages.

As if he could read my mind, Adam handed me his beer again after he took a pull from it himself. I hadn't thought much about sharing his beer before, but putting my lips around the rim when his lips had just been in the same position did something funny to my thoughts, to the already unsteady beat of my heart. I took a longer pull this time. The taste was becoming more bearable and its coolness slid down my throat more comfortably.

"It's an acquired taste," he said when I handed it back to him.

"So is coffee, but I've never acquired it." I licked my bottom lip, already wanting more. Adam took a sip, not taking his eyes off of me.

"Never?" he asked.

I shook my head. "I love caffeine. It doesn't wake me up but it does keep me ... calm, I guess."

Adam handed me his beer again and I took it without hesitation this time, sharing his beer like this felt completely natural. Was the beer having an effect already? It was a light beer, which I knew meant the alcohol content was less than wine would be. So, maybe it wasn't the beer, but Adam's company instead.

As I tried to hand Adam his beer back, someone bumped into me from behind, sending me careening into Adam's chest, and the beer sloshing up out of the neck and onto us. His arm came around my back, steadying me, his other hand trapped between our bodies, clutching the bottle.

I looked up at him, close enough to see the perfect peaks of his cupid's bow. His long, dark lashes were lowered as he stared down at me and his hand was still on my back.

I pulled back first, leaning away from him, but still staying closer than I had before being pushed into him. After a beat, his hand left my back. I realized I didn't even know if *he* had a girlfriend, but I guessed—or, rather, hoped not—from the way he was looking down at me.

"We're covered in beer," he said.

I wiped the back of my hand over my chest, feeling the cool beer trickle down into my bra. Luckily, the olive lace of my tank hid most of the wet spill, like his black shirt had for him. "It's not a big deal. It's warm in here anyway."

He laughed. He actually laughed. One little chuckle before raising the beer. I could see the shadow of a freshly shaved jawline, and knew immediately that he'd be able to grow a beautiful beard if he wanted to.

"Here," Keane said, coming from the side and handing both of us beers. "Tori got roped into beer pong in the garage."

I searched Keane's face for any sign of disappointment. Adam's thoughts about Tori being flighty had stuck in my brain and I was relieved when Keane appeared indifferent about Tori abandoning him. "Since I finished my one beer, I'm done for the night. But I left my sodas in the car," he told Adam. "I'll be back."

Which left us alone again. "Sodas?" I asked Adam, trying to fill the silence.

"He's the DD. He's drinking some god-awful energy drink."

I nodded and twisted the top off my beer at the same time Adam twisted the top off of his and then he tossed his empty bottle into a bin behind him. I bit back the brief bit of disappointment over not sharing his beer anymore but then he grabbed my hand like it was just as natural as sharing a beer. "Let's go outside," he said, already leading me out the back door before I could object. Not that I would.

He threaded us through groups of people until we were at the far corner of the deck, where a tiki torch flamed brightly. He neatly stacked up a pile of discarded plastic cups and set them away from the bench that wrapped the length of the deck, gesturing for me to sit.

Though the seat was cold, it was an incredible relief against the oppressive heat of having that many bodies in that small of a space.

"Aren't you hot?" I asked Adam, nodding at his leather jacket.

"Aren't you cold?" The back of his hand touched my bare arm and I shivered from the touch.

"No," I said. "It feels good after being in there." I took a drink, hoping to come up with something to say that didn't involve Tori, Keane, or the weather. But the thoughts that had rested on the tip of my brain since he said his first word to me at the party poured out of my lips, unbidden. "Don't you hate me? Or something? Why are you being nice now?"

"Hmm." He took a drink and looked out over the deck, where people were assembling around a keg. The music was quieter out here, so I could hear Adam swallow. "I don't really like to think I hate anyone."

But it'd be understandable if he did, for all the grief others at school gave him. "Okay. How about *deeply loathe*?"

He laughed and stretched his legs out in front of him, pulling his jacket off and setting it on his lap. "I had an opinion of you. Have." He looked sideways. "Or maybe had. I'm still working out if it's past tense or not."

"And what is that opinion?"

"That you're just like everybody else."

"But I'm not."

"That remains to be seen. But I'm inclined to agree with you."

"I think I would know who I am."

"But do you?" He motioned toward the crowd by the door. "You're always in those groups of people." I knew *those people* was referring to the ones who tormented him. Adam didn't follow the popular track of high school. He did what mattered to him, regardless of how it made him look to other people.

"I'm still an individual."

"But you're a part of the noise when groups of people do shitty things and you don't stand out from it."

"What do you mean?"

He leaned back, settling in. "I mean that I've been bullied in my life. I don't let it bug me too bad, but when you're silent while witnessing that kind of behavior, you're no better than the ones doing the bullying. Silence makes you complicit."

"But I don't agree with what they do," I argued.

"Do you say anything?" He raised an eyebrow.

No, I didn't. I was a wallflower, staying against the wall. "All right. That's fair," I finally said. "But, do you speak up every time you see someone else being belittled?"

"Yes." He said it immediately. "Mob mentality is real. And the bullshit on social media makes it ten times worse. Rumors start and spread like an infestation via photos or comments and that shit is toxic."

I agreed with him. Which was why the only things on my own social media were boring. "You said that you're deciding whether or not I'm like everyone else," I said. "And what do you think so far?"

"I hope not."

"So, okay, what made you decide that I'm maybe not like everyone else?"

"When you said this was your first party." He tipped his beer back and raised an eyebrow at me. "It's my first one too."

"What?" I couldn't believe that. Adam might not run in the same circles as the people who hosted this party, but he was Keane's friend. Who was Tori's friend. Who attended all the parties. "But you and Keane…"

"Come on, Hollis. Is it so unbelievable that someone like me, a veritable 'band geek,'" he held up air quotes, "has been to many high school parties? Why would I want to hang out with most of these people?"

But he didn't look like some band geek cliché, ripped from the movies we'd grown up on. He looked like someone who stayed up late at night, scribbling music onto coffee-stained pages. He looked dark, maybe a little dangerous. Tori's assessment of him being steel wool was on the nose. "So, the reason you glared at me was because you thought I was like the rest of them?"

He nodded.

"You looked like you hated me."

"You looked like everyone else."

"But I'm not," I insisted. "And," I took a deep breath, saying, "I don't have to convince you of that." And then I held my breath.

There was a change in his face after I said that. Whatever it was, some kind of understanding settled in. He didn't scoff. He didn't laugh. "You're absolutely right, Hollis Vinke. I have to say, I respect you more for saying that." He winked. He actually winked at me. My heart did a little flutter, a flip flop, and I forced myself to keep it cool. It was totally surreal that this guy I had liked for years, who I had only admired from a distance like some lovesick loser, was talking to me. And actually interested in what I had to say.

"That was my assumption of you, that you were like the rest of the assholes in school. To be fair, you never ever speak up."

He wasn't wrong. I felt safer on the sidelines, a member of the audience than a player. "That's true. But if you were in my position, you might be the same way."

"And what position is that?"

I winced, not wanting to talk about my dad. Talk about a buzzkill. "I have an image I have to maintain. At least until college."

"And why do you have to maintain it? Why can't you be your own person?"

"I am my own person." But was I? He was right; I did follow the crowd. I stayed in the back, largely forgotten. There was safety in that. For myself and for the reputation my family expected me to uphold.

"Why do I get the feeling that you don't like talking about yourself?"

I knew I blushed then; could feel the warmth flood my cheeks as I fumbled over what to say. When words failed me, I just nodded and looked down at my beer.

"It's okay, Hollis. Here, I made an unfair assumption of you. Let's even the score: you make one of me."

Oh, no. This was going to creep on dangerous territory. I couldn't make any assumptions about him without revealing how I viewed him. I shook my head. "No, that's okay. I get it. I understand why you might think I'm like them." I looked over at the handful of guys egging each other on to drink more, to obliterate themselves. "I can admit that I probably get swallowed up by those kinds of people."

"Yeah, because you don't use your voice."

It was something Tori always told me. She urged me not to let her steamroll right over me, to stand up for myself. But it was easier to fall into the crowd, even if you didn't agree with them all the time. "I'm working on it."

"I can tell. This is the most we've spoken since, when? Elementary school."

"Probably." I took a sip of my beer, hoping it'd help calm my nerves around him.

"So, Hollis," Adam began before I could swallow. "What awaits you after high school?"

Was he genuinely interested? I wondered. Or was it just a way to avoid awkward silence?

Someone stumbled against the side of the railing, sending reverberations down to where we sat. "I don't know," I said, leaning forward. "I mean, I know what's expected of me, but I haven't made any definite plans. You?"

"I'm getting the hell out of here." It didn't surprise me. I knew—everyone knew—that Adam possessed too much talent to just waste away in our modest little city. He was destined for more, for bigger things, and I ached to have that same kind of calling. "I think Los Angeles is what everyone expects, but I want to go east."

"New York?" I asked, trying not to let disappointment color my voice. In all the years Adam Oliver and I had attended school together, I had never once had a conversation with him the way I was now. I didn't need to feel some misplaced sense of loss when there was nothing for me to grieve.

"Maybe not that far. I've got a kid sister and my gram to look after here."

I knew better than to ask about his parents. His mom had died a couple of years back and everyone talked about his dad. In middle school, the stop sign at the crosswalk had been taken out by Adam's dad one night when he'd had too many drinks. Being that Amber Lake was a smallish town, everyone knew who'd caused it. And Adam, being the son of the guy who had messed up, publicly, many times, had been the butt of many jokes.

I never engaged in that kind of gossip myself, but I hadn't ever taken action to shut it down either. I felt shame, knowing how many conversations I had listened to and remained silent. Too afraid to rock the boat, to even so much as whisper my disagreement.

"You went quiet." His voice was low and beckoning. I met his eyes, saw them searching mine. Much like he had when we'd he'd first greeted me that night, though with none of the contempt he'd held then.

I licked my lips, feeling my breath go heavy as he continued to stare at me. His arm was resting behind me, along the railing. If I leaned back just a few inches, I knew I would feel his arm on my back, the skin that was bared by this pathetic excuse for a tank top. But I couldn't be that brazen, could I? I licked my lips again and this time, his eyes dipped to them and then slowly he looked back into my eyes. I took a breath in, feeling my chest lift and fall in an irregular cadence and every single inch of me came alive like a firework. He looked back at my lips and when he met my eyes again, the crooked smile on his lips nearly undid me. Holy Hannah. Was this sexual tension? I had never felt anything like this. I had little practice in romance, and even less in sexual contact of any kind. My inexperience caused a flurry of feeling to gather in my head: indecision, excitement, and impatience.

When we first sat beside each other, there hadn't been anything intimate about our position. But at some point in our conversation, I had turned my body his way and he'd turned his way to me. In the few inches that separated our thighs rested his hand, close enough that I could feel the cool condensation of his glass wetting my jeans.

But then, in the lightest of touches, I felt his thumb graze my spine. And I did something unheard of for me, I leaned into it.

His head moved in closer—maybe not for a kiss, maybe just for conversation. But I wouldn't ever know what his intention was, because seconds later, a guy double my size fell on top of me, spilling more beer onto my shirt as his beer poured over my head.

"Fuck, Conway!" Adam exclaimed, pulling Ben Conway off of me as I adjusted to the cool shock of the beer completely soaking my tank and dripping down my face. "Get a handle on yourself."

Ben was obviously drunk, based on the way he swayed violently to the side, nearly falling over until Seth, the party host himself, righted him. "Fuck you, Adam," Ben said, but the words were slurred together. He pushed back at Adam, but his hands had the effect of dead fish and Adam didn't budge. He shoved Ben again, and he fell back into his crowd of friends.

I was completely still, feeling the sting of embarrassment on my chest and neck—all of which were visible in this tank. I could feel a dozen people staring at me, but the shock of being completely soaked rendered me unable to stand up and brush it off. I didn't have a spare shirt, and I knew I must reek now. I wanted to go home. I couldn't take the stares, the gossip that was already brewing.

Before I could say anything, Adam was draping his leather jacket over my shoulders and steering me away from the people on the deck. Even with the jacket as protection, I couldn't seem to control my reaction. My eyes filled for a moment, even as I blinked the tears back.

"Asshole," Adam said under his breath as we moved to the front yard, right by a tree that was illuminated by a flood light. "I'm so sorry, Hollis."

"Why are you apologizing?" I said, my lips trembling from cold and humiliation. I couldn't reconcile this Adam, this caring and sincere Adam, with the Adam I'd spoken to hours earlier. He'd switched so fast that even if I hadn't just been doused in beer, I might still be a little shell-shocked.

I couldn't even look at him. I knew my hair was soaked, my shirt was soaked, and I had no idea how I was going to sneak this by my parents. Beer dripped into my eyes and stung, so I squeezed them tight but then a tear slipped out. This was probably the most embarrassing moment of my life. And the one guy I had crushed on forever got to witness it and the impending emotional explosion. I turned away from him, my fingers pulling the leather jacket tight around me. I wanted to burrow in it, to hide from everyone. But the smooth leather smelled like him and I was brought momentarily back to what just had happened. "Here," I said, reluctantly pulling the jacket off of me. "I don't want this to be ruined."

"Shut up, Hollis." He took the jacket from me and then grabbed one of my arms and shoved it through the arm hole. "Think I give a damn about the stupid jacket getting beer on it? You're shivering."

Tears spilled from my eyes. I wanted to snag Tori and run away from here, with my tail tucked between my legs. I would settle for melting into the giant pine tree at my back, but Adam had a firm grip on my elbows.

"Hollis," he said, softer this time and clucked my chin up so he could look at me. I opened my eyes a moment and saw his concern. His eyes were twin black hole abysses, his eyebrows furrowed in concern. He was so beautiful. Poetic, in the way he looked at me.

His hands slid to cup my jaw and he stepped closer. I couldn't even focus on him, not when I was so worried about how I must have looked. His breath washed over my face, but not in an unpleasant way. He was close enough to kiss me. And that sent my heart into a gallop. "Are you okay?"

We stared at each other one long moment. It could have

been romantic, the way he held me, blocking much of the floodlight with his body. This was the moment, the time for something to happen. A little lean in and he could kiss me.

A droplet of ice cold beer slid down my spine and I arched in reaction. This wasn't a moment from one of my books, nor was it a moment from any of the fairy tales I heavily consumed as a child. Adam hated me. I was soaked in beer and too embarrassed to ever admit that the note he received was written by me. The moment was ruined. And I was grieving as much for that as I was the fact that so many of our classmates had witnessed arguably my most embarrassing moment ever. And I had done nothing.

2

ADAM

SHE RESISTED, PULLING AWAY FROM ME.

I wanted to go back to that fuckhole Ben and remind him of the time I nearly kicked his ass last year for similar behavior after a Friday night football game. After spilling his contraband booze all over a row of girls in front of him, he'd just fucking laughed. Back then, I had grabbed him by the collar and shoved him hard against the back of the bleachers, hard enough to create a ripple effect that caused dozens of eyes to turn to us. Because I hadn't needed to get busted for fighting, I had let him go. But there was no one here to keep Ben safe. I mean, apart from the half a dozen meatheads who worshipped him, that was.

Hollis shivered so fiercely that it moved the ground beneath our feet.

"I just want to go home," she said, and I heard the tremble in her voice. I was mad at Ben, not just for humiliating Hollis but interrupting the conversation I hadn't known I needed.

"Okay," I agreed. "I'll go find Tori." I pulled the sides of the jacket so they were covering her front, and she crossed her arms over her chest. Her head was down so all I could see was her forehead, and the beer that dripped down it.

She only managed a nod, so I took her by the shoulders and pulled her in for a hug. There was no doubt she was embarrassed, and it took her several long moments until I felt her hands at my sides, holding me close. I nearly pulled away, but felt her fingers sinking into my t-shirt, holding on like she needed it.

That action from her emboldened me to run my hand over her hair, dampness be damned. She needed a warm blanket, so I made a mental note to snag one from the living room inside. I waited until I felt the give in her grasp before stepping back and giving her one last squeeze. "I'll be right back," I promised.

But once I got inside the house, I realized that promise wouldn't be fulfilled. The house was packed. Wall to wall with people, so many that people stood on the stairs just for room to talk. There was music and yelling and cheering from the kitchen and it was complete auditory overload.

I shoved my way through the bodies, looking in vain for Tori's gold locks or Keane's unruly brown hair. The house had grown darker as the sun has slipped beyond the lake and what few light fixtures were on made most of the partygoers look like they all had dark hair.

Someone grabbed me and then laughed when I turned around. "Wrong person," they said just as I was knocked to the side from behind me. All this jostling was pissing me off, knowing that Hollis was waiting outside in the cold and I had barely made it five feet through the front door.

It was probably too loud for Keane to hear his ringtone, but I tried calling him anyway. And it was no surprise when it kicked over to the voicemail. I didn't have Tori's number, but even if I did I would be surprised if she heard her phone either.

So I kept shoving bodies and after a little bit of time I made it to the kitchen. It, surprisingly, was the least crowded place in what I had seen so far of the house. A few people were drunkenly making sandwiches on the island, but otherwise the rest of the space was empty. Which meant I would have to search upstairs.

If I hadn't been drinking, I would have seen Hollis home myself, maybe calling my Gram to help me. But the last thing Gram needed was to worry over me drinking, to see her son— my father—reflected all over again. I tried calling Keane again, and when it was still unsuccessful, I braved making my way through the people to the stairs. It was absolutely fucking miserable in the house, and it was unbelievable to me that anyone would want to hang out in this space for more than a few minutes. None of the people crowding the space seemed to in any hurry for the fresh air the backyard offered. They were body to body, some even holding drinks above their heads as they swayed to the obnoxiously loud music.

I loved music. I lived, I breathed, I dreamt music. But this wasn't simply music. This was a cacophony.

After what felt like a lifetime, I made it to the stairs and gave up being polite, shoving through people—guys mostly—as quickly as I could. I hadn't seen Keane exit to the outside while Hollis and I had been out there chatting, so I hoped to find him upstairs. And Tori too.

At the landing, the sound was quieter, but still fucking loud enough to obliterate a few eardrums. I opened closed doors and stepped through open doorways, to no avail. It wasn't until I made it down the hallway, to the last door, that I knocked before opening. And sure enough, Keane was in there. And so was Tori.

"What the fuck, Adam," Keane said, and I averted my eyes from Tori, who was topless, focusing my attentions on him. He struggled into his pants and glared at me as he tried to zip them over his erection. It wasn't the most compromising way I had ever found my best friend, but it sure ranked up there.

"I've been looking for you," I said, not wanting to waste a minute.

"You could at least look away," Tori said as she lazily scooped up her bra from the floor.

Putting my hand to the side of my head, I shielded my eyes from her and looked at Keane, whose eyes said he was ready to murder me. "We need to get Hollis home."

"Is she okay?" I heard Tori ask from the other side of my hand.

"She was drowned by Ben Stafford's beer. The fucker was double fisting and fell on her."

Tori gasped and I heard a flurry of emotion. "Where is she?"

"Out front. But the path to the front door is insanely crowded. I would go out of the kitchen door if you want to get out of here."

She was out the door before I could follow her and Keane hurriedly tied the laces of one of his shoes, the glare gone from his eyes.

"I thought you were done with the Tori shit. You kept bitching about how she leads you on," I said, picking up his other shoe from across the room and bringing it back to him.

"She just wants casual," he said, shoving his foot into the second shoe. "It was my bad thinking she wanted something more."

"She's heading far away, Keane. Did you think she'd actually stick around, abandon her college plans?"

Keane glared at me, but it slipped away from his face just as face as it had come on. "I guess I thought maybe I was different for her."

"If you're gonna hold onto that ill-conceived hope, you should probably *not* try to fuck her at random parties." I clapped him on the back. He'd been hung up on Tori for the last couple years, but I knew she'd only seen him in a friendly sort of way. "There will be girls at school," I told him. "In a few months, you'll be saying 'Tori who?'"

Keane eyed me glumly. "Doubt that. Especially when my wingman is gone."

"You don't need a wingman," I told him, skirting the topic of me leaving."

He looked down at my chest and then at my face. "You fucking reek, dude."

"Did you miss the part about Hollis being soaked in beer? I gave her my jacket, but she's waiting outside for us. So calm your dick and hurry up, okay?"

I left him and started down the stairs when I was stopped by someone with a hand to my chest. I could only see a head of blonde hair, so short she was. She wrapped an arm around my waist, but I had been so focused on getting back to Hollis that I was momentarily dumbfounded as to who this was.

"I've been looking for you," her voice purred.

"Oh yeah?" I asked uneasily as I wracked my brain for who it could be. I pulled her from me and she lifted her chin. I had a straight look down the front of her low-cut and very tight shirt and quickly looked into her face instead.

"Hey, Kate."

Her smile curled, blood red lips smiling in a way that felt predatory. I tried to ease back from her hold, but she was totally clamped onto me. "Were you looking for me?"

Speaking of leading on, I had my own situation on my hands. But unlike Keane, I was all too ready to shake Kate loose. We'd gone on one date—if you could even call it that. I didn't. We'd caught a quick bite to eat at her parents' restaurant after a lacrosse game in the spring and she'd attacked me with her mouth in the car as I drove her home, her hands all over the crotch of my pants like her hands and my dick were meant to be best friends.

Don't get me wrong; I was an eighteen-year-old guy with a healthy sexual appetite. But Kate hadn't really done it for me. We'd spent the longest twenty minutes of my life at her family's restaurant talking about her college plans, with no mention of my plans for post-high school life. She was interested in having a boyfriend as long as that boyfriend didn't actually have things to say.

"Actually, I'm looking for Hollis … Vinke." I didn't know why I included her last name. Everyone knew who Hollis was—she was the only person with her name.

Kate's nose wrinkled. "I thought you hated that bitch," she said with an undoubtable pout.

"I … don't." Maybe I had, at one time. Maybe I had lumped her in with the rest of them—the people who'd doused her in beer and hadn't even asked her if she was okay. But I wasn't going to get into it with Kate here on the stairs. I had wasted enough time just getting up the stairs to find Tori and Keane and I didn't want to waste another minute standing here, talking to someone who had no interest in me besides the fact that I played the piano. And I only knew she was interested in that, because she'd said how hot it made her only a dozen or so times that night she'd tried to rip my dick from my pants. I was no ace in science classes, but even I knew the chemistry between us just wasn't there. Or, if it was, it was entirely one-sided. "I gotta go outside," I said, trying to move around her, but her arm was clamped firmly around my middle.

"You never called me back." She pouted again and ran her hand over my chin. I worked not to appear completely repulsed by that unwelcome touch, but internally my anger was building. I clearly wanted out of her hold, but her own aggression was keeping me rooted to the spot.

"Look, Kate. You're great, but I'm just not interested." I said it quickly, hoping the ripping-off-the band-aid delivery would lessen her hurt.

And it did, for a moment and her hand dropped from my face. Her eyes went sad and her pout rivaled any toddler's. "Your dick sure seemed interested."

I pinched the bridge of my nose. "It's a dick," I said by way of explanation, though it was a weak one. Had my dick gotten hard as she'd messily groped it? Sure. But had I done anything about it? No. My dick had stayed locked into my pants like it was fucking Fort Knox, and Kate had crossed her arms over her chest and pouted the rest of the way to her house. "I'm sorry, Kate." I almost said the unbearably cliché, *Let's be friends* line before I thought the better of it. I tried to pull away again and her arm came up, turning so she showed me the fresh ink on her forearm. I peered at it with no little bit of interest, because of its distinctive shape.

"Look at this," she said, and she looked completely miserable as she showed off the rose tattoo just below her elbow. "You like *Beauty and the Beast*, right?"

I had tunnel vision. *She* wrote the note? I tried to reconcile that secret little note I'd seen in my locker, the crude but thoughtfully drawn rose doodled on the front. I had thought someone had listened to my speech and had felt some connection to it.

She hadn't gotten the tattoo to impress me, had she? I never once intimated that I wanted to further get to know her, in a romantic or even a friendly way, but that tattoo made me think she'd assumed a connection that didn't exist. Fuck.

I replayed Kate's words in my head, *You like Beauty and the Beast, right?* It just hadn't been as simple as liking the movie. My speech hadn't been on the movie or the story, but the symbolism of its famous wilting rose.

"The note?" I hedged, wanting an answer.

But she didn't get a chance to answer because my last name boomed from someone's mouth at the bottom of the stairs, and I turned my attention to it.

"I should kick your ass, band geek," Ben said, flanked by two of his friends. They looked warily at me before looking at their buddy, clearly not totally Team Ben's Rage. As far as insults went, *band geek* was an unoriginal one, but it succeeded in doing what he'd intended. A few people had laughed, and some repeated *band geek* like an echo.

"Kick *my* ass? Why? Because you can't hold your liquor?" Many of the people inside hadn't witnessed what he'd done to Hollis, which was evident by the laughs and cheers for Ben.

"Why are you even at this party, band geek? A little above you, isn't it? Did your dad drive you here?" Ben turned to Seth, the host. "Might want to make sure that stop sign is still at the end of your road, Seth. This one's dad is known for taking them out." He pointed a thumb back at me.

That got me. I could deal with being called a band geek. I could deal with jokes about me not being one of the rich kids. But talking about my dad was off-limits. The thing was, I knew my dad was a royal fuck up. I was embarrassed of him. But I wouldn't be like him.

A movement out the corner of my eye had me turning, my gaze colliding with Hollis's. Judging by the progress she'd made into the room full of people, she had to have been there for at least a few minutes. But it wasn't her position in the room I was most surprised by. It was her complete lack of emotion.

Ben and Seth were trading stories about my dad—who was infamous in this small town—but Hollis wasn't saying anything, one way or another. The girl who'd told me she wasn't like the rest of them was silent. And, what was worse, whatever feeling I had seen in her eyes under the moonlight an hour earlier was gone, replaced by something much worse: indifference.

There wasn't an ounce of remorse in her eyes as the half-dozen guys taunted me. She remained silent, still wearing my fucking jacket as she observed the scene from the across the room. Doing nothing.

She *was* the same person I had initially pegged her as. She'd fed me lies I had impatiently gulped down—so eager for a connection that I had believed her lies. I'd wasted my time getting to know her, and I'd felt bad for her for a minute. But I wouldn't anymore. And I vowed then and there, to never drop my guard around anyone, least of all her.

3

NOW

HOLLIS

TORI LEANED INTO ME, HER GLASS OF WINE SLOSHING DOWN HER wrist. "David DeBier's mom is looking at you like you're a snack."

I followed her line of vision and wrinkled my nose. "She is married."

Tori made a nose like that was of little consequence and shook her head. "Well, okay, first of all, have you seen her husband? I have little doubt she wouldn't ditch his cheating ass for your fine piece with little convincing." She sighed and sipped. "Besides, I didn't mean you were a snack for *her*." She waggled her eyebrows and I frowned.

"David is not on my radar and never will be," I murmured.

"Of course not. Your *boyfriend* kind of complicates that, doesn't he?" she teased.

I gave her a warning look.

"Oh, don't be a wet blanket." She leaned back fully on the

sofa in my parents' basement and tugged me down to huddle with her. "Brilliant move, by the way. Pretending to have a boyfriend just to avoid being set up. Can't believe they've bought it for this long."

I casually glanced over my shoulder to ensure my parents weren't able to overhear us. "Yeah, well, I'm a genius sometimes."

"Don't they ask why he's never on your Instagram? Or Facebook? What's that saying? 'If it's not on Facebook, it didn't happen.'"

I rolled my eyes at her. "That's a stupid saying."

"Only because you don't live and die by social media. Speaking of…" she held her phone up in front of us and nudged me. "Act like you actually like me, Hols."

"I do like you, for the most part," I said mildly. "When you've been imbibing, the *like* meter is just a bit lower." I tapped her nose and she nudged me again, so I did my duty and smiled for the photo.

"Loosen up, Hols. It's your first summer party at your parents' where you can actually drink."

"Someone has to drive you home. If I drink, my parents will insist on us staying the night."

Tori coughed on the gulp of wine she'd just taken. "You're right, you are a fucking genius." She pushed her long, honey-colored locks from her face and blinked up at me. "For real, though. How do you explain the fact that you have zero selfies with him on the 'gram?"

I shrugged, watching Mrs. DeBier's movement in my periphery. She circled us like a shark wanting to move in for the kill. When she was safely out on the patio, along with the rest of my parents' guests, I turned to Tori. "I don't post anyone on my social media. Not even my sloppy best friend."

"Hey." She jutted her chin out defensively. "I'm only sloppy when the alcohol is free."

"When is the alcohol *not* free for you?" I laughed.

"If you didn't have a fake boyfriend and a real aversion to the alcohols, you too could benefit from a free drink now and again." She tugged my hair. "Hols, you're so pretty. For real. You shouldn't waste your time with fake people when the real thing is so much better."

"I tried that," I said. I thought of high school, when dating had been fun. For a few weeks. But my reputation for being a brown-nosing bitch preceded me, and thus made me someone that guys weren't interested in. When you were surrounded by people as gorgeous as Tori and my other friends, it was easy to disappear. Which was the way I liked it, anyway. "Besides, the moment I'm *on the market,* my dad will drag me to all of his shindigs and make sure I snag someone he approves of."

"You're his show pony."

"Basically." I sighed and wished, for a second, I could have even a little bit of Tori's carefree nature. To not be worried about anything, to go with the flow and still succeed beyond my wildest imaginations sounded like something out of a daydream. But it was Tori's reality. Not that she hadn't worked for it; she had. She'd graduated college early and now had the luxury of spending a year camped out her parents' place until she figured out what to do with her life. And still, she was easily the most chill person I had ever known.

"Oooh," Tori said. "Adam Oliver liked my photo." She waggled her eyebrows at me and I controlled my face to show no emotion.

"Adam..." I said, pretending to try to place him.

"Ha," Tori said, her attention on me. "We're going to play *that* game? Let me refresh your memory." She thrust her wine glass in my hand and then grasped hair on either side of her head, pulling so she tied it under her chin. Her eyes half-closed and she had the look of someone floating in a daydream. "'I'll take *his dick* for five-hundred. Who is, Adam Oliver.'"

I shoved her, not needing that reminder. "Shut up."

"Okay, how about the notebook you carried through middle school? The one scrawled with *Hollis Oliver* in your best script."

My cheeks warmed. "You're so mean sometimes."

"Remember how we'd go to the sub shop practically every weekend in the summer just so you could stare at him as he layered on your cucumber slices just so?" She sounded breathy and silly and I couldn't help but laugh with her.

"You're awful."

"Yeah, you're hot for Adam Oliver."

"I *was* hot for Adam Oliver. The distinction is important." Because Adam might have found me silly in middle school and part way into high school, but he certainly hated me by the time graduation rolled around. And I couldn't blame him.

"You're still hot for him."

"I am not."

"Oh geez, Hollis. You're as transparent as water."

I crossed my arms over my chest but then uncrossed them when I realized how childish I probably looked.

"That's why Mr. Fake Boyfriend is a piano player, isn't it?" I gave her a warning look, but she had snapped her wine glass back and polished it off. "Come on, admit it."

"Adam plays the keyboard, for a band, a thousand miles away. He's not exactly traveling the world as a solo act."

A Cheshire Cat grin split Tori's lips, and her eyes sparkled. "Look at you. I didn't know you knew so much about Adam Oliver."

"I don't," I insisted, and played with the hem of my shirt. "But he played piano in high school, so of course I knew that about him."

"And you know he's in Colorado. You're not even friends with him. So how do you know so much about Adam?"

I shrugged again, hoping I was playing it cool when I replied, "People talk. I've heard stuff."

"From who? You don't have friends."

Her biting commentary was bordering on aggravating. "You're really going for the jugular?" But again, she wasn't wrong. "Okay, fine. I might've looked him up. Is it really that surprising, since I was once so embarrassingly lovesick for him?"

"No it's not. But since your information is outdated, why don't I enlighten you a bit? He's back in town."

My heart thudded painfully loud. "No. He's not."

"Yes." Her grin spread wider and I recognized the plotting look in her eye. "He is. You can make a move, and then boom— you two are a something. No more fake boyfriend bullshit." She winked and I took her empty wineglass from her, setting it down on the console table behind the couch.

"That's enough wine for you. When you dissolve into ill-conceived and impossible plans, that's how I know you're too far gone."

"Psh." She rolled her eyes. "My ideas are great. You don't need to be a wet blanket."

Ouch. It struck a nerve to have her say that about me. It was the reason I had to make up a fake boyfriend. I was impossibly shy around guys I didn't know, awkward and insecure. Compared to Tori, I was boring. Bland. Which was one of the reasons I gravitated to her. I had a theory that people were closest with those who possessed qualities they wished to emulate. Just not in a *Single White Female* kind of way. I wanted to be carefree and fun like Tori was, and maybe I thought spending time with her would make me more fun.

At my wince, Tori wrapped an arm around my shoulders and pulled me close. "Sorry, that was a real dickish thing for me to say."

"It was." I didn't lean into her hold for a long moment.

"I know you can't help it. Your dad." For the first time, Tori became aware of her surroundings, looking around like my dad was lurking, waiting to analyze our conversation. "I would just love for you to emerge from your shell, reveal the beautiful butterfly that you're hiding."

"Butterflies come from cocoons, not shells."

She waved that off. "You knew what I meant, smartypants." But it was Tori who was the smartypants, not that she rubbed it in your face. She had recently graduated college a whole year ahead of the rest of us. The difference between us was that Tori was easily bored, and finished school quickly to avoid dropping out all together. Tori brushed back my hair and smiled sadly at me before lowering her voice. "It's your senior year, Hollis. This is the time to let everyone see you, the way the rest of us get to."

"Which is why I'm rooming with Navy." It was a small wedge between Tori and me at that moment. The fact that I had chosen to room with my good friend Navy, someone Tori merely tolerated for my sake. They were my two closest friends, but polar opposites in attitude.

"Ugh." Tori slumped back against the sofa with no small amount of drama. "You and that little fairy of happiness, out on the town. When I said I wanted you to get out more, I meant to parties, not to the soup kitchen."

"What's wrong with the soup kitchen?"

"Nothing. But what's wrong with parties?"

I sighed. "I like soup kitchens."

"Of course you do, you baby angel." She tucked my hair again, but it felt mildly patronizing so I leaned away from her. "Nothing is wrong with soup kitchens, duh. It's selfless of you, to spend your free time—what little you get—giving back to those less fortunate. But what about you? What are you doing for *you*?"

"I went to Bolivia this summer. That was for me."

"You helped rebuild an orphanage," she deadpanned. "Come on." She shook me. "I'm serious, Hollis. You're going to be decked in cat sweaters and pearls before you're thirty at this rate."

"Wow, you have such high hopes for the next nine years of my life." I couldn't really disagree with her. But she didn't understand. I had been made aware of my own privilege in high school. I couldn't change my circumstances, my very biology. But I could change what I did with my privilege, with my education and my time. Which was why I had resolved to finish my final year of college and spend the rest of the time traveling to economically disadvantaged communities.

The only kink in my plan was that my parents didn't know that. And couldn't, if I wanted to see a penny of the trust fund they'd set aside for me, like my two sisters before me. "Let me get to graduation and figure that out," I told her simply.

"Are you applying to law schools?"

I looked over my shoulder. "No. But I haven't broken the news yet."

"You get that sack of cash upon graduation, don't you?"

"It's not a sack of cash, per se," I said with a laugh. "But yes."

"Are you gonna pull an Angie and Layla and get the hell out of dodge?"

"That's the plan." Freedom was a mere nine months away, so close that I could practically taste it.

"Well, don't spend every day until then serving everybody but my girl, okay?"

"Hollis." The voice was so jarring that I jumped, turning to look at my dad over my shoulder.

"Dad, hi."

He nodded at Tori once, his first time acknowledging her presence. Which was better than he treated most anyone I brought around, so I knew Tori didn't take it as a slight. "Come meet some people," he said, more of a command than a request.

I stood from the couch and followed his already retreating steps, playing the dutiful daughter. He paused only momentarily at the door to the patio where his guests had congregated, waiting for me to catch up, and leaned down.

"You will behave," he whispered in my ear, his words soft. As if the feel of his words could disguise the venom lying behind them. I knew the venom, I understood the threat. In the tenseness of his jawline, the tightness in his hand that clamped on my shoulder. No, my dad was an actor and I was his supporting cast. And he expected me to win an Oscar today.

"Elodie," he said, his smile stretched in a way that made my own cheeks hurt as I tempted to mimic it. Shaking the hand of David DeBier's mom, my dad launched into accolades and praises for her husband—his employee—but they were thinly veiled insults to my ears. "...Always arrives to work right on time," he said and internally I heard, *but not a moment early.* Punctuality was important to my father, but being early was even better. And after punctuality, good manners followed, which was why he still held my shoulder as he introduced me and squeezed a bit harder when my limp handshake invariably caught his line of sight. "This is my daughter, Hollis. I believe you met her at the Christmas party last year," he said and turned to me. "Hollis, this is Mrs. DeBier." He then tried to list my accomplishments—of which, in his eyes, there were few—and my attention waned until I felt Elodie DeBier's eyes turn to me.

"Oh, and what are you studying?" Elodie asked, face pinched and flushed. My dad had that effect: charismatic to a fault, but still intimidating to the wife of an employee who surely was desperate to keep his job.

I ran my tongue over my teeth, thinking about what I would've liked to say: *I want to eventually become a social worker, but not before traveling the world and studying other cultures,* but instead I opened my mouth and said the lines I had rehearsed a dozen times before. "Cultural anthropology," I said and braced myself for my dad's follow-up which came less than two seconds later.

"She's preparing for law school and this degree is one we mutually agreed on, before she goes to law school, inevitably."

Inevitably: one of my dad's favorite words. I could get it tattooed on myself if he didn't hate tattoos so much. Which was one of the reasons I *should* get it tattooed, if we were being honest. Which we were.

Inevitably, Hollis will ace all her high school classes, including the A.P. ones that she only signed up for under duress.

Inevitably, Hollis will remember to smile in our annual fall portraits, so our family's Christmas card won't look like some sad Jane Austen story, with a family full of spinster daughters.

Inevitably, Hollis will be accepted into the college we've hand-picked for her.

Inevitably, Hollis will graduate with her fluff degree and go onto law school and become someone her father doesn't need to interrupt at parties in order to make her sound more accomplished than she obviously is.

If we were being honest—which, again, we were—I had only managed to reach those first three and only one of them—the first one—had I actually accomplished. So, I was really rating high for dad right then. I was 1 for 3, sinking faster than the Titanic as I slapped mosquitos away from my face at my father's vacation home in St. George, Utah, for his end-of-summer company retreat.

"Cultural anthropology," Elodie said with a widening of her eyes. I could feel my dad stiffen beside me at the interest in her voice. "Why, I've never heard of that. Could you explain it?"

Cultural anthropology rated really low on Dad's approval scale, which was not the reason I loved it as much as I did, but it certainly didn't hurt my own enthusiasm for it. "Oh, yes," I said, "it's really fascinating. In simple terms, it's the study of human cultures, obviously, their practices and beliefs and values but deeper than that it's about studying the diversity between cultures and understanding the causes of diversity. Last year, I wrote a paper about marriage rituals for two different indigenous tribes, continents apart, and how—even though they were uninfluenced by one another—they were similar in their beliefs and traditions."

My dad's hand dropped from my shoulder as he turned to listen to someone else—someone more interesting than me. I wanted to shrug, but I didn't. Elodie's smile widened. "That's incredible work. Or it sounds like it must be."

"It was. I was able to go to Bolivia this summer as part of a humanitarian effort, studying indigenous politics while doing really rewarding work." It was a bone of contention between my father and me—the fact that I was so much like my older sisters and willingly put myself thousands of miles away, so I was glad that my dad's attention was directed away from me for the moment.

"That sounds scary," Elodie said, and her tone changed. With my father's attention away from her, I could only presume she felt less like she was under a microscope. "I can't imagine my David going away that far."

In thinking of it, I couldn't imagine it either. David DeBier, who tried to get in my pants at the last Christmas party? David DeBier, who bragged about stealing some wine from his parents and did I want some? No, David, thanks though.

Keep your tongue and your penis and your mom's boxed wine to yourself, were precisely the words Tori had used.

No, I couldn't imagine David going that far away from his mom either.

Thankfully, Elodie's husband pulled her away before I could answer her follow-up, *Have you met my David?* question, so I was free to roam the appetizers and disappear into the kitchen for the diet soda I had smuggled in. David and I were alike in our preference of contraband beverages, but where we differed was in the fact that I rarely drink alcohol.

I was cracking open the first of hopefully many cans when

my mother walked into the kitchen. I didn't see her, but I heard the tsk leave her perfectly painted lips and I nodded in acknowledgement. "Hollis, really?"

She had the disdain down, but she wasn't intimidating. Which was why I could speak to her more frankly than I could my father. "Yes, really, mom. I've been here for an hour. That's longer than Layla or Angie would've lasted without some kind of their preferred *beverage*. At least mine is non-alcoholic."

My mom sighed and fanned herself with her hand for a moment as she leaned against the white marble-topped island. Not a single white hair on her head was out of place, all tucked away dutifully with some kind of mom-magic only she possessed. My mom wasn't naturally white-haired, no it was more out of fashion than out of respecting her persistent black roots. Like me, she had dark hair before it started going an apparently undesirable shade of gray so she started going lighter and lighter—blonde then platinum then white—and with her twice-a-month salon visits, one would never know that she hadn't gone white *gracefully.* Coupled with her dark brown eyebrows, it was chic, lending itself to her image of a put-together mother of three grown young women, married to an incredibly successful founder of one of the nation's leading tech companies. Mom was a volunteer at several local women's groups and found time to be on the board of three well-regarded nonprofits in the greater Salt Lake City area, hours from our home in Idaho. As my dad liked to say, she was a professional volunteer. It sounded demeaning coming from him, but even as much as my father and I disagreed, I knew he didn't mean it in an offensive way. Mom's work made his look good, especially because the donations came on behalf of his tech company and our last name—Vinke—was uncommon enough that people who didn't know her personally still knew she was a part of my dad's empire.

"That's because your sisters are alcoholics," my mom said

48

lamely and reached for my can of soda, taking one good swallow before handing it back. It was to illustrate a point to me. That anything in moderation was okay—one sip should suffice. But caffeine helped my focus, something she couldn't understand.

"Alcoholics, really?" I asked and finished the can before getting a new one. "Indulging in a beverage or two while in dad's company does not an alcoholic make." My sisters, Angie and Layla, were older by eight and eleven years, respectively, and even with that much time to develop coping skills for dealing with our dad, they still visited rarely and lived the furthest away they could. Which meant shindigs like this one, seven hours south of my parents' fall home—and my home too —was still too far for them to make it.

"Fine, *alcoholic* is a stretch." She sighed again and rubbed an invisible wrinkle between her brows. "They don't exactly make it easier on your dad."

That much I could agree with. Angie, the middle and wild child of the family, was the antithesis of my father. Angie was combative and imaginative and lived off the grid in some modern kind of commune in Alaska. Well, in her words, it was an intentional community of hunters and gatherers and gardeners who coexisted on several hundred-plus acres of communal land. We saw her once a year, if we were lucky.

Layla, on the other hand, studied sharks in South Africa. She was eleven when I was born, and already making an exit strategy when I was entering kindergarten so between my two sisters, I knew her the least. She was secretive, quiet, and preferred animals to humans. We saw her live, in the flesh, once every few years. I hadn't seen her the entire three years I had been in college.

Neither of my sisters were married, much to my parents' growing dismay. And since they'd entered their sixties, the lack of grandchildren was starting to affect them. Hence the spinster

Christmas cards they sent every year, using photos they'd stolen off of their daughters' social accounts because we were hardly ever all under the same roof.

"Dad doesn't make it easier on them, either." I sipped from my second can until she took it from me and poured it down the drain.

"That stuff will kill you. Full of chemicals."

"So is acetaminophen."

Mom wondered why my sisters always hit the wine early into Dad's parties, and as much as it was probably thanks to my dad's unmeetable expectations, my mom didn't exactly help with how overbearing she could be.

"Yes, well, I hardly consume that."

"And your hair dye?"

She leveled me with a look to stop testing her. "What has gotten into you? I think you left part of yourself in Bolivia."

"Or maybe I just found a part there." It was only partly true. Tori's presence had lightened the grip on my tongue. She always spoke so freely, like the censor most people possessed was more or less a hindrance for her. But Bolivia had given me a purpose that my parents couldn't buy. A sense of understanding about the world and my place in it that college alone couldn't enlighten me to.

"Well, that is one souvenir that you could have left behind." She opened the refrigerator and pulled out the remaining few cans I had stashed in there. "I saw you speaking to Mrs. DeBier. You remember her son, David, don't you?"

If her back wasn't to me, she'd have seen the silent groan I made. I *knew* where this was going. "Yes. Please don't throw those away, mom."

She popped the cap on one and, while maintaining eye contact, poured it down the drain. "Everything in moderation, Hollis. Anyway, David spent the summer in Florida but I hear he's back home in Amber Lake now. Maybe you could meet up for coffee."

My mother was just as bad as my dad in many ways, but the difference was her process. My dad went in for the kill. My mom tip-toed along the line, to ease you with her. In this case, I think I preferred my dad's method. "I am dating someone."

Her eyelashes fluttered in the briefest of eye rolls. "Right. Your boyfriend. Who you refuse to bring around your family."

Here we go. I slid my phone out of my pocket and tapped a quick message to Tori to rescue me from the inquisition. "He's not my boyfriend," I said, sliding it back into my jeans. "We are dating, though."

"You've been dating him for, what, two years?"

It was pretty implausible. To casually date someone for two years. But it'd worked for me, so far. "If he was my boyfriend, I would bring him around."

"Are you being safe?"

This time, I audibly groaned. "No, Mom. I'm being reckless. Might be knocked up, who knows."

Her eyes sharpened on me. "That tongue of yours will get you into trouble." She popped the cap on another diet soda and I wished I had rescued one before she could destroy it. "I'm just saying that it would be nice to see you actually go on a date. He's not even on your Facebook or Instagrams."

"No one is." Which was the one thing I had going for me, to give this boyfriend ruse any weight. My social media was dedicated only to my personal pursuits, which meant people only when it was for a project or a purpose.

"Well, since he's not your boyfriend, it wouldn't hurt you to go on one date with David."

"Were you as shameless at hooking Angie and Layla up with would-be suitors?" Where was Tori?

My mom had the nerve to behave like she was shocked. "I'm

not *hooking* you up, Hollis. Don't be so foul." But she knew, deep down I was right. "It'd be nice to see you on a date with anyone."

"I'm not going to be seriously dating anyone until I'm out of school, Mom." It was probably peculiar to anyone on the outside looking in, to hear of a parent pushing their daughter to date. I was only twenty-one, after all, but my mom sometimes behaved like Elizabeth Bennett's mom—not in personality, but in the rush to have her children married. My dad wasn't any better.

"You're so much like them," my mother said, referring to my sisters. "I just wish they'd meet someone to settle down with."

I laughed. "Angie lives barefoot most of the year; I don't think she can settle down much more than that, Mom."

She grimaced, but no lines formed thanks to the fillers she routinely got. "I don't understand how she thinks sometimes. I wish I could." She looked at me when I scoffed. "I do. I'd love nothing more than a peek into her head, just to understand her."

Angie was the youngest child for eight years and then was shoved into that sometimes-overlooked middle child role—I didn't need a peek into her head to understand why she exhibited classic youngest child tendencies, tamed mildly by middle child ones. She wanted to set herself apart from her sisters, and at the same time wanted an escape from my dad. Something I wanted myself. I thought staying north for college when my parents retreated to their three-season home south would give me the freedom I craved, but surprise! I was still close enough for an unwanted drop-in visit, especially when they spent the fall in Amber Lake. "I don't think Angie is going to be a mom any time soon," I said. "And I don't think Layla will let a man close enough to her to touch her hand, much less impregnate her."

"Which leaves you," she said quietly. The volume of her voice carried the same weight as if she'd shouted it. And it was the same expectation I had been made aware of shortly after I left for college. Despite the fanciful origins of their children's

52

names, our parents had laid out expectations for each of us from as young as I could remember.

Mom named her kids after songs she loved. Layla for the Eric Clapton song, Angie for the Rolling Stones and me? Well, I was expected to be a boy. So I was named after a Bob Dylan song. *The Ballad of Hollis Brown*, which chronicles the eponymous farmer who goes on to murder his family.

I should note here that my parents weren't always so uptight. It must have been long before I came around, but judging by their choice of music I knew they must have gotten down in their day. I mean, they named us after songs they loved, but still, I was named after a fictional murderer.

"Well, let me just pop out a few kids before I graduate college then, spice up your Christmas cards." I could only speak with my mother this way. My father wouldn't allow it.

She narrowed her eyes, albeit briefly. "There's your attitude again. And you know that's not what we mean."

"But it kind of is."

"We don't want you to have a child until you're done with college, of course not. But, baby steps wouldn't hurt. Maybe make the guy you've been dating—whoever he is—make an honest woman out of you. Have him come to events, holidays, so we can get to know him. I mean, really, Hollis. I don't even know his *name.*"

Nothing made me feel more ridiculous than my mom asking me when I was finally going to bring a boy around. "I have zero intentions of bringing him around."

"Who?" My father's booming voice reached us from behind me, at the kitchen doorway.

"I'm just talking to Hollis about getting a boyfriend."

He looked at me long enough to make me want to squirm. All the fight I'd given my mom drained out of me at that look. He had the power to make a little girl out of me with just eye contact. "I thought you had a boyfriend."

53

I sighed. "He's not my boyfriend. I've been dating him for a while now, but we're not official." The lie was so familiar to me that it almost felt real. An image of Adam flashed through my brain and I tamped it down.

He shoved his hands in his pockets and stood beside my mom. "Really? Can't seem to snag him then?"

I didn't think it was possible to feel more embarrassment. "I'm focused on school." *So I can finally access my trust fund and get the hell away from your clutches and do my own thing.* "Boyfriends aren't important to me right now."

"That's too bad," he said, rubbing my mom's back. I watched her lean into it, her eyes close for a moment, as if she was bracing herself for a battle and needed that half second to reenergize. "The mistake I made with your sisters, I think, was not properly preparing them for their futures."

I sat down at the island, unease settling over me like blanket covered in needles. "What do you mean? They had trust funds."

"Yes, but I didn't ensure their future by giving them immediate access to it," he said.

Panic flitted over me. Panic born from privilege, I knew, but panic nonetheless. Was this the moment my parents would tell me the trust fund they'd promised me upon graduation no longer existed? The terms had always been that I would have access to it upon completion of my undergrad degree.

I swallowed but a hard lump remained in my throat. The trust fund was more than just money; it was freedom. Freedom from his clutches, to pursue an education that *I* wanted—unconventional, but still valid. Freedom to be me, finally, without the restraints of my father's expectations wrapping me up tight. "Are you saying there's no trust fund?" Better to rip the bandage off, I thought, bracing myself for their response.

"No, of course not. The trust fund exists." My dad and my mom exchanged looks. "But it's a revocable trust."

My chest was heavy, my breaths labored. It was as if I had

just run up a mountain, and I could hardly keep my breathing normal as I processed all of what they were saying. "That makes it sound like you're able to take it away."

He nodded. "It's a living trust. The terms can be changed."

Frustration sunk deep, like an anchor, into my stomach. "What do you mean, Dad?"

"I mean," he exchanged another look with my mom, "that since I am footing the bill for your schooling, giving you access to those funds isn't necessary since you'll be going to law school after graduation anyway."

My cheeks warmed and it wasn't thanks to the oppressive St. George heat. I had to temper my own anger when I asked, "So, when would I be able to access it?"

"Your mother and I have spoken at length about this and what makes the most sense, given your situation. We have concluded," he paused and looked at my mom again—ensuring that I knew she'd agreed to whatever plan he no doubt had concocted all on his own. "That the funds would be best utilized for a wedding or for starting a home with a future husband."

The anchor in my belly pulled me down. I laid a hand on the island for balance. "What do you mean?"

"I mean that we've changed the terms. You'll access the funds when you've announced your engagement."

4

ADAM

"You promise?" Even if I hadn't promised my little sister, the big brown eyes and perpetual disappointment that lingered in their depths would have made me deliver an emphatic *yes*.

"Duh." I tousled her hair and she shrank away, moving to the fridge and pulling out the lunch our gram had made for her. When she reached her hand into the juice box carton and came out empty, I dug out a few singles from my wallet. "Here," I said before she could ask.

"Thanks," she said and stuffed them in the pockets of the jacket that was suddenly looking so small on her ever-growing frame. She was nearly thirteen going on eighteen, and the clothes dad had bought for her seemed to be shrinking every day. A trip to the mall for new clothes was imminent, but the money to make it happen wasn't here. With our grandma in the hospital and our dad ... well, not here, it was up to me to make the money appear. I braced my palms on the worn linoleum counter and stared at my knuckles, which were adorned with the name of my band, a homage to the city I had grown to love.

But guilt bit at me, reminding me that I had been away from home for the last few years, chasing a pipe dream in Colorado. All while my sister and grandma had been doing their best to make it month to month, on my gram's limited income. Unless my dad decided to drop in and play Best Dad Ever for a week or so. That's usually the longest he ever lasted.

Casey pulled her hair into a low ponytail, securing it with a worn rubber band. She should have clothes that fit her better and actual hair things. It didn't seem like a lot to ask, but she wasn't asking. No, Casey was the best goddamn thing my father ever gave me. It was a miracle that Dad was a product of my grandma—who was a saint.

I glanced at the clock on the stove. I'd have time to drop Casey off at school and swing by the hospital before I headed to work. With my wallet still in my hand, I fingered through the remaining bills to see if I had enough to get Gram a few daisies, one of her favorites.

"Dad called me," Casey said, interrupting my thoughts. "Wants to take me out for my birthday in a couple weeks. And," she wagged her eyebrows in a hopeful way, "he said if I get an A on my first report card in math that he'll pay for gymnastics."

I stared at her blankly for a minute until it sank in. Birthday. Casey. Mentally, I calculated. The thirteenth of September was two weeks away, right on the nose. That meant I had one more paycheck coming right before then. Keeping my voice even, I replied, "Oh yeah?" Casey, though older in many ways than her thirteen years, still believed in my dad and his often-empty promises. "That'd be nice." No, what would be nice would be if dear old dad got his shit together so his ailing mom didn't have to take care of his child. But telling Casey... that would be like ruining Santa. She believed so much in him, and me, though we'd both failed her too many times to count.

I didn't know how Casey's grades had been for the last school year, but I wasn't surprised that they had been bad enough for dad to offer an incentive for her to get them up. An incentive he wouldn't follow through with, but one nonetheless. Gram had been sick for a long time, and I didn't blame her for Casey needing tutoring. No, the only person I could blame—apart from my father—was myself. For not being here. "Is math hard for you?"

Casey shrugged, her light jacket slipping over her shoulder. "It's just confusing. They moved to a new way to teach it this year, and so I'm not allowed to do it all in my head like I'm used to doing." There must have been some look on my face, because she quickly added, "But don't worry. I'll get it figured out."

I hated that she felt that way. That she saw my worry and had to console *me*. Once again, I was hit with a wave of disappointment that things had gotten the way they had.

"*We'll* figure it out," I corrected her.

Casey nodded and a few flyaway hairs escaped her ponytail. Tucking them behind her ear, she said, "Okay, but anyway, you should come to the birthday dinner. I bet he'd love to see you."

My back was to Casey as I dug through the fridge for breakfast, so she couldn't see me wince. I thought of the last time I had seen our dad, when I'd grabbed him by the collar and shoved him against my car hard enough to leave a lasting dent in the side panel. "I'll have to look at my schedule," I told Casey as a compromise, though this was one of the few things I couldn't commit to, even for her. "Do you have everything you need?" I asked, wanting to move on from all talk of Dad. "Backpack, lunch, homework, gym stuff?"

"Yes." She shoved a bite of peanut butter and jelly toast into her mouth. "Remember, you have to pick me up for my appointment at noon."

"I know, I promised." I grabbed my backpack and herded her out the door, to the car. Being that it was the end of August, the morning was still warm enough that getting in the car wasn't a hassle. But in the coming months, when winter sent frost across the car, I would need to make sure the radiator was fixed enough to defrost the windshield. I really should start a list of the shit I needed to take care of. Whether I liked it or not, I was going to stay in Idaho for the long term. I tried not to let that thought affect my mood because I knew Casey would sense it and start on her little *I'm a burden* freakout once again. The last time she had, when Gram had been first hospitalized, my reaction had been anger. Not because I was mad at her, but because I was angry with myself. Casey wasn't a burden. Our father, on the other hand, was.

When I tried to turn the engine over, the car sputtered and shut immediately off. Panic quickly prickled my skin, but I tried again. It took four times before the engine rumbled and we were able to get on the road. Having the car break down now would be the icing on the cake that was the last month since I had gotten back into town. It was like I was constantly waiting for the other shoe to drop. For my gram to pass away. For my car to fail on me. For my dad to come back. All three would be just about the worst thing to happen, and unfortunately, the first one was proving to be not so much of an *if* but a *when*. And when it happened, someone would need to become Casey's primary, legal guardian. Even though gram had been taking care of Casey for most of her life, my dad still retained custody. The agreement with my gram was an agreement made by word of mouth and not through any legal channels. But Casey deserved more than my father. She deserved more than me. But Gram, dad, my brother, and I were the last four people in her life and I would fight my own father for my sister before I let him take her.

I glanced over at Casey, watched her take the sights in as we drove out of the little piece of land Gram owned and onto the main road. She looked so much like our mom. Acted like her too. If she hadn't died when Casey was a toddler, all of our lives would look much different now. Better.

59

Shaking the thought from my head, I turned the music up and was thanked with an eye roll from my passenger.

"Do we have to listen to this?" she asked.

"It's better than that country crap you like," I said, teasing her.

"We don't have to listen to country." She dug into the center console and produced a homemade CD. "We could play this..."

I swiped the CD from her and shoved it into the side door. "That's even worse."

"But it's your band," she protested.

"Yeah, and there's a reason why it's not on the radio."

She scoffed and crossed her arms over her chest. "They can't be that bad. You tatted the name of one of those songs on your fingers."

My knuckled flexed on the steering wheel, the words *Mile High* flashing in the early sunlight. "They're not bad. But they're not for thirteen-year-old ears." In truth, the content of the music wasn't the issue. It was my sister listening to the music that was problematic for me. She was the only one whose opinion mattered. And my music had been my life long before I had left Idaho to pursue it. Since I'd left my sister. If she hated it, I'd know. And I'd hate myself a little more for abandoning her for it.

"It's not like I haven't heard it before," she said. "My friends have phones, you know. And there's this website called YouTube. I don't know if you've ever heard of it before, but you can listen to music on it."

I tousled her hair again, earning a 'Hey!' before she quickly smoothed it back into a ponytail. "Okay, smart ass. But that stuff," I pointed to the location of the disc, "is the new stuff." *The stuff that means more*, I added to myself silently. The early shit we had on YouTube was just practice. Also known as: actual shit. If she hated the new stuff, I'd probably toss my keyboard out the window. But, considering that the keyboard cost more than this car, I might rethink it—if only for a moment.

"I mean, it's still the same people. It can't be much different."

Casey didn't get it, but how could she? The first album had been produced in the garage of a place we'd rented on Airbnb. One week. Ten tracks. A thousand bucks in rent and equipment rentals and booze. Each song was fueled by this need to impress but the actual production of it left something to be desired. When you hear that a band is better live, that's how we felt about our band, too.

That is, until the new album. We'd rented a studio. We'd invested in better equipment. But more than money, our hearts were in it. We weren't trying to impress. We'd failed and we'd fallen apart and come back together and we'd built something to be proud of. I was more proud of this album than I could've been of anything else.

But that didn't mean I was ready for anyone else to hear it. My moving back to Idaho had sort of put all our plans on halt. We were just sitting on this album until we knew what was going to happen. Considering that it had been a month and I still had no idea about what was happening, our album's release date was firmly TBD.

"Come on," she protested. "We'll only have time for one of your songs before we get to school anyway."

I raised an eyebrow and glanced at her "No."

Casey reached over and switched the station to country.

With daisies in one hand and an energy drink in my other, I entered Gram's room. The window shade was pulled down and her breakfast sat untouched on the table beside her bed. I set the flowers beside the tray and moved to the window, checking back at her as I raised the shade. Light washed her face, emphasizing the cracks and hollows in her skin. She looked better today than she had the day before. But still, three days in the hospital was wearing on her. The lack of appetite and the dark circles that colored the paper-thin skin around her eyes told me all I needed to know.

She still hadn't woken up, so I went to the nurse's station to ask to see her doctor when she made rounds. I came this early in the morning not just to see Gram before work but to make sure I caught the team of doctors responsible for her care. The clock told me I had thirty minutes before I had to head out the door or I would be late for work, so I hoped that the doctor would speed it up so I didn't piss off my asshole of a boss.

When I returned to the room, Gram was awake but staring out the window with the blankest look in her eyes. It stopped me for a minute. I knew she was sick, of course I knew that. It was the reason I had come back to Idaho. But during the last few weeks before she'd been admitted, she had seemed like her normal self again. She had energy. She went on walks with Casey after she got out of school. She ate really well, constantly scribbling down her salt intakes. So when her doctor had admitted her after her last appointment, I was shocked.

"Gram," I said, grabbing the daisies off of the table and bringing them around so she could see them. "Yellow's your favorite daisy, right?"

Her eyes warmed, but not in the way I was used to, and she reached a hand out for one of the petals, running a shaking thumb over it and giving me a weak smile. "Hi, my boy." It was what she always called me. Not Adam. I was her boy. Considering she raised me more than any other adult had, I was more hers than anyone else's. "How's Casey?"

I dragged a chair close to the bed, wincing as it squeaked across the clean floor. "She's good. Her appointment is today." I tapped my teeth when she looked confused and she rubbed at her forehead.

"That's right. You have her insurance card?"

Shit. I didn't, I'd forgotten it. Which meant I would have to run back home before picking Casey up from school. Which meant I'd need to leave work earlier than planned. Shit, shit, shit. But I nodded and averted my eyes as I set the vase of daisies on the table once again. "All set. Don't you worry about it. Just concentrate on getting the ol' ticker behaving properly so we can break you out of here." I rapped my knuckles on my chest.

"Ah, yes." But she didn't smile. "I'm afraid that it might take more than just an expensive stay in this hospital bed, though."

I was about to ask her for more information when I saw a doctor I had spoken to the day before entering the room. Immediately, I stood up and motioned to speak with her in the hallway. "Back in a sec, Gram."

"Hey," I said to the doctor when we were out of earshot. "Dr. Hathaway, right?"

She nodded and crossed her arm over her chest, hugging the clipboard. "You're Mrs. Oliver's grandson."

"Yeah." I frowned as I pointed a thumb back at Gram's room. "She made it sound like she might not be out of here soon?"

Dr. Hathaway blinked but otherwise betrayed no other expression. "Are you aware of your grandmother's condition?"

"She has heart problems. She has a defibrillator, right? She has been getting better. Getting outside and staying active. My little sister keeps her young." I smiled, like I was trying to convince the doctor Gram was getting better.

"Yes, she has a defibrillator, but hers protects her from death in the event of a cardiac arrest. It is not improving her symptoms, which is why she was admitted." Dr. Hathaway put a hand on my shoulder and guided me down the hallway a bit further from Gram's room. "Your grandmother's ejection fraction last year was fifteen percent." At my look of confusion, she continued. "When your heart beats, it's pumping blood out into your body through your left and right ventricles of your heart. Those are the bottom two chambers of your heart. It takes more than just one contraction to pump all the blood out. The ejection fraction is the measurement we use to calculate the percentage of that blood flow out of those ventricles. We like to see above fifty percent. Hers was fifteen percent. It's now ten percent."

This was where me being a shitty grandson came in, because I assumed her defibrillator was fixing her heart. "But she's been getting better," I said again, weaker this time.

"I understand how confusing that can be. If your grandmother had cancer, we could expect to see a relatively predictable decline in her health. But your grandmother has been in heart failure for over a decade."

"Yeah, but she's been on medication and she does everything her doctors tell her—"

She placed a hand on my shoulder, interrupting me. "She'll have swings that will make you believe she's doing better but ultimately her heart is weakening and is pumping less blood. She will not get better." Her hand dropped and her expression turned concerned. "You do understand, right?"

"Are you saying that she's dying?"

"Well," she swallowed and the concern reached her eyes. "Not today. But she is approaching the end stages of heart failure. You need to prepare yourself for that." She pointed her head toward the hospital room. "We've already informed your grandmother. She took it quite calmly. Now is the time to talk about what's next."

The news was like a hard rock in my throat. "What's next? Like a funeral?"

"I'm not saying that you need to worry about that right now. But we have reached the limit of what we can do for Mrs. Oliver at this point."

"How long does she have?"

"That's not something I can say. Typically, with a fifteen percent ejection fraction, one could have six months or less to live. But I have seen patients live two or more years."

"But you said her ejection fraction is now ten percent."

She nodded and I could finally see the wear behind her eyes in what she was telling me. "I had a patient who was alcoholic and overweight, who went from fifteen percent to forty-five percent after he quit alcohol and began exercising. Your grandmother is not an alcoholic, nor is she overweight. If she's doing everything her doctor has been having her do and is still declining…"

"Then it's not good," I finished for her.

"No. It's not." She touched my shoulder again, but lighter than before. "I am so sorry. I know how hard this can be." She let out a sigh. "You will want to talk about this with your grandmother and any other living relatives. Many patients elect to have their defibrillator deactivated when they are in the end stages. The shock can prove to be traumatizing when the benefit is so small. If you wish, I can help facilitate the conversation to ensure your grandmother's wishes are understood and respected, and to allow you to vocalize your feelings." She squeezed lightly before letting go. "Either way, we are not in the end stages yet. But preparing for it will eliminate any burden either of you feel later on."

What was I supposed to say to that? I had come back to Idaho on the assumption that Gram was just having the occasional problems, not that this might be it for her. For all of us. So, I just nodded and Dr. Hathaway re-entered Gram's room with an enthusiastic "Good morning!"

5

HOLLIS

THEY CHANGED THE TERMS OF THE TRUST FUND.

As I was recovering from the shock, Tori finally waltzed into the kitchen. "I guess it's a good thing Adam's back in town, right?"

Three sets of eyes swung to her, but my heart was hammering furiously in my chest. I couldn't speak. *Adam.*

"Adam?" My mom turned to me. "Who is Adam?"

"The guy who *wants* to be exclusive with our favorite little bean here." Tori joined me at the island, looping an arm around my waist, but I was trying to catch up with what she was saying.

Adam? She'd just told my parents the name of my fake-suitor, and had chosen Adam Oliver, of all people?

"Wait, he wants to be exclusive with Hollis?"

My knees were limp noodles. Were it not for Tori's arm around my waist, I knew I'd crumple into a heap. But were it not for the lies she was spilling, I wouldn't feel as weak as I did.

"Oh yes," Tori said with wide eyes and a nod. "But Hollis is just such a good student, Mr. and Mrs. Vinke. So focused.

Having him traveling all the time for work enabled her to focus."

I couldn't quite fathom what was happening. Tori had just sold me out to my parents, who now dangled the one thing I had been hoping for, for *years*, over my head like a carrot I couldn't—wouldn't—reach. But my parents' gazes on me were curious, searching. I gave them a smile I didn't really feel and placed my hand over Tori's, squeezing. Out of warning or fear, I wasn't entirely sure. "Tor," I said, but she blazed on.

"But now he's back in town. I'm sure you'll meet him soon."

And with that promise, Tori had sealed my fate.

"What were you thinking?" I hissed at her once we were safely tucked away in the guest room two full floors from my parents. I tossed the clothes I had hung in the closet into an open suitcase on the bed when I wasn't pacing. "Adam? Adam Oliver?" I pushed my hands into my hair and pressed against my scalp, hoping the blood would drain out of my face and into my extremities. My limbs felt weightless still, fluttery and weak.

"I was thinking that your parents were about to rip away the *one* thing you've been looking forward to for four fucking years, Hollis. You are welcome." She bowed and grabbed the backpack she'd packed, tossing it onto the bed beside my suitcase.

"You can't really think I'm going to thank you for that," I said, seething. I caught a glimpse of my reflection in the mirror above the dresser. Despite my Mediterranean coloring, my cheeks were still a furious shade of red. From embarrassment, from shock—I didn't know. But I did know that I was pissed off at Tori. So very, very pissed. I couldn't even see reason behind what she was saying.

"You could've denied it," she said with a shrug, dropping to the bed with a bounce. "But you didn't."

"I didn't know how to act! I couldn't believe you were throwing me under the bus, in front of them. What was I supposed to say? 'Tori is lying. There's no one, never has been'? I mean, how do you think they'd take that?"

"Hey, you started the lie, not me. I just..." she twirled her hand in the air, causing her thin gold bracelets to fall to her elbow, "embellished. A bit."

"A bit." I punched a pair of jeans into the suitcase, but the movement did nothing to satisfy the rage still simmering beneath my skin. "You didn't have to *name* him."

"Well, I did. And, for the record, I didn't say Adam *Oliver*. You deduced that all on your own. You could've found some guy named Adam and paid him to play the part."

I couldn't believe her. She was my best friend. Rationally, I knew she always had my back. And, maybe if I stepped back to examine the situation more thoroughly than I had, I could see her motive wasn't malicious. But, again, she was my *best* friend. And she'd practically sold me out.

"I'm..." I pressed my lips together hard enough to cause my eyes to sting. "I'm so angry with you, Tori."

Tori sat straight up and blinked. "Whoa."

I didn't dignify that with a question. I knew why she was surprised. It was rare for me to speak my true feelings with anyone, even Tori. I might elude to it, I might throw tantrums like the epic one I was right then. But rarely did I actually articulate angry feelings into words. It was one of the things Tori pushed me to try, to tell someone when they were taking advantage of me, to speak up when I felt a grade was unfair—yes, I was *that* student. "Bitching to me about your teacher's lazy grading isn't going to help you," Tori always reminded me whenever I launched into a vent session. Well, I had taken her advice and gone direct to the source of my frustration this time: her.

Silence fell over us and my nerves calmed as I folded the last of my shirts, placing them into the suitcase with more care than I had shown my jeans.

"Hollis."

My eyes stung and I refused to look at her. I didn't know why I was embarrassed that I had told her how I felt. I don't know why being honest about my feelings was the hardest thing for me to do sometimes. But still, it was. So I just neatly packed my tank tops and spread my hands across them, making each ripple smooth.

"I'm sorry," she said, scooting closer to my suitcase so that I couldn't help but look at her. "That was a real shitty thing to do." Her hand found my arm and gave it a reassuring squeeze. "I'll go back downstairs and explain it. I can talk my way into a mess as easily as I can talk my way back out of it, trust me."

She didn't have to tell me that. Many times in high school, she'd proved just how good she was at talking her way out of a failing grade. That's probably why she was as successful in school as she was. I looked her over, saw the sincerity in her eyes. She *was* sincere, I knew. Though we had similar backgrounds and parental expectations, in many ways we were completely different personalities. I studied my ass off, she didn't. I didn't have a backbone when it came to my parents, she did. I had been single my entire college career, she hadn't. I couldn't express myself in a way that didn't make me self-conscious, but she could. I knew that in her heart of hearts, she was trying to help. But she'd talked me into a corner that I couldn't see a way out of.

"I'm still pissed at you," I told her, but I felt a million times calmer than I had when I had stomped up the stairs with her minutes before. "I have to figure my way out of this."

"Look. Your dad said revocable trust. Which means he can amend it and change the terms. Again." She laid her hands out. "Convince Adam to be your boyfriend for a little while. Maybe they'll change their tune. Parents think they know what's best for their kids until they're facing it."

I gave what she said some consideration. My initial thought was that they'd never change the terms of the trust now. But then again, I never would have guessed they'd do it this time. "I just need to work this out in my head. Before they come up for the season."

"Let me help."

At my *really?* look she stood and placed her hands on my shoulders. "We'll figure this out. I mean, I'm sure Adam would do you a solid and pretend, at least until you had a 'breakup' that looked believable."

"Adam? Do me a solid?" If I found any humor in this situation, this was where I would've laughed. But I couldn't laugh. Adam *hated* me.

"Okay fine, maybe he'll do me a solid." But her *maybe* was flimsy at best. "I'll talk to Keane. Maybe he still has a crush on me."

"I think you killed your chances with Keane in high school." Though Adam hated me, his best friend Keane did not. Partly because he was so close to my roommate, Navy. And also because I had never done anything to him. Truth be told, I had never done anything to Adam either—but in his case that was precisely the problem.

"I'll talk to him."

I rubbed my temples. "No, don't. Let me sort this out. I'll figure a way through this, I just need time."

"Don't tell me, you're going to make a chart."

"Don't mock my charts," I said defensively. "I've found many solutions by charting out an issue."

"Yeah, I know, you big nerd." To some, being called a nerd might be offensive but I actually took pride in it. I worked my ass off and my grades were proof. Those didn't come easily to me, they required a lot of prep, studying, and extra credit when I could get it.

"Hey, we're not all born with big brains and bigger mouths," I said with a raised eyebrow. "Ready to get out of here?"

She nodded and we left my parents' party without having a long, unnecessary goodbye.

"Are you sure you don't want to stay the weekend?" Tori asked me, after we'd stayed the night at her parents' cabin.

"I'm sure." I looked at the dark, foreboding cabin that was nestled in the tall evergreen trees like they'd given birth to it, like they protected it still. "Navy is waiting on me."

"Ugh, Navy," she said with thinly veiled jealousy. She was always making those comments, revealing to me just how unsettled she was about me moving in with my other best friend. For Tori, I was her ride or die—the only person to put up with her. Her words, not mine. She may have had a tough exterior, but deep beneath the layers of steel was a warm, soft heart, prone to hurt.

"Hey, you're my oldest friend," I reminded her, slinging my arm over her shoulders. "And if we went to the same college, I would've moved in with you in a heartbeat." It was true, but I also knew that moving in with Tori wouldn't bode well for my whole, *get out of my shell* persona. Tori didn't understand that deep-seated need to change. But I didn't see it as changing who I was, but changing how I saw others, how to approach people with more compassion. "I have to finish moving in stuff this weekend. What are you going to do in this place all weekend?"

"I'm going to live up to its reputation as Madame Tori's Pleasure House, of course." She did a regal bow and smirked. "Entertain some gentlemen callers while my roommates are gone."

"Roommates," I said. "You mean your parents."

"Semantics." She plunked down on the stone steps that ascended to the large front porch. "In reality, I'll probably binge all the Netflix romcoms my little heart can take."

"Romcoms." I wrinkled my nose. "You? Has someone kidnapped my best friend and replaced her love for true crime documentary with a newfound love for, as she has so eloquently put it in the past, 'dumpster entertainment'?"

"Oh, I'm your best friend? I thought little miss heart eyes was."

I sighed. Not this again. "Come on, you know that I have different best friends."

"Yeah, yeah, but you're not moving in with me. You're moving in with *her*." The way she said 'her' made her sound like a jealous mistress talking about a wife.

"I've told you why." And I had. Navy, my new roommate, was someone I wanted to emulate more. I was done living in the shadow of who my father had groomed me to be. I wanted to become more comfortable being around people who were not like me. If I was to pursue my passion of traveling the world and understanding more cultures, I would need to push myself out of my cocoon. Unfortunately for Tori, she was so much like me that sometimes it felt like I was having a conversation with myself. Including now, when the jealously lit back through her voice like a trick candle. "You're my oldest best friend, Tori."

She sighed. "I was just hoping that since I graduated early we'd have more time to actually hang out."

"And we will! This is my last year and thanks to the semester I did over the summer, I can take on a lighter load." When Tori quieted, peering out through the trees, I knew it was because she, like me, had to see to believe me. I changed the subject. "What gentlemen callers, by the way?"

Tori laughed. "Come on. Gentlemen callers and me? No. Not in this town. Not in this state."

"Guys here aren't all bad. What about that one guy, Tom?"

"Tommy the Tank? Yeah, that's gonna be a no from me, friend. He was fun to fool around with, but his idea of a perfect date involved gritty protein smoothies and long nights at the gym." She patted her head. "This body was made for advanced mathematics, not aggressive muscles. And the potato chips my roommates bought aren't going to eat themselves. Besides, I've got some plotting to do."

My stomach sank as the realization came to mind. "Plotting." It wasn't said as a question, but it was one.

"Plotting," she echoed. "We've got to figure out this Adam situation."

"I guess I don't like the idea of you plotting."

"Hey," she said, eyes narrowing. "I'm smart, you know." But she said it sarcastically, to get a laugh out of me. I humored her. "We'll figure it out, Hols. Swear."

"I said I would talk to him."

"Yeah?" She pulled a water bottle from the side pocket of her backpack. "When?"

"Navy and Keane are like this." I crossed my forefinger and middle finger. "I'll talk to Keane."

"'Hey Keane! So since you're friends with Adam and all, think you can talk to him and convince him to be in love with me for a little while?'" She laughed. "Yeah, I'm sure that'll go over real well. You need to go directly to Adam."

Just the thought of that made my stomach twist and turn over. A migraine that'd merely flirted at my temples was increasing in its efforts in my head. "I'll figure it out, like I told you. Please, Tori, do not get involved."

She harrumphed and crossed her arms over her chest. "I can be convincing."

"I know you can. If anyone knows that, I do. But you're right; I need to go to Adam, directly. Not you, and not through Keane." But the prospect made my insides quake with fear. We weren't even friends on social media. Would I have to slide into his DMs to talk to him? And how would I begin to word it? I rubbed my forehead. "I'll figure it out, and I'll let you know. But I gotta go, okay Tori?"

"Give me some hugs first," she said with a sigh, standing. Her arms stretched as wide as they'd go as she toddled toward me and then wrapped around me like a straight jacket. "Let me know, okay?" There was a bit of sadness in her eyes and for a moment, I felt bad for leaving her alone in this house. She kissed the side of my head, right at my hairline. I slipped a sticky note into her pocket, something I'd been doing since high school, hoping she'd find it right when she started to feel a little lonely. Along with all the others I had hidden away for her.

I nodded and, after untangling myself from her hold, I waved and climbed into the car.

Once back on the highway, I guzzled as much water as I could, hoping to ward off the migraine early. I had a full load ahead of school, between scheduling my tutoring clients and all the email dodging I'd have to do with my dad. I was so wrapped up in my thoughts, my internal charting on how to approach Adam, that I almost didn't notice the car pulled over to the side of the highway and its driver leaning against the back of the trunk. I had zero intention of stopping, at least until the dark head lifted and those eyes made contact with mine.

6

ADAM

I KICKED A TIRE OF THE CAR THAT HAD FAITHFULLY DELIVERED ME from Denver only a week before. This was decidedly not the time for it to shit the bed, but shit the bed it had. The unsatisfying clunk of my boot hitting the tire did nothing to assuage my own anger at that moment.

The sun was beating down on me, flaming up the back of my neck where sweat had just begun to prickle against my skin. Sliding my phone out of my pocket, I looked up and down the road for a sign of another traveler—especially one willing to pick me up.

I was fresh out of luck that day, which was further proven when my phone proudly displayed "NO SERVICE" at the top of the screen like it was some kind of achievement. I could kick the tire of my vehicle, but I couldn't very well throw my phone like I very much wanted to at the moment. So instead, I growled a swear word that my grandmother would tsk at and tossed my phone onto the driver's seat.

Sullenly, I glanced back at the steam pouring from under my

hood. What the hell else could go wrong? It was nearly eleven, and I was at least an hour from home. Casey would be expecting me, of course, would leave school at exactly eleven-thirty and walk the half mile to the stop sign at the end of the road and look for me. And she'd have to wait for God knew how long before giving up and walking the rest of the way to Gram's empty house. Anger unfurled in me in a spiral of rage. If my dad hadn't been an absent piece of shit, if Gram hadn't been afflicted with a weak heart and if my car hadn't died on me, my sister wouldn't be let down by yet another person in her life.

I shoved a hand through my mop of hair and cursed the fact that this had begun way before Dad skipped town a few months ago. Really, it'd started back in high school when Mom had died. If I closed my eyes, I could very nearly remember the way life had been then, which was to say: much easier than it was now. Which was why I didn't close my eyes. Because the very last thing I needed to be reminded of was how much better life had been before my mom had died. Before my dad had taken off. Before Gram had gotten sick. Before I had been forced to leave the city I had come to call my own and return to the town that held the memories of my broken childhood.

The energy drink in my center console was growing warmer by the second, so I chugged it and tossed the empty can into my backseat. That's when I saw the glint out of the corner of my eye, coming down the road like a beacon to Heaven itself. It was the first car I had seen in twenty minutes, easily, and it was headed in the direction I needed to go.

Hope turned to lead in my belly when I made out the make and model of the car. There was no way that someone with that kind of cash would risk pulling over for someone like me. Admittedly, I wasn't looking my best but to be fair, I hadn't expected to have my car crap out on me. I looked down at my jeans, torn at the knees from use rather than style and the threadbare tee that was soft from over-washing and stained from work. And with the tattoos that covered my hands and arms, I knew I didn't exactly scream trustworthy.

But to my surprise, the car slowed anyway and its blinker turned on as it slowly pulled onto the shoulder. My skin prickled from gratitude and I approached the car with what I hoped was a friendly smile.

Unfortunately, that smile quickly turned sour when I saw who was behind the wheel.

7

HOLLIS

I WANTED TO GO BACK TEN SECONDS EARLIER TO WHEN HE SMILED at me. Even though it hadn't looked completely genuine, it was certainly a hundred times more inviting than the scowl Adam currently wore, which was without a doubt in reaction to the fact that *I* was about to save him.

Putting the car in park, I looked down at my lap for a moment. A whole lot of courage was needed to get out and face him. This was the first time seeing him in, what, three years? And we hadn't exactly parted on friendly terms after that party in high school. I ran my nails over each other and sucked in a breath before turning off the car and opening my door.

"Hey," I said, forcing cheer into my voice as I rounded the side of my car. Glancing over my shoulder, I tried to quickly think of anything—literally anything—else to say other than, *Hey, remember how you hated me back in the day? Do you still hate me too much to accept a car ride?*

But, unsurprisingly, I came up empty. Instead, I turned around and faced him with a smile. "Car trouble?"

"No, I just like standing out here in the hundred-degree temps, kicking rocks for shits and giggles," he spit. "What are you even doing on this road? Don't you live in the hills?"

That made me sound way more primitive than I was. "My parents do. I live just south, on the outskirts of Amber Lake. This route is quieter than the interstate."

"Great for you."

This was going well. "Need a lift?"

He glowered at me from under thick dark eyebrows. His hate for me was palpable and not entirely unwarranted. But he softened for a moment, looking back at the steam of his car and the quiet hiss it emitted. He was contemplating it.. I knew this back road enough to know it saw more tractors than passenger vehicles and that it was often a dead spot for cell service. Which meant the fact that he was debating it explained just how desperately he did *not* want to ride with me.

While he stared stonily at the ground, I asked, "Don't you live in Denver now?" Even though I knew he was back.

He lifted his head and crossed his arms over his chest. "Did. Back now."

"Oh." It was the nicest thing he'd said to me in years, and it consisted of three whole words. "Back to Amber Lake?"

"Yeah." He scratched down the side of his face and looked at me again. "You still live there?"

"I'm going to college there."

"Right." But he was still mulling over the idea of riding with me. "I can take you to your house, if you want. Or to a shop for you to arrange a tow." *Because I know you'd rather cut off your arms than spend any amount of time with me.* "Your choice."

"I don't suppose I have another choice but to ride with you." He sighed heavily, clearly unhappy with the prospect of sharing a ride with me. "Let me grab my shit first."

He brushed past me to the driver's side. He smelled of sweat and something woodsy, like he'd just cut down a few trees or something. I forced myself to act normal, and not like a typical twenty-one-year-old, and climbed back into my car.

When he came to the passenger door, I quickly hit the unlock button. "Can I put my stuff in the back?" He gestured toward the trunk of the car. "I don't want to leave it in case it gets stolen."

Nodding, I hit the button to open the back gate of my car. "Go for it."

He bent over the trunk of his car and came out with a long, rectangular case and another smaller bag—bowling bag, maybe —and put it all in the trunk of my car. When he reached for the top of the door, I hit the button to close the gate and he shook his head. I barely made out his words, "Fancy fucking car," before the back door closed and he returned to the passenger door.

"Ready?" I asked when he climbed in. I pulled my head back to keep his very manly scent from throwing me off balance.

"Yeah. I have to get my sister from school, and then you can drop us off at home." He was quiet for a second and I felt his stare on me. "If that's okay."

"It's fine," I said. "We live in the same town. I don't mind taking you to a shop or—"

"I said I can get someone else, okay?" He cut me off.

Swallowing, I nodded. "Right. Sure." He was like a lit match, searching for gasoline to help him implode. I wanted to help him, but I wouldn't become his doormat. I placed the car in gear and pulled onto the highway.

8

ADAM

"Sweet ride!" Casey exclaimed as we pulled up to the stop sign she was waiting at.

I rolled my eyes at her and motioned my head toward the backseat door. "Get in."

Casey slid into the car, and Hollis turned. "Hey! I'm Hollis."

I'd heard her name hundreds of times, probably, but hearing her say it made it sound fancier than even this car was. She didn't say it any different, but it sounded different in her light, friendly tone.

"Are you my brother's friend?"

"Err—" Hollis began as I gave an emphatic, "No."

Casey nodded once. "Didn't think so. Adam doesn't have friends."

I turned so I was looking at her—or, rather, glaring at her. "Hey." It was a soft warning, so soft that Casey steamrolled right over it.

"Okay, he has friends, but he definitely doesn't have friends as pretty as you."

I sensed Hollis stiffen beside me as she thanked Casey, but seemed to feel awkward about it. "You're pretty too," she said in that impossibly sweet, soft voice. It was stupid to be annoyed by her voice, but I was. I was annoyed to be rescued like she was my white knight—and not because she was a female but because she was Hollis Vinke. One of the assholes from high school.

Not that you'd know that by the way she and Casey were trading compliments and niceties that didn't sound forced. I linked my fingers behind my head to stretch out the tension in my shoulders and said more unkindly than I meant to sound, "Are we going to go or what?"

"I have my dentist appointment," Casey explained.

"Oh, I can take you guys. And," Hollis shifted in her seat so she was facing me, "we can figure out what to do about your car."

I glared, hating her use of *we*.

"What happened to the car?" Casey piped up.

"It broke down," I bit off.

"Why didn't you get a tow from work?"

"Not now, Casey." I clenched and unclenched my jaw. I loved my sister, but she could be a real pain in the ass.

"What? My tablemate's dad works there, if you give me your phone I can try to call her and ask them to tow it."

There was no escaping this, not with my persistent little sister. "I don't work there anymore." I pinched the bridge of my nose.

Casey made a face and her mouth opened to an O. "Since when? I thought that's where you went this morning."

Hollis tried to make a sound, like she was going to interrupt. Why? To spare me the embarrassment? Well, that would be pointless. She was seeing me at my worse. Freshly unemployed. Broken down car on the side of the road. Helping me pick up my sister like we were back in high school. Back to the time when she reminded me that she was just another one of the assholes who tormented me like it was their God damn job. "They let me go, okay Case? Can you cool it on the questions for a minute?" It'd been a long fucking day and maybe my tone showed that. I closed my eyes and let out a breath. "Let's just get to your appointment and I'll figure out who I need to call."

Hollis drove to the dentist appointment and I got Casey checked in. When a woman in pink scrubs called Casey's name from the door, I stood to join her before Casey waved a hand at me, gesturing me to wait. I had been gone for three years but had still stopped back for holidays and weekends here and there, but how had she gone from needing me to *not* needing me in that span of time?

I sunk back into my seat and Hollis turned to me. "Sorry," she said.

"About what?"

"For the Spanish Inquisition in the car..."

I stared into her light brown eyes, saw the sincerity in them and watched the way her lashes fell when I said, "She's not *your* sister, so don't apologize for her."

"That's..." She took a breath and clasped her hands in her lap. "Not what I meant. Casey's great. I just felt bad for being there. I'm sure it made you uncomfortable."

Trying to come up with something to say to that, I stared at her long enough to make it uncomfortable. The anger I felt just ... dissipated. It wasn't Hollis's fault that today had been a royal fucking shit show. She'd only tried to help me. I knew I should throw her a bone, but didn't know how to.

She produced a card from inside her wallet. "I have this for towing. It doesn't matter if the car's mine or not, they will tow it if I say I was a passenger."

"But you weren't."

She nodded slowly and a small smile crept at the corner of her pink lips. "I know. But they won't know that. And it's free."

"Free for me, you mean. Like the ride." *Chill out, Adam.* "Sure. That'd be great. If you can handle lying."

She squinted for a moment and a little wrinkle appeared between her eyes. "Do you think I've never told a lie or something?" She placed her finger on the tip of her nose and then moved it horizontally away from her face. "Call me Pinocchio, especially lately. I'll go make that call. Can I have your license plate and make and model?" She handed me a pen and a paper she pulled out of her handbag, and I scribbled it down for her.

After she left the room, I breathed out a sigh and pulled up my phone, powering it on. Now that I had service again, a few texts came through.

Sarah: Hey butthole. You're awfully quiet today. What's going on?

Keane: Want to come by for a few beers tonight? My roommate's friend left a six pack of something probably gross in the fridge.

Caleb: You didn't call me after Gram's appointment. I'm guessing that means things are ok? Let me know.

I scrubbed a hand over my face. *Fuck.* The last text from my brother reminded me that I had been in a rush when I'd left Gram's room that morning. Between the world-rocking news and the fact that I was fucking late for work, I hadn't thought to text Caleb. I looked to the door Casey had disappeared behind. I hadn't thought to tell her, either. Suddenly, I wasn't in a hurry to be home. To walk by Gram's empty room, to sit Casey down

84

on her worn bedspread and tell her that Gram wasn't getting better.

I texted Keane back first because his was the easiest of the three texts to reply to.

Can't. Want to come over to Gram's Sunday night? I've got Casey, flying solo for who knows how long.

His reply came almost immediately.

Keane: Sorry man. I forgot. 8 work?

I sent him a quick yes and then moved to Sarah's text. She was easier than my brother, but harder than Keane. Keane knew my grandmother, understood her importance to me. Sarah—who happened to be my ex—didn't. She would want to call and chat about things and get me to regurgitate some of my feelings but that was precisely why she moved from being my girlfriend into being *just a friend*. I loved her as a friend, but I wasn't going to unfurl everything for her to pick and prod through.

Sorry, long day. Car broke down. At sister's dentist appointment now. What are you up to?

It was easier to switch the topic to her. And her next text reminded me why, when we'd mutually agreed to end our relationship, I'd kept her as a friend.

. . .

Sarah: Icing Bobby's balls. Your lead singer's gonna sound like he's going through puberty for a while.

I laughed once, felt eyes turn in my direction and typed out a reply.

Literally or figuratively icing his balls?

In response, I got a series of photos. The first was a selfie of her holding a neon green resistance band with handles on each end and Bobby's pained face in the background. The next was actually a GIF of someone getting hit in the balls. The third photo was of her hand covering an ice pack that was against what I recognized as Bobby's paint-splattered jeans.

You're nicer than me. Have fun, you two.

I knew Sarah might scowl a little at my reply, which was both a goodbye and a "I'm not going to be the third wheel to your relationship." It didn't bother me that she'd moved on from me to Bobby—not in the least. But a photo of her hand on his crotch was a little more than I needed to see.

I addressed my brother's text last. Typed out a reply, deleted it and started over again. Before I could finish composing it, a rush of heat brushed my legs as Hollis came in through the front door and sat beside me. "I had them tow it to Maurice's. Have you been there? Maurice is a good guy."

Tucking my phone into my pocket, I nodded. And then, remembering that we were on favor two—or was it three?—I added a quick, "Thanks." I wished I had asked Keane to pick Casey and me up, but I knew he was at work anyway. I'd have to ask another favor of Hollis.

"Mind bringing me to the garage after this? You can just drop me off, I'll get a ride home."

Hollis hesitated and worried her bottom lip between her teeth.

"You know," I waved a hand as if I was breaking up my words, "it's fine. I can get an Uber."

"No, no, no," she hurriedly said. "My pause wasn't because I can't, but because I was going to offer to wait with you. In case your car can't be easily fixed, so I can give you a ride home. I am not in a hurry to go anywhere anyway."

It was increasingly difficult to reconcile this Hollis with the one I had always remembered her as. She was quiet, polite, thoughtful. I stared at her for an uncomfortable amount of time again, enough to see her fidget and tug her earlobe, worry the clasp at the back of her earring before I sucked it up and said, "That'd be great. Thanks." This time, my thanks wasn't rushed, under my breath. She gave me a brief but friendly smile and checked her watch.

"You hungry?" she asked.

As if on cue, my stomach grumbled silently. "I could be."

"I was just thinking…" she twisted her hands again in her lap. "I haven't gotten lunch yet. We could swing through the drive-through on our way. It'll take an hour for your car to get to the shop anyway."

"Okay." I nodded. "But I'm paying."

When she opened her mouth, I quickly shut her down.

"Look, Hollis." Her named sounded funny on my tongue. "You've been really great. It's the least I can do." And it was my pride speaking, definitely, but I couldn't stomach Hollis giving me a ride, a free tow, *and* lunch.

9

HOLLIS

THE WAITING ROOM WAS FILLED WITH PEOPLE WITH VARIOUS expressions of defeat written on their faces. Adam was not unlike them, his eyebrows furrowed with worry. Though, that worry could have been due to the sludge-like coffee in his styrofoam cup. It was very likely eight hours old at this point, but it was all the waiting room offered in the way of beverages.

I was grateful that I disliked the taste, therefore never becoming dependent on its caffeination. Instead, I held a soda from the restaurant that was growing more and more watery as the ice cubes inside of it melted.

The clock on the wall clicked, drawing my attention.

"Do you have to go somewhere?" Casey asked, breaking me from staring at the second hand's movements.

"No." I gave her a reassuring smile. She was adorable, blond hair with hints of strawberry and the biggest brown eyes I had ever seen. But more than her hair and her eyes was the smile she gave me, like she was genuinely interested in what I had to say, what I had to think. With no younger siblings of my own, I

88

didn't really know what it was like having someone look up to you the way Casey clearly looked up to Adam, but it endeared him to me. I glanced at him, where he was sitting in the same position, but rolling the contents of his coffee around his cup like he'd be able to read his tea leaves through the sludge. "What grade are you in?"

"Seventh," she said.

"Boys are still gross in seventh grade, aren't they?"

Her cheeks immediately pinked and she glanced sideways at Adam, who was still lost in thought. She shrugged but wouldn't meet my eyes. I tried to recall my own experience in middle school but couldn't remember having crushes on anyone.

"Are you in any sports?"

"Soccer," she said, leaning forward on the chair, her hands under her thighs as she rocked back and forth. "Maybe I'll do gymnastics too. I don't know. Depends."

"On what?"

Shyness crept over her face and she scrunched her face, running a hand over her hair. I recognized the movement, woman-to-woman, as being self-conscious of something. "If I get my grades up this year." Her voice trailed off and she chewed on her bottom lip a moment, in thought. "If I do, I'll get to go to gymnastics."

"What grades?"

Casey made a face. "Math. I suck."

That seemed to pull Adam from his thoughts, his head snapping up as he looked over at us. "You don't suck. Don't say that."

Casey flushed, but not like she was afraid of her brother. Which made one of us. "Well, it's a new process, I guess?" She twirled her hair thoughtfully. "So they need us to show how we got the answer. But I do it in my head."

I nodded, understanding. "I remember, middle school math

was rough. I can help you if you want. Wouldn't want to miss out on gymnastics."

"I got it, Hollis," Adam said and my cheeks flooded with color. He'd effectively put me in my place. "And if we can't get the grades up, we'll figure it out. I'll pay for it."

Casey looked chastened.

"What?" he asked.

"I mean. I'm not sure if I can do it when Gram's sick and all, in the hospital. And your job…"

"Jesus, Case. Cool it on the job. I'll figure it out." He said the last sentence while looking at me. I was intruding on a very personal conversation; one I shouldn't have been privy to. But there was no way to leave without making it more awkward. His eyes bore into mine, making me feel a tingle in my belly. He *should* be intimidating. He *should* scare the hell out of me. He looked so different from how I had known him in high school. His hair was longer, his arms were covered in ink—all the way down to his knuckles. A tattoo crept up his neck. But those eyes, those deep, soulful eyes that had haunted me since that night at the party were still the same. Instead of friendliness, I saw frustration.

"Yeah, but how are you gonna pay for the repairs with no job?"

When Adam flushed, I finally saw the resemblance in the siblings.

"I can help," I said, eager to alleviate the tension and the embarrassment for all of us. When Adam opened his mouth, surely to argue, I continued. "I mean, I can spot you the money. And you can pay me back." Judging by the look in his eyes, it seemed important, to him, that he'd pay me back. And that's why I decided to lie. "It's just my dad's credit card anyway. It's not a big deal."

It was a tricky line to walk—I knew—saying that money wasn't a big deal to me when it obviously, understandably, was to Adam. But if he knew the money I'd use for the repairs was from my own bank account, which was padded by my income as a tutor, he'd probably never accept it.

"That's so nice of you. Isn't it, Adam?" Casey crooned, her head cocked to the side. "Easy peasy, you can just pay her back."

"Yeah," I said, as sweat slid down my spine. The waiting room was not air conditioned, but the heat had everything to do with the fact that I had lied and Adam was looking at me like I was something to dissect. "It's really not a big deal."

"Won't your dad ask?"

I swallowed the truth and opened my mouth for the lie to spill out. "No, he won't. He gives me an allowance."

It wasn't technically a lie. He did provide an allowance, but not enough to cover car repairs. And the allowance he did provide had strings attached, of course.

Adam still held me captive in his stare, his eyes dark and deep and his lips in a flat line. Finally, he looked away and both Casey and I relaxed, emitting identical sighs of relief. "Fine. I'll pay you back though. As soon as I can."

"No rush," I said, waving him off.

Adam's phone rang then and he stood, walking outside to take the call. A wall of heat followed him in from outside and I fanned myself with one hand as I pulled at my collar with the other. What I wouldn't give to be waiting in my own air-conditioned car.

"He's really not as big an asshole as he acts," Casey said. "But don't tell him I said a bad word."

I held my pinky finger up. "Swear," I said. She grinned and hooked her finger around mine. Age-wise, Casey and I were about as far apart as Angie and me. I had only been in Casey's company for not even an hour and already I could feel an attachment to her. Maybe it was because she was a little sister. Maybe I could see some of myself in her, that sort of unrestrained child that I had left behind so many years ago.

For the life of me, I couldn't remember my sisters doting on me.

"Your car is super nice," Casey said, slumping back in her chair and tapping her feet absently on the ground. She was always moving some part of her body. It reminded me of Navy a bit. But Navy had never outgrown her childlike behavior.

"Thanks," I said, acutely aware of the fact that my car was nice and Adam's was in the shop. I was almost embarrassed, felt an immediate need to apologize for it. "It's my dad's," I said, but knew it didn't really suffice.

"You're lucky your dad cares." She looked sad, but only for the briefest of moments. "I mean, mine does," she quickly amended, like she hadn't meant to be as blunt as she'd been. A smile spread her lips immediately later but it was something familiar to me. I got the feeling that the smile was the only thing hiding her sadness.

"Is your dad at home?" I realized she had only mentioned her grandma, not her dad. I knew her mom had passed away years ago, so naturally I wondered what Adam's home life looked like. And at the same time, I wondered if I was crossing the line by asking.

"I have no idea where he is." She shrugged and my heart broke a little in my chest for her. I complained about my dad a lot, but damn if the dichotomy of my situation against Casey's didn't remind me of my own fortune. "He comes around once in a while. Maybe he'll be by for my birthday."

"When is that?"

"Couple weeks." She sniffed and picked up her soda. "But like what I said about Adam. He's really a big softie. He's just better at pretending than I am." She raised an eyebrow and pursed her lips as she sucked through the straw. "He doesn't like our dad. And my mom died a while ago."

I knew that, but the way she said it, flatly and without

emotion, shook me a bit. "I knew about that but still, I'm so sorry."

"It's okay." She shrugged again, a movement I was realizing was her way of hiding how she really felt. "I was little. And I have Gram. And Adam. And even Caleb, when he comes home for long weekends."

"Caleb," I said, the name knocking around my brain. "He's your older brother, right?" Older than Adam, too, if my memory served. He'd been a few years older than us in school.

"Yeah. It was him or Adam to come home when Gram got put in the hospital again." Casey turned her head so she faced the window. I could see Adam's pacing reflected in the glass. "So, he's nice. He just acts like he isn't."

I took a breath in, absorbing all this new information. I remembered him in high school, before he'd learned to hate me. He had been nice. So nice, that—Tori was right—I had had a mega secret crush on him. But now? Well, being the recipient of his hate had cooled that crush down. Not entirely, because my body still warmed when he so much as looked at me. Like I was burning from the inside out.

"You're lucky to have a brother who cares," I said, hoping longing wasn't present in my voice. I had a dad, and Casey did not. But she had a brother, at least one older sibling who looked after her. And while I had sisters, they were more acquaintances than people I could count on.

When Adam returned, a man at the counter called his name we three approached the counter. As the man went over the car's issues line-by-line, I could visibly see it affecting Adam's face: the tightening of his jaw, the vein protruding in his forehead, the whiteness of his knuckles as he clenched them on the counter. His face didn't register anger, but something more heart-breaking: complete and utter hopelessness.

"How long for these repairs?"

"I can have it done tomorrow."

"This is more than I expected," Adam said, tapping the number at the bottom of the invoice.

"It's fine," I said, my voice coming out meek. Adam turned to me, staring at me like he wanted to climb inside my head and understand why I offered. Before he could protest again, I slipped the closest card out of my wallet and handed it to the man. "Run this."

It was only after I handed him the card that I realized I had handed him the wrong one. Navy and I shared a checking account that we used to pay for our shared bills for the apartment, and I had my own debit card as well. But the card I had given the mechanic was for mine and Navy's account. I debated, briefly, halting him from running it. I knew there was plenty of money in the account—that wasn't the issue—but I would have to pull money out of my own account and give it to Navy to deposit. The debate over correcting my mistake was brief, thanks to the fact that I knew this situation was already unbearably embarrassing for Adam and the last thing I wanted was to explain that I had *lied*, and used another card that still wasn't my dad's.

The mechanic handed me a receipt and the card, which I slipped into my wallet and signed as quickly as I could. "Need a ride back here tomorrow?" I asked Adam as I shoved my wallet into my purse.

"No, it's fine," he said. He swallowed and looked between the mechanic and me. "Thanks, Hollis."

I nodded, not wanting to make a big deal of this. "What say we get you guys home?" I asked them both, looking at Casey and not Adam because his steady stare was making me feel like I needed to confess the lie. But it wouldn't make him feel better, I reasoned with myself as I drove them home.

After stopping at an ATM to get cash for Navy, I headed home.

94

When I finally got home, Navy greeted me with one of her Navy hugs. Squeezed arms around the back and then a side to side motion that could be almost mistaken for a dance. But it was just Navy. She let go of me, taking one of my suitcases before she shut the door. "You made it!"

I glanced at the clock above the television and brushed my hair back from my forehead. "Yeah. Long day."

"I'd guess so. You had planned to be here hours ago." Navy moved into the kitchen, which overlooked the living room where I collapsed onto one end of the super plush gray sectional. I took in the apartment, my eyes traveling over the living room and the kitchen that overlooked it. It was my first time seeing it with furniture and decorations up on the wall. The sectional had fluffy pillows at each end and in the corner and the coffee table was actually a leather ottoman that looked inviting to my feet. On one wall, the television hung, with photos on either side hung up. The stools that sat under the overhang on the kitchen peninsula looked plush like the couch, and on the center of the white countertop was a mesh bowl that I could see fruit peeking out of.

"Oh, you look tired. Rough drive?"

Though too young to be one, Navy possessed the look of a worried grandmother. She also baked, cooked, and possessed more love than I knew one person could contain within themselves. But more remarkable than the amount of love she possessed was the way she doled it out—even to people I would think as undeserving. "No, not really. I came across Adam Oliver. Remember him, from high school?"

Navy nodded, "Oh, yes. I know Adam well. I've been to several of his shows. He's very good."

I chose not to acknowledge that statement, though she wasn't wrong. "Right, well his car was broke down, so I picked

him up and then we got his sister and had to run a few errands."
That sparked an immediate thought and I scooped up my
wallet, combing through my cards. "I almost forgot. I used the
wrong debit card to pay for his car repairs. I grabbed cash on
the way home." I handed her the money and apologized.

"Oh, that's fine. I have to go to the bank today anyway to
deposit my check. It's okay. You paid for his car repairs? You
have such a good heart, Hollis."

Coming from just about anyone else, I would receive a
remark like that sarcastically. But I knew Navy meant it. She
saw good in people who weren't. "I couldn't let him go without
a car. I sensed that things haven't been the best around his
house lately."

"Keane said he moved back to help his gram, who takes care
of his sister." Navy grabbed a white fluffy throw from the back
of the sectional and draped it over her lap, even though the air
conditioning was on and running. "He has had a rough go of
things lately."

"I could tell." I thought of Casey ragging him about his car
and his job and wanted to cringe again for him. "So, I used the
debit card to the account we share, instead of my own. Sorry
about that."

"It's no problem. Rent is already paid. We just need
groceries."

I stretched and yawned. "Make a list, I'll be sure to pick it up
this week."

"Okay," Navy said in her sing-song voice. "But I'm not
worried about it. We are fully stocked. And I have chili
simmering in the slow cooker for dinner."

If I was being totally honest, having a roommate that
actually cooked was another benefit to rooming with Navy. The
one summer I had roomed with Tori, right before going off to
our separate colleges, we'd subsisted on microwaved ramen
noodles and cereal. Having a home cooked meal was something

I missed since moving out of my parents' home at the age of eighteen. "You're the best, Navy," I said as fatigue hit me like a freight train. I nuzzled down into the cushions.

"No, you are," she said, adjusting a pillow under my head. "Take a siesta, dinner will be ready when you wake up. I'm going to the mall with Keane, so I'll be back in an hour or so."

"Okay." That was all I remembered saying before I drifted to sleep.

10

ADAM

"You want another one?" Keane asked as he stood and went to the fridge.

"Sure." I switched the channel to the news, before switching it again seconds later. I was restless, full of listless energy after spending much of the afternoon with Hollis. It didn't sit well with me that she'd paid my repairs. I didn't like owing anyone a dime, much less someone like Hollis. I had a little money in the bank, but it was reserved for keeping the roof afloat when Gram's expenses were higher than usual. Or paying for Casey's much desired gymnastics class—because I *knew* dad would promise and forget to follow through.

Now that I didn't have a job and was indebted to Hollis, I knew there was no way I was going to be able to make gymnastics happen, not for a while at least. It was a knife in the gut, a hard pill to swallow. Casey deserved better than this, and it killed me that I couldn't provide it.

"You okay, man?" Keane asked, handing me the beer. He'd

only been at Gram's for an hour and all we'd done was shoot the shit after eating dinner.

I rubbed a hand over my head. "Got let go today at the shop."

"No shit." Keane sat on the recliner beside the couch. "Why?"

"They're saying seasonal work is down. Since I was a newer hire, I was easy to let go of."

"You haven't even had that job a month. Why did they even bother hiring?"

I took a long pull of the beer. "Beats me." Keane was one of my best friends, but it was still uncomfortable to talk about things like this. Between losing my job, my gram's prognosis being not good, and Hollis paying for my car repairs—all topics that were dominating my thoughts—I was going to be in for a long night if I didn't start talking. "Went to the hospital this morning." I glanced down the hallway and, encouraged by the lack of noise, continued, "Gram isn't going to get better. It's just a time bomb at this point. Ticking away in her chest."

"Shit." Keane sighed and took a pull of his beer before setting it down. "I'm sorry to hear that. No wonder you're quiet tonight." He looked down the hall like I had and turned back to me. "Does Casey know?"

Shaking my head, I said, "Not yet. I don't know what to tell her. I can tell you she's not going to get better, but she's not your grandma. She's not your only stable guardian."

"Does Caleb know?"

"God, not yet. I need to call him but today was just a royal shit show, and I haven't had a moment to breathe. Until now." I tipped my beer toward him. "These aren't as skunky as I expected."

"Yeah, I'm surprised myself." Keane shifted, turning so he was facing me. "So," he said in a voice that told me he was broaching a subject that I'd need to prepare myself for. "I saw Navy. We went to the mall so she could stock up on eighty-seven soaps or some shit. She mentioned that you saw Hollis Vinke this weekend."

Fuck. It was bad enough that Hollis was the reason my car was sitting in my driveway, but the knowledge that she'd told other people was a little more humiliating than I could stomach. Especially after the last few days. But I played it cool, taking a long drink while I thought over my words. "Yeah, I did." It was all I could come up with to say in reply.

"I thought you hated her."

"Yeah, well, when she's the one who saves your sorry ass, anger has to take a backseat to gratitude."

"She saved you?"

Keane's reply was a relief. So he didn't know. That made the bitterness I'd instantly felt dissipate somewhat. "She came upon me when the car was broke down on Little Canada Road. She picked me up, had the car towed, brought Casey to her dentist appointment…" My voice trailed off.

"Wow. Hollis Vinke, being a Good Samaritan."

"Yeah." I drained the beer and set it down. I'd need to slow down before I spoke more freely than I wanted to. I didn't want to tell Keane how good she'd looked. Something about her was just … fresh. It sounded stupid when I said it to myself. The last thing I needed was my best friend ragging me for it. "Good thing too—Casey's dentist is hard to get into." I debated telling him about Hollis paying for the repairs, but put the thought away for the meantime.

"Did you call me?" Casey asked at the end of the hallway.

"Hey, squirt." Keane held up a hand for her to high-five, which she did. She loved Keane probably as much as I did. He was the kind of best friend I would've hand-picked for myself growing up. Never giving judgement or unwanted advice. But he commiserated in the utter shit show that life could be when it wanted to be. "What's with the outfit?"

"Oh, this?" Casey grabbed the fabric around the knee of her

shorts, pulling them away from her body and then letting them snap back at her skin. "Just preparing."

"For what?" Keane asked.

"The olympics." She brushed her hair over her shoulder. "I'm gonna be there one day."

"Oh, yeah? You have tickets or something?"

"Athletes don't need tickets." She brushed hair over her other shoulder in a dramatic move that was meant to incite laughter. I knew she didn't really believe she'd end up the Olympics, not at her age and especially with her lack of professional training. But it was something she wanted enough that sometimes when she said she was preparing for the Olympics, there wasn't any laughter in her voice. It simultaneously lifted me up and broke my heart. I hated my dad all over again for being the asshole who could have but never had provided her. Not just in the instance of having gymnastics practice, but emotionally and physically. He wasn't the dad she needed, he definitely wasn't the dad she deserved.

"Well," Keane smiled at me and leaned toward her conspiratorially. "I believe it. When does practice start?"

Casey glanced at me and then shrugged. There was the slightest slip in her expression, from delight to the briefest pass of solemnity before she put on a smile that wasn't genuine. "I'm not sure yet. I mean, it's not a big deal. It's okay, I've waited this long and I can wait longer."

That was why I wanted more for her. Because she didn't think she needed it.Yes, on the list of needs for an almost thirteen year old, gymnastics lessons were low. But everything was low on the list for her. She was constantly promised one thing by our father before it slipped away. All I wanted—even more than a steady job—was for her to have a break from the bullshit.

"You about ready for bed, Case?"

She slumped, chagrined, against the wall at her back. If it

wasn't a school night, I would have let her stay up. But I wasn't going to be like my dad, not when it came to my sister. "When's Gram coming home?"

I hadn't told her yet because, quite simply, I didn't want to tell her. Really, I didn't have anything to say. There was no news. At least, that's what I told myself. "Nice try stalling." I waved my hand toward the bathroom at the back of the house. "Brush those teeth with all that new dentist swag."

She sighed and rolled her eyes, but complied. When she was out of earshot, Keane turned to me. "Gymnastics?"

"Yeah." I leaned forward, elbows on my knees as I cradled the beer in my hands. "She's been wanting it forever, but of all the extracurriculars, she chose one of the more expensive ones. And of course, my dad promised it to her. He makes all these fucking promises that leave everyone else on the hook to fulfill them." Talking about money made me feel sick. The feeling had settled low in my gut when Hollis had offered to pay for the repairs, and the feeling hadn't left since. Talking to my best friend about it made me feel even worse.

"I can—"

"No," I interrupted. "I'll figure it out. I always do." But I didn't. Not really. Because if I had, Casey would've had lessons years ago.

"They're always hiring down at the plant, you know. Especially with harvest season just passing." Keane tipped the beer back and lifted a shoulder. "I could get you in." My hesitation made Keane shake his head. "It's a job, Adam."

I knew his tone. I wasn't too good to work a factory job. Far from it. But the hours would be rough. Keane worked extended shifts sometimes. Swapping the afternoon and the late shift, which was eleven at night until seven the following morning. I'd be fine working it if there was someone to stay with Casey, but because it was just me her and me, my options were to hope to get a morning shift or have someone stay with Casey while I worked overnight. I thought of my brother Caleb but knew that he wouldn't be able to help. Classes were about to start, and he was hours away.

Before I could give an answer one way or another, Casey returned and Keane stood to give her a big ol' bear hug. "Goodnight, squirt."

Casey wrinkled her nose at him and then went into my arms. "'Night, Adam."

I kissed the top of her head and patted her on the back. When Keane and I were alone again, I grabbed the last two beers from the fridge and motioned toward the front door, where we could sit out on the porch in the quiet, far from Casey's ears.

I loved Gram's house. When I thought of 'home' I thought of this place. Small but tidy. Many nights I sat on the front porch with Gram, talking about everything from my dad to girls to school and my future. "My boy," she'd always say, "you've been dealt a bad hand. But that doesn't mean you can't play like you haven't." Gram always wanted more than the life I had been given, and had sacrificed so much for me to get it. Lately, it felt like all I was doing was falling back into the cycle I had grown up in. I wasn't afraid of being poor. But I was afraid of allowing my sister to grow up that way.

When Keane and I were settled on Gram's white wicker furniture, our gazes straight ahead at the park that was across the road, Keane spoke up, confirming once again that he was more than just a best friend: he was a mind reader. "Maybe Casey could stay with my mom at night."

I shook my head, simultaneously grateful for Keane and annoyed at myself for pride being my Achilles heel. I *knew* I didn't have the luxury of letting my pride get in the way, but I let it all the same. "Let me call Caleb," I said. "He knows things haven't been good with Gram. Maybe he can transfer to college here." But even as I said it, I knew it would be a fruitless phone call.

"Maybe," Keane replied, but I could tell from his tone that he didn't necessarily agree. Keane didn't really like my brother, which wasn't a surprise since my brother didn't like him much either.

"I'll figure it out," I repeated.

"Maybe you can figure out how to work 'we' into that statement, instead of 'I.'"

I sighed. "You know it's hard for me to accept help, Keane."

"You're basically a single dad right now. You have to do what's in Casey's best interest." I knew I appeared crestfallen at that statement, and he continued. "You know that. That's why you came home. You're helping your gram and your sister. Let me help you. I'll get you the job. We'll figure out how to help your sister."

When he put it that way, how could I say no? "I owe you." And I thought of what I owed Hollis too, for the car repairs.

"What's that look for?"

I lifted my head, blew out a breath. "Uh..." I began, and stared at the playground across the street. "I seem to be owing a lot of people these days."

"Well, for one, you don't owe me. I'll see about getting you on, but I'm sure I can. Who else do you owe?"

Pride told me to shut the hell up, but this was Keane. I couldn't lie to him. "Hollis."

Keane sat back and waved a hand at me. "For the ride? Don't sweat it. I'm sure she isn't."

Running a hand through my hair, I breathed out and leaned forward, elbows on my knees as I stared at the leaf rustling away, across the driveway that was cracked and needing to be replaced. One more thing that needed tending to around here. "It's not just the ride. She paid for my car repairs."

Keane was silent, taking a long pull of his beer.

"She insisted," I added. "Saying it was her dad's card anyway, and he wouldn't notice." I wondered what that must be like. To have money within reach, without worry or work to produce it. It was a bitter thought, turned to acid with the final swallow of my beer. "So, I've got to pay her back of course. I'm not in a position to turn down any job right now."

"Oh..." Keane finally spoke. Sort of. I looked at him and he held up his phone. "That's what Navy meant."

I went still. "What do you mean?"

"Navy and Hollis are roommates. You knew that, right?" I shrugged and angled my head toward him, prompting him to continue. "When we went to the mall, she was carrying a wad of cash like she was some drug dealer, said she had to deposit it while we were there." Keane rolled his beer bottle between his hands. "She said that Hollis used the wrong card to pay for repairs of some kind. That she used the debit card attached to her bank account with Navy. And she pulled out cash from her savings for Navy, to make up for it."

The beer in my stomach rolled, turning thick like syrup. "What?" It'd been bad enough when she'd claimed the money was her dad's, *his* credit card. But now, knowing it was actually Hollis' savings, didn't sit right with me. She'd lied to me.

"Whoa there," Keane said. He set his beer down and held up his hands. "I'm sure it was a misunderstanding."

"She used her savings to pay for my repairs? Not her dad's money?" I blew out a breath. Anger lit through me quickly and thoroughly before I tamped it down. "That's fucked up."

"I mean, does it matter?"

I nailed Keane with a look. He knew how much lying bothered me. And he knew my pride often got the best of me. "Why didn't she tell me the truth?"

"Would you have accepted it if she had?"

The answer was quick. "No."

"That's why." Keane tilted his head back toward the house.

105

"She knows what Casey means to you. Anyone in your presence for five minutes knows that. She took one look at Casey and did what anyone would do, and approached it in a way that you'd be more willing to accept it." He picked up his beer, draining it. "Don't let it get to you that a girl helped you out. Like you said, you're going to pay her back."

"Yes, but it makes a difference that it was *her* money. I don't even like her."

"Come on, Adam. You're not being very fair."

I gritted my teeth and shook my head at him. "You don't get it. Her little cronies in high school made my life hell. And she never did shit to stop it."

Keane made a face. "You're right. High school sucked for you. But it's incredibly generous of you to assume that she'd have any kind of power over everyone who made her acquaintance back then."

"They were, are, her friends. You're *my* friend. If you were being a dick, I'd tell you."

"Yeah, and when you are being a dick, I tell you." He looked at me pointedly. "Like now." He slapped me on the back. "Look. I get that you hold a grudge against her. Your grudges are legendary." I knew he was talking about my dad. "Maybe her paying for your car repairs is a small way of her making up for high school bullshit."

"I'm going to sell my keyboard," I said and Keane looked at me like I was out of goddamn mind. "I'll pay her back tomorrow."

"You're a real piece of work, Adam. She was trying to be nice and I know you—you're just going to throw it back in her face." He stood up, jingled his keys until his headlights flickered in the dark. "You know what? That high horse you're riding on? It's actually a donkey." And then he left.

11

HOLLIS

"You saw him?" Tori squealed. "Holy shit. You actually saw Adam *I'll take his penis for 500,* Oliver."

I cringed, remembering the one time I had said that—in a drunken stupor, naturally, in high school. Before he hated me. "Yes, I saw him. But he hates me, so…"

"Oh, I'm sure he doesn't *hate* you. How can anyone hate you?"

I picked at the hem of my shirt, remembering how he'd looked at me with eyes so dark that I would've done anything to avoid looking into them. "Well, he hates me. For sure. No doubt about that." I glanced at the work on my computer waiting for my attention and sighed. "My dad emailed me," I said. "I haven't opened it."

"Ugh, don't. You're just going to have your good mood darkened."

"Am I in a good mood though?" I asked her. "Adam hates me, I've got so much to do until class starts tomorrow, and I already have a line of people wanting my help."

"You mean you have a line of people waiting for you to do their work for them. Hols, you're really such a pushover."

"I'm not." But I was.

"Did you tell Adam about how you two have been hot and heavy the last couple of years?"

"No." My face soured. "Somehow, I didn't have a chance to sneak that into the conversation."

"That's surprising," she deadpanned. "But you should. You could be well on your way to accessing that trust fund."

"That's upon my engagement," I reminded her.

"Yeah, but you can't be engaged until you actually start dating someone, like for real."

"I have been dating someone, a fake someone."

"Yes, so you need to bring that fake someone—Adam— around the 'rents to make it look real. Maybe your parents will realize their antiquated ways and amend the trust again so you still get it after graduation."

"Unlikely."

"Why is that unlikely? They amended it once. They could do it again."

I sighed, pinching the bridge of my nose. "I'll just own up to the fact that I lied."

"Technically, I lied. I told them his name was Adam."

"Yes, well I told them there was a *he* to begin with. And there isn't. Or wasn't."

"Oh come on, Hols. You need a boyfriend."

"Oh sure, let me just order one on Amazon. I'm sure I can find one with good reviews and two day shipping."

"Ooh, feisty Hols, I like it. But I'm serious." I could hear her clicking and I imagined her searching Amazon for gently used fiances. It was almost enough to make me laugh. "You paid for Adam's car repairs, right?"

"Yes…"

"Then maybe he can do *you* a favor. You know. Pretend."

"Sure, my dad would just love that. Also, how convenient that I go to school and immediately have a fiancé."

"Well, ease into it, dum-dum. They already think you have a legit relationship. Start slow. I bet you could pull off a believable engagement before graduation."

Glancing at the calendar I said, "Oh sure, just keep up the ruse for the next seven months. No sweat!" I sighed, flopping onto my back on my bed. Papers flew up around me and I winced, imaging the mess they were making. "I am not seriously entertaining this idea."

"But you should."

"Isn't it pretty slimy for me to tell him he doesn't have to pay me back for his car repairs, just as long as he pretends to like me enough to convince my dad we're on track to get engaged?"

"How much were his repairs?"

"Irrelevant," I huffed. "Drop it, Tori. I'm not going to go along with this. No way."

"I'm just saying. It's not a terrible idea. You scratch his back, he scratches yours."

"Yeah, and I'm pretty sure he'd rather just claw my back."

"Ooh, kinky. I like it."

She was trying to make me laugh, so I obliged her. But in the back of my mind, I knew my dad's ultimatum for the trust was going to have to be dealt with one way or another. That's what my tutoring income was for. It wasn't enough to completely live off of, but if I kept socking it away, maybe slowly I'd be able to build up enough money that I could do what I wanted: not go to law school. "Maybe I should just listen to my mom and meet up with David." But that felt more like sending myself off to be slaughtered.

"David?"

"Come on, you know David. His mom was at my dad's party."

I heard the crunch of her chips. "Give me a hint."

"Box wine."

"Oh, hell. Dick pic David?"

I blinked. "*Dick pic* David? What dick pic?"

"I didn't tell you?" Tori sighed. "Well, that's probably because it was unmemorable. Unsolicited, and unmemorable. Two strikes before he even went up to bat. Not that it was an impressive bat. Ugh, he dropped one in my texts. Anyway, your mom wanted you to hook up with David?"

"I'm still processing the fact that he sent you a dick pic."

"Yeah, well, don't. Clearly, I forgot about it because I never told you. You're not missing anything. Big yikes."

"I'll have to take your word for it. He just got back from Florida, I guess."

"Really? That surprises me. He was on his mom's tit *before* he left the womb. I thought he was still there."

I laughed. "He only leaves long enough to steal her wine, I guess." My phone chimed a notification for another email and anxiety filled my chest. "I got to go, Tori. I have a lot on my plate and I still need to go to sleep at a normal time tonight."

"I get it. Call me after class! And don't worry—you're going to have the best first day."

I hung up and sat up, staring at the mess that awaited my notice. My phone pinged with yet another tutoring request. Tutoring was how I made money—yes—but some people liked to think their "five second question" which was never five seconds, didn't merit compensation for my time. For my friends, I would've helped in a heartbeat. But for people who only texted or called me for help, I knew I should be more assertive about charging them what I charged my actual tutoring clients.

Overwhelmed and under pressure and I were in a threesome. It was pretty much life-long at this point, but the pressure was only getting more intense—which exacerbated the feeling of being completely overwhelmed. I was really good at playing it off like I had my life together. Never overreacting, always complying—at least when it came to my dad. And my friends, really. I loved my friends. But I was a yes girl.

"Hey, Hollis. Can you edit my paper? I know it's last minute and due tomorrow."

Yes, I can.

"Hols, I'm short fifty bucks. Can you spot me?"

Yes.

"I really need a tutor for class. Can you meet me when I'm not hungover on Sunday night to go over the course?"

Yes.

"Can you share notes with me? I don't really feel like going to class today."

Yes.

"Can you be my partner? I don't know what to do and you're so good at it."

Yes.

It was my own fault, of course. It was if I had been preprogrammed as a child to say yes even when I only wanted to say no. To do everything asked of me even if it was my last fifty bucks, even if I hadn't slept for three days, even if I was sick with pneumonia and unable to get out of bed. I was motivated by my fear of failure—and in succeeding for everyone else, I was failing myself. I knew I needed boundaries, but I'd created a monster. In looking at my email, and the three emails with proofreading requests from people who weren't actually friends but who felt like I was their friend when they were in need of something, plus the two requests from people who wanted me to make a resume for them based on their information, and staring down at my tutoring schedule for the following week, I knew I had taken on too much. Way too much.

I blew out a breath through my nose, practiced some breathing techniques, but no number of inhalations would clean out my inbox to my satisfaction. I clenched my fists and released, hoping the blood flow would cool me down. But it was no use.

And the cherry on the sundae of shit was the email from my father, with links to four acceptable law schools and the personal numbers of three tutors for my LSAT. The email ended with a note:

Your mother indicated that you have not yet hired a tutor for your LSAT. I wish I could say I am surprised, but I'm not. Here is a list of tutors who come highly recommended from my legal team. Interview each of them and see which one would be acceptable. We will pay for it, of course, but you don't have much time. One month until the test. You will have to devote much of the next few weeks to studying.

Expecting your answer by tomorrow.

The thing that made me laugh was that he didn't sign the email with "Dad." No, he used his standard company-related email signature, like this was a business transaction. I guess, really, it was. I wasn't his child, I was a product to improve.

My mom was right; I hadn't hired a tutor. Because I hadn't had any intentions of taking the Law School Administration Test. It was stupid of me, really, I knew. Dad wasn't going to go quietly, especially not with the recent trust fund amendment. Before, graduation had been the stipulation. But now, knowing that he could change the circumstances if I went against his wishes, I had no choice but to take the damn test. There was no way I could procure a fiancé by the end of the school year, eliminating the issue of taking the test and continuing on to law school. I had to keep Dad happy if I ever wanted to see a drop of that money. And I did.

I wished I could say to hell with it all, but I wasn't a girl who gave up. Someone better than me might turn up their nose at my father's—let's just call it what it was—bribe. But I wanted that money. I justified it by reminding myself that I wanted to do good things with that money, things that I simply could not do without it. There was no way I'd be able to afford to go help poorer countries rehabilitate after disaster or misfortune. Money was my opportunity and I hated that I wanted it as bad as I did.

I closed my eyes and sucked in a cleansing breath. When I released it, I looked around my room, grateful for the privacy. Dorm living had been fine except instead of plastering on a smile when I was in class or in a group, I had to do it all the time. Here, in the apartment I shared with Navy, I had a space dedicated just to me and my breakdowns. I could be me in this room—it was the only place on earth I felt I could safely be me. And the real me was shaken by the load on my plate, which was growing taller and more overwhelming by the minute.

I had no choice but to take the LSAT. I had no choice but to apply to law schools and hope to find a boyfriend who didn't find me cold or insensitive or boring. That last one was the most worrisome one, really. Because *I* knew I was warm and sensitive, but I also knew I was relatively boring.

My phone pinged and I glanced at it. Another email from another student—former dorm roommate this time—asking for free tutoring this weekend. Classes hadn't even begun and people were already banging on my figurative door, asking for favors that they weren't certain they'd need.

When Navy knocked on my door a few minutes later, I was mid temple rub, trying to release the migraine that was growing larger by the minute. "Yeah?"

"Hollis?" Navy pushed the door open and stood there for a moment, looking me over. "Are you all right?"

I gave her a weak smile. "Headache is all. What's up?" I couldn't even be honest with her, because she'd want to sit on my bed and pet my head while I unloaded. But I simply didn't

WHITNEY BARBETTI

have time to unload in that way, nor was I comfortable dumping my woes on Navy.

"Well." She clasped her hands in front of her and her expression took on one of concern. "I did a bad thing, Hollis."

"What?" The pressure was mounting in my head and I struggled to keep my cool.

She blinked and sat on my bed anyway. I'd have to keep my head away from her so she couldn't deliver this likely emotional blow with a hand stroking my hair. "I was talking to Keane this weekend when I was at the mall. He was with me when I had to deposit the cash you used for Adam's car repairs and anyway…"

I sighed, but it did nothing to alleviate the stress that was mounting in my brain. "So you told Keane who told Adam who now knows I lied," I deduced.

"Yes. And he decided to come over here."

I stared blankly at her.

"He's downstairs now. He wants to talk to you."

I was torn between crying, screaming, and tossing my books off my bed to bury myself under the covers. But because I was not reactionary, I told her, "Well, send him in. I'm in the mood to be yelled at."

12

ADAM

SHE HAD THE PRESENCE OF MIND TO LOOK AT LEAST A LITTLE remorseful as she stood in her doorway.

"You sure you don't want to have the fight downstairs?" Navy asked, braced at the top of the stairs as she looked between us. It would be comical if I weren't so pissed off.

"No, because there are knives there. I'm sure Adam wouldn't hesitate to use them," Hollis said. She looked different than she had last week. Not necessarily her appearance; her clothes were perfectly pressed, and her hair looked neat and tidy. But her eyes. There was something in their depths. Something uncontrolled.

"That's fair," I said, looking from Navy to Hollis. I watched the delicate lines of her throat shift as she swallowed, her only tell to her own anxiety, as she stood aside and let me enter the room.

"We'll be down in a minute, Navy," Hollis said, confidently for someone who looked like she was preparing for a guillotine.

"Okay, well if you hurt her," Navy pressed a finger in my

chest, "I'll hurt you back." Navy was probably the gentlest person I had ever come across but because I knew she was also sensitive I just nodded my understanding.

Hollis shut the door behind me and moved to her bed, sitting down perfectly straight as she stared at me. "I lied to you."

"Yeah, you did." I was angry on the way over, which was why Keane had insisted on accompanying me. But now that I was here, standing in her sparsely-decorated bedroom, I tried to remember exactly what had driven that anger.

"Would you have accepted my help if I hadn't lied?"

"That's not something I can answer. It doesn't matter because you lied to me." Ah, there it was. The anger I had been overflowing with before I'd called Keane.

"Kind of a moot point now, isn't it?" she asked.

"I don't like liars, Hollis. I'll sell my keyboard and get you the money tomorrow."

She waved it off and shook her head. "That's stupid, don't do that. I told you, I'm not in a rush for the money."

There was that word. Stupid. It wasn't a word I took lightly. Too stupid for college, too stupid to get a job in a town where Gram and Casey were. "I'm not stupid."

"I didn't say you were. I said selling your keyboard would be stupid."

I clenched my jaw. "Lying is stupid. Is that how you get by in life, by lying?"

"Oh," she said laughing without humor, "I *wish* I could get by on lies. I wish I could dance around the truth and fool everyone but I can't."

"I remember how you were in high school. The people you hung around with." Her eyes flared at that.

"Who, like Navy? Tori?"

"Ah, yeah, Tori."

Her back straightened. "What's wrong with Tori?"

116

"Nothing is…" I ran my hand through my hair with frustration. "She's flighty."

"She just knows what she wants; she's self-assured."

"Is that what all your little high school buddies were? Self-assured? So sure of themselves that they had to belittle others?"

"I never belittled anyone."

"Maybe. Maybe not. Regardless, you kept the company of bullies. You should take full responsibility for how you were in high school."

A light went into her eyes. It wasn't confusion or frustration. It was anger. "What do you mean?"

"You know what I mean." When she stared blankly at me, I gritted my teeth. "I thought you were different. But it didn't take long for me to see who you were. You might have been nice at one point."

"I'm not claiming I was a saint. But I didn't go out of my way to be mean."

"No, you just supported those who were."

"I didn't support them."

"Sure you did. By being silent. Your silence spoke louder than dissenting words could." I shrugged. "You were different," I repeated, as if that said enough. "Until you weren't."

She had a jawline sharp enough to cut glass and its edges were only sharper when she set her jaw like she was doing then. But it was the fire in her eyes that pulled me in, fire I hadn't seen from her. Was this the same person who'd quietly given me a ride despite my biting remarks, who had been kind to my sister when she didn't have to be? "I'm the same as I've always been." But something flitted across her eyes, telling me that wasn't the entire truth. "I'm not a product of the people I spend time with, but Tori is a good friend of mine. She has never once made you feel less than. And you know it." She was standing, pointing a finger at me, inches from my chest.

"But you did," I said and nearly regretted it. It was the truth, but it was *my* truth and not hers, judging by the hurt that shone in her eyes. Her eyes grew wide, searching.

"What do you mean?" she asked. "When?"

"It doesn't matter," I said, waving her off. "It's old news."

"Obviously it isn't if it's still bothering you." Her arms tightened across her chest, her jaw set harder and her chin lifted. There. That was the way I had thought of her after that night at the party.

I pointed to her face. "You're doing it right now. You might not think you are, but you're looking down your nose at me. Literally and figuratively." I thought of her family, of the eyes that matched her father's, the eyes that were shooting daggers at me. "Once your dad fired mine, I was real trash. You merely took pity on me in high school, at that party."

At that, she really looked confused. Was I lying to myself? No, I knew. I remembered how she'd looked at me at the party, when I thought I had cracked her surface to see what was underneath. She'd watched as I had been made a fool of. She hadn't stood up for me. She'd been silent.

"I've never once thought that." The fire seemed to go out of her and her arms dropped. I didn't know if I could believe her. She'd switched so fast before. She was more than met the eye, more than I had ever assumed her to be.

"You watched. You did nothing." Instantly, I wanted to snatch the words back. I had my pride and nursed it more than I probably should, but disarming myself in front of her wasn't something I had ever wanted to do. "But like I said, it doesn't matter. You're you and I'm me."

"If that's supposed to allude to something that actually makes sense, I don't get it." The fire was back again, stoking itself just behind her thick lashes.

"You're Hollis Vinke, daughter to the town's most well-known philanthropist. I'm Adam Oliver, son of the town's most gossiped about philanderer."

"I think you're giving your dad too much credit."

I didn't know what it was about that wording in particular that made anger light up in my veins. Perhaps it was the delivery, like she was better than me, always had been, because her dad was rich and well-admired. "Okay, right, let me make this simpler: your dad is rich and better than my dad. I'm just some stupid kid who you toyed with in high school for a few minutes at a party."

"I never toyed with you."

"But you did."

I watched her jaw clench, briefly hollowing out her cheeks. "I did no such thing. I think the problem is that you put me on a pedestal I didn't ask to be put upon and when I made a mistake I was suddenly some kind of jezebel, worthy of your stones." Her phone rang and she glanced at it before tossing it on the bed. "I didn't ask you to talk to me at that party and I don't know what I did to make you think I was some asshole, but I promise you that I *wanted* to talk to you. Okay?" She was breathing heavily like she'd just run a marathon. Like the words had been an effort for her to say. To admit.

"Oh, don't try to nurture my wounded pride now, years later, Hollis. I'm a big boy. I don't need to you make me feel like you actually thought I was special."

"You really have a low opinion of me, don't you?" Her eyes shined with fury. "Well, get in line."

"Don't give me the poor little rich girl sob story, Hollis. You know you're better than that."

"Am I? You're not painting me in a very good light right now. I feel like I'm on trial for something I didn't do." The uncontrolled look in her eyes I had seen before was wilder now, and I saw it reflected in her body, in the way her hands shook as her own anger took her over. Was I an asshole for wanting to see her angry? For wanting to see her as anything but the unfeeling image I still held of her, seared in my mind?

"Do you deny that you had friends who looked down on people like me?"

"Navy and Tori never did that."

"I'm not talking about them," I said, unable to keep the frustration from my voice. "I'm talking about *you*. I'm talking about the people you joined in mocking me at that stupid fucking party that night. After we'd talked on the deck and after you'd let me in. Just a little. Was it all an act? Is that who you are? Just another fake person in a crowd of frauds?"

She had the nerve to actually look hurt by that, as if what I was saying wasn't true. She'd spent a good chunk of our conversation that night telling me she wasn't like the rest of them. But her actions had proved otherwise.

"You are so..."

"What?" I held my arms wide. "Mean? Am I a dick? A loser? No... what was it they were chanting that night? Band geek?" I scoffed. "Pretty fucking unoriginal insult. Or do you want to take a dig at my dad, too?"

The phone rang again and she picked it up. In slow motion, I watched the scrunching of her eyes and the grimace that curled her mouth and then—most spectacular of all that—when she sent her phone flying across the room until it crashed unceremoniously into a bookcase. Woven dolls, books, and frames fell to the ground and I looked back at her.

Her hands clapped over her mouth as she stared at the destruction. Well, *destruction* was really exaggerating the mess she'd made. A toddler could've done worse. "I've never done that," she said around her fingers. She seemed genuinely shocked by her own outburst and turned to me. "I'm sorry you saw that."

What the fuck. I had no clue what to make of her then. Who was she? She wasn't the girl I'd talked to at length at that party, the one I thought was so composed, so tightly-wound, until she'd loosened during our conversation. But she also wasn't the girl who'd accepted my verbal barbs in the car several days ago and hand't stood up for herself. She was someone else entirely. Someone who was so closed off that their outbursts were rare and shocking to even themselves.

"It's fine," I said, not really sure what to say. But she stood, frozen, staring at the mess. I found myself dropping to my knees in front of the bookcase and picking up the frames and books and knickknacks, not sure how they went back on the shelf but trying my best to arrange it the way it was.

"No—don't." She collapsed next to me, taking the doll from my hands and running her long, delicate fingers over the clothes it wore, brushing the doll's hair back from its face. It didn't look like a doll Casey had ever had. This one looked homemade and not like a child's toy but a souvenir of some kind. I picked up a picture frame, inspecting the glass for cracks. There were three girls in the photo, their heights so distant that it looked like a papa bear, momma bear, baby bear arrangement. "Is this you?" I asked, pointing to the smallest.

"Yes. My sisters," she said, tapping the other two girls. "They're a bit older than me."

"I figured," I said. She took it from my hands and I picked up the next one. "Your mom?" I asked. I could see Hollis a little in her, in all the ways she didn't look like her dad, at least.

"Yes." She placed the frame on the shelf next to a stack of biology books. Their spines were creased and the lamination was peeling, but still they appeared to be in neat order. "Sorry," she said again. "I shouldn't have let my anger get the best of me."

I didn't necessarily agree with her. Seeing that little burst of anger from her was oddly refreshing. I couldn't explain it really, except that she was different—multi-faceted in ways I was only beginning to discover. "Stop apologizing."

"Okay." She took a breath and I knew she was about to fucking apologize again so I put a hand on her knee for a brief moment before removing it.

"I suppose this is where I say I'm sorry for making you so angry."

"You suppose?" She arched one perfectly groomed eyebrow.

"Yes, suppose. But, since I'm not sorry…"

"If you're trying to get me angry again…" she began, but was interrupted by her phone trilling. She picked it up and huffed, throwing it on her bed. Where it was safe from causing damage.

"I don't think *I* was the reason you were so angry," I said. "Your dad?" I had only glanced at the text enough to see the sender, not the contents of the message.

"Yes, well, you're not the only one with Dad problems." She winced, like she hadn't meant to say that.

"Are you saying you don't get along with your dad or something?"

She was still crouched beside me, her hands braced on the floor, as she turned to look at me. She waited a breath, one long moment as she searched my eyes. "My father has expectations of me."

"Don't all parents?"

"I don't know. Does your dad?"

At my shrug, she continued.

"Sorry, that was a rude thing to say. I know your situation. Or, Casey told me." When I didn't say anything, she barreled on. "I mean, she didn't divulge every detail to me or anything. But she gave me a good idea." When I still didn't say anything, she kept rambling to fill the void in our conversation. "My dad cares —yes, but one could argue he cares too much. And his care is essentially control."

"At least he cares," I said, wondering what it would be like to have my dad give a shit about me.

"Okay, well at least your dad doesn't hold your very future hostage over your head, like mine does."

"And how does yours do that?"

"My sisters," she said, pointing to the photo frames. "They

122

each received access to their trust funds upon their college graduations and then took off. They only visit home under duress. Me? Well, up until a couple weeks ago, the plan was the same for me. Once the diploma was in my hands, I'd finally have access to that money."

She wasn't looking at me, but at the doll she still held in her hands. If pity was what she was looking for from me, she'd have to do better to get it. Money was the biggest worry of my mind. The idea of having access to a large sum at some major milestone in my life wasn't something I could relate to. But I let her continue without interruption, waiting for it to get better. For me to understand her better.

"But my dear sisters, having gone off to live in a commune or swim with sharks aren't producing the one thing my father wants most: grandchildren."

That perked my ears up. Surely, he wasn't pressuring Hollis to get knocked up at this young age?

"I know what you're thinking and the simple answer is *no*. But the not simple answer is, in a way, yes. I won't have access to my trust fund upon graduation. Rather, I'll have access when I've announced an engagement. My dad has traditionalist values in that he sees life in steps: college graduation, engagement, career beginning, wedding, children. It's his thought that having his daughter engaged will earn him what he most covets."

"So you don't get this pay day until someone puts a ring on it."

"Right." She rubbed her lips together and a line creased her forehead. "And it's all the more laughable to them because I'm virtually a spinster in their eyes."

"A spinster? What is this, the 1700s? You're no more of a spinster than a—what was it you called yourself earlier?—a jezebel. You're twenty-one."

"Exactly. Nearing twenty-two. Practically ancient, in my father's eyes at least. And because his eldest two have not had kids nor have the idea of marriage on the horizon, my dad is pinning his hopes and dreams on me. So, I must deliver in order to access that money."

"So you have to inspire a man to propose in order for your dad to surrender your money?" I asked. "That's first world problems at its finest."

She waited for a beat, eyes flashing. That anger was back, brighter than before. She still held the doll in her hands and I eyed it with suspicion, hoping she wouldn't feel so inspired to hit me with it. I didn't think she was capable of violence, but then again I didn't know her all that well to be the judge of that, did I?

"It gets worse." She sat back on her haunches and rubbed her temples. She looked defeated, like she had nothing left to lose. "Are you ready to hear one of the bigger lies I've told?"

"What?" More lies? It would surprise me to hear she was anything less than perfect.

She laughed, but it wasn't reflected in her eyes. Instead, there was a shining in there that had nothing to do with humor. "My parents have been trying to set me up for years now. With a variety of people they're acquainted with. Like this is some Regency time period. So," she swallowed a breath and wouldn't look me in the eyes. "I made up a story, a couple years ago, that I was seeing someone. Not a boyfriend, necessarily. But I made them believe … I was not single. And therefore, unavailable for their match-making."

I mulled that over. "That doesn't sound highly unreasonable."

She barked another laugh so sharp that she clapped a hand over her mouth. Her normally well-put together hair was fraying along her crown, with tendrils curling over the gentle slope of her forehead. When I stopped to really take her in, it was striking to me just how beautiful she was. A fact I resented, for complicated reasons.

"I hate to echo myself, but it gets worse still."

"Try me."

She laughed again, but moisture was collecting at the corners of her eyes. "When they dropped the bombshell, about altering my trust, Tori was there."

This *was* taking a twist. I was equally interested in hearing her continue and also, strangely, dreading it. What could she possibly say that made this worse? But, judging by the way she kept side-eye looking at me, I had a feeling something big was coming.

"And Tori," she swallowed, "unhelpfully told them the name of my fake suitor."

"She did?"

Her eyes met mine, that flash of brown looking wholly terrified. "Yes." I watched the column of her throat as she swallowed. "She used yours."

Silence fell over us. As I absorbed this new knowledge, her eyes grew wider and wider, like I was an oncoming semi and she was a deer, frozen in its headlights; waiting for its inevitable demise. She was bracing herself. For me.

"Tori named me," I finally said after a while. "Why?"

Hollis's eyes darted to the side and I reached out, touching her chin, making her look directly at me.

"You've racked up quite the number of lies as of late. Let's try on the truth, Hollis."

"This is embarrassing," she whispered. A pink tongue darted out, wetting her lips. "It's not my fault she said your name."

"No," I agreed, but hadn't let go of her chin. "It's not. But the question remains. Why did she say *my* name?"

"Because, once upon a time, I had a crush on you." When I said nothing, she hurried on. "After that party." She winced. *That* party. It seemed unbelievable, given the way things had turned out.

I held her chin a moment longer, searching her eyes and

only coming up with the knowledge that this time, she wasn't lying. "Okay," I said and let go. I didn't really believe it—or at least, that's what I told myself. But deep down, I knew—I just knew—there'd been something between us at that party. Some unspoken set of feelings. Emotions that had laid dormant until we'd spoken to one another. "Well, that's awkward."

She flinched and pulled away from me. "Yeah. It was supposed to be one little lie."

"Your lies have the effect of a snowball becoming an avalanche." I gestured to myself, reminding her of why I was even here in the first place.

She flinched again. I started feeling a little sorry for her. I was still sorting through the rest of my feelings, but she'd definitely found herself in a pickle.

After we were both silent for a little while, she said, "Are you done yelling at me?"

I realized we were still on the floor, and the wreckage from Hollis's little burst had been cleaned up entirely. "Yeah, I think so." I stood to leave, but Hollis stopped me with her hand lightly touching mine.

"Please don't sell your keyboard. I'm not worried about the money. I understand and acknowledge that that's a fortunate thing for me, to not have to worry about. I don't say that to make you hate me even more, but to tell you that I want to help you, in the only way I can."

I stared at her, but she wouldn't lift her head to meet my eyes. So, I left.

On my way home, I called Caleb. I hadn't had a real conversation with him in a while and I needed an answer one way or another from him, so I'd know how to proceed with the job and with Gram. I had filled him in on Gram's status the

126

day my car had broken down, but we hadn't discussed next steps.

"Hey," he said. "What's up?"

There was an explosion of sound on the other end of the phone, and he laughed and hollered something away from the receiver.

"Caleb," I said, impatience simmering in my voice. "This is serious."

"What?"

"The Gram stuff. You get what I told you, right? She's not in great shape." I swallowed, staring out the windshield as the sun set beyond the mountains. "I need to know the plan." I rapped my knuckles on the steering wheel, already bracing for the answer I expected.

"Well, I'm not coming home."

Right. Of course he wasn't.

"I've got school."

And I had a band. "I thought as much."

I heard a sigh on the other end of the line. "Hold on a second, Adam. I can barely hear you."

I stopped at an intersection and watched as the railroad crossing began blinking lights. Of course, I'd take the wrong route home right during the train's nightly run. Amber Lake had boomed in the late 1940s and as a result the town grew faster than it had adequately prepared for. The railroad tracks crossed over nearly every major roadway intersection, causing backed-up traffic in a town that didn't have that kind of traffic normally.

I moved the car into park and waited for Caleb to stop saying hi to people who weren't me on the other line as he navigated to a quieter area.

"Hey," he said. "What did you say?"

What had I said? "I guess it's on my shoulders to figure this out, right?"

"Well, you don't have to put it that way."

"What other way is there to say it? You're staying across the state. Casey has been struggling in school for the last year and Gram is dying. Do you get that, Caleb? She's dying."

"Calm down, Adam."

I clenched my jaw, willing myself not to explode on him. Caleb had been lucky enough to get out before Dad had deteriorated, becoming the man he was now. He wasn't ever home often enough to see how bad it had gotten, or he did see it and ignored it. "Did you hear what I said?"

"Casey's always struggled in school."

"No, she hasn't." I rubbed a hand over my face. "She was doing well until the last couple of years. Right when Dad stopped taking care of her." Taking care of her was a gross misrepresentation. Casey was used to fending for herself, had to be in order to survive the few years since I had left. Gram did her best, but no one could fault her for not being there for her granddaughter when her heart was failing her.

"What do you want me to say?"

"What do I want you to say? I want you to fucking help me, Caleb. I don't know what the fuck to do. I left everything in Colorado and came home to a shit show. I don't know how to take care of Casey."

"Jesus, she's not a baby. You don't have to mix her formula or give her baths."

"No, I just have to raise her." Could I blame him for choosing to stay at college? I would be a boldfaced liar if I claimed that leaving my band, my life in Colorado, hadn't been hard. If Caleb had said he'd take care of Casey, would I rush home to help? I couldn't say for sure. But he hadn't volunteered, the day Gram had asked me to three-way call her and Caleb for a mini family meeting. It was a choice I had made, and I didn't regret it. But if I was being honest, there wasn't another choice on the table.

"Just help her with her homework. She's a good kid. She's practically an adult already."

"She's not yet thirteen," I reminded him. "And me, help her with her homework? Do you not remember how school was for me?"

"Of course I remember. That's why I'm in grad school and you chased a dream." He said it almost patronizingly, not that I was surprised. Me leaving town and joining a band had made me a spontaneous child in his eyes. "Come on, it's middle school shit. It can't be that hard."

"I also have to get a job, keep up on the bills."

"You chose to go back, Adam," he reminded me gently.

"Because you wouldn't."

"That's not fair. If Dad was there—"

"But he's not," I interrupted bitterly. "And if—no, when—Gram dies, Dad has to step the fuck up. Do you think he will? Or, is it more likely that he'll OD on some bullshit pills that hold more worth than his own daughter?"

"Addicts deserve compassion, not judgement."

"I don't need a fucking lecture from you, Caleb," I spat. "Trust me, I've been to enough meetings with Dad. I've sifted through enough pamphlets, hoping to find some kind of answer in those glossy pages. But Dad doesn't *want* to get better."

"He showed me a sober coin the last time I saw him."

"Oh yeah? When was this?"

Caleb was quiet for a moment. "Last year. Summer, I think."

"Yeah, well, he's homeless in Utah right now. Or at least that's what he claimed when he hit me up for cash three months ago."

Caleb was quiet again. He didn't see the side of Dad that I saw. He saw Dad more human than I could. "Did you give it to him?"

"Fuck no." I had told him I could buy him groceries on an app, for him to pick up, and I had directed him to one of the men's shelters. But he'd angrily refused and I knew why—because the shelter required sobriety. And because despite what he'd claimed he needed the money for, what he really wanted money for was drugs. My dad was as predictable as the moon. I knew his MO.

Caleb was my big brother, but I always felt like the responsible one in the things that were practical and necessary. I wanted Caleb to be my big brother. To tell me everything was going to work out. To talk me through this in an actionable way.

I replayed the conversation I'd had with Hollis and found myself coming up with a plan.

"Don't worry," I found myself saying. "I'll figure it out."

I always did.

13

HOLLIS

ON MY WAY OUT OF CLASS, I WAS ACCOSTED BY A STUDENT WHO tried to schedule me for one-on-one tutoring later that day. I tuned out his words and instead acknowledged just how exhausted I was. I could feel it in my bones, the kind of tired that sleep can't solve. When the flow of students out the door caused him to bump into me, alarm flitted up my spine, and I took a big step back.

"No," I told him, interrupting his *You know how it is* pity speech. "I am unavailable today." Saying the words felt like prying them from my tongue and I had a knee-jerk feeling to take them back with an apology and a smile, but I bit my lip to keep my mouth from opening and rushed away from him and everyone else that was waiting around him, like vultures waiting to pick the meat from my bones.

I practically slammed into the doors to exit, sucking in the air that awaited me outside, replacing every bit of stale air I'd been forced to breathe for the last hour.

That's when I saw him.

He was sitting on one of the benches just outside the doors, his head down as his thumbs danced together in his palms. He hadn't seen me yet, but I knew he wasn't a student here. There was only one reason he was waiting outside this building at this hour.

I thought of our conversation the day before, how I had let my temper get the best of me. Maybe it wasn't even temper but pure frustration. My hand found its way to my back pocket as I recalled throwing my phone and the shock that he wore on his face at my lack of composure. I never slipped. I always held it together, even if the seams holding me together were stressed and taut.

A gentle breeze ruffled his hair before it reached me and his head lifted, eyes connecting with mine. He braced his hands on his knees and stood. "Hollis."

He never said hi. Not to me, at least. I took a tentative step forward, taking in his dark jeans and dark t-shirt. "Adam," I returned. "Hi," I said, because I wasn't accustomed to not saying it.

"Can we talk?" He motioned to the bench and I walked over to him, taking in the lack of anger or any other negative emotion. If anything, his slouched shoulders and worrying hands made him appear resigned. He sat down with a sigh.

"Yes, I suppose."

The side of his mouth quirked up in a crooked smile and he patted the seat beside him.

When I was sitting, he handed me an ice cold can of diet soda.

"You don't drink coffee," he said by way of explanation. But the way he said it, with almost a question enunciated at the end made it sound like he wasn't totally sure.

I took the can from him. "That's right." I stared down at it, wondering if this was some kind of peace offering.

"You like lemon poppyseed muffins, right?" This time, he

sounded less sure as he produced a paper bag with my favorite bakery's logo across the front.

I didn't touch it, and set the diet soda down between us to pull the binder I was holding closer to my chest, a kind of plastic shield. I didn't know what his game was, but I'd be lying if I said I wasn't suspicious.

"Look, think of these as a peace offering." He'd read my mind.

"Are we at war?" I asked him, meeting his eyes for only a moment before looking away. Anywhere but at him and at the muffin and soda. My chest hurt, embarrassment from the night before but also because breathing was more work than I could allot just then.

"Maybe not at war. But I was a dick yesterday. And you..." his voice trailed off and I met his eyes again. "You looked tired."

Just what every girl wants to hear, I thought.

"Not tired like you hadn't slept but tired like the weight of the world was on your shoulders. So I looked at your Instagram when I got home and didn't see photos of coffee but I saw a lot of photos of this soda and these muffins." He lifted the paper bag in my direction again but I was still processing everything he said.

"I *am* tired," I conceded, sitting beside him. He handed me the soda and muffin and I took both with a smile of thanks. After carefully peeling back the muffin paper, I hesitated for a moment before I tore it and handed one half to him. "But the soda is mine," I said, my attempt at a joke.

"I bought it for you," he said, his eyes piercing mine. "This too, but I'm not gonna give it back to you since you're sharing." He popped the entire half into his mouth and smiled with a big ol' lump in his cheek.

"I'm sorry I freaked out yesterday." I took a careful bite of the muffin, brushing my fingertips over my lips so they'd capture the crumbs left behind. I chewed carefully, swallowing thoroughly before continuing. The last thing I needed was to embarrass myself for the third time in front of him. The muffin, while delicious, went down my throat like a rock when I thought of my dad's email. I snuck a glance at Adam. "Thanks for this." I lifted the muffin and took another bite.

Adam relaxed back against the bench and I envied him, his ability to be chill after the tension that had been simmering between us. I imagined that the differences in our body language made it hard to discern exactly what was happening between us, what with him reclined back, his ankle over his knee, and me with my back straight as a pencil and my legs pressed together. I tried to relax, I did. But I still wasn't entirely sure why he'd brought me the muffin and soda. I mean, that was casual right? It's just a muffin and soda. Three bucks. But why did it feel like a much bigger deal? Why did I feel a tiny slice of anxiety snake its way into my belly?

He gently tapped my arm, pulling me from my thoughts. I whipped my head to him, taken aback.

"Sorry." He held his hands up in front of him. "You're so deep in thought that I didn't think words alone could pull you out of it."

I blinked, still a little shocked that he'd touched me. Granted, it was a finger tap, gentle, but … oh, I was doing it again. "I guess I've got a lot on my plate."

"Yeah, you mentioned as much yesterday." He drummed his fingers on the back of the bench, looking at me like I was a puzzle he was putting together. "So listen, I've given it a bit of thought."

"What?"

"What you said yesterday. About your parents, your situation."

I took another bite of the muffin to keep myself from saying anything stupid, waiting for him to continue.

"And I think I can help you. Be your…" He waved a hand in

the air between us. "Fake boyfriend, for a little while. But we have to be clear about this." He looked away then and I saw his Adam's apple bob as he swallowed. Was he as nervous as I was?

He was *agreeing*? In all the possible plans I had plotted since Tori had let it slip, I'd never once banked on him actually going through with it. "What are your terms?"

He laughed then. "Terms. Like this is a legal transaction or something."

"It's important for us to be on the same page, so there is no confusion." I was already trying to think of what to do first. My parents wouldn't be in town for a couple weeks, which meant we'd have two weeks to act as a legitimate couple.

"Right. Sure."

"What do you want in exchange?"

He stared at me, long and hard. "You're a tutor, right? That's what Keane and Navy have said."

I nodded, not sure where this was going. Adam wasn't in school. What did he need a tutor for?

"It's for Casey," he explained. He dragged a hand through his wild dark hair, and the pieces fell back into place like my hair did, after I had assaulted it with half a can of hairspray first. "She's got her heart set on gymnastics lessons. I hoped I'd be able to buy them, but with the way things have been going, and my gram... Well, anyway, she's had a rough couple years, thanks to my dad." He didn't elaborate on that part, because we both knew he didn't need to. "Now he's promising to buy her gymnastics lessons if she gets her grades up." He laughed. "The first responsible thing he's done as her father in a long time."

I nodded, remembering my conversation with Casey. "Okay, sure. Of course." I licked my lips and ran my tongue over my teeth, hoping to remove any traitorous poppy seeds. "Casey needs tutoring." I thought that through, deciding I needed to make a plan sooner than later before my schedule filled up. "I can do that." He smiled gratefully. He was asking me to do something for his sister, not him, and it warmed me in a way the morning sun could not.

"I feel weird about this, to be honest. I don't like the idea of using your services for free, but using it for her feels better to me."

I wanted to tell him I did it all the time—work for free. And for people who weren't asking out of care for someone besides themselves. But helping Casey meant more time in her presence, which wasn't a bad thing at all. I had enjoyed what little time I'd already had with her.

"There's another thing." He coughed and looked around, as if suddenly aware of our setting. "Shit, do you have another class to get to?"

I shook my head. "I have another hour."

"Okay. Well, this one is a big ask." He gazed at me sideways. "So if you say no, I get it. I'll figure it out."

"What? Money? I don't mind paying you. It's a big ask of me to have you pretend to like me for as long as this lasts."

"No. I'm going to work with Keane. His job has openings. I'll figure everything else out." At least he had the dignity not to protest that he actually did like me. This was a business transaction, and the help he'd be giving me far outweighed what I was doing for him. As far as I was concerned, he hadn't asked enough of me. "But I'm going to work some late shifts. Gram will be home soon, but I can't really count on her if there's an emergency—for her or for Casey."

"Casey needs company while you're at work," I said. "I got it. Just tell me when."

He hesitated a minute before nodding. "Is that going to affect your schedule?"

"I don't think so. Most of my classes end before one in the afternoon. If this late shift is after then, I should be available."

"Okay." He paused. "If you're sure?"

"I'm sure." I stuck my hand out and he waited a beat before taking it. "We'll figure everything else out later."

He'd lost that carefree posture in the last few minutes. It was like we were back to being strangers, but strangers who had to feign romantic interest in one another. "I guess I'll need your number then." He handed me his phone and I put the numbers in and sent a text to my phone, so I'd have his.

"One thing," I said, suddenly remembering why Adam had come to my apartment the day before and started this entire conversation. "We can't tell anyone, apart from Keane, Tori, and Navy."

He let out a frustrated breath. "I don't like lying."

"Well, you'll have to get used to it. At least for the time being. Our fake relationship has to look real to everyone—not just my parents."

"Why everyone?"

I raised an eyebrow. "Do you know my dad?"

Realization dawned over his eyes. "Yes, he fired mine. But okay. I get it. So we have to post on Facebook and Instagram and all that shit."

"Yes. Build it up until their visit in two weeks."

"There's a party tonight," he said out of the blue. "Mike Summers's house. We could go, our first outing." He said the last word with air quotes. "If you're game."

It was on the tip of my tongue to say *No*. An instant, knee jerk reaction. But there really was no time like the present. Delaying the inevitable would only lead to nerves haunting me every hour leading up to it. I still dreaded going to the party tonight, but at least I didn't have to agonize over it for days. Only hours. "Okay," I finally said.

"I'll pick you up."

That was it; we were done. I stood and retreated with a hasty "Bye."

"Hollis," he called.

I paused, holding my binder to my chest as I turned around.

Adam rose from the bench, walking to me with confidence I didn't possess myself. I swallowed as he came closer. Somehow, when we'd been sitting beside each other it felt easier than it did when he was standing, face to face, looming over me.

"You forgot this." He held up the can of diet soda. "I figure, if I'm going to be your pretend boyfriend, I'm going to have to get better at bringing you snacks." The side of his mouth lifted in a rare smile and I took the cold can from him.

Without saying anything, I turned and walked away, waiting until he was out of earshot to exhale the breath I had been holding.

14

HOLLIS

MIKE SUMMERS'S HOUSE WAS SET BACK OFF OF AMBER LAKE, LIKE a space in the mountains that wrapped around the lake had been made precisely for the footprint of his palatial family home. The dock that stretched down to the lake seemed a mile long, judging by the number of bodies from the house to the edge of it the boat landing. Out on the water floated a dock, and from the laughter and splashes that carried across the lake the party was out there as well. The sky was darkening enough that the presence of the dozens of tiki torches was welcome. Out on the water, bugs were as present as people this time of night.

I glanced at Adam as he looked out over the water, wondering what was on his mind. If this was a normal relationship, I could ask him what he was thinking. I could pick his brain and he could pick mine and maybe we'd even hold hands as we walked through the large glass double doors into the foyer. But instead we were so far apart that if we hadn't arrived in the same car together one might think we just happened to be here at the same time—not that we'd come, together. Adam looked around the grand entrance, taking in the curving staircase and the high ceilings, while I sought out a more familiar and friendlier face at the back of the house, in the kitchen that overlooked that long dock and the water beyond. Navy was there, picking up plastic cups and rinsing them out, laying them upside down on a tea towel so they could dry. She leaned over and asked someone if they needed anything and to anyone else, it might've seemed like she was the lady of the home or—at the very least—Mike's current girlfriend. But she was neither of those things, she was just Navy.

I wrapped an arm around her waist, grateful for the break from Adam.

"Hey," she murmured, leaning into me. "This party is kind of a snooze fest," she said under her breath.

"It looks busier outside." I nodded at the large glass windows that faced the deck.

"It is. But still, snooze." Navy mimicked snoring for a beat. "Mike wants to take his dad's new boat out but thankfully Keane has the keys out of reach. Mike's been looking for them for the last thirty minutes."

"Oh, Mike must be in the sauce."

Navy's eyebrows reached so high I thought they'd disappear into her hairline. "Oh, is he ever." She looped an arm through mine and led me away from the kitchen out to the near-empty living room. It was an actual formal living room—no television in sight, just two white leather couches and a wall of books organized by color. With its plush, white rug and white marble fireplace, it looked like a room my mom would've pinned on Pinterest for inspiration, if she didn't already have two completely decorated homes. Navy and I lowered onto one of the couches and she immediately tucked her feet under her. "Are you here alone?" she asked, looking around.

"Adam's here somewhere."

"Oh," she said, in a knowing way. Knowing, like she was

actually cheering on this relationship. When I'd given her the rundown of what was going on, surprisingly she'd clapped excitedly for me. "Adam's a catch!"

"Yeah, well, I haven't really caught him, per se. He and I have a business transaction," I'd told her.

"Still." Navy had clutched her hands to her chest and gazed up at some invisible spot on the ceiling. "He likes to read; you like to read. How romantic."

"Navy, you need to get out more if you think that's romance. Or, maybe, read one of my books."

So, at least Navy was on board for the farce. I still needed to tell Tori, however.

"Where is he?"

"Probably getting a beer." I propped my elbow up onto the back of the couch, not wanting to talk about Adam at all. "Where's Keane?"

"Probably distracting Mike outside." She looked over her shoulder to the foyer as more people spilled in. Unsurprisingly, I didn't recognize them either. "Best to keep him distracted so he doesn't get pissed that he can't find the keys. Want a drink?"

She had slipped so easily into a hostess role that I had to smile. "I'm okay, Mom," I said, tugging on one of the braids that lay over her shoulder.

"If I was your mom I wouldn't be offering you alcohol."

"Maybe," I said, but not entirely sure. I was fairly convinced my mom medicated with wine throughout the day just to stand being around my father as much as she was. She was so judgmental toward my sisters about their own alcohol intake, so it made sense if she was actually a hypocrite. Though if I had to be around my father as much as she did, I suspected I'd be the same in her shoes. "Is it bad that I already want to go home?"

"It's not bad," Navy said. She nearly reached for my forehead before I stopped her.

"I don't have a fever. I'm not sick. I just…" I shrugged, looking around the space. "I don't want to be here."

"Is that why Adam has abandoned you for a beer?"

"He hasn't abandoned me," I said, trying to make sure I was careful with my words. He and I hadn't spoken the entire way over to Mike's party. This party was for appearances only, so that it wasn't such a shock when photos of Adam and I together started popping up on social media."He wanted a beer and I didn't."

"But you're here." Navy tapped the couch. "With me. Not hanging on your boyfriend."

"He's my fake boyfriend."

"He's not trying very hard, even for a fake boyfriend."

I looked at her in confusion. "What do you mean?"

"He asked me a little bit about you," Navy said coyly.

"What did he ask?" I wasn't aware Adam was going behind my back to converse with my roommate.

"Just… stuff. Likes. Dislikes." Navy said it like it was the most romantic thing. And under different circumstances, it would undoubtedly be. But I knew that Adam could use those dislikes to his advantage when no one else was around.

I was beginning to feel actually sick. This was such a bad idea. Our first outing together and I was not prepared to lie through my teeth. Sure, I did it all the time for my dad's fundraisers and functions. But this was different. I actually knew a lot of these people. I tutored some of them. I had classes with many of them. Lying would be harder since these people knew us both.

"There you are," Adam's voice rang out from behind us. Like twins, Navy and I turned at the same time. He approached us, a beer in each hand.

"I don't drink beer," I told him.

His eyes stilled on me for a minute and he pursed his lips. "You did once," he said, reminding us both of that night.

"I did, until I practically drowned in it."

Adam raised one dark eyebrow. "That's a little dramatic, isn't it?"

"Is it?" I cocked my head to the side. "Maybe you don't remember, but I was a little bit shocked by that."

Adam took a sip of his beer and then deadpanned, "You seemed to be back to your regular self before the night was over."

I knew what he meant by that. Because I had said nothing when the cronies from high school had taunted him. But he'd been so busy wrapped up in another girl that he'd forgotten all about me.

"Besides," Adam continued. "You assume too much. I brought this beer for Navy. Not you."

"Oh, Adam," Navy said with a laugh like his joke was the funniest thing in the world. She took the beer from him and stared up at him adoringly. She looked between the two of us when neither of us laughed. "Oh, well, it's nice to see us all getting along so well." Turning to Adam, she said, "We were just talking about you."

"Oh?" He sat on the back of the couch so that I had to crane my neck to look up at him. "Only good things, I hope."

"That'd be a terribly short list of topics to discuss," I said with a fake smile plastered on my lips.

"Hols," Navy said admonishingly. Why did she nudge me when I took a dig at Adam, but laugh when he snubbed me? I glared at Navy a little and she laughed. "You two make such an interesting pair," she said, standing. "I'm going to go find Keane and see if I can rescue him."

"Has he got himself into trouble?" Adam asked after her.

"He's hiding Mike's keys before he decides to drive and inevitably crash his dad's new boat."

"Ah," Adam said to her retreating back.

We were alone then, Adam sipping his one remaining beer

and me beverage-less. When he glanced at my hands, he held up his bottle. "Want to share?"

"No."

"Okay." He took a long pull and I turned my eyes away from the way it made his throat move, his sexy little veins pushing against his skin. "Not even a sip?"

"No," I said, wrapping my arms around myself.

"You do that a lot."

"Do what? Say no?"

"Wrap your arms around yourself." He nodded at my posture.

"Only around you," I countered and hesitated, briefly, before uncrossing my arms.

"Don't care to share?" He held the beer up.

"No."

"You liked sharing my beer back in high school."

I felt the blush and hoped he didn't see it climbing my neck to my cheeks. "Yeah, well that was before you hated me."

"Fair point."

"We should probably go outside," I said, nodding toward the door.

"Oh, right, because no one can see us acting like a *real* couple in here." He finished his beer and held his hand out for me. I stared at it, wishing I could take it and make it seem careless and free. But like he said, there was no one in here to witness us. Why put either of us through hell for no reason? I ignored his hand and moved back toward the dining room.

I was almost through the French doors before I felt the hand on my back. Looking over my shoulder, I met Adam's eyes. That look seemed to be the invitation he needed and his hand slipped over mine, fingers pushing their way between mine so that our fingers were laced.

I wanted to pull away. The very last thing I wanted in the whole world was his stupid, warm, large hand holding mine.

And it rattled my bones realizing that, knowing that I *wanted* this. I wanted his hand holding mine. And not just for appearances.

The air outside the dining room on the deck was warm—not humid—which made it easier to relax. The sky was melting into the water, and the laughter and splashes coming from the sandy beach below made this situation more bearable than if I'd been alone.

"What do you want to drink?" he asked me after we walked over to one side of the deck. It was less crowded here, away from the beer pong table and the kegs. But it was still visible.

"Nothing," I said, leaning my forearms on the railing as I looked below, where a few people lounged on chairs.

"What do you want to do?"

"What do you mean?"

I felt his hand lay gently on the middle of my back. "This is your scene. How would you like this to play out?"

"I'm not a director," I said quietly. This would be easier if he didn't hate me so much. If the chemistry wasn't tainted by his disdain for me. Then, we could be natural, unchoreographed. But he had a point. I turned around so my back was at the railing and we were facing one another. "Cage me in with one arm. Not both."

He waited for a beat before stepping closer. "Spread your legs," he said softly.

"Why?"

He gave me an impatient look. "I'm not after that, Hollis. I just need to put my foot between yours. My arm span isn't ten feet."

I was so tense, I could feel it knotting my muscles. This really was the last place on earth I wanted to be, but this was my show. I had to play my part. After a pause, I lifted one leg back until my foot hit the solid spindle of the railing. He stepped forward again, his jeans brushing my leg as he came closer. I leaned back, so that the brush of his stomach against mine remained that, and not a solid press. His leaned to my right, his left hand braced on the railing and our arms pressing against one another.

"There," he said. "That feels natural."

I wanted to tell him to speak for himself. I didn't make a habit of standing so close to any man.

"What should I do?" I asked, hoping he'd help me. I could feel eyes on us, but I did my best to stare up at him. The angle of my neck caused my hair to tumble down my back, catching between it and the railing.

"Just act natural," he said, his warm breath fluttering against my cheek as he leaned forward, inch by inch, until our chests were pressed against each other and his lips touched the shell of my ear.

I held my breath, not wanting to exhale and further push my chest into his. Holy…mackerel. When I tried to tilt my head down, my hair stuck in the wood behind me. "My hair," I said breathlessly against his ear.

His fingers trailed against the thin fabric at my back, freeing my hair from their confines and pulling it forward, over my shoulder, as he too pulled away. His hand lingered there, with my hair, for a moment too long. Well, too long if he hadn't been brilliantly playing his part.

We were close enough to whisper but he didn't say anything as he looked at me, hand slipping over my shoulder. From the intensity in his eyes, the slight parting of his lips, I could almost allow myself to believe there was something stirring there. Perhaps, the very thing that was stirring for me.

"Adam!" someone yelled, effectively breaking both of our attentions as we turned to the voice.

"Blake," Adam said with more warmth than he'd ever used for me. He stepped away, leaving me leaning against the railing awkwardly. I brushed a hand down my skirt and stood straighter.

I peered at the guy clapping Adam on the back. He looked genuinely happy to see Adam, and Adam looked happy to see him too. They exchanged hellos and *what are you doing here*, both completely oblivious to me. Which was fine. Because the smile Adam gave him was so brilliant that it made my own teeth hurt. And, maybe my pride just a little. If he ever leveled that kind of affection toward me, I'd surely be in trouble.

"Hollis?" the blonde guy said as he turned to me. "Hollis Vinke?"

I blinked a little, silencing cursing the growing dark which made it impossible to see him. The long blonde hair, scraggly like it was drying and attempting to curl didn't look familiar at all to me.

"It's Blake. Blake Miles."

I knew the last name. One of my dad's employees. "Oh, right. Your dad is Rob."

"Yeah," Blake said enthusiastically, giving me a wide mouthed smile. "You're here with Adam?" He gave Adam some kind of bro smile.

"Yes," I said, carefully minding my words.

"You dating?" He asked Adam like I wasn't even here.

"No," I said at the same time Adam said, "Yes." Adam's eyes flared as he looked at me. But he knew I couldn't make this too obvious, too fast. My dad might be hundreds of miles away, but he wasn't an idiot.

"Well, she says no," Adam said, squinting at me in challenge before turning his gaze to Blake. "But I say yes." His arm came around me, pulling me so we were stuck side to side. "I just have to convince her."

"I'm sure you will." As quickly as he'd said hello he practically said goodbye to me with his body language. "What about Sarah?" he asked Adam.

Sarah. I didn't know any Sarahs, not well anyway. I mentally went through our senior class, trying to remember a single Sarah—such a common name, I should've come up with at least a couple, but I was spared the search when Adam said, "We're still friends. She's in Denver."

Who the hell was Sarah? And what was this weird little burn I felt in my chest? Heartburn, surely. No way was I jealous.

Okay, fine, if I was jealous at all it was of the life Adam had that I wasn't privy to. Something we'd have to amend if we were going to make this believable at all.

"Let's take a photo," Adam said. "I'll send it to her. She really liked hanging out with you when you came to our show."

"Sarah's great," Blake confirmed, pulling out his phone and opening up the camera. "Hollis?" he asked, holding it out to me.

I stared at the phone like I wished it'd spontaneously combust, but took it anyway and snapped the photo—hoping my lack of care made it blurry. I could breathe again, being away from Adam and his hold around me.

"Now let's get one of the three of us," Adam said, hooking an arm around my waist and pulling me close. I didn't know what to do, being this close to him again. It felt like I had just taken my first deep breath before he pulled me back under, against his heat. In the frame on his phone, I could see our faces and Blake's just behind us. Adam's shoulder lifted, brushing my cheek.

I got the memo. I lowered my head so I was resting on his shoulder and after a moment the flash captured us. I didn't even have a chance to make sure it was a decent photo when Blake was taking his phone back from Adam.

"I'll text it to you," he said to Adam, typing away on his phone.

"Oh, just put it on Facebook." He was still holding me. "I'm getting a new number now that I'm back in town for the time being."

"Okay, cool. I'll tag you. See you around. Bye, Hollis."

He'd barely paid attention to me, but the goodbye seemed sincere enough. When he was gone, Adam's hand loosened so he wasn't holding me so tightly.

"That was smart," I said, grudgingly.

"What?"

"Having him post online and tagging us."

He raked a hand through his hair. "Thanks."

"Who's Sarah?"

He arched a brow.

Shrugging, I hoped I looked the very picture of nonchalance. "Blake practically gushed over her while I looked on like a fish out of water. I probably should learn a little bit about your life in the last few years."

"Sarah's my ex," Adam said. "She was our band manager. Unpaid gig, that."

"Slave worker. Got it."

"Ex-girfriend," he corrected me. "Still a good friend."

I didn't have much—any—experience with former relationships to know if this was normal or not. But it didn't settle well on me, knowing that there was a woman familiar to Adam's friends, one he apparently kept in touch with. "What's she like?"

"Oh, she's great. Warm. Tough as nails if you fuck up though." His lips spread. "She threw a drink in my face once."

I swallowed the bitterness that had pooled in my mouth. He looked totally smitten with her. "Wow, that's nice." I didn't know what else to say.

"It was vodka and I had road rash from an unfortunate stumble home the night before. Nice isn't quite accurate." He ran a finger over the side of his neck, over his chin where the facial hair looked slightly patchier. "I've got a scar here. Hair doesn't grow quite as proudly here as it does elsewhere."

"I'm sure you deserved the drink."

"Oh, I did. Like I said, she's tough as nails."

So, nothing like me. At least, not in Adam's eyes. No, I was some American princess with first world problems whose most dramatic outburst had been throwing her phone at a book case. Bad ass, I was not. And I didn't really know why it bothered me so much, hearing him talk about Sarah like she walked on water.

"What does she look like?" I asked, wanting a picture in my mind. Inexplicably, I imagined some dark-haired Angelina Jolie nymph, in leather like he was. But when he turned his phone to me, I didn't quite believe he hadn't just Google searched "Blonde angel woman," and shown me one of the first results. Her hair was long, blonde—duh—and she had the biggest, bluest eyes I had ever seen. She looked exactly the opposite of me. Once again, disappointment lit through me at my own inadequacies.

"She's pretty," I managed, meaning it. Because she was. Whatever my own insecurities, I didn't need to twist them and aim daggers at this innocent woman. No, my daggers would be saved for Adam. After all, he had plenty for me.

15

HOLLIS PULLED A BOTTLE OF WATER OUT OF HER PURSE AND chugged it. "You bring your own water to parties?"

Capping the bottle, she looked sideways at me. "What, you don't?"

She was trying to be funny so I rewarded her with a half-smile. "You seem tense." I glanced around, but few people were actually paying us attention. "Parties still aren't your scene, are they?"

Ignoring me, she turned to look out over the balcony. Below us, Keane was carrying Navy on his back as he ran down to the beach. Navy squealed—in excitement or protest, I couldn't tell—and both of them ended up in the water as people laughed around them.

"Maybe," I began, "you need to blend in."

"I'm not drinking any alcohol." She shrugged, glancing at me. "I just don't drink. Especially when I have school." When I didn't say anything, she said, "Yes, I know I'm boring."

It wasn't the first time she'd said something unkind about

151

herself. "Chill," I said without heat. "I didn't mean to make you feel pressured."

When she said nothing, just stared out over the water, I got an idea.

"Okay. I'll be right back. Don't move." I said it jokingly to myself, but Hollis didn't even turn to acknowledge what I had said. In the kitchen I grabbed another beer and two plastic cups before venturing back out onto the deck.

Hollis hadn't moved. I approached her and tapped her gently with the cups.

"I'm not sharing your beer," she said, eyeing the cups and my beer, back and forth.

"No, you're right. You're not. This beer is mine. The cup, one of them at least, is for you."

"I don't need a cup." She waved her water bottle at me like I was dumb.

"You don't need it. But it might make you feel, I don't know, one with the people." I opened and closed my hand, gesturing for her to give me the bottle. When she did, I set the cups down on the railing.

"I want this one," Hollis said, choosing the one nearest to me.

"Fine." I uncapped her water and she watched me with shrewd eyes as I poured the contents into the cup. I tucked the empty water bottle into my back pocket and poured my beer into the other plastic cup. "Ready?" I asked, handing her the cup.

"For what?"

"To join the fun." I angled my head over the railing. "Down there."

"Oh, I don't think we have to…"

"We don't *have* to, Hollis. That's not what we're doing here. We should be seen though." I held out my hand to her and she looked at it warily before taking it. "Come," I beckoned, drawing her down the stairs to the ground below. Her skin was soft and cold. I brushed my thumb over the back of her hand, the instinct to warm her being at the forefront of my mind as I pulled her toward the throng of people. Off one side of the long dock above hung a tire swing that somehow was unoccupied.

Steering her toward it, I glanced at my watch. "Hey, sit here for a minute with your cup. I gotta give Casey a call and check up on her." Hollis nodded, sliding her legs through the hole of the tire and resting her arms over the top of it. Tanned legs kicked against the ground, backward, and then she sailed forward. The hem of her skirt fluttered little a little, showing only another inch of skin, before she realized and tucked it down, between her legs.

I shouldn't stare at her like that, I admonished myself as I walked away. She was too uncomfortable, too tense. If she caught me looking at her I'd only confuse us both. And potentially piss her off.

Before I made the call to Casey, I shot a text to Keane.

Get some candids of Hollis and me, please. She's over on the tire swing.

His reply came quickly.

Aye, aye.

"Casey," I said when she answered Gram's house phone.

"I'm fine," she said on a sigh and I imagined her rolling her eyes.

"Good because I wasn't calling to check on you," I lied easily. "But now that I've got you, how's it going? Hanging out with Keane's mom?"

"Yep. She's cool. She just lit a joint for us to share and now she's telling me about what a loose lady she was back in the day."

It caught me so completely off guard that I was speechless for a moment until Keane's mom barked a laugh and then some kind of remark that incited Casey to apologize. "What shit are you watching on television?" I asked her.

"Oh, just preschool stuff," she said innocently and not at all believably. "We're fine here. But can you bring me something to eat?"

"What about the lasagna?"

"I pigged out and finished it all."

"Yeah, yeah." I looked over at Hollis. She'd folded her arms over the top of the tire swing and rested her chin on her hands as she watched everyone else careening into the water. "I'll get something," I told her. "Don't forget to do your homework, okay?"

Casey said something but I wasn't listening to her anymore. Someone had approached Hollis and in the dark, with his back to me, I couldn't make him out. But Hollis had stopped swinging, and her head had lifted. I said a hasty goodbye to Casey before sliding my phone back into my pocket and approaching Hollis from behind. I heard murmured words, but Hollis looked worse than when I had left her. Her brow was furrowed, and her eyes looked tired.

"Hollis," I said, but it came out like a question as I came closer. Whoever was talking to her left, walking up the hill toward the front of the house. "Who was that?"

"No one," she said. "How much longer do you think we have to stay here?"

"Who was it?" I asked again.

"Just someone who wanted tutoring."

"Look at you, networking even when you're not trying."

She smiled, but it didn't reach her eyes. "Yep. That's me." She was unsettled, resigned, and looked like she didn't know if she wanted to curl up and sleep or cry. I had seen her cry once before, long ago, and had no desire to witness it again.

"You look nice, by the way."

She lifted her head, confusion on her face.

"Your outfit." I nodded at it, specifically at the skirt that showed off her long legs. "It's nice."

"Oh." Her hands smoothed down the skirt. "Thanks."

"Are you ready to get out of here then?" I asked her, when she stared numbly at her phone.

"I mean, do you think we accomplished anything?"

"We got a photo on Facebook," I said, showing her the photo Blake had tagged us in. "That's something."

"We need more," she said with great resignation. "Just us. We need a paper trail."

If her face wasn't in such a frown, I'd have laughed at the way she said it with such professionalism. A paper trail? Who even talked like that?

"Come on then," I said. "Let's go down to the water with everyone else and get a few more."

She didn't want to and if she decided to give up on tonight altogether, I wouldn't push her. Whatever the guy had said to her while I had been away, it'd exhausted her. But if he was one of her students, why did she look so defeated? She fumbled her way through the hole of the tire swing until I held my hands out and gestured for her to put her arms through.

"Give me your hands and slide through," I said, standing in front of her.

She grabbed hold and she slid through—legs first, upper body next. We were toe to toe, chest to chest. "You can let go now," she said.

"You know," I said, not letting go right away, "for someone so concerned with making this believable, you keep making excuses to avoid actual displays of affection."

"Fine," she said, setting her jaw as she peered up at me. In the moonlight her skin glowed like golden marble. Her eyes were impossibly dark, deep in a way that made me want to stare into their depths until she released even a small part of herself for me.

But I didn't really want that. No matter what, she and I were fundamentally different. Her goal was money and mine was to help my sister out. Hollis wanted to be seen with me, but not really *with* me. I wasn't sure if she felt like she was slumming it with me, like I was convenient but not the first pick. Which only made me more defiant in my attempts to treat her—at least when we were around others—like she was a woman I was actually romantically interested in.

I pressed a thumb to the center of her palm, our fingers still clasped, just to see what kind of reaction she'd have. When she was frozen in place, still staring up into me, I leaned down a couple inches, hovering above her face. Her eyes widened and her lips parted. Slightly, but enough that I noticed. I felt a tremble in her hands. "Are you cold?"

"The sun's gone down." Her voice was hushed like a secret. I supposed to anyone looking on, we appeared to be in an intimate discussion. But I wasn't really thinking about anyone else. I was thinking about her eyes, and how her long bottom lashes kissed the tops of her cheekbones. I was thinking about her mouth, berry pink and just the lightest gloss coating them.

The wind picked up, brushing hair across her face. I felt the flex of her fingers in mine and knew she itched to push it back, but I tightened my hold on her. The moment she let go of my hands, she'd have an excuse to stop looking at me in the eyes the way she was.

Her tongue wet her lips before retreating back into her mouth. Her mouth parted, and she squeezed my hands back. When her chest heaved, brushing her breasts against my chest, the feeling rocketed straight to my groin. Fuck.

I let go of her hands to run mine up her arms, to her

shoulders. I was testing the waters, slowly, getting her accustomed to me touching her. Technically, I wasn't holding her in place any longer. She could step away at any moment. But since she hadn't, I moved my hands to her shoulders. All the while, I maintained eye contact. My intention was to make sure I wasn't scaring her. The last thing I wanted was to make her feel pressured.

I grazed my thumb along the curve of her neck and her head tilted, giving me access to more skin. My caresses were smooth, gentle. The ground shifted beneath us, the sand pouring over my feet as she stepped closer.

Was I setting myself up for failure with her? Was this arrangement going to ultimately embarrass me? And, at that moment, why did I not give a damn if it did?

A clap on my back had me letting go abruptly to turn around. I was getting really sick of being interrupted, even though Blake's interruption had actually helped our ruse. But it was just Keane.

"Where's your beer?" he asked.

I swooped down, retrieving our two cups from the ground and handed Hollis hers.

"How's it going?" he asked, looping an arm over each of our shoulders, sandwiching himself between us as he steered us toward the water.

Hollis looked at me over his back, willing me to speak first. "Good. Fine. Where's the boat keys?" I asked.

"Nuh-uh. I just got done babysitting a two-hundred-pound drunk dude. I am *not* giving you those keys."

"Was worth a shot," I said, grinning at Keane. "Maybe another time."

"Maybe," Keane said and turned to Hollis. "Having fun? You never come to these things."

"A blast," she said through her teeth. She shivered, wrapping her arm around her waist.

"Cold?" Keane asked her and then whipped his head to look at me. "Your girl is cold, Adam."

"She's not my girl," I told him at the same time that Hollis said, "I'm not his."

"No shit, Sherlock. You two couldn't look more standoffish right now. Why do you think I've got you wrapped together?" He squeezed his arms, bringing us closer, into a huddle. "Get down by the water. Ricky Aiken is showing off his water-resistant phone by doing stupid shit with it like taking photos under water."

"Water resistant doesn't mean waterproof," Hollis retorted.

"Exactly. Now, come on kids. Join the others. Be young and free while you still can."

"I really do need to head home soon," Hollis protested, her feet dragging on the sandy shore as Keane led us toward everyone else. "I have studying to do."

"Classes just started, Hols."

"Yeah, well, I've got a lot on my plate." She shuffled her feet, staring at her toes dug into the sand. I wondered if she chased perfection naturally or if it was expected of her. I thought of her bedroom, how put together it was. How shocked she'd been when she'd knocked over a few books and pictures. And, unconscionably, I took pity on her.

"Let go, Keane," I said, ducking out from under his arm. In a second, I grabbed his other arm and gently pulled him away from Hollis. "We're probably going to leave soon." I wrapped an arm around her to stifle the shivering.

"Leave?" Blake asked, coming toward us from the water's edge and clapping me on the back. Again. "But dude, we got kegs."

Even though I'd poured a bottle of beer into my cup, I held it up like it was directly from the keg. "It's flat beer. No go, man."

"Yeah," Hollis added weakly, holding up her cup, which she poured out onto the sand. "It's been fun, but I do have a lot to do this week." This time, she reached a hand to me, and I took it without hesitation. "I'm ready to go," she said, looking me in the eyes meaningfully.

"That's our cue," I said to Keane and Blake. "Send the host my thanks," I added, already backing up toward the house. When we were out of earshot, Hollis tugged on my hand.

"Thanks."

I nodded.

"Mind holding on a sec? I need to get the sand out of my sandals."

"Sure." I tightened on her hand when she started to pull as she leaned over. "Use me for balance."

She did, bent forward to grab her shoe and shook it out. I looked around, not wanting to leer at her cleavage. It was tempting, but Hollis and I weren't *that* kind of fake boyfriend/girlfriend. I was brought back to the first party we'd attended together—the first high school party we'd both experienced. My thoughts trailed from me like a cat chasing a ball of yarn and I struggled to hold on and reign it in before I thought of how that night ended.

"Okay, ready," she said, flipping her hair over as she straightened. She had hair like a damned shampoo commercial. Under the spotlight shining off the house, it looked glossy, soft. The kind of hair that beckoned hands to run through it. But we were out of reasonable eyeshot now. I didn't need to be running my hands through her hair. Or even holding her hands. So, I let go.

"Do you mind if we get burgers on the way back? Casey asked for some."

"Sure." She pressed a hand to her stomach. "I'm starving myself."

"So who was it you were talking to when I called Casey?" I asked, trying once again to get an answer from her.

"No one."

"You looked upset."

She sighed. "It's not *him*. It's my situation. I've done it to myself, really." She glanced at me and looked away. "Why do you care anyway?"

She had me there. "I don't."

"Exactly."

We didn't speak in the car, which was probably for the best. My body was still on edge from being so close to her, from staring into her eyes under the moonlight. In Colorado, I had attended my fair share of parties. I had had plenty of good memories, had spent time with many women at and after those parties. Those relationships were usually brief blips of my life. Forgettable moments in the grand scheme of it all. So why was I so hung up on the spring break party from high school? The hour I had spent with Hollis had been unremarkable. It'd simply been light conversation. So why did it stick to me as long as it had? Was it because of the quick stab of betrayal I had felt when she'd played me, convincing me she wasn't like the rest of them when she was? I was used to my dad playing me. I didn't need it from anyone else.

The cashier handed my change back to me at the drive-through and then the bag of burgers and fries.

"Thanks," I said and handed a soda and a burger to Hollis.

She took the burger but looked between me and the soda as I pushed it toward her. "That's for you. I don't drink diet soda."

"Oh." She seemed she wasn't sure how to take it. "I have money," she said.

"It was a whole dollar, Hollis. Not a big deal."

But it was, to her, I could see it. And I wondered at it. It was just a damn fast food soda. I'd be willing to bet she had enough change in the bottom of her purse to buy a dozen sodas. But still, she fingered the plastic lid, her fingers tracing its circle shape. "Thanks," she said. "Fountain soda is the best."

I tucked away that little admission for future use. "Diet soda tastes like chemicals, but whatever you say."

She laughed and pulled out of the parking lot.

"What's so funny?"

"That's funny. The argument that certain foods are disgusting simply because of the chemicals in them." She nodded at the bag of burgers in my lap. "I'm sure there are dozens of them in there."

"Those for Casey," I said defensively. It wasn't a lie, necessarily, because *some* were for Casey. But I'd definitely eat my fair share of them before going to bed.

"So the chemicals are okay for Casey, but not you?"

She had me there. Before I could come up with an argument, she continued.

"And how many beers did you have at that party?"

I clenched my jaw. Was she judging me? I would never do what my dad did. "Two light beers. Over the course of three hours and on a full stomach."

"I apologize. I didn't mean to imply you shouldn't be driving. Your blood alcohol level is definitely in a safe range. What I meant was, did you know that fermentation is a chemical change?"

I relaxed for a moment. "Sorry, not all of us have gone to college."

"Okay, well I learned that in high school."

"Sorry," I said again, "not all of us stayed awake for Mrs. Croft's chemistry lessons."

She laughed lightly. "Mrs. Croft. Do you remember when there was that mini explosion in the fume hood in her class?"

"Remember it? Yes, it was one of the few classes I was awake for."

Her jaw dropped. "You were *in* that class when it happened?"

"Oh yeah. Never fell asleep again after that."

"We had to evacuate the school," she said, and her eyes took on a dreamy look like she was remembering. "And we just saw black smoke coming from that end. Everyone knew it was Mrs. Croft's class."

"Yeah, those were the days. I don't know if they ever figured out what caused it, either."

She laughed again, and I found myself laughing with her. It felt good to do that, when smiles were so rare for us. It was almost too easy for me to forget why I didn't particularly like her.

Almost.

When we pulled up in front of my house, we both looked toward the windows, where Casey's frame was silhouetted against the curtains as she sat on the sofa in the living room.

Hollis's hand hovered on her seatbelt button. Did she want to be invited in? Again, if this was real, I might invite her in for chemical-laden, greasy burgers and the company of my sister. Who obviously liked Hollis. But I didn't want to get Casey's hopes up for something that was completely fake anyway.

"Stay here," I said, "I'm going to drop these off and then bring you home." I exited the car before either of us could make it awkward.

16

HOLLIS

AFTER THE PARTY, I WANTED TO HIDE IN MY BED FOR DAYS. I settled for five hours upon waking up the next day.

Adam had seen the longing in my eyes when we'd pulled up to his house. He'd seen it, and he'd rejected it just as fast. He must *really* hate me.

My phone had been vibrating all morning, but I just knew it was a bunch of tutoring requests. I didn't want to deal with looking at my schedule, going through another monotonous day. When it vibrated again on my nightstand, it fell to the floor. I debated leaving it there for a solid hour, but remembering that I still hadn't responded to my dad had me sighing and reaching over the side of the bed, scooping it up and resigning myself to the frustrating day that awaited me.

But the notifications that lit up my home screen were not tutoring requests. Nor were they a million emails or texts or missed calls from my dad. I scrolled down the screen, a little in awe at the sheer number, before I selected one.

Blake had uploaded the photo of Adam and me standing

with him at the party onto Facebook. There were a hundred likes and twenty comments. I remembered Adam showing it to me last night, but I had been dismissive of it then.

But looking at it now, I couldn't believe it. I wasn't on the radar of guys like Blake. After all, he'd come over to talk to Adam, not me. But the fact that he posted that photo, and that so many people had commented made my chest fill up with held breath. I expected a snide comment about me, but there were none. A lot of "Small world" comments, and other "Where was my invite?" Okay, so the picture didn't shout WE ARE DATING.

I clicked on my notifications, surprised to see so many. Most of the older ones were related to the photo Blake had posted, but one notification stuck out: a photo Adam had tagged me in.

The breath I had been holding whooshed out of me only so I could suck it all back in as I clicked the photo.

It was a candid photo of us standing toe to toe, our fingers linked as we stared at each other. I knew exactly when it'd been taken: immediately after he'd helped me off of the tire swing. There must have been a breeze, because my hair was flying behind me. But it wasn't my hair that held my attention. It was the look on our faces. The posed photo with Blake was one thing; this was … well, not that. This was … what was it? I was mesmerized by the height difference between us, the way Adam's eyelids were lowered as he gazed down at me. "Are you cold?" he'd asked, and the truth was that being that close to him had made me warm.

Where had he gotten this photo from? I almost couldn't believe it was really us. The way we stood, the way we looked at each other, there was no mistaking it. We were definitely dating.

Breathless with anticipation of the growing number of comments under the photo, I scrolled down. Lots of comments with just hearts—by girls I didn't know.

A comment with an eggplant and "That's a lot of big dick

energy in one photo." There were replies to that comment: "Adam or Hollis?" asked someone which was followed with Tori's reply, "Hollis, duh." And then there were at least a half-dozen comments by Tori herself:

FUCKING FINALLY JESUS CHRIST
seven tongue emojis
Who took this photo because it's A-R-T
Can't wait to third wheel this bitch!
tricycle gif

And the last comment by Tori, the one that made me laugh so hard tears sprung to my eyes, was the same photo of Adam and me, except with Tori's face photoshopped over the tire swing, smiling hysterically.

Once I had recovered, I scrolled down a bit more, reading the rest of the comments—most of them seemed surprised by Adam and me, "Who knew?" And I stopped on the comment by someone named Sarah. I recognized the thumbnail of her face, from the one Adam had shown me last night. "Is this why you're not returning my messages?" There was a winky face after that comment. My lips made a flat line and I wished I hadn't seen her comment. Not that I had anything against her, as a person, but I'd be a liar if I didn't admit to a little irrational jealousy. This was a woman who knew Adam more than I did, who'd been in a *real* relationship with him. She had something I didn't. The real him, not the Adam who guarded himself against me.

I scrolled back up, wanting to see Tori's comments again. And, as if she knew I had been thinking of her, a text message came through: *What's up? Gonna break the internet today, you think?*

I looked back at the photo, which had already well over four-hundred likes.

I didn't even know that photo existed. I don't know who took it, I replied. She called me immediately after the text delivered.

"Okay, spill."

I shrugged, then remembered she couldn't see me. "There's nothing to spill. He agreed to the fake relationship ruse for now. We'll see how long it lasts, but it's not going to get to engagement territory. We're just going to play it long enough, hoping my parents amended the terms of the trust. Like you said."

"'There's nothing to spill,'" she mimicked me. "Just that I'm dating the guy I've had moon-eyes for since before I even had a period."

"*Fake* dating," I reminded her.

"Suuuure. But that photo wasn't posed. So, let me tell you: there's nothing fake about the chemistry you're emitting in that photo. I mean, you're looking at him like he's a snack, and he's looking at you like you're a feast. It's so hot. Until that photo, I didn't know I could orgasm without penetration."

"Oh my gosh, Tori," I said, knowing pink was staining my cheeks. "What a thing to say."

"I almost wrote that on the photo," she said with a laugh. "But then I remembered your parents are gonna see it. So I kept it tame."

"Yes, I could tell, talking about my big dick energy was really tame."

"To be fair, I didn't bring up the big dick energy. Someone else did. I just made them aware that it was you with the big dick."

"Thanks," I said, a smile forming my lips. I nestled into my big, heavy comforter and put the phone on speaker, laying it on the pillow next to mine. "I can't believe this, really. It feels so fast."

"Well, according to your folks, you've been seeing this guy for a couple years now. So you've gotta appear like you've got the hots for him."

I didn't think that'd be too hard. I *did* have the hots for him. And I had it in a bad, bad way. It wasn't just every day that you got a chance to date the person you'd lusted after for years. Even if it was fake dating.

"What's on the agenda this week?"

"Tutoring…"

"Yeah, snooze. What else?"

"Class…"

"Yeah, I don't think you get what I'm referring to. What about Adam?"

"I don't know. I guess we'll need to get together a couple more times before my parents come into town this week."

"Speaking of your parents, I see your mom liked the photo of you and Adam."

"She did?" Admittedly, I hadn't looked through all the likes, but the fact that my mom had liked it and not said anything made me feel no small amount of anxiety. I half expected to hear the doorbell ringing so she could come grill me about being safe. Again.

"Yep, she did. When are they coming up to visit?"

"Thursday." I rubbed my eyes, mentally making a list of everything I needed to do before then.

"Yikes. Big yikes. Is Adam ready?"

"Can anyone ever be ready to face my parents?"

"True, true." I heard the crunch of something over the line. Tori was always eating. She wasn't picky, either—fruits, vegetables, grains, proteins, and junk were on a heavy rotation in her diet. "By the way, I miss you. I know it's only been a week, but it's been one hell of a week, huh?"

"I miss you too," I said. And I did. Living with Navy was nice. She was tidy, she was quiet. But she wasn't Tori. Living with

Tori required an ability to be comfortable with at least a little bit of chaos. She got bored easily, or distracted, which meant mess followed her like she was leaving a trail of crumbs in case she got lost. "When are you going to come up here and visit?"

"Eh. I'll probably surprise you," she said, and I heard another crunch. "Like your little sticky notes. I keep finding them. You sentimental little shit." She was teasing, but it was something I'd done ever since we'd been kids. Leaving her little notes for her to find, notes reminding her of how funny and wonderful I thought she was. "Surprise visits are my sticky notes. Hanging with my roommates—"

"Parents," I corrected, and smiled.

"—is like hanging out at a sad nursing home, except there's no bingo so it's even worse."

"It can't be that bad," I said. Tori had a flair for the dramatic. "But I'd love to have you visit. The apartment I share with Navy is only two bedrooms, but I have a big bed."

"I don't want to encroach on Adam's share of the bed."

I stared at my empty half of the bed, my Adam-less half, and said, "Well, I don't think there's any worry of that."

"Don't you wish you hadn't lost your virginity to that guy on the junior year camp trip? What was his name?"

"Willy."

"Oh, God, that's right. I mean, there were worse choices."

"Thanks," I said insincerely. "I just wanted to get it over with."

"I know, I know. I'm just giving you a hard time. Before Adam gives you a *hard* time. If you know what I'm saying." I rolled my eyes and she said, "That was a joke."

"Yeah, a bad one," I told her.

"You're not wrong." She sighed, the sound blowing air into the receiver. "Okay. I'm going to try to make it up one of these weekends. I might have to borrow one of my roommate's cars until I get off my ass and get a job, but I'll be there."

At the knock on my door, I turned off the speakerphone and said my goodbyes to Tori before I told Navy to come in.

Navy strolled through the door, a shit-eating grin on her face. "Saw the photo." She waggled her eyebrows. "Keane did a great job."

"Keane took that?" I asked, pushing myself up to sitting. I patted the bed so Navy could sit beside me. "I was wondering who did."

"Yeah, I think he took a couple and sent them to Adam."

It made me want to text Keane and ask for them too, but for some reason that felt almost desperate. So I pushed the thought to the back of my mind and pulled my hair into a low ponytail. Navy was already moving around my room, picking up my empty diet soda from the nightstand and tossing it. "Did you stay late?" I asked her. When Adam had dropped me off, her car was still gone.

"Until about two. Mike was so drunk he started crying and talking about his life problems, so I stuck around while Keane consoled him. Did a little cleaning so his mom wouldn't have a surprise when she comes home this week."

That didn't surprise me. "Any plans for today?" I asked her, noticing that she was already dressed.

She glanced down at her ripped shorts and her white crochet button down shirt. "Oh, well that's why I came in. Adam decided kind of last minute to throw a birthday party for Casey. Her birthday's next weekend, but he's pretty busy with the new job starting next week and Gram comes home right after her birthday, so he wants to do it before."

"I should go," I said, pushing up out of bed. "I don't have a present for her. What should I get her? She's going to be thirteen, right? What do thirteen-year-old girls like?"

Navy shrugged. "I got her a Target gift card. Everyone loves Target."

"I can't get her one if you got her one." I wracked my brain as

I grabbed clothes from the closet, pulling on a pair of skinny jeans and one of my black peplum tops. It was somewhat dressy, but not over the top. "This look okay?" I asked Navy as I pulled my hair into a cleaner ponytail and slid some thin hoops into my earlobes.

"Great." Navy reached over to my nightstand and picked up the book I'd read last night. "What's this one about? Explain it to me badly."

"A man accidentally kidnaps a woman and he spends the rest of the book trying to bring her back to where she belongs but she isn't having it and they fall in love."

"That was explaining it badly?" she asked, her eyebrows shooting up high on her forehead. "Because this sounds like something I actually want to read." She opened the first page and began reading as I applied some makeup. "I wish I read more," she said on a sigh as she read the first page. "This sounds wonderful."

"It is." I grabbed the one necklace I wore regularly and paused. It was gold, with the tiniest, most delicate rose charm that hung just at the base of my throat, between my clavicles. I thought of the weak rose I'd drawn on that note for Adam almost four years ago, and wondered if he ever thought about it himself. Sliding the chain around my neck, I wondered if I'd ever tell him it was me.

"Where do you want to go for her gift?" Navy asked, pulling me from my thoughts.

I pictured Casey in my mind, and knew instantly. "I've got an idea."

17

ADAM

K<small>EANE HAULED A HELIUM TANK FROM THE BACK OF HIS TRUCK.</small> "You know," he said, his breath heaving from exertion, "we should've done this at my house instead of here. What if this shit blows away?"

I grabbed the bag of balloons I had picked up at the party store and the string that went with them. "It'll be fine. I'll hold the balloons while you fill them, and then you'll tie them off.

Keane grunted and dragged the tank to the gazebo overlooking Casey's favorite park. As far as birthday parties went, this one was kind of lame. But it was cheap, and cheap was what I could afford. My last check from my job deposited the day before, which meant I had enough to pay Hollis back, throw this little party for Casey, and cushion my account until my new job at Keane's work paid me. I hated the stress of living paycheck to paycheck, hated having to stalk my bank account to make sure everything was functioning in there the way it was supposed to. Gram was on a fixed income herself, but that money wouldn't last forever and it was really only enough to cover the essentials.

In the darkest hours of the night, when I lay awake in bed worrying over what was coming next, I wished for my life in Colorado. I wanted the peace of mind I had back there. The roommates, my bandmates, and the mostly steady flow of cash from the paid gigs we had, especially over the summer when our wallets were padded by festivals and small outdoor concerts.

But when I thought of Casey, and how happy she'd been upon seeing me again, and the ease that had settled over her when I had told her I was staying, I erased those thoughts as wishes that I wouldn't want to come true.

Pulling the cake from the backseat of Keane's truck, I glanced over the decorations. The grocery store bakery didn't have time to do anything special just for her, but they'd offered to pipe in name in purple frosting over the front of the cake. It wasn't a fancy cake, with layers of decorative fondant, but it was her favorite flavors: dark chocolate and whipped cream frosting.

I carried the cake and the plates I had picked up to the table, setting the cake on top of the plates so they wouldn't blow away. Amber Lake was a widespread town, with small clusters of residential neighborhoods separated by acres of farmland. The mostly-flat terrain made it great for farmers and ranchers, but it made the wind a real bitch without having any natural shields for it.

Keane ripped open the balloon bag and handed me a yellow one before opening the valve on the helium tank. As he began to fill them, he looked up at me. "So it's you, me, my mom, Navy, Hollis and…"

"That's it," I said. "Wait, Hollis?"

Keane looked away from me, rolling out a string as I tied the balloon. "Yeah, Navy's bringing her."

I hadn't invited Hollis. I had invited Navy. I mean, it made sense that Hollis would come along since she and Navy were roommates, but I didn't feel right having Hollis around my sister when it was all just a lie between us.

I thought of how adoringly Casey had looked at Hollis when she met her, like a girl observing a big sister she never had. And that was the only reason I didn't text Hollis not to come.

"I can see the 'I'm gonna be a dick' face forming already," Keane said, tying the first balloon to the picnic table he was sitting on. "So, why don't you knock that off right now. You should've invited her."

"Why? She's not my real girlfriend."

"Because, you dick, this party isn't about you and your stupid labels, it's about Casey. And who Casey might want here." He held his hands out, gesturing to himself. "Now, I know I'm pretty great. Navy's great. My mom's great." He eyed me. "You're okay, I guess."

I glared at him as I prepped the next ballon.

"And Hollis is… well, she's Hollis. A girl. And Casey doesn't get a lot of girl time."

"She hasn't really needed it."

"Oh, so we've moved from 'I'm gonna be a dick' to 'I'm gonna be a dumbass' then? It'll be hard to keep up if you keep this up."

"Ass," I said back, my flat reply practically falling on deaf ears as he continued.

"Casey's going to be a teenager and she doesn't have a mom. She has Gram, but Gram…" He paused.

"It's okay, I get it." I knotted the next filled balloon and held it out for him to tie on the ribbon.

"It's good for her to have stability, and I don't know about you but Hollis doesn't strike me as someone who's going to flit in and out of her life."

"Did you forget that this thing between her and me is temporary?"

"Did *you* forget that today isn't about you? Jesus, Adam, I know you went and became a rockstar in Colorado but I didn't think you'd assume the rest of the world revolved around you."

"You do a good job of humbling me, man," I told him and prepared the next balloon. "How much helium is in there?"

"Probably enough for that whole bag, but do you think you can fit a lot more balloons in your car to take home?"

"Probably not. Maybe three more."

We set to the task, filling the rest of the balloons. "That photo you posted is a good one," Keane finally said. "Of you and Hollis."

"Yeah," I said, trying not to think about Hollis. She'd only been revolving around my thoughts for the last forty-eight hours, since she'd dropped the bombshell about her parents thinking we were in a relationship. And already, we *were* in a relationship. Facebook official, even.

Sarah had been blowing up my phone since last night, but I didn't want to talk to her. She wasn't stupid, she'd know something wasn't as it seemed.

"You two looked totally natural together."

"Yeah," I said again, grabbing a handful of the balloons and moving to start tying them to the two picnic tables we'd snagged. "We're supposed to."

"Right." Keane helped me tie off a couple and then said, "Except those photos weren't posed. You didn't know I was taking that shot."

"I asked you to take photos."

"You didn't know I was taking that shot," he repeated. "You didn't even see me. It's okay, I get it. You don't want to admit you have the hots for your fake girlfriend." He held up his hands as if he was conceding. "That's fine."

"I didn't say that," I told him, then wished I could take it back.

"So, you do have the hots for her."

Hollis, with her dark, thick hair and wide brown eyes. With her pink lips, her long limbs, and the natural grace she exuded when she didn't even realize it. Yeah, I had *something* for her. But it was purely physical, and I told Keane so.

"You weren't looking at her like that in the pic, Adam. But whatever you say. One day, you'll admit it. And I cannot wait for that day." He rubbed his hands together like he was scheming.

"You're going to eat your words," I told him, checking my phone for a text from Keane's mom. Casey was on her way, would be at the park in ten minutes. "Hey, I meant to ask you. Gram's coming home next Monday. Would you mind helping me do a little furniture rearranging? We're going to move her to the living room, so she's nearly never alone. I don't like the idea of her being locked away in her bedroom where we can't easily hear her."

Keane's expression sobered and he nodded. "Of course."

"I was thinking this Thursday, if that works for you?"

"Yep. I'll bring my truck. We can move a lot more that way."

"Good." I nodded. "Thanks, man."

"Look who's here," Keane said, and I turned. Hollis's car pulled in and Navy popped out, skipping across the grass with bags of cheeseburgers in her hands.

"Casey loves cheeseburgers, right?" She held the bag out to me. "I figured she needed something besides just cake."

Something I had completely spaced. I gave her a grateful smile, taking the bag and putting it beside the cake on the picnic table. Hollis followed behind, albeit at a slower pace. She carried a drink cooler in one hand and a small gift bag in the other.

"Hey, Hollis. What's that?" Keane asked when I didn't say anything. Hollis looked nervously at me before turning her head to him.

"It's a punch, sort of."

"Like the one we had in middle school," Navy said excitedly, and pulled plastic cups out of a bag she carried. "With the lemon-lime soda and sherbet. So good. And fun! It was Hollis's idea."

"Here," I said, taking the beverage cooler from her hand and putting it on the picnic table.

Hollis stood there, hands clutching the present as she looked at everyone except for me.

I felt Keane's elbow in my ribs and elbowed him back before stepping toward Hollis. We hadn't spoken since I had dropped her off at her apartment, and even then it'd been a terse goodbye. Hell, she'd been out of the car within seconds of me pulling to a stop.

"Thanks for coming," I said to her. "Casey will be happy to see you." I sounded robotic. "I'm glad you're here," I added as an aside.

"Wow, you two are a couple of teddy bears," Keane said, wrapping an arm around Navy. "I guess I missed the part where this was a formal shindig."

I glared at him, but the heat wasn't really there because he was right. I turned to Hollis, to offer her a hug, but she was already moving away from me, back to the parking lot where Keane's mom was pulling in, with Casey excitedly waving at her from the front seat.

Huh. It was a little odd to see Casey so animated for someone she didn't know that well. But she was out of the car and hauling ass to Hollis before I could blink. And, to add to my surprise, Hollis wrapped her up like they were old friends.

Keane's mom made her way over, a bag full of plastic silverware and napkins. More shit I had forgotten. I looked at Keane who shrugged. "I didn't see it in the backseat, so I asked her to bring it along."

"Hey Mrs. C," I said, giving her a hug when she offered one. "Thanks for bringing stuff. I guess I'm not really good at this."

She squeezed me and then let go, her hands coming to my elbows. The smile she gave me was tinged with just a bit of sadness at the corners. "You're doing great, Adam."

Hollis and Casey joined us, and Casey poked one of the balloons. "Wow, real balloons! With helium."

"Yep. I have the tank, too, if you feel like making your voice sound like a thirteen-year-old *boy* experiencing puberty."

"Oh, heck yeah. And burgers!" Her eyes lit up as she spied the bag. I had been so worried about the low budget party, but she was already delighted by the simplest parts of it.

"Dig in," Navy said, sitting at the table. She patted the seat beside her and Hollis moved out of the corner of my eye toward it before Keane took the spot. Keane's mom and Casey sat opposite of them, leaving Hollis and me to sit at the lone table next to them.

"Give me two of those," I said to Keane as he passed out burgers.

"Oh, I'm good—I ate on the way here," Hollis said when I had both burgers in front of me.

"That's good, because these both were for me anyway."

Hollis eyed me like she wasn't sure whether to run or to laugh. Her eyes darted left and right, and from how straight she was sitting I knew she was uncomfortable. If Keane had been sitting beside me, he'd have elbowed me in the ribs again. "I was kidding," I said to Hollis, but the humor had passed. "Are you sure you don't want one?"

"No, but thank you." She shook her head violently fast, so fast that her dark ponytail swung left and right like a whip. Not a hair on her head was out of place, not even one lone tendril across her forehead. Was it exhausting to be that put together all the time?

I leaned forward on the table and my knees knocked with hers. We exchanged eye contact for a moment. I expected her to avert her gaze, to look away as she often did, but she didn't. No, she held my gaze, her eyes heavy-lidded and dark, but confident.

Her knee grazed against mine, but this time it was intentional. The side of her mouth lifted, briefly.

The bite of burger lodged itself in my throat as I stared at her. Had we ever held eye contact for so long? I didn't think so.

My gaze dipped to the charm that flashed. A rose. It suited her. Her features were classic, delicate. She seemed poised, like someone who'd been trained to balance a book atop her head. But it didn't seem forced. It was a natural grace she carried, a quiet kind of confidence in herself. I was struck, as always, by how beautiful she was. It was no hardship to be in a relationship with her, especially when it meant being able to look at her all the time.

That didn't mean I'd warmed up to her quite yet.

"What's that?" she asked me, eyes on my bicep. "A rose?"

"Yeah." I swallowed the bite of burger and turned my arm to show it more clearly.

"Do you … like roses?"

What a weird thing to ask. I had it tattooed on my body, hadn't I? I thought the answer to that question was obvious. Instead, I turned it on her. "You do." I nodded at her neck and took another bite.

She looked down, fingering the gold charm. "Yes. That's why I noticed your tattoo. Did you get it for any reason in particular?"

What was she getting at? I felt, perhaps irrationally, that I was being tested somehow. Again, I redirected what she asked me. "All my tattoos have reasons."

"Like your knuckle tattoos?"

My hands splayed out on the table in front of her. "Mile High, it's the name of one of the songs we wrote."

"After the city?"

"Yeah." I held my right middle finger out toward her and laughed when she looked at the lone finger curiously. "No, I'm not trying to flip you off. I wanted to show you. Here," I reached with my other hand for hers and brought her forefinger to the skin between two knuckles. "I wasn't going to get the tattoos on my hands, but I had a little accident and had to get pins in my fingers here." She touched the skin carefully. "I lost a lot of feeling in this finger and the scar was pretty gnarly, so I got the tattoo to cover it, but also to see if I could feel it."

"So, you subjected yourself to pain just to see if you could still feel it?"

After a beat, I answered her. "Yes." No one had ever put it that way, so succinctly. It struck me a little, and for the first time since I got the tattoo I wished I *hadn't* regained feeling there. Because her little touches, the grazing of my skin, was starting to get to me. But I had invited it, hadn't I? The smile that played on her lips made me feel fidgety. "What's funny?"

"Oh." The smile dropped from her lips. "I mean, it's not funny per se. I just found it interesting. Because it seems like as our advancements in medical science continue, we, as a culture, are always seeking ways to eliminate pain, whether that's physical or emotional pain. And yet there you were, seeking pain to make sure you could still feel."

"It was just my finger. A small thing," I said. "I'm not someone who voluntarily seeks out other kinds of pain."

She looked me over, her eyes thoughtful. "No, I don't suppose you are. And that's not what I meant." Her knees brushed mine again, and this closeness was starting to do my head in. "I just meant that I admire that. Putting yourself through pain—even a small bit, to give you the peace of mind that you can feel it."

"You said that was your most painful tattoo," Casey blurted

out, her mouth full of burger. Keane's mom handed her a napkin. "That's what you told me, when I said it was cool."

"It was my most painful tattoo," I said, "but you're a little kid. I'm not going to talk you into getting a tattoo."

Casey's eyes narrowed. "I'm not a kid. I'm thirteen. Teenager."

"Still a kid."

"Aww." Hollis squeezed my hand gently. "She's a young lady, Adam. Here's a true test: do boys still have cooties?"

"Cooties aren't real," Casey said.

Hollis and I exchanged looks. "Shit," I said.

Hollis's touch moved up my arm, distracting me, and I felt like I had been zapped with some kind of electricity, through her. "This one is pretty," she said, tracing its valves and curves.

I smiled. "I got that for my gram. She didn't want me to get tattoos, so I thought if I got one for her, as my first one, she might cut me some slack." It was an anatomical heart, with tiny teardrops for each heart surgery she'd had. "I always said she was the first woman I had ever loved."

"And did she?" Hollis asked. Her eyes were wide, and the smile that had only been a whisper on her lips returned. "Cut you some slack?"

"Oh hell no," Casey said, drawing all our eyes to her.

"Casey," I admonished. "'Hell,' really?"

"You say it."

"Yeah, well I also drink beer and drive a car and that doesn't mean you can do those things."

Casey rolled her eyes and took a big bite of her burger. "Those aren't even the same thing. It's just a word, Adam."

Yeah, and you're just a kid, I thought. But she wasn't, not like the rest of them. She was growing older every single day— obviously—but it seemed accelerated now. When I had been away, in Colorado, my memory of Casey had been of a girl with braces and unruly hair and a Tomboy streak that didn't quit.

Now, she was experimenting with makeup, she brushed her hair more regularly, and she said swear words around other adults. Where had the last three years gone?

Hollis's knees knocked with mine under the table again. Fucking hell. It wasn't like the rattle was jarring. Not at all. But it was the fact that Hollis and I were close enough to be knocking knees under the table, that she kept touching me like it didn't have an immediate effect on me. Which it did.

"Can I have some cake?" Casey asked after she'd swallowed her final bite.

"Uh, sure." I rubbed my hands on my jeans and then eyed her uncertainly. "Do you want us to sing? We have candles."

"No, that's okay. I just want cake." She licked her lips and her eyes closed halfway as her smile spread. "Caaaake."

"I brought some punch," Hollis said, standing. "I can get everyone a cup?" She looked around for the nods, smiling at the enthusiastic one Casey gave her. When her eyes landed on me, I just shook my head. I didn't want anything sweet right now, not when my stomach was in knots being this close to her.

I opened the lid on the cake, the smell of sweet engulfing us immediately. As I sliced the first portion, Hollis handed out cups of punch with orange and pink sherbet floating on the top. It was nostalgic, and I felt like a dick for being the only one who didn't partake in it.

"Where are the plates?" Hollis asked, already grabbing forks.

"Oh," I said. "Under here."

I lifted the cake box and three things happened in quick succession:

1. A gust of wind flew through us, sending the plates up into the air and across the playground.

2. Everyone gasped or shouted as the plates rolled away, dancing in the wind and leaving us entirely plateless.

3. Hollis took off running after them.

I felt I had no choice but to follow her. We didn't have any other plates. We had napkins, but those were sure to blow away even faster than the plates had.

"Shit, shit, shit, fuck," I mumbled under my breath as I chased down a single plate. Hollis was several feet ahead of me, and had secured two plates. Well, at the very least we'd have to share a plate with two other people.

But she was still chasing after them, already at least a couple dozen yards away from the gazebo. In fact, we were nearly out of sight as the plates trailed behind a giant shed that belonged to the parks department.

I watched in shock as Hollis dove over a rogue plate, landing right on top of it. She yelped in triumph and rolled to sitting, clutching the now three plates to her chest like hard-won medals. Which, I guess, in a way they were.

When I caught up to her she was laughing and her hair had come undone in the wind.

"I only rescued three," she said, laughing. Had I seen her laugh like this? So openly, so uncontrollably? I didn't think I had, because I'd have remembered feeling the surge of heat through my body at what that kind of laughing did to her face. The sun warmed her face, glittering off of it like it shone only for her. The tendrils of hair that whipped around her made her look like some woman on the edge of a cliff, embracing the wind that rushed around her. She was roses and cream, with dark, enticing hair—hair that made me ache to tug, to twist, to bury my face into. She was, in a word—okay, *two* words: fucking stunning.

I set my jaw, annoyed at myself for being so fucking turned on right then. And then I was even further annoyed with myself for being annoyed, especially when I saw the look in her eyes as she gazed at me, like she was damned delighted I had chased her.

Holding a hand out, I tried to think of something—anything —to distract me from doing what I wanted to do.

But then she took my hand and came to standing, her body bumping against mine and the loose tendrils licking both our faces and I thought, *Fuck it.*

I slid my hand up her arm, feeling her go still, and erased whatever distance there'd been between us as I stepped forward. She could run. She could back up. I told myself that as my hand moved further up, until I was cupping her chin, fingers splayed along her jaw.

And I did the unthinkable.

I kissed her.

18

HOLLIS

I WASN'T SOMEONE WHO SAID SWEAR WORDS ALL THAT OFTEN, BUT the moment Adam's lips closed on mine at least a half-dozen swear words flitted over my mind. And then there was silence, punctuated by a persistent beat, as his hands slid into my hair and the pounding of my heart drowned out even the strongest voices in my head.

Later, I would be so glad I'd committed that kiss to memory, so I could replay it over and over. Because while the kiss had begun tentatively, it quickly grew urgent and seeking. I held the plates to my chest with one hand and with the other I held his wrist, anchoring him to me simply so he wouldn't stop.

Adam Oliver was kissing me. And it was everything I had never known to hope for. I tingled everywhere, like my skin was coming alive all on its own. His fingertips pressed gently against my scalp and sensation exploded there, blossoming out over my head and making me dizzy.

Almost as quickly as it'd begun, it'd ended. Adam pulled back and stared at me. The shock I felt seemed echoed in his eyes.

I opened my mouth to say something—anything—but nothing came out. It was as if he'd robbed me of the words I wanted to say.

He pressed his forehead to mine and a shuddering breath from his lips washed over mine. "One more," he whispered, surprising me, before he leaned back in and claimed my mouth again.

This time, the kiss was slower. Like he was seeking, like his mouth was getting to know mine. The first kiss had been a test but this was more than that—this was exploratory. I angled my head when his hand guided me to and the kiss deepened, his tongue brushing over mine in the lightest of touches. It was as if I could feel it all the way in my low belly, like he was stoking a fire that lay dormant for years. I knew, without a shadow of a doubt, I had never been kissed like this—like I was something to be savored, something to enjoy.

And that train of thought led to another, unbidden one: if kissing was this incredible, what would the sex with him be like?

This time, I broke the kiss. I shouldn't be thinking that. This wasn't a real relationship. It was completely inappropriate. But the thought nudged me harder, especially when he searched my face, his hand holding the back of my head for several long moments. It was if speaking them in my subconscious had seared them there.

"I'm sorry," he said, but he was still holding me.

"Liar," I said, my voice sounding hoarse to my ears.

"Yeah." A smile tipped the side of his mouth. "I'm not sorry."

"Okay." I swallowed. "Me neither."

"Good." He nodded once. He brushed hair from my face, tucking it behind my ear. "Because I want to do it again."

I placed a hand on his chest and tapped a finger on the plates I held in my other hand. "We need to get these back. They're going to think we got lost."

He stared at me, unblinking. Warmth filled me from my belly outwards. "I'm not entirely sure we didn't." But he let go of me and I felt the cold from the wind sweep over me instantly. His body had shielded mine from the worst of it, and I felt a deep longing to have it again.

We stared at one another for a long moment before he reached a hand out to me, as if in a truce, and I took it.

When we rejoined the group, I could feel Navy's scrutinizing gaze like a brand. Without a compact, I had no way of knowing if my lips betrayed what'd happened. But really, so what? We were bound to kiss at some point. No relationship—fake or real —could be believable without certain exchanges of physical affection.

But that wasn't a kiss between two people trying to make their relationship look believable, because we'd done it out of the sight of everyone. That kiss hadn't been a show, it'd been for us and only us. I bit my lip to keep from smiling.

"I only managed to rescue three," I said sheepishly, holding them up.

"Well, the birthday girl and I can share," Mrs. C said with a smile for Casey. "And Navy and Keane can share, too."

"I'll share," Adam said, bumping into my shoulder gently. "Unless you're afraid of catching my cooties."

I chewed on my lower lip and could only shake my head. I wished I had some witty retort, something I could shoot back at him playfully. But I had nothing.

"Are you guys dating or something?" Casey asked with a mouthful of cake.

"Yes," Adam said before I could say anything. "And Hollis is going to start tutoring you this week. If Dad isn't able to get home to make gymnastics happen for you, I will. As long as you get those grades up."

Casey's eyes lit up and with the frosting on her upper lip, she looked like a small child. My heart squeezed, realizing how much gymnastics meant to her. "We can start tutoring after school on Wednesday," I told her. "If that works for you?"

Casey nodded happily. "Thanks, Hollis. Thanks, Adam." She looked as if she'd already been given the whole world.

"Ready for presents?" Keane's mom asked, handing a gift bag over before Casey could say no.

She opened her gifts one by one: new earrings and hair accessories from Keane's mom, the Target gift card from Navy, and a stack of her favorite book series in hardcover from Keane. When she opened the gift from Adam, she held up the remote with a look of confusion on her face.

"Gram and I got you a new tv for your room. It has all the bells and whistles, so you can watch your shows in your bedroom."

Casey squealed and launched herself at Adam. When she pulled back, a wrinkle formed between her brows. "Is this because Gram is going to be in the living room from now on?"

Adam nodded once, and the light in his eyes darkened slightly. I had an overwhelming desire to be the one to put the light back into his eyes, but this wasn't the place or time to talk to him about it.

"And this one is from…" Casey held up the last gift bag and I nodded.

"Yup. Hopefully you like it."

She yanked the pink tissue paper out of the top and tossed it. Peering into the bag, she said, "What's that?"

I almost answered before I realized it was a rhetorical question. She pulled out a card and fabric. As she unfolded it, I explained. "That's a leotard. The lady at the gymnastics studio picked it out for you, and said if it's not the right size we can exchange it. And the card is a gift card—enough for one of the balance beams they sell. I wasn't sure what your favorite color was, but I thought you could at least practice until your lessons begin." I was so unsure about the gift, if I was stepping on Adam's toes, or if I was too presumptuous with it. But I barely made out Casey's grin before she launched herself on me.

"This is perfect," she said into my hair. My arms came around her and I squeezed her. She wasn't related to me. She wasn't *mine* in any way, but at that moment the warmth that filled my chest reminded me of what I felt for my own sisters. I ran a hand over her hair, feeling strangely connected to this girl, the sister of my fake boyfriend. I looked over her head at Adam's face, and wished I could sort out the puzzle of feeling there. Everyone else was smiling, but his face held so many layers that I couldn't discern a distinct, singular emotion.

After the punch was gone and the cake was reduced to crumbs, Casey left for the second part of her gift from Keane's mom: pedicures. That left the four of us to pick up the mess, until Keane abruptly turned to Adam and said, "I'm going to take Navy home. I've got some errands to run."

I didn't know if Adam saw through it as clearly as I did, because I kept my eyes on the task at hand. But I could hear Adam arguing with Keane about me driving him home and whatever warm feelings I had been developing for Adam quickly turned cold once again. Hadn't he said he wanted to kiss me again? Why was being alone with me suddenly so terrible?

I might've shoved the stack of dirty plates a little too forcefully into the trash. And I might've been a little aggressive when I smashed up the cake box so that it would fit, too. He was just so hot and cold, which meant I couldn't get a handle on him. I wanted to, because he was such a loose wire that he made *me* feel out of control. And I was never not in control.

"Hollis."

I turned around to his voice. "What?" I didn't mean to snap, but I had. "What?" I asked again, softer this time.

"I didn't mean that I didn't want to spend time with you, when I was talking to Keane?"

"Yeah?" I asked, averting my eyes as I stacked the plastic cups. "Whatever, it doesn't matter."

"Yes, it does."

I shoved them into the trash and squirted hand sanitizer into my palms, attacking my fingers like I could see all the micrograms burrowing into my epidermis. "No," I said, through gritted teeth. "It's fine. I get it. Trust me."

"No, I don't think you do." He placed a hand on mine, stalling me for a minute. "I wasn't trying to get out spending time with you. I mean, we *should* spend time together. Your parents come this week, right?"

I nodded. "Thursday. For a visit. Which means we have to put on a performance long enough to last a dinner." Ugh, even just saying that made me wince.

"Right, so it's good we're spending time together now. It makes sense." I watched his throat move as he swallowed and the hand on mine turned so our fingers were linked. "But what doesn't make sense is whatever it is that's between us right now."

I wanted to play dumb, to protect myself. But I knew exactly what he was saying. The kissing had meant something. I just didn't know what that was, besides real attraction masked by the fake whatever-we-were. But I didn't feel safe with him yet, to let him know that I was as affected as I was.

"It's just kissing," I said, as a compromise to myself. "It's not a big deal."

In his eyes I witnessed a whirlwind of emotion, but again—nothing specific I could pin down. "Right," he said after a moment. "It's just kissing. At least we're good at it, right?"

I swallowed, wanting to go back to that pocket of time we'd had together out of everyone's view, under the warm sun, when he'd wanted another kiss, and I had stopped him.

Oh, how I wished I hadn't stopped it.

But instead, I nodded. "Yep. At least we're good at it."

19

ADAM

Casey and I walked into the hospital Monday morning, arms laden with cake and balloons and roses and Gram's favorite throw blanket. I felt bad for not visiting as often as I'd have liked, especially considering everything that had happened. But then again, knowing Gram would be home after the following weekend, it seemed only a matter of time until things were somewhat back to normal.

When we entered her room, her face was pink, flushed. She looked...vibrant, and healthy.

Casey ran to her bed, balloons streaming behind her, and launched herself at Gram. "Oh, I missed you, sweet girl," Gram said. Even her voice sounded strong. Maybe this week in the hospital was doing her some good.

"Hey, Gram." I set the cake on the small table in her room and set the vase beside it.

Gram gave a happy little sigh. "Daisies last time and now, roses. You know my favorites."

I moved the table so the vase got a little bit of sunlight. "I know. And these ones I didn't steal from your yard."

Gram laughed, surely remembering all the times she'd hollered at me for swiping roses off of her beloved bushes. "I tell you," she began, "I wouldn't have minded if you had. I miss home." Her smile turned wistful and once again, I felt like shit for not being here more often, for longer.

She reached a pale hand toward me and I took it, rubbing her cold, papery skin until it warmed. "What kinds of shenanigans have you two been up to while I've been here?"

"Adam has a girlfriend," Casey said and grinned like she'd just told Gram a secret. It wasn't a secret, but I didn't really want to explain Hollis to Gram. Not when it was confusing for *me*. "Her name's Hollis and she's really pretty, Gram."

"Oh?" Gram lifted one of her eyebrows and her lips puckered. Her eyes were pale blue, icy blue, and they saw right through me. "Is that why you haven't been around to visit?"

"No…" I began. I looked around the hospital room, its antiseptic smell burning right through my nostrils. I took the blanket we'd brought and laid it over her legs. "I'm sorry, Gram." It was a pathetic response, but it was all I had to offer. Visions of my mom in this same hospital, and the reminder that she hadn't come home, made being here difficult. But Gram looked good. Her pale skin had pink color in the cheeks, in her chest. She looked better than she had in a while.

"Adam had to get a new job," Casey volunteered again.

Gram was used to Casey steering the conversation, so she gave her a small smile before looking at me, again raising her eyebrow.

"Yeah." I rubbed the back of my neck, giving her a sheepish smile. So much had happened since I had last visited, and Gram was getting the abridged version of it all. "I'm working with Keane now."

"Who's helping with Casey?" she asked me. She knew Keane

and his work schedule, so she knew what those kinds of hours meant.

"Keane's mom. Casey can walk to their house after school. It'll be a little bit of an adjustment in the beginning, but we'll get it figured out."

"You know, I have all that savings from your grandfather."

I knew what she was talking about. After her husband had died ten years prior, his life insurance had paid off her house and she'd invested the rest with her late husband's financial advisor handling it all. Gram received a small pension from her job as a teacher—just enough to pay her monthly expenses.

"Can I use your bathroom, Gram?" Casey asked, her fingers covered in frosting after she'd served up three slices on paper plates.

"Of course, darling," she said, motioning to the door on the opposite side of the room.

"I don't need your money." Since Casey was currently out of hearing, I said, "Dad promised Casey gymnastics lessons if she got her grades up. But he hasn't called her. Her birthday is this week. We celebrated it yesterday, but still."

"He has all week," she reminded me softly. "But I understand." She did. Gram had exhausted herself apologizing for her son. I imagined most parents wanted to be proud of their children, but hers had only succeeded in burdening her with children of his own. "But I do have savings. I know you spoke with Doctor Hathaway. She's a good doctor." She squeezed my hand. "She's honest. Do you understand?" She waited until our eyes locked. "I'm not going to get better, my boy." She squeezed again, and this time I felt the tremble in her hand. I didn't want to think about the possibility of losing her, not right now, not in this hospital.

"But you look great, Gram." Arguing with her was futile, but I didn't know what else to say. Besides, "I can't do this without you."

Her bottom lip shook and she gave me a watery smile. "Hopefully you have a while yet. You are a good man. I'm so proud of the person you've become." She squeezed my hand more urgently this time. "I'm so sorry for the responsibility you have to take on. But I know you *can* do it. You already are."

I felt the back of my eyes sting, but blinked it away. "I don't know where to start."

"Just be there for her. Like you already are. You left a good life in Colorado for your sister—for me." She reached a hand for my face, and it was then that I saw her weakness as the arm fell onto the bed before she lifted it again, determination glittering in her eyes. "I have a will, you know. You don't get to this age with an ailing heart without one." She patted my cheek, drawing me closer to her. "I'm leaving you in charge."

A million protests formed on my lips but she shook her head. "Your dad obviously cannot be trusted, and I love Caleb but his head is in his studies. Always have been. So, you're in charge."

It was an enormous responsibility and when I tried to tell her all of the reasons I couldn't do it, she shook her head again.

"Stop being so stubborn. Caleb already knows. He agrees. The only one who won't agree is your father, and that's to be expected. But don't worry, my lawyer is well aware of his criminal record and will do what needs to be done, if it needs to be done."

My stomach twisted. Gram loved her son, of course she did, so the decision she must've made to make about his competency in managing her estate couldn't have been an easy one.

"You will do the right thing, my boy," she said as I heard the bathroom door open from behind me. "You always have."

"Who's ready for cake?" Casey asked. "This isn't the birthday cake we had at my party, but it's better because it's *your* favorite!" She produced a piece of German chocolate cake and handed it to Gram. "I wanted ice cream, but Adam thought it'd melt in the car."

"Oh, that's all right." Gram's eyes were shining as she looked at Casey, her only granddaughter and, for the last half-dozen years, her full-time partner in crime. "I've missed you so much."

Casey hopped up on the side of the bed with her own slice. "Me too, Gram." She took a bite of cake and grinned at me, completely oblivious to the conversation that had just taken place. A heaviness settled over my heart, of what the future would be giving all three of us. "Hollis is tutoring me, on Wednesday," Casey said, reminding me of that fact.

"Oh? She's a tutor?"

"That's how she makes money. Cool job, right? She doesn't have to flip burgers or wake up at the buttcrack of dawn to deliver newspapers."

"That is a cool job. So, Adam's hooked himself a smarty pants girlfriend then?"

Casey nodded, her hair swinging all over her shoulders. "She's super smart. Like, Caleb smart. And she's really pretty. Prettier than Caleb." Casey laughed at her own joke. "Right, Adam?"

Did we have to talk about Hollis right then? I was feeling hollowed out, my mind spinning with everything Gram had said, which had forced a reality I didn't want into my subconscious. "Sure."

"Well, which part?" Gram asked. "Is she Caleb smart?" Gram looked at Casey. "Growing up, Adam was so mad at Caleb for, in his words, 'being the smart one.'"

"Yeah," I said, "because he's so focused on himself that he doesn't think about anyone else." Was that why I resented Hollis sometimes? Because she was so much like Caleb, so laser-focused that she seemed selfish to everyone else? But the more I got to know her, the less selfish she seemed. She was more than met the eye, more than her reputation of being her dad's little princess painted her to be.

"Oh, my boy," Gram admonished softly. "It's his passion. Surely you can't begrudge him for it. I wouldn't want him to begrudge you for yours." But the thing was, Caleb did. He thought of my music as my hobby, something I did for shits and giggles. Because he was the brains, and I was less than. "But you didn't answer the question," Gram continued. "Is she pretty?"

Was she pretty? It was such a childlike word for someone who wasn't a child. "She's beautiful," I said, regretting saying it the moment Casey turned and grinned.

It'd been a while since I had played my keyboard. I had pretty much resigned myself to selling it to pay Hollis back, so I'd put it in the back of the closet so I couldn't look at it with regret. But now that I didn't have to sell it, I wanted to feel the keys under my fingers again, to let my mind pour into it the way I often did when things were confusing or difficult.

And things were difficult with Hollis. What the hell was going on with her? Why had I kissed her?

I could better answer the second question than the first, but even then I didn't understand the answer. I'd kissed her because I'd wanted to. Ever since years ago, at the party. Something had happened between us at that party, but we'd never been able to explore it.

There was no denying I was still insanely attracted to her. Physically, she was stunning—of course. But when that facade she maintained cracked a little, I felt like I could really see her. And I liked what I saw. I *more* than liked what I saw. The moments she showed her own vulnerability were few and far between, but when she did, I was a lost cause. She was doing my head in, invading my thoughts and my sleep. Maybe I just needed to exorcise her—these feelings—in a song, and I would be cured of whatever she'd afflicted me with.

I set up the keyboard in my bedroom after Casey had long gone to sleep, and poked at a couple of keys until I found the right tone. I started slow, testing and scribbling things down, until I found the right melody. It started to come together, and when I felt I had a good handle on it, I closed my eyes and let my fingers lead me where they needed to go.

20

ADAM

BRINGING GRAM HOME WAS PROVING TO BE MORE OF A FEAT THAN I had anticipated. There was the equipment to set up, the furniture to move around, and the schedules we'd have to manage so she wasn't home alone for long. Which was why, when Keane showed up bringing Navy and Hollis, I was grateful for the help. Even if I was still a little annoyed with Hollis.

She'd been so fucking dismissive of our kiss. Like it hadn't meant shit to her. I didn't know which reality I preferred: the one where a kiss like that only affected me or the one where Hollis lied about how it'd made her feel.

"Don't be a dick," Keane huffed as he moved a recliner in through the front door. He said it quietly so it wouldn't be heard over the music Navy had put on the stereo. "They're here to help."

"Why would I be a dick to my *girlfriend*?" The word slithered off my tongue, and I hated the way it made me feel. I was lying to everyone—Casey and Gram included—and it didn't sit right with me. Even though I had been the one to agree to do it when she hadn't actually asked, I was still uncomfortable with the idea of looking at Hollis like she was someone I was supposed to have feelings for. Well, okay, I did have feelings. But not *girlfriend* feelings.

Then why do you look at her lips like you want to taste them again? The thought was unwanted, and I tamped it down as Keane dropped the recliner outside the door.

"I think this has to come in two pieces," he said, flipping the back of it up and disappearing under the fabric. "Yeah, here." With a grunt, he lifted the back piece fully off. He set it down on the seat and looked at me. A bead a sweat dripped down his forehead. "Because you don't think of her as a girlfriend. That's why." He looked back over his shoulder for a moment. "I can't claim to know her dad very well, but he's not exactly obtuse. He'll see your contempt and he'll use it as a weapon against you. You're gonna have to convince me that you actually like her if you want even a shot at convincing her dad."

"Yeah, well, when I agreed to do this, I wasn't thinking about my acting chops."

"You're a bad actor." Keane shrugged. "But you are a good friend. Try treating her like one. And touch her from time to time. Brush her hair away from her face. Grasp her hand. Things like that."

"I think I know how to touch a woman, Keane." I picked up the seat as he carried the back of the recliner. "It's not like I've never had a girlfriend before."

"Are you sure?" His face was puffed up from holding a breath as he eased the piece of furniture down in the living room.

"Yeah, I had Sarah. In Colorado, remember?"

"Oh, right. She's dating your lead singer now, isn't she?"

After setting the other half of the recliner down, I punched him in the arm. "What happened to 'Don't be a dick,' huh?"

"That was for you. Not me." He gave me a cheesy grin and

punched me back playfully. "It's not like you're heartsore over her."

"No," I agreed.

"And that's exactly why I'm reminding you to be affectionate. Thoughtful."

I frowned. "I am those things."

"Yeah?" He looked beyond my shoulder to where Navy and Hollis were carrying in Gram's mattress from her bedroom. It was more convenient to have her set up in the living room, in a hospital bed, than tucked in her bedroom, alone, in a queen bed. Gram had asked me to get one of those adjustable beds, the ones that could be moved to a sitting position with the touch of a button. She'd asked me to get rid of her queen bed, because she wouldn't need it. She wanted me to eventually take the master— but I wasn't ready to talk about that, not right then.

"Truck?" Navy asked, her words breathy from exertion.

Keane nudged me from behind, and I approached them both. I pressed a hesitant hand to Hollis's low back and said, "Let me get this."

"Thanks," Keane added, coming up behind me and taking Navy's end. "Why don't you guys get her bedding?" The smile he gave Navy was warmer than one I could summon for Hollis, and he wasn't even dating Navy.

I turned to Hollis, prepared to give her an Academy Award winning smile. She had her dark hair pulled back into a high pony and had some kind of silky blue scarf wrapped around her hairline. Her cheeks were pink from the heat and the effort, and her lashes were long and dark, her eyes fluttering closed when they met mine.

Well, so much for smiling at her, I thought. "I got it," I told her in a gentle voice, nudging her around me. She only nodded, not opening her eyes at all, and moved away.

Keane raised an eyebrow at me as we began to carry the mattress outside.

"What?" I asked. "I was going to smile at her."

"You're fucking hopeless, man." I turned to the pickup and lowered myself to the ground to grab the bottom of the mattress.

"How am I hopeless? She was the one who looked away."

"Because you make her uncomfortable. I'm sure that shit is gonna be real believable when you meet her parents for the first time. Her not even being able to look at you is gonna scream, *We've been dating for years!*"

"It's still new," I told him, irritated. "Besides, it's on her to warm up to me. I can't force her to make eye contact."

"No, but you can make her feel comfortable enough to do so."

"*I'm* not even comfortable with this shit."

"Well, you're gonna have to get comfortable. And quickly."

"How the fuck do you suggest I do that?" My aggravation was sharpening my words. It wasn't just the conversation, but the knowing that so many things were happening all at once. Gram was coming home, but not the way we'd all hoped for. Hollis was going to be a fixture in Gram's house for the time being and on top of that, I had to impress people I didn't even fucking like. To help her.

"Come to the cabin this weekend. We're all going. Me, Navy, a few people from the plant."

"Is Hollis?"

"She will if you invite her."

I scowled, and Keane held his hands up.

"Hey, man. You want to know how to make her comfortable with you? You gotta make an effort to actually spend time with her."

"I can't go away this weekend." I nodded toward the house. "I've got Casey."

"Oh, let my mom take her. They can do some girl shit together. It'll be great."

"I like how you volunteer your mom for everything."

Keane slapped a hand to my shoulder. "Because she's offered, idiot. A few times. She *wants* to hang out with Casey. She doesn't have any daughters, after all."

"Gram's coming home soon."

"Yeah, that's why we're doing this now. She doesn't come home until next week. You can afford a little bit of fun." He stood back, crossed his arm over his chest, and left the mattress on the ground. "Come on, what other excuses do you have?" He held his hand palm up, beckoning his fingers. "I know you've got at least one more."

"The new job—"

"Starts Monday." Then he stood back and held his hands up. "I'm just saying—it'd go a long way if you invited her."

I picked up the end Keane had abandoned and pushed the rest of the mattress into the truck and then tucked my head down when Hollis and Navy appeared from the house. Hollis was holding a clear Tupperware that held my Gram's wedding quilt. "Did you fold that?" I asked her, realizing too late that I hadn't exactly said it kindly.

"Yes," Hollis said, meeting my eyes for a brief moment. Of course she had. Hollis was Type A; there was no way she'd leave a quilt unfolded.

"Sorry," I said, "Thanks." From behind her, Keane mouthed 'invite her,' before he grabbed Navy and disappeared back into the house. "Here," I said to her, holding my arms out for the plastic container. She stepped close, and my hands closed over hers, which were securely holding the lid down. I felt her jerk from the touch and was more than a little annoyed with myself for being the kind of person that barked at someone who was only trying to help. That wasn't me. That wasn't the person Gram had raised me to be. "Hot day, right?" I said, and then felt like a total idiot. I sounded more awkward than a middle schooler trying to ask a girl way out of his league for a dance.

I realized that was how she made me feel. Out of my league. Not that I wouldn't have gone for her on my own. But she was smart; she was worldly in ways that I wasn't. She worked hard, and she showed me kindness even when I didn't deserve it. While I wouldn't devalue my musical talents, I was man enough to admit when things didn't come naturally or easily for me. And showing kindness when it wasn't given in return was still something I was working on.

I rearranged my hands to let hers loose and heaved the plastic bin into the back of the truck.

"Yes," she said, and I had forgotten that I had even mentioned the stupid weather. "This weekend it'll cool off."

This weekend. What Keane had mentioned flitted through my brain and though I wanted to swat it away like an errant fly, I opened my mouth and found the words to segue into what he'd suggested. "Speaking of. Do you have plans this weekend?"

Hollis had been preparing to turn back into the house but stopped short and looked me over for a moment. "No..."

"Is that a for sure no, or a depends-on-what-you-want no?"

She blushed. And damn, if I didn't find that even a little bit endearing. Even when I didn't want to. "I guess it's more of the latter of those two."

"At least you're honest." Her smile disappeared and I realized the effect those words in particular had had on her, for all the lies I knew she was holding onto. Shit. "That's not what I meant." I pushed a hand through my hair. "Fuck."

"What can I get next?" she asked. She stared at the ground, where our toes were inches apart. She took a step back and I placed a hand on her shoulder, preventing her—in a gentle way —from stepping further away.

"Before I fuck this up any further, is it okay if I get straight to the point?"

After a moment's hesitation, her gaze lifted until she was looking at me. She gave me one short nod.

"Want to go to the cabin this weekend? Navy and Keane are going, and I guess a few people Keane works with." When she didn't say anything for a moment, I continued. "It might be nice to get away right after school has started. And after the thing with your parents, before they're up here all the time. Casey can stay with Keane's mom. She practically thinks of Casey as a member of her family anyway. And it'd give us a chance to get to know each other a little better."

Her eyes searched mine for a long moment as she mulled it over. "Okay. Friday through Sunday?"

I nodded, though Keane hadn't exactly given me the details. "We can all ride together, if that'll make you more comfortable." At her questioning look, I added, "You seem uncomfortable being around me."

"I am." She swallowed. "We can take my car."

"So it's settled," Keane said, coming up behind Hollis and wrapping her in a loose hug. "Weekend at the cabin!"

21

HOLLIS

MY DAD'S TEXT CAME THROUGH RIGHT AS I PULLED INTO THE driveway of Adam's place.

I assume we'll be meeting your boyfriend tomorrow. We will also discuss your LSAT, since you've failed to respond to my emails. I assume that you're ignoring them, not that your phone has gone missing. Which is why I'm texting. See you tomorrow.

Texting was beneath my father. He'd never said it verbatim, but the disdain was there every time he saw me texting my friends. "Don't you get sick of being glued to your phone?" he often asked me.

Realizing I was going to see my parents tomorrow, with Adam in tow, exacerbated the nerves I felt after this week of school. My phone was blowing up already, with repeated texts from classmates.

I tucked my phone away, not wanting to answer my classmates or my father. What would I say to him? *Actually, I am not interested in law school and Adam is not really my boyfriend but someone who took pity on me.*

Before I made it to the front door, Casey swung it open. "You're here!" she said, as if she was surprised I had actually shown up.

"Hey," I said, wrapping an arm around her shoulders and following her into the house. "What kind of homework are we looking at today?"

"Ugh," she said. "Social Studies."

"That's my favorite," I said, smiling as she led me to the couch.

"Then I guess I'm lucky."

A noise drew my attention to the television where none other than *Beauty and the Beast* played. "Oh," I said, feeling instant nostalgia. "The cartoon version."

"It's the best," Casey said.

"I agree. My favorite movie." I fingered the little rose at my throat as I watched the scene where Gaston plopped his feet onto the table for Belle to rub.

"Hollis," Adam said from across the room. Why did he never say hi? A simple hi. I lifted my head, eyes connecting with his. He looked … different. It'd only been one day since I had seen him, but his eyes were darker, haunted. And the smile he gave me was purely for Casey's benefit because it didn't reach his eyes.

"Hey, Adam." I settled onto the couch while Casey opened her backpack.

"Hollis's favorite Disney movie is *Beauty and the Beast*," Casey said, motioning to the television. "Adam got me this DVD when I was still in diapers. I've watched it at least once a week ever since."

"I can quote the whole thing thanks to that," Adam said. Was that why he'd written an essay about it in our Fairytales class in high school?

"We're learning about the Native Americans, before the explorers came over to North America," Casey said, pulling my attention back to the book in her hand. She handed me a pretest and I noticed the way she held her thumb over the failing score on her pretest.

"This is just a pretest score, to see what we know before we learn," she quickly said.

"Of course," I reassured her. "How would you know these things if you hadn't studied them previously?"

"Well, Arcadian, in my class, knew all the answers." Casey glanced at her brother before saying under her breath to me, "Arcadian is kind of a dick."

"Casey," Adam said in a warning voice.

"It's not really a bad word, Adam," she argued. "It's just a nickname for people named Richard."

"It's not a nickname for 'Arcadian' though," he said, coming toward us. I could feel him drawing closer, his cologne enveloping me. If I didn't focus, I'd lose my head and go moon-eyed for Adam.

"Okay, so you're learning about how the geography and climate influenced Native American culture. Well, that's something I find fascinating anyway so this should be a piece of cake."

We went over that week's lesson and when I felt Casey had a pretty good grasp on the key points of the lesson, we moved onto the next one. Normally I wouldn't have moved on to new lessons with one of my other tutoring students, but Casey's struggle wasn't comprehension—it was confidence. She looked to me before answering the questions I came up with after we'd read the text, making sure she was saying it right. She *wanted* to be right so badly that she tripped over her sentences and got mired down in the details rather than the big picture. "That's very good," I encouraged her when she came up with her own hypothesis about why Europeans sought to explore the rest of the world. Little by little, she understood more and answered more of the questions—including the test ones the teacher likely lifted from the back of each section we covered. I covered the answers with a sticky note and went by each question one by one until the confidence within her bloomed and she answered them with ease and understanding.

"You totally got this, Casey."

She smiled, and I could see the change in her mood from when we'd begun to where we were now. "The pretest for next week is tomorrow. I'll kick Arcadian's ass this time."

I looked around for Adam, but he hadn't heard her. I gave her an encouraging smile. "I'm sure you will."

"I'll be right back," she said, dashing down the hall. I heard the door to the bathroom close and looked down at the book one last time. The sticky note still covered the answers and so I scribbled a little encouraging note for her on it and moved it to the front of the section before closing the book.

"You're done?" Adam asked, coming in from the kitchen.

I nodded. "She's really smart. I'm sure you know that. I think she just needs to work on her own preparedness, and organization." I showed him the backpack already stuffed with papers, some shoved in so they crumpled and others folded unequally like they'd been slipped into the backpack in haste. It made my eye twitch slightly, and if it was my backpack I would set it to rights immediately.

"Have you ever seen her room? It's probably a lost cause." He laughed, sitting on the couch beside me. "But I'll work on it with her. At least if we can start small with her backpack, maybe some organization will echo in her bedroom."

He was sitting so close to me that I could hear the gentle hum of his breathing. He bumped into me, in a friendly way, and said, "You hungry?"

It was on the tip of my tongue to say no immediately. He'd been so wishy-washy with me lately, and the last thing I wanted was to spend more time with Adam—not knowing which Adam I would get—even with Casey as a buffer.

But my dad's text came to the forefront of my mind and I realized we still needed to talk through what to expect, to get our stories aligned.

"Sure," I said. "Want me to order something?"

He laughed. "I already cooked."

"You cook?"

"Sure." He said it like it was the most obvious thing in the world. "I mean, I'm not a chef, but I do okay. For Casey and me, at least. How are you with chicken? And pasta?"

It surprised me that he'd cooked, and had thought to include a portion for me. "Pasta is one of my major food groups."

"As it should be." The haunted look that had been in his eyes earlier had disappeared, leaving him looking more relaxed, settled.

"Thanks for helping her out. It means a lot."

I swallowed. "Well, it's only fair." My breath got shallower, looking up at him, and I felt my limbs go a little stiff. "You get to meet the parents tomorrow night."

"Fuck," he said, and I saw it dawn on his face. "That's right." He looked down at his clothes, which were his signature black. "What should I wear? What will your parents expect?"

It bothered me that he asked that, that he worried about that. "You don't need to dress up for them. Just be yourself."

"Well, what have you told them about me?"

"I mean, technically Tori gave them your name. I'd never given my mystery suitor a name in the two years I lied about having one."

"When she gave them my name, were you surprised?"

"That's an understatement. I mean, it worked out fine, I

suppose. I did tell them my fake sort of boyfriend was a musician, so you already have that down."

He held his hands out, his ink on full display. "I bet they won't expect this."

He was right, but he didn't appear embarrassed by his tattoos—which he shouldn't be. They might've given him a bad boy look, but he was far from it. "They won't, but they've already seen the photo. No doubt my dad has already looked up your family."

"Which means he'll remember my dad. Who he fired."

I hadn't thought too much about that, admittedly. "You have an uncommon name for this area, so I am sure it would've come up eventually anyway." My fingers fidgeted on my lap. In some ways, I felt like I was preparing to lead him into the lion's den. My dad would undoubtedly interrogate him—another reason I hadn't dated in years—and I didn't know how Adam would stand up to that kind of pressure and stress.

"So, you want me to be myself?"

"I don't expect you to act."

"Well, there will be some degree of acting, right?" His arm draped across the back of the couch, behind my head. "After all, they'll think we have been dating for the last couple of years."

"Oh." I swallowed, feeling his warmth encroaching on my space in an unexpected but welcome way. I licked my lips. "Yes, I suppose."

"Why won't you look at me when we're talking?"

I did. "Because you make me nervous."

"Good." I felt his fingers playing with the ends of my ponytail. Though he was gentle, it was as if I could feel it all the way to my scalp; a kind of acute awareness of his proximity and all the tension between us.

His eyes searched mine, like he was watching to see where I cracked from his ministrations. And maybe he'd exploit that weakness, use it to his advantage because he'd have the upper hand then because he was a closed book, except for the warmth in his eyes when he looked at me. It unsettled me, that he could affect me with just his gaze.

"Ew, get a room," Casey said coming out of the bathroom and breaking us up.

"We weren't even kissing," Adam said, standing up.

"But you had that look on your face?"

"What look?" Adam asked, looking at her with skepticism.

"This one." She made her eyes all heavy-lidded, tilted her head to the side and pursed her lips. It was, well, pretty spot on, so I laughed. "Hollis gets it."

"Whatever." He shoved his hands in his pockets, looking adorably uncomfortable from his sister's teasing. "You hungry?"

"Only always," Casey said and grabbed my hand. "You can sit next to me, so Adam can play footsies with you under the table."

"Footsies?" Adam groaned. "We're not in middle school."

He'd set the table, complete with a short, fat candle in the middle. The table runner was blue gingham and the ivory plates were laid out neatly, with forks and knives on pretty gingham napkins.

"Wow," Casey said, echoing my thoughts. "You must really like Hollis."

Adam looked at her the way I imagined most siblings would look at their younger ones when their balls were being busted. "You can eat in the old dog kennel out back."

Casey led me to the seat beside her and scrunched up her nose. "That thing is haunted."

"It's a kennel, it's not haunted."

"Caleb buried Goliath under it."

"Goliath?" I asked.

"Gram's Yorkie. He died a couple of years ago and Caleb thought we should use his kennel as a sort of headstone, I guess, so he buried him under it."

Adam looked less than amused by that. "Should've buried him out by the other animals, along the fence line."

"Caleb does what he wants," she said, and I saw Adam control his mouth to not say anything in response to that. "This looks good, edible even."

"You're really going for the jugular aren't you, Case?"

"Doesn't he usually cook for you?" I asked, trying to prevent more sibling bickering. Using tongs, Adam held up a chicken breast for me and I lifted my plate. "Thanks," I said to him, feeling suddenly, strangely, shy.

"Yeah, but he doesn't go to the trouble of setting the table and using real plates." She shoveled a forkful into her mouth and mumbled, "It's good."

I turned him, feeling an unfamiliar kind of warmth, sitting at the table with them both. Adam and I seemed to be settling into a comfortable kind of peace. We hadn't really talked about what happened back in high school, but I hoped that whatever grudge he'd held against me had been buried for the time being.

"Tomorrow, you're going to stay with Keane's mom," Adam said after a moment. "I've got to go to a dinner with Hollis."

"Oh, you're finally taking her on a date?" Casey said around a mouthful of food.

"Ehhh," he looked at me. "Not a date."

"Well, isn't that what you guys are doing? Dating? Kinda requires a date, doesn't it?"

I smiled at Casey's boldness, wondering what kind of person I might have been if that same independent streak had been nurtured rather than stifled growing up. "Okay, well then maybe it's a sort of date," I said, wanting to let Adam off the hook.

"Have you played for her yet?"

"No." Adam cut into his chicken breast with a heavy hand. "You know you have to go to bed at some point tonight, right?"

he said to her, pointing at her plate with his fork. "Eat up, Chatty Cathy."

"Who's that?" Her mouth was full of food.

Adam eyed her.

"What?" Her shoulders lifted. "I'm *eating,* like you told me to."

"Hollis," Adam said, directing his attention to me. "How is school? How are classes?"

I chewed carefully, hoping there were no flecks of food in my teeth. "Good," I said after swallowing. I waved at the plate. "This is really good, Adam. Thank you for dinner."

"I was cooking anyway," he said, but I knew from what Casey had said that setting the table was an extra step he'd taken for me. "We're eating dinner at your parents' house, right?"

"Yes. I have to bring a meat and cheese board with me. Would you mind coming over early tomorrow to help me prepare it?"

"I've never done one before." I could see the unease settling in. He took a large sip of his water.

"It's okay," I said. "I'll show you. We'll do it together." With that last word, I scooped up another bite so that my mouth was full.

Adam cut into his chicken breast and looked at me thoughtfully. His gazes were warmer lately, and if I thought having him look at me any way other than contempt would be a relief, I was wrong. Because the look he gave me, like I was a puzzle he was putting together, made me feel vulnerable, naked in front of him. And it'd been a long time since I had been naked in front of anyone.

"You're doing it again," Casey said.

"What?"

"Looking at her like you need to get a room."

At that, Adam stared down at his plate for the remainder of the meal.

22

ADAM

Hey stranger. What's going on? I'm starting to feel like you're avoiding me. Don't make me go to Idaho just to talk to you.

I STARED AT SARAH'S TEXT FOR WHAT FELT LIKE AN ETERNITY. I *was* avoiding her. I knew she'd see through the Hollis stuff, and she'd bust my balls for it and the last fucking thing I needed was my ex-girlfriend poking her nose into my business. So I ignored the conversation for now, promising myself to reply eventually.

"Who's that?" Casey asked as I got ready. I tried a tie and then ripped it off my neck in frustration. Hollis had told me just to be myself.

"Sarah," I said. "My ex."

Casey scrunched up her nose. "Why is she texting you when you have a girlfriend?"

"Because she's a friend."

"Then why'd you make that face before tucking your phone away?"

I sighed. Casey was too damn astute for her age. "Because she wants to talk about Hollis, and I don't want to talk about Hollis with her right now."

"Why? Maybe that'll get her to back off."

Casey had no idea how far off base she was. "I doubt that."

"Well, I think Hollis is great. The best decision you made, asking her to be your girlfriend."

Except I hadn't asked. A fact that made me more than a little agitated that I was lying to Casey, as well as everyone else. And there was still more lying to come.

"You know what she did?" Casey asked me when I didn't say anything. "She left me a little note in my textbook. Telling me I was going to kick butt on that test." Casey grinned. "It's funny that she doesn't say swear words."

"I'm sure she does." I frowned, trying to remember when she had, but couldn't remember hearing a single bad word from her mouth.

"She even drew a little thumbs up emoji thing on it." Casey smiled at me. "I know it was just a little note, but it helped me focus. Reminded me that she believed in me."

I was trying to retain what Casey was saying, but her last sentence threw me. "I believe in you, you know."

She rolled her eyes in a "duh," kind of way. "But you're my brother. You're supposed to believe in me. Having her believe in me, I dunno, meant something I guess."

"Glad to know my opinion means so little," I said drily.

"That's not what I said, butthole. I meant that she has no reason to believe in me, but she does."

Casey needed more female influences in her life, besides Gram and Keane's mom. As she was getting older, growing into herself as a young woman, she'd need a steady presence in her life. And not for the first time, I mentally kicked myself in the shins for bringing Hollis into Casey's life. Once this ruse was over, Hollis would have no obligation to stick around. And just like our father and Caleb had done, she'd leave Casey without another thought.

But there was a little voice in the back of my head, asking me if that was even true. Would she abandon Casey when she and I were done? If you'd asked me a week ago, my answer would have been resolute: YES. But now? It was if I was peeling her back, little by little, understanding how she worked all the more. I knew that meeting her parents would help me understand her more clearly.

A knock at the door surprised me. I was going to Hollis's house, to help her with the cheeseboard. Keane was at work, and Keane's mom was expecting me to drop Casey off.

"I'll get it!" Casey said, skipping off to the door.

I attempted one more tie before giving it up. My black button up was fitted and long sleeved, which felt formal enough. Hollis had told me to be myself, so fuck the tie. I opened the bottom dresser drawer, where I kept things I never used—like ties—and a tiny slip of paper in the bottom of the drawer caught my eye and held my attention. Gram hadn't changed my room since I had left for Colorado, so my bedroom was really a time capsule for my high school life. Upon pulling out the square note, I was instantly flooded with memories.

Adam. I loved your speech.

I looked over the crudely drawn rose and briefly debated tossing the thing, but something nagged at the back of my mind, so I smoothed out the note. A high-pitched squeal of glee from Casey pulled my attention away from the note and back to the task at hand.

"Who is it?" I called out as I pulled my first boot on. When Casey remained silent, I rose from the bed and exited the room.

Instantly, red colored my vision and anger flooded my veins. I should have fucking known.

"Hey, bud," my dad said as he let go of Casey, setting her on the ground and turning to me. "Well? Miss your old man?"

I struggled to keep my anger under control, for Casey's sake alone. In his hand he held a few mylar balloons, wilted and used up. One of them said, "It's a girl" as it tried to decide whether to be up or down.

"The, uh, grocery store didn't have a great selection." He held them up. He looked, surprisingly, put together. His beard was gone, his hair was trimmed, and his clothes looked clean. Casey stared up at him adoringly, as if he was some saint sent to rescue her.

"I don't have to go to Mrs. C's house after all," she said. She looked happier than she'd been in a long time, and for a moment—one selfish moment—I wanted her to see him the way I did. I wanted to rip her hand from his arm, so that none of her light was wasted on him. He didn't deserve an ounce of her love, her affection, her attention. And yet, she loved him. But loving my dad was asking for hurt, and that was what I wanted to shield her from.

"Maybe you should still go to Mrs. C's house," I said, still not speaking to him. I was looking at him, all right, like someone would watch a wild animal. My dad was unpredictable, and that was why he was such a threat.

"No," she said, her voice high pitched and borderline whiny. "I want to stay with Dad. He's taking me to dinner!"

"For her birthday." My dad folded his body onto the couch, arm draped over the back of it like he fucking belonged there, like he was going to stay there. "House looks different." He stared at the bed we'd moved in for Gram.

"Gram comes home on Monday," Casey said, sitting next to

him. "We could go see her," she said. "After dinner? Maybe we could even bring her dinner!"

Casey's excitement was on a runaway train, and nothing I could say would stop her hope. That was the tragedy of childhood—you hoped and you hoped until someone let you down. While my friends had learned how to play basketball from their dads, I'd learned how to wait in vain for a day that never came.

"Mrs. C is expecting you."

"The kid wants to spend time with me," my dad said, and I wanted to remind him of her name. She wasn't a *kid,* not really, not anymore. But he only saw her the way he remembered her, in some technicolor dreamland where he was the good guy, the guy who showed up, who kept his promises, the guy everyone loved. Unfortunately for him, I stopped having that kind of blind faith when I was younger than Casey.

What was I going to do? It wasn't like I could tell him no. Technically, he was still Casey's only guardian in the eyes of the law. If I dragged her to Mrs. C's house, Casey would only find a way back here. And he would follow. It wasn't like Amber Lake was a big town. If he wanted to find her, he would. He looked clean, he didn't reek of alcohol, and his eyes were clear.

I didn't want to go to dinner with Hollis's family, not now. With my dad being in town, I wanted to watch him, to protect Casey from the hurt he'd inevitably give her. But the time was ticking, and if I didn't leave soon, I'd be late.

I had promised her, I reminded myself.

"Okay," I said, even though I didn't really have a choice. "I'll be back late, but I will be back."

"We'll be fine," Casey said, but somehow I knew—down deep —that he'd only break her heart. My promise to Hollis was the only reason I left.

23

HOLLIS

"You know, you have to actually pretend to like me, right? I'm not asking you to be my Jack Dawson here. But maybe a little less hostility would be a good start." It was a weak attempt at humor since he'd been in a mood upon arriving at the apartment, but he didn't laugh.

"What hostility?"

"Well," I began, sucking in a deep breath. "The moment you walked in through the front door, you've been kind of pissy. And now, you're holding a butcher knife and looking at me like you're wondering where my softest spots are for you to sink the knife into."

"I don't have to wonder about that." He leveled me with his dark gaze, and my legs trembled. "I already know."

I bit the side of my tongue to keep myself from saying anything to that. Why did him talking about stabbing me sound so sexy? It made no sense. "I-I thought you didn't pay attention in science class," I choked out.

Oh, there it was. The smallest crack in his armor. His lips

lifted, betraying him, and he struggled to keep a smile from fully forming. "You got me there." He looked me over. "Nice dress, by the way."

I looked down at myself, as if I had forgotten what I had chosen for my parents' house. It was more flirtatious than I usually went, but then again I didn't usually bring a boyfriend around my parents. I had chosen the red, off the shoulder A-line thinking it was the perfect balance of sexy and classy. "Thank you," I said.

"Hand me the brick of cheese would you?"

"Which one?" I asked, gazing at the line of white and yellow and orange cheeses on the counter.

"I don't know. The one that looks like it belongs on this board. This is your deal, not mine." Annoyance flitted through his voice and at my quick glance, he exhaled through his nose. Watching him trying to calm down was easily in my top five favorite Adam Oliver moments. It was like an orchestra, really. He braced his hands on the solid wood butcher block, the ropy muscles in his arms tensing and un-tensing. The rise and fall of his chest, like a drumbeat solo, sent my gaze further up, to his face, where I got to witness a quick hollowing out of his cheeks before he inhaled again and looked back at me. For just a moment, just the briefest of pauses, I saw something there in the dark, that made me think he didn't hate me as much as he seemed to.

I calmed my own tone. For Christ sakes, we were about to come to blows over a charcuterie board. "Sorry." The absence of "I'm" from that felt insincere so with a quick wince, I corrected myself. "*I'm* sorry. This board is a mix of cheeses, meats, nuts, jams. So, they'll all go on it in some fashion." I grabbed the wedge of gouda and brought it around the counter to him. "This is gouda." I reached over him, brushing his skin just slightly and completely unintentionally, and sliced off a sliver of the cheese for him to try. "Here."

He stared at me stonily, and I worried he thought I was mocking him.

"It's good," I insisted and tore off a piece. I held it up and worried for a second that he'd make me feed it to him. I very much wanted to keep my fingers attached just then. But he relented, taking the piece from my hand and setting it in his mouth. The entire time, his eyes were locked with mine. The room felt suddenly too small, with Adam here taking up so much space. And it wasn't just because he was tall. It was his presence that filled the room, that made it more intense.

"Do you like it?" I asked when I couldn't take the silence between us any longer.

"It's fine."

I deflated a bit. "Well, it's really good on grilled cheese."

He scoffed a little but took the wedge and sliced it identical to the slice I'd given him to try. "American cheese suits me fine."

I knew what he thought of me, by making that comment. I had to take a different approach if I wanted to get him to talk to me. "Have you ever had goat cheese?" I asked, grabbing the log from beside the other cheeses. "I had the best goat cheese in Bolivia this summer."

"Do I look like the kind of person who would know what goat cheese tastes like?"

I knew what he meant, but his attitude was grating. "I don't know what someone who has had goat cheese is supposed to look like. It's not like it's stamped on your forehead, *Oh, hey, I have tried goat cheese!* So I have no way of knowing."

"Well, no. I haven't. I am not someone who eats fancy cheese." He stepped away for a moment, returning with the cheddar cheese that he seemed much more comfortable using, completely bypassing the goat cheese in my hands. "Not all of us get the opportunity to go gallivanting off to another fucking continent on vacation and waste our days lounging on a beach."

I squared my shoulders. "I didn't go there for vacation. I paid a lot of money to go, sure, but I wasn't exactly spending my days tanning on the beach or shopping or whatever else you assume I did." I yanked the goat cheese out of the wrapper, aggressively rolled it in a cranberry and walnut mixture my mother had shown me how to do once, and slapped it on the board, hard enough to rattle many of the nuts off. Adam took a step back and looked at me. "I went there to help orphans with homework. To teach them that the world isn't so cruel, especially for those who have only known cruelty." Rage boiled beneath my skin and I could feel its heat climb to my face. "For someone who has such disdain for my privileged life, you sure deliver your insults with a lot of smugness. For your information, Bolivia is landlocked. There are no beaches, you jerk." I thought of all the children I had worked with, and how grateful they would be just to be standing here, in an air-conditioned room discussing the trivialities of cheese, of all things. Shame colored my cheeks and I turned away so he wouldn't see. Swiping my water bottle from the counter, I could hear him move behind me and I closed my eyes, taking the first swig and setting it down. "Look," I began, "I get it. I know I'm privileged. More than the average person—forget a country full of orphans. The life I lead looks better than yours right now. But I am no more at fault for being born in a wealthy family than you are for being born into yours. I'm trying, okay? It may not be my best because yeah, sometimes I have to check myself, but I *am* trying to be a better human in all the ways that count to me."

"I knew Bolivia was land-locked," he said and I nearly choked on the next swig of water. He made no mention of anything else I said? Really? I turned around and was greeted with a hand held up, palm out. "And you're right," he said, and again, that annoyance burned. "I shouldn't have assumed."

I took another swig of water. "It's so hard for you to say I'm right about anything, isn't it?"

"Is that what you're after?"

I set the bottle on the counter and turned to him. "No. I just want to explain myself. You're going to my parents' house, you're going to see their expensive things. I'm their daughter, but," I waved a hand over myself, "I didn't ask for this. And because of that, I do try to use what's available to me to do good. You wouldn't know because you haven't seen."

"You don't post any of that on Instagram, so how would I have known?"

So he was still looking at my social media? I digested that carefully before answering. "Yes, because that kind of cheapens it, doesn't it? I didn't go to Bolivia for likes or hearts. I went there because it's what I'm passionate about and posting it for some kind of limp validation from people who don't get what it felt like to be there would cheapen it." I shrugged and grabbed another wedge of cheese, needing to do something with my hands. "Besides, it's not like you post about your family on your Instagram."

"You've been stalking me?"

A smile tugged at the corner of my mouth. "You've been stalking me, since you admitted to it first."

"Yeah, well." He shrugged and took the cheese from my hands. "I had to make sure you hadn't gone off a deep end."

"I'm not entirely sure I haven't." A headache beat at my temples and I ached for some caffeine. I packed one can into my purse, knowing if I brought more than that, my mom would drain them in the sink. "I just don't think I can stand you thinking so little of me."

He was quiet for a long moment as he attempted to spiral slices of prosciutto and layer them in the gaps on the board. "I sometimes feel like you've got the upper hand on me. You're developing a relationship with my sister, and I guess I hadn't expected that when I agreed to this."

"I like your sister," I said. "If you're worried I'm going to hurt her, I won't."

He looked directly into my eyes. "I am worried about that. She's been abandoned too much in her life."

And so have you, I thought, understanding him more. "I won't."

"You can't make that promise. When this thing between us is over, you'll have no obligation to her."

Oof. I wanted to press a hand to my chest, where his words punctured the deepest. *When this was over.* I mean, that part was inevitable, right? Soon, this would just be a blip in both of our individual memories. We'd probably never speak again.

Why was I mourning a loss that hadn't happened yet?

"Okay," I conceded. "You're right, I can't make that promise. But I see in your sister what I saw in myself at her age. My middle sister and I are the same age apart as Casey and me." I grabbed the nuts that had spilled on the counter. "I would've given my left arm for my sisters to pay attention to me." I took in a breath and grabbed the brie. "I won't abandon her."

He stared at me for a long while. "Okay." But he didn't fully believe me, I could see it. "You understand that it's a little hard for me to get why all this effort is necessary, right? The fake relationship, the fact that you haven't dated for years and have held up this lie that whole time?"

"The short answer is that I haven't had time to date." *Or the interest,* I added to myself. I showed him how to slice the brie. "As far as the trust fund, I'm not exactly dying to stay under their thumbs the rest of my life." I adjusted a few slices of the cheeses and then added little spoonfuls of jam in little white pots, strategically around the board. "I want to do more with their money than go to law school and pursue the career my dad wants for me."

"So you're lying to them to get access to that money?"

WHITNEY BARBETTI

"I know it isn't honorable. I have to make my peace with that." I shrugged, as if it didn't bother me as deeply as it did.

"Do you even like your parents?" He turned away from the board to allow me to continue with my little piles of nuts.

"I love them, of course. But there's a reason my sisters went MIA after they graduated. And since my parents changed the stipulations of my trust, I don't have a ton of options here, even when I do graduate. Not if I want to make the impact I want to."

"So money is your barrier from causing change?"

"When you say it like that, it makes it sound so sleazy. So cheap." I stepped back and regarded the board carefully. I wanted this board to be perfect, so that not even a tiny bit of my confidence wavered when we walked into their house. "But money is really only a stepping stone for me. If I get to do what I want to do, I won't be able to get very far on the salary."

"You mentioned once that your degree was in cultural anthropology?"

"Yes. It's the study of human societies, their histories and cultures. Eventually, I want to travel to more remote areas of the world, to obtain hands-on education. And then I want to work for a nonprofit that helps empower indigenous people and preserve their culture. It's such a rare thing these days, for these cultures to exist as they did thousands of years ago. Diversity is beautiful, but for those people who wish to keep their customs, to live far from our modern world, I think we need to do what we can to protect them and their ways of life." I shrugged. "I don't know anything about my familial history. I don't know when my family came over from Europe, I don't know their stories and it bothers me greatly not to know where I came from or the things my ancestors did. When I met people in Bolivia, I heard their stories. They knew what their grandmother's grandmother had done for work for their village. History is passed down through those kinds of stories."

He was quiet for a long moment, regarding me carefully.

"You make me wish I talked to my gram more, about our own stories."

"It's not too late," I said. "Now, are you going to tell me why you stormed in here like you wanted to murder something?"

There was a tick in his jaw. "My dad showed up at the house," he said after a while. "Surprise. He had a handful of sad, not-birthday balloons and insisted on keeping Casey instead of me bringing her to Keane's mom's house." He took the plastic wrap I handed him and pulled off a length of it. "I don't like that he's at Gram's, alone with her. But she's not a baby, and she's not *my* baby at that."

"Your dad is still her legal guardian?"

"Yes. So no matter what *I* want, it doesn't fucking matter." He blew out a breath and braced his hands on the island as he looked at me. "Sorry I was a dick."

He was actually apologizing to me. "Don't be sorry. If you want, we can swing by your place after we leave my parents'. It's closer, and I know it'll give you peace of mind."

He regarded me for a long moment. "Yeah. I'd like that."

24

ADAM

HOLLIS PULLED UP IN FRONT OF HER PARENTS' HOUSE. I LOOKED up at the mansion before us and wondered what the hell I had gotten myself into. Hollis turned to me, worry straining her face, in the crease of her brows. "Are you sure you're ready for this?" she asked. "Because if not, we don't have to do this. We can leave. We can go back to my apartment and we can pretend that this night never happened. I can let you out of our deal. I'm not worried about it. The last thing I want is for you to feel uncomfortable."

I placed a hand on her knee, calming her. "It's okay. It'll be fine." But the truth was, I did feel uncomfortable after the showdown with my dad and what ensued. It was like there was this itch, to crawl out of my own skin, to be someone else, to not be the son of the man that was known famously for drunk driving around town, the man that was fired by my fake girlfriend's dad back in high school.

But I had promised Hollis, which meant I had to see this through because I would not be like my dad.

I just had to keep my eyes off of Hollis's legs, which were on full display in the red, off the shoulder dress she wore. It exposed vast expanses of skin, most of her legs and her shoulders, and it was all I could do not to stare in a way that might incite a father to violence.

Hollis unlocked the front door, letting us both into the house. She called for her mom and dad, poking her head into a wide room off the side of the entryway. As I looked around, what struck me the most was how much space there was. Light wood floors as far as you could see, sunshine pouring in from directly across the front door, from windows that took up floor to ceiling real estate. The white walls looked completely free of smudges or fingerprints, as if they were freshly painted. Hollis set the charcuterie board on the front entry table, drawing my attention to the flowers arranged in the vase there. They were so well put together that I wouldn't have been shocked if they'd grown from the ground exactly like that, as if Mother Nature herself had always intended for them to belong in an arrangement.

Everything about this house screamed—in a soft, careful voice—perfect. Clean. Like if I just touched the walls with the briefest of fingertip grazes, I would impart stains.

I looked down at my clothes, seeing little bits of lint on my black shirt and the little bits of scuff at the hem of my jeans. My clothes screamed imperfection.

Hollis once told me that she'd had a crush on me in high school, which I now found unbelievable. She stood, her hands clasped gently in front of her, her rich brown hair pulled back into a taut ponytail. Not a hair was out of place. Not a wrinkle or lint or imperfection in her clothing. We were complete opposites. Did she enjoy slumming it with me? Is that why she'd harbored some kind of weird crush?

Hollis led me into a living room where I sat down on a very plush light gray leather couch. I didn't even know leather came in this color. I pressed my hands on the cushions feeling its bounce. You couldn't feel any springs. This wasn't at all a place I would be comfortable relaxing in, but I supposed I wasn't there for relaxation, was I? I was there to perform. Perfection would not be natural for me, but I'd try, for Hollis. She gave me a smile that bordered on concerned and I knew that concern was for me. "I'm going to go see where they're hiding," she said, casually, but I knew by the little wave she gave me that she was not comfortable.

I didn't want to sit on the couch by myself anymore, so I stood and walked across the room, which felt like a football field in length, to a white marble mantle. Atop that mantle were photos of Hollis and her sisters, each photo displaying their achievements. I found it so interesting that each photo was posed carefully, revealing that each photo was specifically taken —for a purpose, not candidly. There was one of Hollis in her cap and gown, holding a diploma in her hands, but the smile on her face didn't quite reach her eyes. The photo beside it I assumed was that her sister, same pose, same smile. The last photo again I assumed was her older sister, based on the date of the diploma, and she too wore the same smile. If it wasn't for their slightly varying shades of hair color, one would think they were cloned.

I tried to imagine what it would be like to live in that kind of pressure, to feel that kind of innate responsibility to perform and to be perfect. I could not relate.

"So you must be Adam," came a voice behind me.

I turned and immediately knew who I was looking at. Hollis's father, the reason half of Amber Lake's residents were employed, was staring at me from across the room. He wore very neatly pleated slacks and a tucked in dark gray shirt. He was tall, fit, and clean shaven, with an air of wealth that was evident even if you didn't look at his house. I approached him with a hand out. "Good to meet you, sir."

After a moment, he pulled one hand slowly out of his pocket and reached for mine, but his eyes were measuring and calculating. "Where's Hollis?" he asked. I turned around, wondering the same thing. It was one thing coming here with Hollis, but being alone with her father made me feel like I was a lobster in a restaurant's tank and he was eyeing me for his next meal.

"I think she went to look for you," I told him. I looked around the room trying to calm my own nerves. I hadn't felt as nervous walking up to the house, but then again, Hollis had been beside me and now that she wasn't, I felt scrutinized. It was like a job interview, but this was a hundred times worse.

"Do you watch sports?"

"No, I don't." With the same measured gaze, I watched his response to that. But unlike me, he didn't betray a trace of anxiety. Why would he? He didn't have to impress me. "My sister is into gymnastics, so I do watch that from time to time with her, but my interests don't typically fall toward athletics."

"What interests you?" he asked me. He seemed immensely calm, comfortable, which I supposed I would be too if I had money and power and people who bent to my will.

"I'm a musician. I have a band in Colorado." But did I? I wasn't really sure that I could call myself part of the band anymore. Not after leaving as abruptly as I did, and I knew at some point I'd have to address that with my bandmates and have them seek out a new keyboardist. Nothing felt real yet. Gram being in the hospital felt like a pause, not a period. It was as if I was under some delusion that she'd come home, be better, and we'd move on about our normal lives. But there was nothing normal about our situation.

Hollis's dad took in my tattoos, betraying nothing on his face. Unlike his daughter, Mr. Vinke was a closed book.

Just then Hollis came in, accompanied by whom I assumed to be her mother. Her shocking white hair was sleek and stylish, and she had the same measuring look in her eyes when she reached a hand out to shake mine.

"Mrs. Vinke," I said, and for some strange reason it felt like I should bow. If the air that surrounded her husband spoke of wealth, hers spoke of royalty.

Hollis came to my side, and instinctively I put my arm around her, only to remember where I was and drop it. Fuck. I was supposed to play this part, so I put my arm around her waist and she shifted closer, subtly. I took that as a silent sign that this was okay.

"I left a charcuterie board on the front table," Hollis said when silence ensued.

"Perfect," her mother replied. "I will go fetch that. Let's go into the rec room."

In a house as pristine and showroom worthy as this one, I couldn't imagine what a rec room must have looked like. But Hollis's hand over mine on her waist squeezed reassuringly, and we followed her father into a room off of a formal dining room.

The room looked opposite from the house, darker with wood on the walls and echoed in the beams that stretched from one side of the ceiling to the other. On one end of the room was a billiards table and on the other was a bar and a collection of plush couches. Everything matched well, but judging by her father's ease with the room, this was his domain. "Pool?" he asked me, holding out a stick. I didn't play pool well, but I felt as if I had no choice to agree to something, anything, so that I didn't become some kind of wallflower.

"You can go first," he said. He arranged the balls on the table for me while Hollis rubbed my back, reassuringly. She stood beside me and handed me a blue cube of chalk. It was like she was subtly guiding me on what to do without trying to make it overly obvious because she placed the white cue ball on the table for me next. I'd happily let her choreograph the rest of the evening if it meant I did everything right.

"Good luck." She gave me a small smile, but just like the photos on the mantle, it didn't reach her eyes.

Hollis's mother returned with the charcuterie board and placed it on top of the bar. "This looks lovely." She uncovered the plastic wrap and looked over each chunk carefully. Maybe I imagined it, but Hollis seemed to relax a little bit at my side. Was she really this nervous over a damn cheese and meat board?

"What have you been up to?" her mother asked. "I've been trying to call you, but you haven't returned my calls." Well, if Hollis had been relaxed before she was stiff as a board once again. So, we were already going to launch into the inquisition, I realized as I struck the cue ball and watched all the other ones go flying.

"Stripes," Mr. Vinke announced.

"Well, I've been pretty busy with my tutoring schedule and my schoolwork and I've been looking up the LSAT."

"Oh really?" Mr. Vinke turned to her, his voice deeper than it'd been when he'd been talking to me. "That's good to hear because you didn't reply to my messages for me to know one way or another."

I could already tell that it was going to be hard for me to be quiet and to not say anything to her father. The passive-aggressiveness was already a little bit over the top in just the five minutes we were there, and we were supposed to be here for hours more? At least long enough to enjoy a charcuterie board as well as dinner. It was going to be a long fucking night.

Hollis turned to her father and I could just see how she worked to hold herself tall, with pride. Shoulders back, head straight. That posture and elegance or not just innate to her, but expected. "Yes. I'm sorry. I've been very busy." I wished I still smoked, if only to use it as an excuse to seek relief from this torturous tension.

Hollis waited for her dad to reply, but I decided to butt in first. "Hollis has started tutoring my sister."

Whatever her dad had wanted to say, he'd abandoned for now. I was luring him in, so that his attention and his passive aggressive remarks could be lobbed at me instead. "How old is your sister?"

"She's going to be thirteen this weekend."

"We had her birthday party on Sunday," Hollis added.

"Is she your only sibling?" he asked.

"No, my brother Caleb is in Boise." I almost left it there, but it felt necessary to validate myself somehow by using my brother. "He's going to medical school."

"And what about your parents? What do they do?" I was deeply regretting changing the subject to my family. I glanced at Hollis's father, wondering if he already had made the connection about my dad or if perhaps she had told him. "My mother is gone." It was always such a weird thing to explain and the pity and looks I often received didn't make it any easier to say. "And my father is in Utah." Better to leave it at that, than explain what he was doing in Utah. I was sure my father's current exploits would scandalize them both.

"Then who takes care of your sister?" Mrs. Vinke asked.

"My grandmother does, but she's in the hospital right now, which is why I'm back in Idaho."

"Where were you before?"

I could feel sweat along my spine and wanted to loosen the collar of my shirt. "I was in Colorado with my band."

"Oh," Mrs. Vinke said. "Well, have we heard any of your music?"

"That's unlikely. It's a small band—mostly local—but we do okay. Mostly shows Denver and the surrounding areas, festivals, that sort of thing."

"Are you the singer?"

I laughed, feeling ease in talking about the band. "Oh, no. I'm not on the vocals."

"Oh, Hollis told us you were a musician."

"Yes, I play the piano. I'm not really good on the singing bit. So, the piano is it for me."

"And," Mrs. Vinke said, "your grandmother is in the hospital. Will she be coming home soon?"

"Yes, but she has a weak heart and as of now, my plan is to stay in Idaho indefinitely. At least until Casey, my sister, has graduated and moves off on her own."

"That must be very hard for you." For the first time, Mrs. Vinke's facade of sleek perfection cracked enough for me to see a sliver of genuine compassion. Hollis's father, on the other hand, still eyed me like a lobster in a tank. "But what about your older brother? Will he come and help take care of your sister? Or maybe your father?"

Hollis's fingers entwined with mine. I could feel Mr. Vinke's gaze on me as I addressed his wife's questions and I wondered if I should tell him who my father was. Already, he was forming an opinion of me and it didn't seem to be a good one.

"My father will not come home." It was the most honest thing I had said aloud about him in years. I was never even that frank with Casey, lest I break her heart. "He hasn't been home in years."

I sunk one ball, then two, then three.

"Well," Mr. Vinke said, lining up his stick for his shot after I had missed.

"Want some goat cheese?" Hollis asked from beside me. "It's great with a little bit of the jam." She made a motion with her fingers, like she was drizzling something with them.

I nodded, and she let go of my hand with a squeeze. When her father missed his shot, I lined up for the next one. I sunk three more balls, leaving me facing the eight ball. As I looked at the table, trying to decide which hole to aim for, Hollis returned.

"Here." She held up a cracker up for me. There was a smear of goat cheese and a dollop of jam on top. She motioned for me to open my mouth, so I did, and with exquisite care she fed it to me.

I chewed, staring at her, willing her to keep staring at me. Something was shifting between us, redefining us inside of this relationship. I had been feeling it since Casey's birthday, but it'd been building since then. I didn't have many memorable relationships, but they'd all started from a place of straight-up lust. This thing with Hollis had begun with a lie but had been built by respect, patience, and attraction. My hand found her waist and squeezed. "This is good."

She stepped closer, closing the gap between us. "It is, isn't it?"

"The tangy cheese is balanced by the jam." Words I never thought I'd have ever said, but there they were, spilling from my mouth anyway. Hollis had that effect on me.

"Are you going to call it?"

I turned to the interruption. Mr. Vinke was pointing at the eight-ball and he looked more uncomfortable than he had the whole night.

"That corner pocket," I said, and bent over the table, aimed, and sunk the final ball.

Hollis made a funny little half-cheer, half-whoop sound behind me and I turned to her, proud that I had won a game against her dad, feeling for the first time like this night might be okay.

25

HOLLIS

AFTER THE GAME OF POOL, MY DAD LEFT US TO TAKE A PHONE call and my mom disappeared into the kitchen. Adam and I picked at the charcuterie tray until I finally said, "Want a tour?"

"Sure," he said, popping one last cracker with goat cheese into his mouth. He grabbed my hand before I reached for his, and that connection was everything I needed to ground me to him, to convince myself that whatever this was, it might be something real after all. It hadn't been long, but we'd spent every day together since.

"This is the rec room," I said, holding my hand out like I was a game show model showing off a brand new car.

"Oh wow," he said, playing along with my cheesy tour guiding. "There's a pool table in here."

"I know, amazing right?"

"And even a board with cheese and meats and shit."

"No shit on this board," I corrected him. "Though some of the cheese is kind of stinky."

"You said a bad word." It pulled me out of my fake spiel.

"I say bad words."

"Not to me you don't."

I looked over my shoulder, half expecting to see my mom spying on us. "I guess I just don't say them as often as I'd like to." I lifted a shoulder. "Come on, the tour doesn't end here." I led him out the doors opposite from the ones we'd come through, into the family room where my dad watched his sports every night.

Adam paused in his steps and when I followed his line of sight, I saw what captured his attention.

"That's a Steinway, isn't it?" He left my side to approach it.

"It's my mom's."

"Does she play the piano?" he asked, running a hand over the gleaming rosewood.

"No, but this one has been in her family for a couple of generations."

"I can tell. This is early nineteen hundreds." He looked at it reverently, like I imagined some guys looked under the hoods of muscle cars. "Beautiful," he said, and it was like I didn't exist for the moment. Which I didn't mind. Seeing him like this, awed by something I took for granted, gave me a new appreciation for it myself. He walked all around the grand piano, his hands roaming over the keys. When he finally looked at me again, there was a smile on his face I hadn't seen before. "I want to play it."

"It would be a shame if no one did." I approached the piano and patted the bench in invitation.

"Sit with me." He slid on the left side and gestured for me to sit on his right. "Do you know if it's been recently tuned?"

"She gets it done at Christmas every year, that's when she hires a pianist for one of her parties."

He pressed down on one key and closed his eyes as the sound reverberated in the empty room. "Ahh." It was a treat to experience the piano through Adam's eyes. "You hear that? It's

so fucking cliché, but they don't make pianos like they used to."
He played another note. "During the Great Depression, so many
piano makers went out of business. But they were in decline
before then, thanks to the phonograph and then the radio
replacing them in the home." He played another note. "Just
listen to that. There's nothing like that sound." He turned to me,
a smile on his face. "I paid thousands for the keyboard I have,
the one I play with my band, and it's great, but this sound."

I wanted to listen to him talk more about the piano, about
why it was so great. "How is it different?"

"Well, first of all, the keyboard doesn't have the hammer that
strikes a string to produce this sound." He pressed down on a
key. "On a digital piano, it's actually a digital file, so it doesn't
have the same effect. It's warmer, it's a deeper sound on an
acoustic piano. And this kind of piano is touch sensitive."

"What do you mean?"

"I wish I had my keyboard to show you the difference, but
here." He took one of my hands and placed it on the keyboard.
"Let your fingers go lax, so I can show you." He covered mine
with his and then pressed down on my forefinger. "Hear how
loud that is? That's due to the pressure of our fingers." His
finger pressed down over mine again, but with a lighter touch.
The sound that it produced was less powerful, lighter somehow.
"On a keyboard, you get don't get this kind of range from the
pressure of your fingers. You can't control the sound as easily as
you can here." He played something that sounded somewhat
upbeat for a minute. I was so lost in watching him, watching his
concentration as his head moved to the beat.

"'Someone Like You' by Adele?"

He smiled and stopped. "Yeah. It's pretty unmistakable.
Notice how the louder parts are more pronounced than the rest
of the melody. That's not due to the tone necessarily, but the
pressure I'm applying to the keys."

He played something else, something that initially sounded

more like a nighttime lullaby. It took me a minute to figure it out. Without the lyrics, it wasn't as recognizable, but then it built up to where I guessed the chorus was and I knew it instantly. "'Against All Odds.'"

"Good ol' Phil Collins," he said, grinning.

"Do another one," I said, hoping not to sound too desperate. Casey had asked him at dinner if he'd played for me and considering that was one of the things I found most attractive about him, the fact that he hadn't played for me had stuck in my head.

"Okay, but you have to sing the lyrics or else I stop."

"Oh, okay," I said. "So this is a game?"

"Yeah. I stop when you get it wrong." His smile was infectious. I wanted to stay here, next to him on the piano bench as long as possible.

"I won't get it wrong."

"Let's see." He winked, took a breath in and out and then placed his hands on the keys. What erupted from his fingers was completely unmistakable.

"You're making this too easy," I told him before I started to sing along to Bohemian Rhapsody.

"Am I?" he asked.

"Why does it sound so good like this? It's so unique."

"Freddie Mercury spent years developing it. Years of work for this song. Okay, next one."

I knew it immediately after the first notes were played, but since the lyrics took a minute to come through anyway, I just enjoyed watching him. He might've been halfway in love with this piano. His eyes were closed and his head moved to the beat. From time to time, his arm brushed against mine, bumping into me, and I wanted to lean into it. But I let him enjoy, pouring himself into the song, before I joined in with the chorus to 'Drops of Jupiter.'

"That one took you a minute."

"No," I said. "I just liked watching you play."

We were so close, sharing the same breathing room. Our legs were inches apart, and he didn't seem so much taller than me when we were seated, side by side.

The attraction I felt for him was a persistent hum, nearly to the point of distracting, but it swarmed when he looked at me the way he did. I was never more intimidated than when he stared deeply into my eyes, deep enough to see all the way through. Like he knew my secrets, without me saying a single word. Without taking his eyes off of me, his hands returned to the piano and he played another unmistakable tune.

I couldn't sing along to this one. No way, no how. I swallowed, trying to get the courage to sing the lyrics, but I was overcome with the sharpest kind of intimidation. "You're brilliant," I told him, and because I was nervous it came out a whisper. "That sounds beautiful."

"What's the song, Hollis?"

I shook my head, and he continued to play, continued to look into my eyes.

The tension was building along with the melody on the piano. He was waiting, testing me. I didn't mind play singing along to the other songs, but this one was too close to the truth for me to sing it like it was nothing. "I can't," I said.

"Want me to stop playing?"

"You're a real jerk," I said. "I can't do Alicia Key's song justice."

"You don't need to do it justice. You just need to sing it." He closed his eyes briefly, bopping his head to the beat. "Come on, you can do it. I believe in you."

The words struck me, especially coming from him. But since his eyes were closed, I gave in and let the lyrics to 'Fallin" pour out of me. It felt better to sing along with my eyes closed, so I gave into that as well.

"Keep going," he whispered, when he probably would've

stopped. So I did, I kept singing, hoping my voice didn't sound like a raccoon dying, until he stopped playing.

Opening my eyes, I felt my stomach twist. His were open, probably had been for a while. "You're not half bad, Hollis."

"I'm not talented like that," I said, feeling shy. I looked everywhere but at him.

"Don't say that."

"It's not a big deal. I know where my strengths are, and I'm very comfortable with myself. I'm not going to make a career in music, and that's okay." I was rambling. I shook my head and gave him a smile. "This isn't me fishing for compliments, Adam. I'm awed by your talent, but I recognize that I lack the same talent."

His eyes didn't look settled, however. He was on the verge of frowning when I nudged him. "Play another one."

So he did. It took me a little bit longer than the others to get, but after he played for a little while I recognized it and started singing softly along with it.

He stopped playing, abruptly, and I looked at him in confusion.

"You know this song?" he asked.

"Yes…" Why was he acting so weird?

And then it hit me, right when he said, "That's one of my songs."

There was no backing out of this. I couldn't feign ignorance, couldn't pretend I hadn't listened to his music over the years. "Yes. It is." I folded my hands on my lap, willing myself not to be embarrassed.

"So…you know my stuff? I mean, my band's music?"

My face warmed. "Yes. I've listened to your music."

"You knew the lyrics to that song. The piano is just background in that track, but you caught it and sang it anyway." It wasn't a question, but it was posed like one.

I took a deep breath in. If I got ahead of it, if I admitted it, maybe this would be less embarrassing. "Yes. I told you, I had a crush on you."

"You did, but I didn't believe you."

I licked my lips, feeling claustrophobic on this bench. "Hopefully you do now."

"Why are you clamming up on me, Hollis?"

I hadn't realized it, but I had gone board-straight, and my hands clasped in my lap were tight enough that they'd start sweating in an instant. "Because," I said, "I'm embarrassed. Obviously." I hated that I couldn't control my face when it came to my emotions. For someone as much of a control freak as I was, my cheeks flooding with color when I was embarrassed was exceptionally frustrating.

"Don't be embarrassed." He gently bumped against me. "I'm flattered. But if it'll be easier, I'll play another one." And he did, something slow and sad, almost. It started slow, crescendoing into something strong, powerful, before it ended on a few higher notes that he played softer and softer until you could scarcely make them out.

I didn't recognize the song. It wasn't any of the ones on his band's album, or a song I'd heard on the radio. "Maybe I'm a little rusty," I said. "I was gone most of the summer, so I haven't caught up on all the hits right now."

"Did you like it?"

"It was beautiful. Sad, a little."

"That's interesting." He rubbed his jaw. "I didn't think of sad when I started writing it. It was more confusion than anything."

"You wrote that?" I shook my head. "That was gorgeous. Really, something special."

"I'm glad you think so." He played the beginning riff again and then turned to me. "I wrote it after we kissed for the first time." He glanced at my mouth before meeting my gaze again. "I guess it's kind of your song."

That truth pummeled into me, robbing me of any intelligent

thought. He'd written a song partially inspired by me. What did someone say to that? I was flattered, shocked, and felt entirely inadequate. "You did?" was all I managed. I wanted to hear it again.

He nodded. "I couldn't get my own thoughts out of my head. So I wrote them down."

"Did it help?"

"Music always helps," he said. "But it doesn't solve my confusion. It just makes it sound pretty." He gave me a crooked grin.

"I want to hear the lyrics," I said.

"I'm not a singer," he replied.

"Neither am I." I held his gaze this time, saw him look slightly less at ease than he had before.

"Touché."

"Are you ready to eat?"

I turned to where my mother stood at the entrance to the kitchen. I didn't know how long she'd stood there, how much she'd heard. Her face betrayed nothing.

"Ready?" I asked Adam, feeling a little rubbed raw and completely *not* ready for a dinner with my parents.

"I guess." He stood and held out a hand for mine. When I took it, I wished to have the kind of outlet Adam did, to translate my own feelings into something beautiful the way he could. I had my studies, but what else?

My mother had set the table for our four places, complete with crystal goblets she'd filled with wine and impeccably white cloth napkins. My father was already seated opposite of where Adam and I were to sit.

Adam pulled out my chair and I gave him a grateful smile as I sat and prepared myself for what was sure to be stressful dinner. The intimacy of our four place settings and low lighting in the room should have made it feel comfortable and cozy. But instead it felt more like a face-off between two sides, with an interrogation looming.

"Was that you playing the piano?" my mother asked as she dished out salmon to each of us. "Hollis was right, you're very good."

I would not blush. I would not blush. I mean, when I had told my parents that my sort-of boyfriend was a pianist I hadn't exactly been referring to Adam. But in a way, I had. He was the one I thought of, the guy I modeled my fake boyfriend after.

"Thank you, Mrs. Vinke." He sounded stiff. Maybe he was intimidated by the opulence of the room and the stare of my father. In what I hoped was a reassuring touch, I placed my hand on his thigh under the table and rubbed my thumb gently. Before I could pull my hand away, he'd captured it with his, flipping it over and entwining our fingers.

A stupid, giddy little smile tried forcing its way onto my lips but I bit them to keep it from happening. I was being scrutinized by my father, who hadn't said a single word, and I didn't want him to question anything about my facial expressions.

"How long have you been playing?"

"Since I was small. My gram had an upright piano when I was growing up. She was the one who taught me." His thumb caressed mine in a slow gesture and I wriggled a little in my seat. "And when I was in middle and high school, I was in band."

The memory of him being called band geek was enough to sober me. I'd have to eventually talk to him about that night at the party, the night that had shaped his opinion of me for so long.

"Oh, to further your piano skills?"

"Well, no, actually. I tried out a few instruments. Renting whatever was available until I got bored. I wanted to understand how they worked together, how the layers of each instrument affected the others. You know, learning how identical notes layered together create fat sounds in a song."

"That's fascinating," my mom said, and I actually believed her. "You know, Hollis's father and I were quite the music buffs back in the day. That's why our daughters all are named after songs."

"Oh?"

"Yes, Layla for the Eric Clapton song."

Adam nodded. "That's a good one."

"Angie for The Rolling Stones."

"Of course," Adam agreed. "A classic." But then he frowned and turned to me.

"'The Ballad of Hollis Brown', by Bob Dylan."

Adam looked up the ceiling, as if he was mentally going through a catalog of songs that lived up there. "Isn't that one about a murderer?"

"Yes," I said, when my mom tsked.

"You're looking at the lyrics too simply," my mom protested. "I didn't name you after a murderer. I named you after a feeling I had. You see, Adam," she said, ignoring me as she addressed him. "My dad was a bit of a musician himself, but he played the banjo and guitar. I grew up on that song, listening to him sing it. The notes are simple, but I can still hear him strumming along to the beat."

"My wife's father came from poverty," my dad added. "The song is about the effect poverty can have on a person, and my father-in-law saw it firsthand." He looked at me. "As someone so interested in cause and effect in society, the song is really perfect for you."

He'd never actually talked to me at length about his own feelings for the song, and I couldn't disagree with him. "Yes, I imagine Grandpa wasn't immune to poverty. And so that song might have hit home for him. A farmer deep in poverty, so deep that he can't afford to feed his children. Bob Dylan's song was an expose on social problems and the tragedies they can cause. Things we don't always think about when we're reveling in our own wealth and our investments in the very things that are forcing others into poverty."

"You're talking about Bolivia," my father said. Sometimes, he acted as if he was blind to the problems of the world unless they directly affected him.

"I'm talking about everywhere. Poverty exists everywhere. Navy volunteers her free time at the women's shelter, at the soup kitchen, wherever she can."

"Don't be so self-righteous, Hollis. You certainly enjoy the opportunities we've given you, thanks to our financial support."

He wasn't wrong. I couldn't claim to always be doing what I should be. I didn't always recycle, I didn't always choose to walk instead of driving. I was far from being a leader on protecting our planet *and* its inhabitants, but I did what I could, with what I had. I was imperfect, but I was trying. "Yes," I finally said. "I've used the money you've given me to fund an education. I've used the money you've supported me with to go to Bolivia and help the people there." And, if I could, I'd use the money to fund my education in less formal ways. Instead of in institutions, I'd do it in small villages, in camps, in places my parents wouldn't travel to, wouldn't approve of, to make a small impact in the ways that mattered most.

"Adam, tell me about your...artwork. On your hands." My mother was not subtle in changing the direction of the conversation. But Adam, whose grip on my hand had remained firm through my verbal battle with my father, took the bait immediately.

"Mile High is the name of one of our songs. One of the first we composed music together for. The heart is for my grandmother, because hers is ailing. There are others, too, but some of them I got when I was younger and dumber."

I held my breath, waiting for my dad's response. I knew

what he thought of tattoos. When Angie had come home with her first at seventeen, he'd made it very clear his opinion of them while we lived under his roof. But my mother continued on, probably suspecting my dad's rising annoyance.

"I always wanted a tattoo," she said, but I didn't believe it. "When I was younger, of course. It's a good thing I didn't, or else I've have gotten it right over my belly before getting pregnant and watching it go to ruin."

"Isn't it hard to find employment when your body is covered in ink like that?"

Adam shook his head. "No. I mean, before I started working back here, I was in a band so I was kind of my own boss."

"You're working at Russell and Sons Construction, correct?"

Adam stilled. "Well, I was." He cleared his throat and I continued eating. "I start work at the potato plant on Monday. The one west of town."

"Ah." My dad fingered his glass, looking over Adam in a way I recognized. "Hard to hold down a job?"

"Dad."

Adam squeezed my hand. "It's been a rough adjustment being back here, I'm not going to lie. I've been doing my best for my sister and trying to keep up on things for my gram so she can come home on Monday."

"Have some more salmon," my mom said, holding the platter toward Adam. But Adam had barely had a chance to eat a bite of the salmon on his plate. He took another portion anyway.

"You know," my dad said, after he'd polished off his dinner. "I thought your name was interesting."

Awareness prickled every inch of my skin. I had been waiting for this to come up, for my dad to mention something about it, and unfortunately this was the time.

"Adam?" Adam asked, and I knew he was playing dumb. My dad was about to have the upper hand, but Adam didn't have to admit defeat to him.

"No. Oliver." My dad sipped his water, and I hated that he was being so calculating. I gripped the seat under the table with one hand, bracing myself. "I remember your father. Mark, is it?"

"Yes. He was fired. By you, I believe."Adam's voice was cool, his posture relaxed. He even sipped his water calmly, as if this topic didn't cause him even one iota of distress. Maybe it didn't.

"That's right. Do you know why I fired him?"

"Dad," I started, feeling the ascension of my father's condescension.

He simply held up one hand, effectively shushing me. "He drove to work drunk. He was late, which would've been forgivable, but it was his inebriation that was, well, not."

I squeezed Adam's hand, humiliated for him and for the show my dad was putting on.

"Sounds like my dad." Adam lifted his chin, perfectly highlighting his beautiful jawline. The light danced over his cheek when he clenched his teeth, but otherwise he showed no outward signs of being unsettled by this conversation.

"I see he was arrested recently for public intoxication," my dad continued.

"Dad," I said again, firmer this time. His bright eyes flipped to me, with *that* look, the one that told me to shut up. But I wouldn't. "Is that what your phone call was? You were investigating my boyfriend?"

"Are you really surprised?" He folded his hands neatly in front of him, his face placid.

"I guess not, but I don't really see the point of this conversation, especially right now."

"The point is that you brought your boyfriend to my home, your boyfriend who knew that I had fired his father. Was this to get back at me for some reason?"

"I don't know what you mean."

"I'm asking if you're dating," he motioned to Adam with a

flippant wave of his hand, "this, just to aggravate me. You knew this would embarrass me."

"Enough." *This?* He'd referred to Adam so flippantly, like he was some broken toy I paraded around my dad just to piss him off. Fury burned bright through my limbs. I stood, my legs shaking, and faced my father. "I brought Adam here because he's my boyfriend." I barely spit the words out without my voice trembling. I gripped the table for stability. "I brought Adam here because I thought you might like to meet my boyfriend and because I thought you'd behave the same way you expect me to behave around the guys you practically shove down my throat."

"There's nothing wrong with those young men. They come highly vetted—"

"There's nothing fucking wrong with Adam," I said, my voice like razorblades on my throat. It was louder than I had ever spoken to my father. I saw the shock immediately in his eyes, and my eyes flipped to my mother who mirrored his expression. "If anyone here needs to feel embarrassed, it's you. You've tried to humiliate my boyfriend, for something that has *nothing* to do with him, and you've embarrassed your own damn self." I turned to Adam, felt the harsh breaths sawing in and out of me, as if I had just run some kind of marathon. Adrenaline was coursing through my veins when I reached a hand to him. "Ready to go?"

"Yes." He stood, setting his napkin on the table. "Thank you for dinner, Mrs. Vinke," he said before taking my hand and practically hauling me out of the room when my legs were too shaky to walk.

We ran through the living room, through the foyer, and out the front door and down the giant concrete steps all the way to his car. I felt Bonny and Clyde-esque as we raced across the lawn, like we'd just barely escaped and were on the run for our lives. I knew it was the adrenaline causing that feeling, propelling me forward when my legs felt weak. I nearly slipped in a puddle in the grass, but Adam caught me before I fell and then half-carried me to his car.

It had started drizzling while during dinner, and a fine mist coated us both before we were safely tucked into the car.

We didn't say anything for several minutes as Adam drove off. I felt completely discombobulated. I couldn't think about anything except what had just happened.

The adrenaline abated, leaving me weak, clammy, and rattled to my core. "I need a bathroom. I think I'm going to throw up," I said.

"I'll stop at Deb's Pizza, right up here."

I nodded, the shakes fully coming on. I wrapped my arms across my chest, and clenched my teeth to keep them from chattering. I had just yelled at my father. I never yelled. I'd thrown my phone, that one time, from sheer frustration. But never had I reacted so dramatically in front of my father.

Deb's Pizza was pretty quiet at nine p.m., thankfully because I wasn't entirely sure I could keep it together for much longer. "Here," Adam, said, leading me down to the bathrooms. It'd been a long time since I had been to Deb's, and in my current state I couldn't discern where the bathrooms were.

"Fuck."

I looked to what Adam was talking about, seeing the out of order sign on the ladies room. My stomach pitched and I braced a hand on the cool tile wall. I wanted to press my face against it, to let the tiles cool my inflamed skin.

"Here," Adam said, pulling me into the men's room. Before I could protest, he led me to the lone stall, past one urinal, and said, "I'll stand at the door, make sure no one can come in."

If I had been thinking clearly, I'd have given him a grateful smile at that. But my focus was on getting into the stall and facing the music.

I wasn't even sure if I had locked the door. The bathroom

floor was probably disgusting, but I sank to my knees anyway and stared at the toilet, waiting to vomit.

But strangely, the nausea went away. I stared at the surprisingly clean bowl and felt no desire to empty my stomach. It must have been a fleeting feeling, a side effect from the adrenaline wearing off.

"You okay?" Adam asked.

I swallowed and tested my voice. "I think so." I pressed my palms flat on either side of the stall walls to stand. One leg wobbled, but I attributed that to being hungry after barely eating any of the dinner we'd been served.

Remembering everything my dad had said, I did something out of character for me: I pressed my forehead to the stall's wall and flattened my hands against it. My eyes closed and I said, "I'm so sorry, Adam." It was a pathetic apology, not at all the kind of apology he was owed.

"Don't be," he said. I heard the squeaky approach of his steps across the linoleum and when I looked down, I saw the tips of his shoes almost touching mine under the bottom of the stall wall.

"If I'd known that was going to happen—that way—I'd never have taken you along."

"I don't expect you to be a mind reader, Hollis."

"But still. What he said to you was inexcusable." I winced thinking of how he'd referred to Adam like he was somehow less of a person merely due to his paternity. "I really am sorry."

"Would you stop saying that?" I felt a slight give of the stall wall, and realized he was pressing on it from the other side. "Stop saying sorry. You didn't do this. And besides, you're no more responsible for your father's behavior than I am for mine."

I closed my eyes again and released a shuddering breath. "I said a bad word."

"You did. Two, actually."

I pulled away from the wall and buried my face in my hands.

"It was pretty fucking great." He chuckled lightly from the other side of the door. "A damn sight."

"I never say those words, not to my parents."

"They had it coming." He paused before asking, "Are you going to come out, or are we going to hash this out in the men's restroom of a pizza place?"

I exited the stall and looked up at him sheepishly. "I'm embarrassed, Adam. Really. I didn't expect…" My voice trailed off and I winced, realizing my face must be a mess. "I probably look terrible right now."

"Hollis," he said in a hushed voice. He framed my face in my hands. "All of that at your parents' was bullshit anyway. Your family photos, all posed and perfect, are bullshit. Seriously, fuck them. Fuck that whole museum they call a home." He tucked a stray hair behind my ear. "I like you like this. You don't have to be embarrassed or apologize for not being perfect, Hollis."

I swallowed, hoping the movement would uncurl some of the tension that lived deep in my gut.

His thumbs brushed along my cheekbone, rendering me speechless. "Let's grab a couple pizzas and go back to my house for a little while. Okay?"

I could only nod.

26

ADAM

When we pulled up in front of the house, most of it was dark. Dread ripped through me, acute and aching.

I threw the car in park and barely said two words to Hollis before I was out of the car and sprinting toward the entrance.

"Casey?" I called out when I entered the house. I looked around, searching for any sign of her or my dad, but saw none until I went to Casey's room.

She was curled up in bed, facing the wall, her knees pulled all the way to her chest. I wasn't sure if she was awake until she said, "I'm fine, Adam." But she didn't sound fine. She sounded miserable.

I sat on the edge of her bed to get a better look at her. Her eyes were clear—thank God—but her face was blank. She wouldn't even turn her head to look at me. I wanted to kill him. A rage I was all too familiar with lit through me. "Where is he?"

"He said he was going to get dinner, but didn't come back."

"How long have you been here alone?"

"About an hour. Not long." She rolled onto her back, staring up at the ceiling. "He was in Gram's bedroom for a while before he left." Her head rolled to the side, and she finally made eye contact with me. "He probably stole her pills."

I wanted to call him a dozen very creative swear words. I wanted to find him and force him to sign off on custody papers. I wanted to tell him what I really thought of him, the kind of person and father he was. But I couldn't do any of those things. No matter how I felt about my father, I had to be sensitive to Casey's feelings about him.

She blew out a breath. "I should've gone with Mrs. C. You were right. I just thought he was here for my birthday." She rubbed her lips together, blinking back a sheen of moisture on her eyes. "He sucks."

"He does. I know he loves you, though." It physically hurt me to say the words, because while I knew he loved her in the way he could, I couldn't understand how his love for anything else could surpass the love for his own daughter. It was a hard thing to understand, from the side of someone related to an addict. I supposed unless I was in his shoes, I would never get it. But I wouldn't support him, not anymore. Not after seeing how resigned and unsurprised Casey was. When he'd bailed on her years prior, she'd always been surprised by it, as if he had ever proven himself to be anyone other than a fucking flake. But the fact that she didn't seem shocked, that she seemed almost indifferent, told me exactly what I'd do the next time he came to town to bond with her. "I'm sorry he left you alone."

She lifted a shoulder, looking so weary that I wanted to shake my dad until he physically hurt in the ways his daughter hurt deep down.

"I'm a teenager. I'm not little anymore, Adam."

"You're still my little sister. Always will be." I vowed then and there, to never abandon her the way my dad always did.

"Little?" She scrunched up her nose. "I might be taller than you one day."

"Keep dreaming, shortcake."

"Dad probably just wanted you to leave so he could get Gram's meds."

"Maybe," I agreed, though I wanted to tell her an emphatic yes. I should've locked the meds up, I supposed, though I doubted that would have prevented him. If anything, it might have meant him being a bigger dick to Casey when he couldn't find them.

I just wanted to make this better for Casey, to make up for my dad, but I knew that I couldn't. "Are you hungry?" I asked. "I brought pizza."

"No. I made some canned soup a little while after he left. I had a feeling he wasn't coming back." She pulled her comforter up higher and rolled back to her side, facing the wall. "I just want to go to bed, if that's okay."

"Of course that's okay." I brushed a hand over the back of her head. "Let me know if you need anything, okay?"

She merely nodded.

In the living room, Hollis was setting up the two pizza boxes on the coffee table and had already grabbed plates and beer from the kitchen. "There was beer in the fridge. I hope that's okay."

I looked at the beer a moment, well aware of my dad's inability to control his addictions. "I could use a couple," I said.

She handed me one after popping the cap. "I take it your dad is gone?"

I nodded and she rubbed her lips together. "Pepperoni or cheese?"

I pointed the beer at the pepperoni pizza and eased onto the couch. What a fucking night it had been. I knew Hollis must be thinking the same, but appreciated that she hadn't pressed me for details about my dad.

"Mind if I sit next to you?" She motioned with her plate at the empty spot on the couch.

I gave her a half smile. "If you don't, I'll just have to put you here myself."

She settled beside me on the couch and put her feet up on the coffee table as I was doing. "I almost never do this," she said, wiggling a little like she was delighted.

"Do what exactly? Seems like it's been a night of firsts."

"Okay, that's true. But I mean this." She held up her plate. "I hardly ever eat on a couch. I'm used to eating at a table."

That was what had delighted her? I couldn't help but laugh. "Sometimes, you seem so...alien to me. You don't eat at a couch? I eat at least a couple of my meals here every day."

"You set the table that night I ate here."

"Yeah, well, that was for you."

Her cheeks pinked adorably and she stared intently at her plate, boring a hole through it. "Why..." she started, but didn't continue.

"What? What were you going to ask?"

Her tongue darted out, moistening her lips. "Why do things feel different?"

I pondered that for a moment. "I think we're starting to get more comfortable with each other."

She nodded and picked at a piece of pepperoni. "I guess that's probably true. I do feel more comfortable around you in some ways. Less in others."

"Which others?"

She chewed on her lip thoughtfully. "Mostly when we've been close enough to kiss. I feel awkward, like I don't know what I'm doing."

That sent off bells in my brain. "Are you a virgin?"

Her eyes widened and I worried for a minute that she would drop her pizza.

"I mean..." I continued, feeling like I was backpedalling on a stationary bike. "You don't have to answer that. Sorry for asking."

"No, I'm not a virgin." She popped the piece of pepperoni in her mouth and chewed for a minute. "But I wouldn't say I'm whatever the female equivalent of a lothario is. I don't have a lot of experience. So, I'm sorry if I seem awkward or whatever."

"Stop apologizing, Hollis." I waited until she looked me in the eyes. "I just don't want you ever to feel like I'm taking advantage of you."

"You don't," she replied quickly. "I like kissing you." Her voice had gone softer. "I just don't know how to take you sometimes. You're so hot and cold. One minute you're kissing me and the next time I see you, you look like you want to see me struck by lightning. It's quite the conundrum."

Shit. Did it really feel that way for her? I could admit to being hot and cold, but had I really made her feel like I wanted to see her hurt? "I know. I can be pretty moody." I thought of all of Sarah's recent texts, her accusing me of avoiding her. "I guess there's just a lot happening right now, with my gram and Casey and the new job and now my deadbeat dad briefly making an appearance. And us, of course."

"Us," she repeated.

"Yeah. Us." It was becoming clearer and clearer to me that *us* wasn't just some show pony we needed to parade around her parents to benefit her. We were something more, something real. The feelings she brought up in me were definitely real, and the song she'd inspired was more real than I had known in a while.

She shifted her position on the couch and looked contemplative. "Can I ask you something?"

"Go for it."

"If things were different—say, if we hadn't entered into this with the purpose of deceiving people. If all the stuff from high school hadn't happened. Would you take a second look at me?"

I pulled my head back. "What do you even mean?" Would I take a second look? No, I'd take a third. And a fourth. And a fifth. And as many as it took until I got her out of my fucking system. But then again, I didn't really believe any number could accomplish that.

"I mean, you know, I'm not the girl you take a second look at."

"No, actually. I don't know that. Who the fuck says you're not a girl someone would take a second look at?"

She gestured a hand down herself. "I know I'm not ugly. I am perfectly pleasant looking. But I am unremarkable."

When I opened my mouth to protest, she shook her head and put her fingers to my lips, shushing me.

"You don't have to say anything, Adam. It's okay."

It was fucking *not* okay. I grasped her wrist and pulled her fingers from my lips. I probably looked at her like she had lost her marbles. "You are beautiful, Hollis."

I could tell she didn't believe it, didn't lap it up like someone thirsty for validation might.

I set my pizza and beer down and turned my body toward her. I paused long enough to watch her squirm. It was my favorite thing, watching the effect I had on her, and feeling it on her skin when I touched her. "You are beautiful," I repeated, the words heavy in my throat, like I was carrying something I couldn't articulate. "Your skin is creamy and golden, and your lips are the kind people write love songs about." I swallowed away the nerves I felt for being as honest as I was. "Your hair, well," I wrapped my hand in her hair, tugging just a little so that I made sure I had her attention. "It's like a shampoo commercial. It's lush, long, completely *remarkable*." Still holding her arm, I brought it to my mouth and did something out of character even for me: I kissed the delicate skin where palm met wrist. She was warm and her pulse fluttered beneath my lips. "And your eyes, when I do something like this…" I kissed her wrist again, and dragged a finger over the back of her hand, "Are so fucking expressive." I leaned closer, close enough that our breath mingled. "And the only thing stopping me from kissing you right now is knowing I won't get to see into your eyes when I do."

She took a deep, shuddering breath. "Oh."

I loved the curve of her lips when she said that. "Yeah." I scooped up the pizza and beer. "Oh."

"That's the nicest thing any guy has said to me."

Was I going to have to set my pizza and beer down again? Once again, I looked at her like she was out of her mind. "Come on, Hollis. You meet guys all the time. Or, at least your dad brings them to you."

"Right. But they're not really interested in me. They feign interest long enough to get on my dad's good side, to get an internship or a highly coveted position in his main office."

"And do they?" I asked. "Get an internship or a job after fake wooing you?"

She dabbed her mouth with a napkin. "Sometimes, yes. I would never accuse him of it, but sometimes I think he hires these guys thinking I'll be impressed."

"But you're not."

"Power doesn't impress me." She shook her head, staring at her pizza. "My dad has power and I see what it does—it makes people fearful. I haven't really had time to seek these guys out, to even hear them out, if I'm being honest. I'm very focused on school."

"That's why you're such a smarty pants." When she winced, I frowned. "What's that face for."

She picked at the side of her crust. "Everyone assumes that because I get great grades and because I was in honors classes in high school that it's because I'm smart. And maybe I am, but not in the way everyone assumes. Good grades don't necessarily mean there's some kind of innate intelligence. At least, it doesn't for me. My good grades are from my natural inclination to stay organized and prepared and my own drive to be my best." Her head whipped up, eyes searing into mine. "I know, that sounds stupid."

"No, it doesn't." I took a large bite of my pizza so I had the time to mull over what she'd said as I chewed. After swallowing, I said, "So you believe intelligence isn't natural for you, but your drive to push yourself is what makes you such an all star on paper."

She nodded solemnly. "Exactly. It's a lot of pressure when people expect that you just know the answer because it lives somewhere in your head. I know, this is a first-world problem. But I can't tell you how many people say, 'Hollis knows,' or 'Hollis can do it, she's smart.' I don't think I'm *not* smart, mind you, but it's not like calculus comes easily or that I have some kind of photographic memory where the answers to every test problem are scorched into my brain. I work really hard. Maybe harder than I ever need to."

I chewed again and after swallowing, I nodded. "And you claimed there was nothing remarkable about you." I tipped my beer at her. "That, Hollis, is remarkable."

"What? That I try?"

I ignored her sarcastic reply. "That you have the drive to keep working, even when it isn't easy. You know how many people I know who give up at their first attemp? In Colorado, I saw so many guys who gave up when they went weeks without booking a gig. Guys who came on the scene thinking it was easy, a walk in the park. Guys who later left and instead of taking ownership for realizing it wasn't their true passion, they blamed the industry or some other external factor other than the fact that they didn't want it bad enough. If you want something bad enough, if you work hard enough for it, I can't call that anything but passion. And passion, that's what is remarkable."

I took a long pull of my beer, realizing I was on a slippery slope with Hollis. I admired the hell out of her. She was beautiful and she was strong, and she spoke freely when it was just the two of us. She didn't play coy, she didn't tease or test me. She wasn't starved for anyone, and she had goals that didn't fit into any kind of neat box. It'd been a long fucking day, a day of discovery, of disappointments. But Hollis hadn't been one.

"What about you?" she asked. "Everyone has expectations about you, too."

"What, like band geek?"

She frowned a little. "No. I've never thought that about you."

"Okay, I'll play. What *did* you think of me?"

"In high school, I guess I kind of thought of you as a poet, maybe. Like you were a little bit of an old, tortured soul."

My throat went dry. It was a little too on the mark and I didn't have enough alcohol for this conversation. But she continued on.

"I never saw you as a geek. I guess I saw you more like a bad boy." She laughed and covered her face. "That sounds so stupid. But I mean, like in an uncontrolled, *I'm not afraid of you* kind of way."

"I was a little bit of a shit in high school, to be fair. I didn't try to pick fights, but I did insist on ending them."

"Exactly. You weren't afraid of those assholes in high school."

I held up three fingers. "Wow. Swear word number three. In one night. What a rare pleasure."

She laughed again. "I know. I'm so out of control." She chewed another bite and after blotting her mouth with the napkin, she continued. "And then you went off to Colorado, joined a band and got all these tattoos." Her gaze traced my arms, all the way up to my face. "I guess that sort of solidified my *Adam Oliver is a bad boy* image."

I couldn't help it, I laughed. "I think you're the first person to accuse me of being a bad boy."

"I don't mean it in a bad way. And not even in a, *I want him to throw me on the back of his motorcycle and ride out of town* kind of way."

"That's good," I said. "Because I don't have a motorcycle." But I would, I knew. I had barely left her parents' house with any rubber still on the tires. If she'd asked me, I'd have thrown her on the back of my imaginary bike and ridden off to wherever she wanted. That realization was a weight in my gut, but it wasn't all too unwelcome. Strangely, it was if Hollis had only anchored me to her.

"You asked." She shrugged and finished her slice of pizza.

"I did. And I'm glad to hear what you thought of me." I set my discarded plate on top of hers and settled back onto the couch. "I'm not a bad boy," I said, a smirk playing the side of my mouth.

"I know."

"And now I know that you've listened to my music."

She squirmed a little on the couch. "Yes. I have."

"I never would've guessed."

She let out a sigh. "I told you I had a crush on you. How else should I prove it?"

"I don't think you need to anymore. I believe you." And even if it didn't make sense, I knew that as expressive as she was, she still held some things buried beneath the surface. I couldn't deny I wasn't nurturing my own little crush on her. When I caught her eyeing my beer, I held it out. "Want a sip?"

Her cheeks were that pretty pink. I loved that she didn't duck her head to hide it, that she didn't lie about her own attraction to me. She was realer than I gave her credit for; she was only boxed in by circumstance. "Sure," she said. She dabbed her mouth with her napkin again and gave me a soft little smile as her hand reached for my beer.

I had the urge to kiss her, stronger than I had felt before. But she was still shy, and maybe felt a little run over from what had happened earlier. When her hand clasped the bottle, I did the next best thing, I grazed my finger over the back of her hand.

"I love it when you do that," I said just as she took the first sip.

She immediately pulled the beer back, putting her hand over her mouth as she swallowed. "What?" She reached the beer toward me.

"When I do this," I said, taking the bottle from her with one hand and capturing hers with my other. Our hands came to a rest between us, my thumb playing over her knuckles. "That," I said, and my voice sounded hoarse to my own ears. "There." Her lips shuddered open a hair, her eyes went soft and heavy-lidded. Like she'd been put under some kind of spell—which was exactly the way she made me feel when I spent any length of time with her. "You're so fucking expressive." Why did my voice sound so raw, like the words were tangled together as they left my throat? My attraction to Hollis wasn't just a physical reaction, it was deep, something so intrinsic to my DNA that I couldn't decipher it for myself.

I couldn't wait any longer. I leaned in and claimed her mouth with mine.

27

HOLLIS

HE WAS DOING THAT THING AGAIN, THAT THING THAT LEFT ME dumb and slow to speak. His hand slid through my hair and his fingers pressed into my scalp. It was as if he sparked something in me, something that lay dormant. As if he was unlocking a secret door by pressing in just the right places. Because, before I knew what came over me—before I could analyze it too deeply —I had slid from my spot on the couch to straddle his lap, the sides of my dress blanketing us as I balanced on my knees.

He made a noise in his throat that echoed into mine, a sound that spoke of hunger, of desire. It did something to me, that sound, sent my hands running up the back of his head and into his hair. I wanted to press the same buttons in him that he pressed for me, to ignite him in a way that he did for me.

He pulled away and tipped me back a hair, and I almost stopped him—so greedy I was for the connection I had only ever felt with him. But his mouth was on a journey, and its destination—after a long scenic route along my jaw and down the side of my neck—was the hollow of my collarbones, from one shoulder to the other. He nipped, he caressed, and he even licked the edge of my collarbone. I wasn't usually so controlled by lust. In fact, I had eschewed lust for so long, knowing it'd be hard to control.

I was wrong.

It was impossible to control.

"I love this necklace." His whisper fluttered across my skin, blowing air across the areas his mouth had sampled. "The rose."

"They're my favorite," I said, without thought. I couldn't think. Words spilled out of me like they'd been pushed to the top by others, like I was merely a container filling up too fast to contain.

"Mine too." An echo of a memory whispered through my head, but I couldn't pay attention to it, not when his hands were sliding up my waist to my back. His fingers curled in at where the zipper met my spine, so that his fingers replaced the fabric along my skin. "You make me think of clichés," he said.

"Like what?" His hand swept my hair over my shoulder and his mouth moved back up the way it had come, leaving a trail of kisses along my sensitive skin in his wake.

With his fingers still looped around the back of the dress, he pressed me forward, closer and closer, until our lips touched— but we weren't kissing. "Like how *you* look like some kind of wild rose right now, with your red dress and your pretty pink skin, and the shadows of your hair." He nipped my bottom lip. "I told you I wasn't the bad boy you'd envisioned me as." His tongue darted out, teasing the seam of my lips. "But you make me want to do bad things."

I nearly lost my balance then, almost fell right onto his lap. "Oh."

He laughed, and his head fell back onto the couch. "Shit, Hollis." His hands left my dress to drag down his face. "You and your 'oh' get me every time."

My body was rapidly cooling from the heat that he'd caused my skin. "You stopped."

He tipped his head back. "I had to. I'd have embarrassed myself right here if I didn't."

But I didn't mind, and something in my face must have told him so.

"Trust me," he said, pressing his forehead to mine and his hands on either side of my face so I couldn't move away. "I *want* to. Badly. But Casey is just down the hall. And…"

"Oh."

"Yeah. Oh." He laughed again, the motion echoing in his thighs that I was straddled around. "So. Not today."

It wasn't a no. It wasn't a never. I'd just have to remember that. I climbed off his lap and stood, desperately needing to fan my face. I was warm all over, especially between my legs, and the fact that I couldn't immediately soothe it was a unique kind of torture I had yet to experience.

"Are you okay?"

"I think so…" I pressed a hand to my face, hoping to accelerate my cooling. "I'm just warm."

"Yeah. Me too." He dropped a pillow on his lap and looked up at me sheepishly. "I just wanted to make sure I didn't rush you. Or hurt you."

"Hurt me?" I laughed, but it sounded choked. "I'm not a piece of tissue paper. I'm not fragile."

"No," he said, agreeing. "You're a rose. Hardy."

I couldn't stand hearing him compare me to a rose. It did something to me, made me want to leap with joy and cry simultaneously. Because I knew something was different, that my attraction to him was not one-sided, that something else was blooming between us. Even though I hadn't had enough experience to see where this could go, I knew enough to be afraid.

"Hollis."

"Hmm?" I turned, looking at him.

"You look sad."

I shook my head. "I'm not. It's just…" I waved a hand vaguely in front of me. I didn't really have the words to articulate the mess of emotions I was feeling.

"I know what you mean."

"You do?"

"I do."

I took a deep breath in. "Did something just change between us?"

He waited a long beat before reeling. "Not something. Everything."

28

HOLLIS

"What do I even pack?" I asked nobody as I faced my still-empty duffel bag. If Tori was here, she'd rifle through my closet before concluding it was as hopeless as my dating life.

Well, she might not say it in those words, but it would be implied nonetheless.

"Hey!" Navy knocked on my open door and moseyed in before plopping onto my bed. "Not packed yet?"

"No." I stared glumly at the duffel bag I had taken to Bolivia. There were buttons on one end of it, from all the airports I'd stopped in on my way there and back. The handles were worn from the times it'd fallen off the back of a truck and had been dragged for several feet. It was so completely opposite from the rest of my luggage, but it was my favorite.

Navy fingered one button in particular—the Peruvian flag button I had picked up. "It's going to be really casual, if that helps? Jeans. Sweaters. It gets cold at night."

That made me feel better. This wouldn't be a repeat of the

267

party where I had been doused in beer while wearing a flimsy tank. Sweaters and jeans I could do. I opened my closet and grabbed two pairs of jeans—one dark, one light.

"Hiking boots, if you've got 'em. And it's probably a good idea to dress in layers. If we go hiking, you'll want to take your sweater off."

I studied my closet, taking in the basic tees and dress slacks. My wardrobe was boring but functional. It didn't require much thought to put things together. I didn't have a ton of free time as it was, spending what little I did thinking about what to wear or how to clothe my body didn't serve me.

"What are you worried about?" Navy asked, reading my mind.

"I don't know what to pack." It was such a waste of time, to even worry about this. I'd rescheduled my tutoring clients for the weekend, though there were few since school had just begun. But spending the few minutes I had free studying the LSAT book my dad had sent, angered me.

"It's just Adam and Keane. And some other guys."

I envied Navy's ability to be blasé about this. *Just* Adam wasn't something I could say, or believe.

The difference between this time and the last time I'd dressed with Adam in mind was significant. Before, I wasn't sure if he even knew who I was. Now, not only did he know—or at least had some semblance of an idea of who I was—but he was my boyfriend. The basis of our relationship may be fake, but it didn't feel fake anymore. And I felt compelled to dress somewhat nice, like a real girlfriend might. I tried not to think about the last time we'd been together, and how much I still tingled in all the places he'd touched. On occasion, I'd catch my hand drifting to my neck, to run my fingers along my collarbone. And then I'd snap right out of it.

"You don't need to sweat this, babe." Navy placed her hands

on my shoulders. "It's a casual weekend. I've packed tees, jeans, and sweaters. That's about it."

I took her in, the outfit she'd picked to wear to the cabin. Cut-off shorts, a black tee that said Hello Sunshine across the front in loud letters, and a long gray cardigan.

"Aren't you going to be cold?" I asked her, eyeing the shorts.

"I've got leggings to change into when we get there. It's just too hot to wear them now. What you're wearing right now looks good."

I looked down. Black jeans with a white v-neck that fit snug. I wore my little gold rose necklace, but otherwise I wore no other jewelry or accessories.

"Grab that cozy-looking thing," she said, pointing to the closet. I slid the chunky knit maroon cardigan over my shoulders and pulled my hair out from under it. "Perfect." She beamed. "Get your chucks and pack some boots and you'll be all set." She grabbed fuzzy socks from the top drawer of my dresser and tossed them in. When a sleep tank fell out of the drawer, realization hit me.

"What are the sleeping arrangements?"

"Oh." Navy wrung her hands for a moment, considering. "You and Adam will probably want to bunk together."

"Uh…"

"Any normal boyfriend and girlfriend would room together," Navy gently reminded me, scooping the tank up and holding it out. "You don't have to have sex, Hollis."

I wasn't entirely sure I didn't want to have sex. But I knew, for certain, that I didn't want anyone else talking about us having sex. "The implication is there, if we share a bedroom."

"The implication will be there, since you've been dating for as long as you have."

She was right. I rubbed a hand over my temple. "I'm not bringing sexy lingerie." Not like I had any, but if I had—they were most certainly not invited. Maybe my sexy pajamas could come, though.

"Then don't. I'll probably room with Keane. He's warm."

It was sometimes hard for me to believe there were no romantic feelings between Navy and Keane. Maybe that was just because I couldn't even reasonably talk about sharing a room with my supposed boyfriend—much less a friend. But Navy was a cuddler by nature. So what was perfectly normal for her was foreign to me. "You don't have your eyes on any of his coworkers?"

Navy shook her head and grabbed my trusty pajamas, the ones with the faded school logo, and tossed them into the bag. "I'll let you grab your underwear," she said with a smile and took the shirts I'd pulled from the closet and began folding them. "And, no. I'm just not interested." She shrugged and took my hiking boots and placed them in the handy shoe compartment section of the duffel bag. "I just like to cuddle, you know that. And Keane really is the best cuddler. No offense."

I held up my hands. "None taken. I'm not much for cuddling myself."

"Maybe Adam can break you from that." She waggled an eyebrow but when I didn't return her smile she frowned. "Are you okay with this? It's a lot of pressure. We don't have to go if you don't want to."

"I do want to go." I pushed my hair away from my face. "We've already put on the performance for my parents, but I'm not sure they bought it." But did it really matter if they had? My phone had remained silent since shit had hit the fan, which was unusual for all of us. Maybe they thought they were calling my bluff with Adam. I didn't exactly want to prove them wrong, but I also wasn't ashamed to spend time with him—like he was someone to be embarrassed about. I shook my head, re-folding my jeans and placing them into the bag. "But lying like this makes me feel icky. I've never told a lie this big. And for such a dishonorable reason."

"Oh, come here." Navy tugged me to the bed, so I sat beside her. She took my hand in hers and squeezed it reassuringly. "On the surface, it might *look* dishonorable. Because it's about money. But that money is more than just padding for your bank account. It's freedom. It's choice. It's going to be used in honorable ways. You're going to help people with it."

But no amount of encouragement made up for the lie that was growing bigger and bigger. If I could go back, way back to when I first lied to my parents, I would. I'd change my story. I'd be brave and tell them I simply wasn't interested in any of the guys they'd found suitable. But it was too late for all of that. "I just don't know how I'm ever going to be able to act like a girlfriend around Adam." My feelings felt bigger, louder than that. I couldn't look at him the same as I had even a week earlier. So much had happened between us. Our relationship had meant to appear much further along than we normally would've been. But the problem was that my feelings seemed to eclipse what they were even supposed to be. He was so much better than I'd ever even imagined him to be, and it made me a little sick to think about it.

"You're so worried about acting that you should take the acting out of the equation. How would you treat Adam if he was your *real* boyfriend?"

I couldn't answer that definitively. I didn't know what that was like. "I guess I'd hold his hand."

"Yes, and?" She said with a nod.

"I'd kiss him from time to time."

"Probably a lot of the time."

I closed my eyes and slapped a hand over my face. Groaning, I said, "I don't know why I thought I could do this. I most certainly cannot do this." I was chickening out, when my body was telling me to shut up. This right here was why I never had any boyfriends. I couldn't deal with the indecision, the way my body and my mind fought against one another.

"Why? Don't you find him attractive?"

"Yes. And that's exactly the problem."

"I fail to see how that's a problem. You wouldn't ordinarily date someone you weren't attracted to, would you?"

"Ugh. I guess you're right."

"So you've already hurdled over the hardest part: attraction. What you have to do now is accelerate the feelings you have and the way to manifest that kind of intimacy is by treating him like you would any other boyfriend. Who knows, maybe you won't just be fake dating before long. Maybe it'll be real."

She didn't know how true that was, at least for me. "We've never talked about what happened in high school," I reminded her. "He holds my hand and it feels different—real, maybe—but it's sometimes hard to believe he doesn't harbor some contempt for me after what happened."

"I'm just saying, treat him like you would if he was your boyfriend for real. Jump over that sexual tension and bone him."

Just the very thought made my entire body flush with warmth, remembering the kisses we'd already shared that I hadn't told anyone about. Strangely, I felt protective of them. Like telling Navy or even Tori would diminish their impact somehow. "No. Way."

"If you don't think Keane isn't convincing Adam of the very same thing I'm talking you into, you're dead wrong." She squeezed my hands. "Adam doesn't hate you, not anymore at least. He just needs to get to know you."

"That's what I'm afraid of." We had the same chemistry we did in high school. And it had all been ruined when I had let jealously snake through me at the sight of him talking to a girl when he was supposed to find my friends. I guessed if I was afraid of anything with Adam, it was getting to know him only to be let down by him.

"I hate to tell you this, but you gotta suck it up, Hollis. You've struck an agreement. You both have to make this relationship believable. That means people this weekend will have to see you guys acting all couple-y." She ran a hand over my hair. "You can do this. Be brave, Hols. I know you've got it in you."

When we stopped at Adam's Gram's house to pick him and Keane up, I was instantly transported back to high school. The scene was a mirror of high school, if you swapped Tori for Navy. But as if she sensed my discomfort, Navy stayed in the front passenger seat instead of getting out and inviting Adam to sit beside me. I blew out a breath, grateful to be eased in.

Adam looked good. His trademark black clothes were switched up a little with the white and black checkered plaid flannel he wore over his black shirt. His jeans had tears in the knees and his black hiking boots looked broken in, unlike mine. He ran a hand through his hair as he approached the car with his backpack slung over his shoulder. He looked carefree in posture, but as he got closer I could see the apprehension in his eyes. He was nervous, too. Which settled me for some reason. At least I wasn't alone in my nerves.

"Cool to sit in the backseat?" Navy called to them as I hit the unlock button. In answer, Keane opened the door and slid in, with Adam right after him. Which left Adam diagonal to me in the back seat. I could look over my shoulder at him. And as I adjusted the rearview mirror, I could see him clearly. He met my gaze and gave me a smile. A real, genuine one. So I smiled back. And warmth settled those nerves.

"Do you have the address?" Navy asked, my navigator for the trip.

Keane read it out to her and leaned in, looking over her phone as the various suggested routes popped in "Don't go this route. It goes over the Teton pass and your boy is afraid of heights." He patted his stomach. "Don't need to begin this weekend with some vom-vom, do we?"

"I have plastic bags back there," I said and pointed to the well-stocked seat organizer hanging behind Navy's seat. "If you get sick, I mean."

"Hollis, were you a girl scout?" Keane asked. At the shake of my head, he patted my shoulder. "Well, you'd have made a great one. Always prepared."

Normally, I'd feel a sting at a comment like that because it was usually mocking. But Keane was just a good guy, through and through. He was the kind of guy you brought home to your parents, the guy you brought to keggers, the guy you brought as a plus-one to a wedding. He had a way of making you feel comfortable, of taking the pressure off. Which was probably why he and Navy were so close.

"We should stop here for dinner," Navy said, showing the GPS route to Keane as I pulled onto the road. "I hear there's a really good barbecue place there."

"You're speaking to my stomach."

"Like the Teton pass speaks to your stomach?" she said on a laugh.

"Not at all the same way," Keane said and tugged gently on her earlobe.

"Sit back and buckle up," Navy reminded him, playfully shoving him back to his seat. She turned to Adam, nodded when she saw his belt securely fastened. "How's the new album going?"

I looked at Adam in the rearview as I drove the route the GPS indicated. "It's done. But it's on hold for the minute."

I felt bad for not asking more about his music, but when I caught Navy's eye, I knew she was asking for my benefit as much as her curiosity. "Do you think you'll be able to go back to Denver when things settle down?"

Adam looked out the window and I focused on the road as I awaited his answer.

"Probably not. I think they'll need to move on without me. I've gotta stay here, help my gram. And Casey has a few years before she graduates."

There was silence for a moment. There was no mistaking the longing in his voice. Giving up the band was no doubt going to be disappointing for Adam. It was akin to me giving up my own dreams for the time being, but on a nuclear level. I could always travel. But I knew it'd taken a while for Adam to find his bandmates, and that putting out an album must have cost more time and money than I could imagine.

"You could tutor," Navy said. I felt her look at me. "Like Hollis does. That way, you can keep making music. My aunt has that music shop on Capitol Ave. They're always looking for new tutors."

"I could," Adam said, but there wasn't conviction behind his words. "I don't think I'm cut out for teaching. I don't have the patience. Hollis does, in spades."

Was that a compliment? I glanced at him in the rearview and he was looking squarely at me. "Thanks," I murmured.

"You'd need to have the patience to put up with Adam," Keane said, elbowing him in the backseat. "But Navy's right. I'm sure it's something you could try to do, at the very least."

"Maybe," Adam said, but then he changed the subject. "How was the first week of classes?"

Navy turned in her seat. "Fine. I've got homework I'll have to disappear to do, but my teachers seem pretty great so far."

"Hollis?" Adam asked, and I got the feeling when he'd first posed the question, he'd intended it for me.

"It's good." I had completed my homework before this weekend, even though that had meant staying up until midnight the night before, after Adam had brought me home, in order to do so. There was no way I'd be able to relax at all this weekend if I had to worry about incomplete assignments. "But I have a feeling next month my schedule will be slammed."

"Tutoring schedule?"

I nodded. "There are a lot of people in my Psychological Anthropology class that seem ill-prepared."

"Just don't let them take advantage of you this year," Navy chided me. She gentled her response with a squeeze on my arm. "If they want you to help, they should pay you for it."

"I know," I said, at the same time that Adam said, "What do you mean?"

Before I could answer, Navy spoke up. "Last year, people would act friendly with Hollis. You know, like invite her to parties or whatever. But it was all a ruse."

"Well, I don't know that for sure."

"But I do," she said, facing me, an eyebrow raised. She turned back to the guys. "But really, they just wanted to be chummy with her so they could ask for help. Free help."

"And did you? Help them?" Adam asked.

I nodded. "I can admit, that sometimes it bit me in the butt. But it's hard to say no when someone who calls you their friend asks for help."

"No, it's not." Adam leaned over, so that he was inches from me. "It's one syllable. Two letters. Try it out."

It felt silly to shake my head, so I said it. "No."

"Good job. Now that you know how to say that word, use it more often."

"It's easier said than done."

"So then don't just say 'no'. Follow through with that no. If someone wants your help for free, let them know your tutoring hours are pretty full but they can try to get on your schedule," Navy piped in. "It's not unkind to ask to be compensated for work. It's unkind to ask for it for free, especially when you don't have a real relationship with them."

The *real relationship* bit of her sentence sunk in and, judging by Adam's reflection in the mirror, it had for him too. "I'll try," I said, noncommittally.

"Don't just try, do it. It's not shameful to say no, Hollis." Adam stared intently at me. "The sooner you start saying no, the easier it will be."

I gave a curt nod. "Okay."

29

ADAM

By the time we made it the cabin, it was dark. The cabin was situated on a lake, not dissimilar to Amber Lake, but it was infinitely quieter up in the mountains. We were backed up to the Tetons, and the lake spread out before us wasn't crowded like the lake back home was in the summertime.

Keane's parents owned this little cabin and during the summer months they rented it out to the flocks of tourists who wanted a bit of wilderness. But in September, tourism had started to die off as this part of the state saw cold weather sooner than other parts.

The hazy light by the front door of the cabin greeted us but rooms were also lit up inside. Keane's friends from work had arrived already, and the plume of smoke from the back yard wafted over to us.

"S'mores," Navy said and clapped her hands. "It's been so long since I had one!"

Hollis opened the back of the car but before she could grab her duffel, I had it in my hands. Keane grabbed the cooler he'd packed and Navy grabbed her bag as well, leaving Hollis bagless. She wrung her hands.

"It's fine," I told her, adjusting the bag to my other hand so I could put an arm around her. "This is what a boyfriend would do."

She gave me a small smile, but I could already sense her retreating into her shell. I squeezed her a little, leading her behind Navy and Keane into the house. "Do you like s'mores?" I asked, trying to tap into her a little. She'd kept quiet most of the ride and now that we were here, I could see her clamming up little by little. She didn't like crowds, I remembered that from high school.

"Yes. When we were kids, my sister Angie once used our gas stove to make a s'more. She caught a bag of bread on fire. My dad had to use the fire extinguisher to put everything out."

"How old were you?"

She furrowed her brow. "Maybe six or seven? Angie was fourteen. Needless to say, that was the first and the last time she cooked."

"Does she live in Amber Lake still?" I held the door open for her, ushering her in ahead of me.

"No." She shook her head. "She lives in a kind of commune, up in Alaska. With a few dozen other people."

"A commune?" I raised an eyebrow and set my bag on the empty bedroom we came across. Hollis didn't seem nervous about being in a bedroom with me yet, so I let her continue before she was hyper-aware and then, as a result, anxious.

"Yes. I guess they all have roles as gardeners, builders, and hunters."

"That sounds like the opening of a dystopian novel."

At that comment, her eyes lit up, which made them look larger, and more innocent than I was fully prepared for. "You read?"

I was struck by her question. "Yes…" What kind of question was that?

"I love to read." She placed her hands in her lap and looked up for a moment, the softest smile on her lips. "When I was in Bolivia, we mostly stayed in tents. I brought five books with me, and my e-reader. I'd charge it during the day and at night I'd just stay awake to read."

"Was it hot there?"

"Yes, it was a scorcher." She held her arms out to me, and shoved the sleeves of her heavy-weight sweater up her arms. "That's why I'm so tan."

She had a dozen little freckles lining her arms, and I didn't know why I found that so attractive. When she pulled her sleeves back down, color filled her cheeks. All I wanted to do was talk to her. We were at the cabin to spend time as a group, but after that last kiss, and the feelings we'd both discovered, I wanted to just sit with her, navigate those waters until we figured a way through.

I sat beside her on the bed, wanting to talk about last night.

She pulled out her phone. "Let's take a photo for social media."

I nodded, but didn't lean into her as I held the phone up to take the snap. When I pulled it back, I showed her and said, "What a great picture of two people who have zero romantic chemistry."

She frowned as she looked at the picture too. We looked friendly enough—but that was it. Friends. The inches that separated us were as distancing as a mile.

"Let's try again," she said, hitting the delete button.

"Okay. Well, this time, how about you act like you like me. That'll help."

She leaned into me, her head coming to rest on my shoulder. I tilted my head down so there was no white space between us and took the pic. "I do like you, you know. It's you who hated me, remember?" She said it so quietly, I wasn't sure if I had heard her at first.

What did I even reply to that? Especially after what we'd gone through just the day before. Maybe in high school, I hadn't really liked her. But it was hard to imagine that I ever hated her. "I don't think this is a good time to talk about that," I said diplomatically, like a coward.

"You're right. We've got a bunch of people to visit with. More photos to take and post." She stood and something about her words unsettled me.

"Okay," I said, but my answer had come slowly. I extended a hand to her. "You ready?"

"Yes."

By the time we joined the rest of the group, they were at least a couple drinks in, gathered around a metal fire ring in Adirondack chairs. The smell of burning marshmallows permeated the air and the sounds of laughter and the low beat of some music made everything feel cozy, despite being so out in the open.

"Hey," Keane said, standing.

"Hi guys," I said to his coworkers who were in a cluster of chairs surrounding the fire. I'd met them once, at orientation, but hadn't talked to them since. I scanned the rest of the group, taking in the severe lack of chairs. Only one remained.

As if he'd seen my thoughts, Keane patted the chair. "Here, buddy, one chair for you both."

"You can take it," I immediately said to Hollis. "I don't mind the ground."

To my surprise, her hand found mine and clasped it, unsteady at first until I squeezed her once. "We can share it," she said, as the flames danced in her eyes. She was silhouetted against the fire, her eyes bright and her lips red and her face flushed. She was beautiful in a way that distracted me.

"Okay," I said, and cleared my throat when I felt my voice go froggy. "Sure."

She led me by the hand to the chair. The only way we'd both fit into it was if she was on my lap. I gave her another look, to make sure she was sure, and she surprised me again when she placed a hand on my chest and gently pushed me to sit. "Like last night," she said at my ear and I smiled.

I remembered what Keane said when he'd helped me move things around at Gram's, about touching her and making this feel natural—so that it looked natural. But when Hollis took a careful seat sideways across my lap, this didn't feel natural. It felt intimate. It felt private. But most of all, it felt fucking right.

There was a war of emotions battling it out in my head. Things between us *were* different, everything was different. But where I was struggling was deciding what was real for Hollis or a show for everyone else.

I forced myself to play it cool and wrapped an arm around her back, securing her to my lap.

"Want a drink, Hollis? I've got those cans of Moscato?"

I felt, rather than saw, her nod at Navy.

"And a stick, please, Navy?" I leaned my head back so I could look at Hollis. "She wants a s'more."

"You got it," Navy replied. "What do you want to drink, Adam?"

"I already got it," Keane said from my left, tapping my elbow with an ice cold beer bottle.

"Thanks, man." I had a feeling I was going to need a few of those. I took a long pull and set it in the cup holder attached to the side of the Adirondack chair just as Navy returned with a can of wine and a metal stick with a marshmallow already shoved onto its pointy end.

Hollis twirled the stick in her hands. "Do you want one?"

I shook my head and Hollis stuck her stick over the fire, so far from the flames that Keane laughed.

"You think it's even going to get cooked that way?" he asked her.

Hollis nodded and I held her canned wine with one hand while she cracked it open with her lone free hand. "I don't like just shoving it in the fire. It burns up and the middle doesn't get ooey gooey."

"She's right," a guy from across the fire—the one I recognized as Todd—replied. "Low and slow is the way to go."

I saw the small smile that stretched Hollis's lips as she nodded at Todd. "Exactly. It'll get brown, but on its own time. A good s'more should be earned."

Keane shoved a marshmallow onto the end of his stick and attempted to hold it above the fire like Hollis did, but after less than a minute he gave up and stuck it right through the flames. "I like it burnt."

"But then it gets stuck in your teeth," Navy protested. "Gross."

"It's called a toothbrush, Navy." Keane laughed and popped the whole stick into his mouth, biting the end of the marshmallow off.

"If you'd just waited, that middle part would've been soft." Hollis rotated her stick and I found myself mesmerized by her long fingers, how they delicately turned the stick like she was operating heavy equipment, something that needed precision and patience to be operated. "Like this," she said with a little sigh as she pulled it back from the fire.

"Here," Navy said, handing me a graham cracker topped with chocolate. She handed another graham cracker square to Hollis and I held up my half to her as she carefully placed her marshmallow right on the center of the chocolate and brought the top down. As she slid it out, Keane groaned. "Wow, that looks sexy." The stick came out clean and she set it aside. The marshmallow oozed out of the sides, coating her fingers with it.

She laughed, seemingly delighted by the mess she'd made.

I didn't know if it was the sweet sound of her laugh or the way she looked, or a combination of both that caused me to take her hand in mine and bring her thumb to my mouth. The smear of marshmallow was almost as irresistible as her, but when I slowly brought it into my mouth, I saw the surprise in her eyes and the little O her lips made. I grazed my teeth across her finger, feeling parts of me wake up now that I had done such a sensual thing. When I finally released her thumb, the bubble she and I existed in popped.

"Get a room," Todd said from across the fire, earning a few chuckles from his friends. But I sensed some jealousy in his voice.

"We have one," I said, giving him a toothy grin.

It took him a minute to think of a reply. "Well, might as well go make use of it."

"Oh." I leveled him with my gaze, my arm tightening around Hollis. "That wasn't near enough foreplay for me, Todd. I feel sorry for your dates if that's enough for you."

Navy gasped.

Keane laughed and spilled his beer all over himself.

Keane's friends laughed and punched Todd in the shoulder.

And Hollis, most shockingly of all, leaned until she was resting her body weight on me.

HOLLIS

I DIDN'T KNOW IF IT WAS THE WINE OR THE COMPANY OR THE warmth of the fire, but I felt myself soften and relax. Even with the addition of the guys Keane had invited, the group still felt cozy. Maybe it was the fact that they were complete strangers. I didn't feel like I had to act for their benefit, so instead I could just *be*. "What's the plan for tomorrow?" Navy asked, snuggled up in a flannel blanket, her legs pulled to her chest on the chair. The air had cooled over the last hour we'd been outside, but being on Adam's lap, with his arm securely around me, kept me warm enough that I didn't take the blankets Keane had offered earlier.

"I was thinking of a hike. There's a well-worn path on the other side of the lake that zip zags up into the mountain." Keane looked across the fire at Todd. "Or we could take the straight up route, though that's a bit harder on the ol' lungs. The switchbacks are a bitch, but they're not gonna exert you as much."

"It's fine," Todd said with a wave. "I can do whatever everyone else wants to do."

"What do you mean? Are you injured?" Navy asked him.

"I had ankle surgery about a year ago, but I need a revision eventually. It's still a little rough on inclines."

"If you don't mind me asking, why did you have surgery?"

Todd rolled up the bottom of his sweats, revealing a long scar along the side of his leg. "Car accident in New Zealand last year. Broadsided."

"New Zealand?" I asked, my interest piqued. "What were you doing there?"

Todd turned to me. He was attractive, close buzzcut, well filled in beard. He gave me a smile that was warm, friendly, and made me feel—for the first time since joining them by the fire—slightly self-conscious. "I was there surfing for a competition. Nothing big leagues, mostly for fun." He set his foot back on the ground and leaned forward on his knees, the muscles of his shoulders and arms straining against his tee. "You've been?"

I shook my head. "But I'd love to go."

"Hollis went to Bolivia this summer," Navy offered and I felt a half dozen eyes turn to me. "She loves to travel."

"Bolivia?"

"I helped rebuild an orphanage," I said. "And studied. It's my major—cultural anthropology. I wanted to study the culture, too."

"That's fascinating," Todd said, and he seemed genuine. "Where to next?"

Adam's legs shifted under my butt and I put an arm around his back to steady myself. His arm around my waist tightened, gluing me solidly to him.

"I'm not sure," I said, and the reminder of my dad's expectations soured whatever warm and cozy feelings I had. "I might go to law school," I said, but my heart wasn't in the statement and I knew Navy was desperate to say something. I glanced at her, waiting until we held eye contact, so she wouldn't utter a word.

"Law school," Todd said, exhaling. "So I can call on you the next time I need to sue someone for an injury?" He laughed.

"Sure," I said, but again there was a distinct lack of enthusiasm in the one-word reply. I wanted to be hopeful about a future where I pursued what I wanted, but I couldn't be full of hope when that freedom came at a cost. I had three options: I needed to convince my parents that I was serious about Adam and hope that they amended the terms of the trust so I could still receive the benefit upon my graduation; I needed to suck it up and go to law school; or, I needed to tell the truth and figure life out on my own. Could I deal with my dad constantly reminding me of his disappointment in the person I'd become if I chose the first or third option? Could I live with disappointing myself if I chose the second option? The first two options meant I would be lying to someone: my parents or myself. And the third option sounded unbelievable. I had never been fully independent. I was the youngest child, the sheltered child, the child who shouldered her parents' expectations. Could I shake that part of me and grow up enough to take care of myself?

It was such a first world problem I had, which was why I didn't like to talk about it. *Boo hoo, your parents pay most of your bills including your college. What could you possibly have to complain about?* I had heard it enough from most of the people I ever tried to talk to. They didn't understand the crippling pressure, the expectations to be perfect, the lack of choices I really had.

But listening to my internal dialogue whine about my problems when I had witnessed, first-hand, problems that I would never have to experience—a lack of fresh water, for example—made me feel very small.

"I guess I'd need your number for that, though, right Hollis? That's your name, isn't it?"

Adam stiffened under me, so I turned to look at him. There

was a tick in his jaw, and his lips were in a flat line. Was he mad? He shifted again, this time rubbing a hand up my back. The touch was so comforting that it was easy to press into it, to relish it fully.

"I'm beat," Keane said, standing and stretching. "Ready for bed, Navy?"

His friends made noises across the fire at that and Keane shot them a look. "We're *friends*, dickheads." But Navy paid them no mind, standing and looping her arm in Keane's. She looked back at me and I nodded, knowing she was checking on me without saying a word.

"I'm tired too," I said, slipping off of Adam's lap and waving goodnight to Keane's friends. I turned to Adam and he caught my hand as I waved and tugged me closer. My heart fell and I nearly tripped over it as I leaned down. With his eyes locking with mine, Adam turned my hand over and pressed a kiss at the center of my palm. Tingles shot through me, starting at my wrist and ending low in my belly as I stared at him, more than a little stunned.

"I'll see you in a bit," Adam said, and his eyes held a promise I was equal parts excited and nervous for.

I pulled away from him and jogged to catch up with Navy and Keane. I slung my arm around her shoulders and she said, "I gotta pee. You?"

"Why do girls pee in groups?" Keane asked. "Are you afraid the toilet's gonna suck you in?"

"Maybe we believe in safety in numbers," Navy said, pushing Keane away. "Put on a movie—a good one—I'll be in in a minute." She led me down the hall, into the master bathroom.

"Whose room is this?" I asked as she closed the door. "You'd think that Keane would get the master."

"Three of his friends have to share this room. Not sure how they're all going to fit on that bed."

"Maybe one of them will be on the floor," I said, facing the mirror. What little makeup I had worn that day looked like it had already melted off my face. I rubbed the skin under my eyes, noting the dark circles I needed to do a better job covering up.

"You tired?" Navy asked as she peed in the water closet, the door slightly ajar.

"A little," I admitted. "It's been a long week."

"You're the only person I know who goes so hard to study the first week of class."

"'By failing to prepare, you are preparing to fail,'" I replied. "The more I read, the easier the class comes to me."

"And that's why people take advantage of you." I heard the toilet flush and she came out to wash her hands, meeting my eyes in the mirror. "You shouldn't let them do that; you work hard for your grades."

It was the same argument we always had. Tori would have approached the topic more directly with, "Fuck 'em," but Navy was more pragmatic. She had a big heart, gave love even to people who treated her unkindly. "Easier said than done."

"I think you're so preoccupied with pleasing people that you don't think about what pleases you. What would please you?"

"Right now?" I rubbed the circle under my eyes. "Sleep."

"Are you nervous about sleeping in the same room as Adam?"

I shook my head. "It's weird. I'm more comfortable with him than I've been with any other guy. But the tension..."

"You know how you get over the tension?"

I raised an eyebrow. "What, are you going to suggest sex again?"

Navy's eyes widened and she put a hand over her mouth comically. "Of course not!" But then she winked. "It's just sex."

"You sound like Tori."

"Really?" She opened a cabinet. "I mean, if it's something more for you then that's different. But your first real boyfriend—Willy, right?—wasn't something more for you, was he?"

I hated reliving that five-minute meeting of flesh behind the bathrooms in Wyoming—not just because the location wasn't exactly romantic but because the guy had been someone chosen somewhat randomly. "No, he wasn't."

"So, is Adam?"

I didn't want her to see the blush I knew was creeping up my neck. "Yes, he is. But I don't know. It's basically like I'm a virgin anyway, for as much experience as I have."

She handed me a washcloth, turned on warm water, and pulled some fancy makeup remover from the cupboard, squirting it onto the washcloth. "I don't want to pressure you, but if Adam is someone you want, then why not? You're an adult, for goodness sakes. If you want the sex, and if he wants the sex, get the sex."

I was glad to have my face covered by the warm washcloth, so she couldn't see my expression. Did I want that with Adam? I think the answer was an obvious and emphatic yes. But we hadn't spoken alone, at length, since last night. And I already felt awkward, not knowing what exactly was going on between us.

"But at least take the first step in giving him a kiss," Navy said on the other side of my washcloth. "That'll help to get the tension out of the way."

I pressed my hands over my eyes, feeling the heat of the washcloth more firmly against my skin. "No, it won't."

Navy was silent for a long moment, like she knew I'd just confessed something. Then, I felt her fingers at the side of my face as she began to peel the washcloth away. "Um, what?"

I let the washcloth go, feeling my cheeks go pink. "Yeah..."

"When? Tonight?"

I shook my head. "At Casey's birthday, when I chased after the paper plates."

A light dawned in her eyes. "I *knew* something had happened.

You looked even more flushed than usual. I thought you two either bickered or almost kissed. But you actually kissed!" Navy clapped, absolutely delighted. "How was it?"

Needing to occupy my hands, I rinsed the washcloth and met her gaze in the mirror. "It wasn't bad."

She frowned. "That's not a glowing review."

How did I explain to Navy that it'd been the best first kiss I had ever had, but then I'd gone and ruined it? I didn't understand my own feelings. I'd wanted it—but hadn't known I'd wanted it. And then I'd been afraid of it, so I'd minimized the effects of that kiss to protect myself. I said as much to Navy and she sighed, placing her hands on her hips as she looked me over.

"Of course you're afraid. This is all so new."

"Well. And last night…" I rinsed the washcloth. "After dinner with my parents, we went back to his house and…"

"You little minx!" she exclaimed. "What did you do?"

"Nothing." But I frowned, because nothing was far from the truth. "We kissed. It was…great. And then it stopped and then I think I realized that I had bigger feelings for Adam than I am prepared for."

"Maybe he has those same big feelings for you. I saw the way he looked at you, the way he held you, tonight."

I knew he found me attractive. He'd surely paid me enough compliments the night before, but that didn't mean he was at the same level I was.

Not something. Everything.

It's what he'd said. But maybe everything for him looked different than it did for me.

"Maybe he has feelings that aren't *hate* feelings," I finally said. "But I don't think they're advanced far enough to be *like* feelings. If we weren't forced together, he wouldn't even be this far."

"You know, for someone so smart you sure say not-so-smart things."

I rolled my eyes and dried my hands on the towel. "I just don't want to get my hopes up, Navy. I don't want to fantasize. Lord knows I've done enough of that already." I thought of how silly I'd been in high school, when I'd slid that note into his locker. What had I expected? That he'd fall over in excitement to talk to me? Telling him now it was me would only be more humiliating. "I don't want expectations."

When Navy remained silent, looking me over curiously, I shook my hands impatiently. "What?" I asked.

"It's just that you always have expectations. You never plan anything without an idea of how it might turn out. You weigh pros and cons and you make lists and you exhaust every detail of your plans until they're executed. To hear you giving up expectations sounds unlike you."

I shrugged. "Maybe I'm trying to let go a little." If I wanted a future that included traveling to countries in need of humanitarian aid, I'd have to let go of expectations anyway. I glanced at my watch, realizing the late hour and turned to Navy. "I really am tired, and if we're going to hike tomorrow I need at least a few hours of sleep." I didn't include the part about wanting to get to bed before Adam did, but that was the real reason.

Navy wrapped me in a hug and it was pure instinct to resist, to pull myself back. Maybe it was because I was tired: emotionally and physically, but I melted into it, letting her warmth warm me too. Hugs from Navy were like a sedative when you desperately needed one.

It took me a minute to navigate my way to the bedroom Adam and I were sharing, as the house was darker than it'd been when we'd arrived, but when I found the door, I pushed it open and immediately closed it. I took a deep breath in and began rooting through my suitcase.

"That was a heavy sigh," came a voice from the far end of the room. I nearly jumped out of my skin, pressing a hand to my speeding heart. "Adam," I gasped. "I didn't know you were in here."

A lamp turned on and he sat up in the bed. He was wearing pajama bottoms and an old concert tee, his hair ruffled like he'd spent a few minutes running his hands through it.

The bed was king-sized, so realistically we could each take up our respective halves and not even touch one another. But Adam stood and motioned to the bed. "I wasn't sure how long you'd be, but if you're more comfortable with me sleeping on the floor, I'm fine with that."

"No," I said with a vigorous shake of my head. "It's a big enough bed, it's fine." I wrung my hands on the tank and the shorts I'd brought to change into. I could go back into the hall to the bathroom and change, but then again the room had been pitch black before Adam had spoken. Did it matter if I changed in the room, in the dark? "Would you mind turning off the light?" I held the clothes up in my hand.

"One sec." Adam climbed out of bed and walked over to the foot of the bed, where a small cooler sat. He reached in and produced a can of diet soda, then walked to my side of the bed and set it on the nightstand. I tilted my head, eyeing it with confusion. "Navy said that you usually drink a diet soda right before you fall asleep."

I knew that he'd asked Navy some things about me, but the fact that he'd remembered that detail, among all things, surprised me. "I do. Helps me sleep."

"It's funny—most people I know cut off their caffeine intake after noon or else they're up all night."

"I know. But strangely, it helps me fall asleep." I set my clothes on the side of the bed and touched the top of the can. I turned to Adam, who was close enough for me to reach out a hand and touch. But I didn't. "Thank you. That was really kind of you." It was one of my nightly rituals, but I had been so frazzled about the trip to the cabin that I hadn't even thought to pack extra sodas.

"Of course." He swallowed and looked me over a moment. "Look, about last night." He ran a hand over the back of his neck and looked down at the ground.

"I liked it. A lot," I blurted out. I didn't want to have an awkward conversation right before bed. I wanted to get it out in the open, because at least I could feel reassured that he'd liked it as well. "All of it. But it's new for me, I don't really understand things. I'm sorry if I made it awkward or anything."

"You apologize a lot." He took one small step toward me, and I had to tilt my head back in order to look up at him. With the small light from the lamp, all of the angles and planes of his face were more pronounced. Shadows settled in the little dip in his chin, and along the line of his jaw. When one side of his mouth tilted up in a smile, a dimple made a small canyon in his cheek. What was it about dimples that made a smile even more attractive?

"What are you thinking about?"

"There's a theory that dimples are caused by a divide in the large muscle along the side of your face."

It was so quiet for a moment that I swore I could hear crickets outside, but then his half-smile spread wider and he laughed—a real, from the belly, laugh. "That's what you're thinking?"

I nodded. More or less. Really, I'd been thinking about the weird desire I'd had to kiss that little crevice in his skin, but admitting that was definitely going to make things awkward. So I went for the secondary thought I'd had, when I had been wondering at my own lustful thoughts over a tiny patch of skin.

"That's interesting," he finally said. "I guess I didn't think about it too much, but it does make sense. Do you have dimples?"

As if to illustrate my lack of them, I smiled. "Nothing."

"So your muscle here," he said, and glided one finger over my cheek, "is intact."

I couldn't speak. My smile fell from my face as I stared up at him. This was what I meant when I told Navy how sharing a room didn't make me anxious. I felt completely safe in Adam's company, as far as any kind of danger went. But I didn't feel safe in ignoring our sexual chemistry. Which, there was no doubt of. I mean, he had a single finger on my cheek and I could feel the tingle spread through me like wildfire, igniting every nook and cranny of my body.

"I want to hear you say it again."

I just blinked dumbly at him. "What?"

His smile went soft, his eyes went soft, and his lips went soft. My body went soft too, with his hushed words and the soft glow of lamplight. "That you liked it."

Those four words had an immediate effect on me, roping around me and pulling me to him like a magnet finding its match. He still only touched my cheek, gently gliding over my skin like he was testing its texture. He wanted to hear that I had liked it when he kissed me? Like was such a mild term for how I felt.

I forced myself to keep my breathing even so I didn't act like a dog panting, but it was an effort to say the words, "I liked the kiss." Luckily for me, those four words had an effect on him too because I barely got them out before his lips came down on mine.

Like the first time, and the second time, and the third time, kissing Adam was surreal. His hand moved into my hair, cradling the back of my head as he tilted it, warm lips testing mine, teasing them open. He took such care with me, like I was an instrument he was learning to play. His other hand met my spine, fingers pressed there like the keys of a piano he was holding down. I swore, if I listened closely enough, I could hear music too. In the breaths we exchanged, in the swish of our clothes as they moved against each other, in the thrumming of my heartbeat in my head.

I held him at his waist, unsure and tentative. My hands curled around his back, climbing and climbing until my fingers met the back of his shoulders and we pressed together, solidly as one.

He pulled back, blowing a shaky breath across my forehead as his hands slid from my hair to glide along my chin. I wanted him to keep touching me in the reverent way he was, to keep holding me like he was learning my body and how it responded to each caress, to each press. It was sensory overload, in the best possible way.

"If I keep kissing you, I'm going to get us both in trouble."

"And you said you weren't a bad boy," I said, forcing my voice to be light and teasing. "You know, for someone who claimed to hate me as much as you do, you sure like to kiss me an awful lot."

He pulled back, allowing the light to fill in the space between our faces. "I don't hate you at all, Hollis."

"You did."

"If I hated you for real, I wouldn't have agreed to this."

"In high school," I said, reminding him. I swallowed a lump that formed in my throat.

"I don't think I hated you even then. I was just ... disappointed."

I thought hearing that he didn't hate me would give me some relief, but what he'd said was actually worse than hate. Hate was a powerful yet fleeting emotion, but disappointment was bitter and lingering.

"It's late," he said, stepping away from me. Coming off the high of kissing him to the low of knowing I'd disappointed him were two intense and different emotions, so jarring that I felt the breath whoosh right out of me. It's a terrible thing, knowing you've disappointed someone you care for. Especially when you've only just realized the depth of your care for them.

He made it over to his side of the bed and switched off the light.

I changed into my pajamas—not the sexy ones—in the silent dark and after crawling into bed, I replayed our conversation over and over in my head, on a loop. If Tori were here, she'd know exactly what to say. She'd give me a pep talk, cheer me on. And because I missed her so much then, I shot her a quick text before shutting off my phone, finishing the can of diet soda, and settling in for a long night in the same bed as Adam Oliver.

ADAM

I WOKE BEFORE HOLLIS THE FOLLOWING MORNING. I GLANCED AT her as I climbed out of bed, not bothering to change out of my PJ bottoms and tee before I left the room.

She was going to drive me fucking crazy. One minute she was putty in my hands—and let's be real here, I was putty in hers too—and the next, we were cold with one another. It was the strangest shock to my system, from hot to cold in an instant.

The kitchen was empty, thank Christ, which meant I was able to drink three cups of coffee before anyone else had a chance to, the last of which I drank outside on the deck.

I spent many weekends growing up with Keane and his family at the cabin. It was a nice break from the small city we lived in year round, and out here on the water, it felt calmer than back home in Amber Lake. Because this lake was smaller, with fewer houses having access to it, the water stayed mostly undisturbed. The rising sun reflected off the water, stretching across the widest part of the lake. Mist covered the rest of the lake, fat little clouds that seemed to hover just inches off the surface.

My phone buzzed in my pocket and I pulled it out. Another text from Sarah. I didn't mean to ignore her as long as I had, but she wanted to talk about things she'd seen on Facebook. I'd known as much when she'd sent me texts that were just a stream of interrogations, asking about Hollis and why I hadn't told her about her. Even if the whole thing with Hollis wasn't a ruse, I doubted I'd have had the time to explain it all to Sarah anyway.

It wasn't a ruse anymore, was it? The scales had tipped after dinner with her parents, and I could no longer discern where our fake relationship ended and this new one began. I liked to think that if Hollis and I hadn't been tied together by the fake premise of our relationship—forced to spend time getting to know one another—we wouldn't have ever gotten to this point.

She was more than the girl I'd maybe hated in high school. Much, much more. And it was hard to reconcile the girl who'd betrayed my trust that night at the party with the woman who had chased down a bunch of paper plates in a park. The girl who had stood up for me to her dad, who'd trembled with a kind of fury that I wanted to bear witness to. The past and the current versions of Hollis didn't even exist in the same reality.

Except they did. And I didn't know what was real for her anymore.

The screen door opened and I heard Keane's unmistakable yawn and the creak of his steps across the deck floor. "Morning," he said as he approached.

I looked sideways at him. He, like me, was still in his pajamas, but he wore a robe that looked like it belonged in some fancy pants hotel, and not on Keane. "Nice slippers," I said, eyeballing the unicorns on each of his feet.

"These are my mom's. All I could find." He brought a coffee cup to his lips and sipped, looking out over the water with me as he leaned on the railing. "It just feels good out here, doesn't it? Like there's extra oxygen or something. The air just fills your lungs, with no side of smog."

"You're in a good mood this morning," I said, sipping my coffee.

"You're … pensive." His eyes narrowed as he took me in. "Trouble in paradise?"

I laughed without humor. "It's hardly paradise. It's confusing."

Keane laughed, but with humor. "Oh, poor Adam, having to cuddle and kiss Hollis. I get it, man. Rough life."

I elbowed him. "Feel like going swimming?" I asked him.

Keane raised an eyebrow. "What?"

Before he knew what hit him, I grabbed him by the legs and tossed him over the railing and into the sure-to-be-freezing lake.

"You fucker," he spat when he surfaced. The back of the robe floated behind him as he eyed me angrily. "The least you can do is help me out. This robe weighs like fifty pounds soaking wet."

He had a point. "Don't patronize me next time and you won't end up in the water, dick." I set my coffee cup on a nearby table and reached down, wrapping one arm securely around the railing and held my hand out for his.

Keane clasped my arm, but he winced and I could tell he was struggling to tread water. "I need your fucking help, man," he said, encouraging me to reach for him with my other hand.

Which proved to be a mistake because the next thing I knew, I was in the water along with him.

"Asshole," I spat water when I came up for air.

"You put me in here first," he reminded me, grinning like an idiot.

"You didn't need help getting out?" I asked him, teeth chattering from the cold.

"Oh, no, I'm gonna need help out. This robe is an anchor."

"Dumb ass," I said without heat. "I would've helped you out. But now we're both fucked."

"Navy's up, I'm sure she'll help us."

"You think I'm going to help you after watching you both act like idiots?" Navy asked, coming into view as she walked toward the end of the deck. "Nope. You'll have to swim over to the beach." She motioned to the sandy beach on the side of the house, a solid ten yards from where we were.

When I glared at Keane, he shrugged and grinned. "Your fault, brother."

By the time we'd hoisted ourselves onto the sandy shore, Navy was calling us in to eat breakfast.

Keane stripped out of the robe and laid it on a chair to dry off. "I'm going to need a shower," he told her as he took off toward the upstairs.

I would need one too, but I settled for the towel Navy laid on the back of the couch. My clothes felt twenty pounds heavier and my cold limbs made moving difficult, but the towel was warm, fluffy, and dry, so I relaxed into it as Navy dished plates of eggs and sausage.

"Smell's good, Navy," I said, reaching for a sausage link.

She slapped my hand away. "You're not getting lake water all over this food. If you're not going to shower, at least change." She cocked her head toward the front bedroom, where Hollis and I were, so I trudged across the floor and into the room.

Hollis was rubbing her face when I entered the room. She slid glasses onto her face and then her eyes went wide as saucers as she took me in. "What happened?"

She looked fucking adorable in glasses, her hair mussed up and her face flush from waking up. "Keane and I went swimming."

"In your clothes?" She eyed the soaking wet flannel pants and the shirt that clung to me like a second skin.

"Sure, who doesn't? I need a shower." I wrapped the towel around my waist and moved to pull the shirt off, but it was so heavy and stuck to my skin that I struggled. "Can you help me a sec?"

She hesitated a moment before coming to me, grasping the hem of my shirt and lifting it up.

If it wasn't for the fact that pulling off the wet shirt felt like a workout, I might've found myself awkwardly hiding a boner. But as it was, every part of my body—including *that* part—was ice cold. It'd take an act of God to even get a tremble in my dick, and I didn't think God was eager to make that happen for me.

"I'll pull the neck hole out, just dip your head down so I can get it off and over your head," she said, stepping so close that her chest brushed my bare one. I wanted to press more fully against her, to feel that warmth, but I didn't want to get her wet as well.

R-rated images of Hollis flitted through my mind with that thought and I pushed them down, along with the feel of her breasts against my torso as she pressed her front to mine. She was struggling with the neck, so I obliged her request and dipped my head down. Which put my eyes so I was staring directly at her boobs.

Fuck. Me.

One of her warm hands cradled the back of my head as she tugged the neckline over it, releasing me from the freezing cold of the shirt and into the warmth of her.

Well, it hadn't taken an act of God after all. My dick twitched all thanks to her. At the most inopportune time.

"Your lips are turning blue," she said, her brows creasing as she frowned. "You need a shower right away."

I did the only thing I could think of doing at that moment. I placed my hands on her shoulders and dipped down to kiss her.

I might've kissed her longer than I'd intended. My hands might have roamed her back, along the teasing bits of flesh her tank top exposed. My kiss might've deepened, shifting from a *thank you* kiss to an *I want you* kiss. And after that, even though I didn't want to, I pulled back, belatedly mindful of the coldness of my skin against hers.

"Sorry," I said, dropping my hands from her.

"I'm not," she returned, surprising me. She grabbed an extra towel from the top of the dresser and pressed it into my chest. "Shower."

32

HOLLIS

LEAVING ADAM TO THE SHOWER, I EXITED THE ROOM WHEN I heard a loud commotion from the kitchen area.

There were feminine laughter and loud male voices—one of which I recognized: Keane. And the female voice that followed was unmistakable, so I quickened my pace into the kitchen.

Tori stood with arms outstretched and laden with grocery bags. She had sunglasses on and a giant hat, like that crazy aunt that always followed you on vacation.

"Babe!" she shouted from the kitchen island upon seeing me. She shook the bags loose, a cacophony of glass bottles rang all over the counter, and then she ran to me, launching herself onto me seconds before I braced myself for the impact.

"You're here," I said, half-stunned and half-confused.

"Yep. The party has arrived." She let go of me and stood back, cocking her head to the side as she took me in. "Just wake up?"

I had. I never slept in late, but being without an alarm and in a new place had meant that it was already well past eight. "What are you doing here?"

Navy was busying herself at the kitchen island, but kept glancing our way. She didn't have a problem with Tori, but Tori hadn't ever been welcoming toward her.

Tori pulled off the wide-brimmed hat and tossed it aside, along with her sunglasses. She wore skin-tight jeans and a black crop top; not exactly mountain weather appropriate, but Tori didn't pride herself on behaving appropriately, ever.

"I got your message. Read the subtext of it. So I said goodbye to the roomies and high-tailed it up this way. Stopped at the convenience store for libations, of course. Why are you looking at me like that? I thought you'd be happy to see me."

I *was* happy to see her. I had missed her, of course, but Adam and I were on tenuous ground and I didn't think Tori's presence would strengthen our status. Yes, he'd kissed me before getting into the shower and we'd done that quite a few times now, but that didn't change the history we shared. I forced cheer into my voice, knowing she'd see right through it, when I said, "Of course I'm happy you're here."

She pouted and looked around for a moment before she looped an arm through mine and pulled me outside onto the deck. I waited until the glass door was closed behind us before whispering, "What are you really doing here?" I thought she was over Keane. They'd played around in high school, but it hadn't ever been serious between them. "Is it because of Keane?"

She looked at me like she'd just smelled something bad. "What? For real? No way, toots. I'm here for *you*. You texted me at like ten last night, sounding super sad." She held her arms out. "Ta-da! Like your fairy fucking godmother."

"Am I going to a ball I don't know about?"

She tucked her fist under her chin as she looked me over. "No, but you've got a distinct smell of the sads on you."

"The sads?"

Tori looped her arm through mine again and we continued across the deck until we were out of sight from everyone gathered in the kitchen, our view being the side of the house. "Yeah, the sads." She made a show of sniffing me and then pulled back. "Did Adam already break your heart?"

"What? No. No way." Where had she gotten that from? "I'm *not* sad. It's just confusing. Everything is." I had so much to fill her in on, I realized. She didn't know what had happened at all. And suddenly, as I took her in, I realized I had missed her. And I was glad she was there.

I wrapped my arms around her, giving her the hug I should've when she'd first shown up.

"Oh god, please don't tell me you're crying on me right now."

"What?" I pulled back and gave her a look. "I am not crying. I'm just happy to see you. I am. It shocked me, but I'm actually glad you're here."

She pursed her lips, considering what I was saying, before she leaned back against the railing. "Yeah, I knew you'd say that eventually. Didn't think it'd happen so soon, but I'm not complaining." She nodded at something behind me and I turned, half expecting Adam to be standing there. But it was just the side of the house.

"What am I looking at?"

"See that dumpster over there?"

I squinted, straining my eyes through the trees until I saw it, nestled in a little alcove. "Yes, I see it."

"I was in that dumpster once."

I swung my head back to her. "What?"

"Long story." She shook her head, like she was repelling the memory. "But that's how I know, you've got the sads too."

"I do not have the sads. I'm confused."

"Aren't they the same thing, for you? You don't relish lingering in confusion, babe."

"Are we going to talk about how you ended up in that dumpster, or…"

"You're changing the subject." She wrapped an arm around my shoulders and turned me away from the view of the dumpster. "Talk to aunty Tori, tell me your woes."

"I don't have woes," I insisted, but Tori was already leading me to one of the patio chairs and all but shoving me into it. "I wouldn't call them woes."

"Go on." She twirled her hand as she sat across from me.

"We kissed. A few times. More than a few, I don't know. I stopped counting."

"Okay, keeping it rated PG, I dig it."

"But it's just that we run so hot and cold. He's mad one minute at me and the next he's got his hands on me."

Tori raised an eyebrow. "Are we venturing into rated R territory?"

"We are firmly in PG still."

"Okay, fine. Why does he get mad?"

I mulled it over. "Maybe mad isn't the right word. He's just so moody. Two days ago, he was cutting up cheese with a very sharp knife, looking at me in a very murdery kind of way."

"Oh, murdery sounds hot."

"I guess it was more broody than murdery. But they can be similar."

"Yeah, broody sounds even hotter."

She wasn't wrong. It had been hot. I was never the sole focus of any man, and the fact that it'd been my childhood crush was not exactly something I acted blasé about. "It was hot. And that's why it's so confusing."

"Well," she said with a laugh. "That part isn't so confusing. You want the D."

I rolled my eyes at her. "As I was saying, he was cutting cheese and looking at me like that and then we went to my parents' house and…" I waved my hand in front of my face, already cutting my own self off. "I don't want to talk about that right now. But anyway, that night we got pizza and went back to his place and I sort of straddled his lap and—"

"Hot damn!" she cheered. "NC-17, let's go!"

I couldn't help it. Even though she'd interrupted me, laughter poured out of me. I needed this. Time with Tori, to digest everything that had happened and help me figure a way through it. "No," I said, shaking my head. "Nothing happened besides some kissing and lip grazing."

"Oh." Tori frowned. "So you guys are playing it like it's middle school?"

"I'm not in a rush," I told her. "That didn't work out well when I rushed things with Willy."

"Yeah, well, to be fair he thought your name was Hannah, so." She held up a hand. "And he was a grown ass boy who chose to go by Willy."

"That's fair." I dropped my head against the back of the chair I was sitting in. "We are decidedly in PG territory, but maybe a little bit of PG-13 chatter. And, like I said, we go from hot to cold so fast, like something is always there, lingering in the periphery ready to douse us with ice cold water."

"What's causing the cold then?"

I racked my brain, searching for a discernible explanation. "I think it's gradually getting better, but I feel like maybe some of it stems from high school. That party." I was sick of talking about that party. I wanted it to go away, to exorcise the memory from my brain.

"Did you guys ever talk after? I knew you were upset with him, but I didn't really know why."

"Ugh. I don't want to talk about this."

"And that's why you should. Get it off your chest, and then there won't be so much weirdness between you two. Come on, tell aunty Tori what's up."

"Well, you know I was soaked in beer."

"Yes. Keane bitched about his car smelling like shit for weeks."

"And Adam had been there, when it'd happened."

"And he didn't do anything?"

"No, no." I shook my head. "Ben did it. He grabbed him by his shirt and shoved him back."

"That's good at least."

"Yeah. But then we went to the front yard and he left, telling me he was going to find you so we could go home."

She was nodding with each thing I said, recapping the night. And she continued to nod. "Yes, I remember. He saw me half-naked."

I was on the verge of continuing with my story when what Tori said stopped me in my tracks. "What?" This was new information. My story had been that he'd abandoned me for another woman on the stairs, someone who had a rose tattoo and who showed it off to him.

"So, he found us upstairs. Surprised us both."

"Who is 'us'?"

"Me and Keane." She rolled her eyes. "We were fooling around. Anyway, he snagged me, told me how to get to you fastest. I guess he assumed you were still out in the front yard, which is why it took me a bit to find you."

I stood and pressed my fingers to my temples, absorbing this new information. "When I came through the front door, he was on the stairs, talking to whats-her-name."

Tori lifted her shoulder. "I wasn't there, I don't know who he was talking to."

"Some girl. Well, I was jealous and I basically proved his prejudices about me right soon after I found him." I leaned over the railing and sucked in a deep breath of mountain air. "Ben and his cronies started taunting him, and I did nothing. I just stood there, letting them egg him on." No wonder Adam had hated me. All this time, my narrative of that night had been so different than the truth.

"It sounds like you need to talk about that night," Tori said, coming up behind me and wrapping an arm around my shoulders.

"I don't want to."

"It'd be better than letting this fester between you. So what, you were jealous. What girl doesn't have a jealous moment once in her life? Cut yourself some slack, and then tell him the truth."

"Ugh," I said again.

"Tori," Keane said from behind us. When I turned, I made sure to watch his face. If there was any lingering attraction between him and Tori, it was long gone. "This is a surprise."

"Sorry for crashing your party," she said. "Again."

They exchanged a look, telling me that there was so much history there that I wasn't privy to. "It's okay. You staying the night? I can put up an air mattress."

"I don't have to stay the night," she said, but Keane stopped her, wrapping an arm around her and squeezing.

"No, stay. I'm glad you're here. There's a lot of dudes, it's nice to have another lady around."

"No one's ever accused me of being a lady, but if it's a lady you seek, it's a lady you'll get."

"You gonna hike with us today?"

"Hike? Me?" Tori looked down at her clothes and then back at Keane. "Do I look like a person who climbs mountains for fun?"

"Oh, come on," he said. "You never go hiking when you've come up here. Once wouldn't kill you."

"You only really die once, you know. So, best not take any chances."

Keane laughed and let her go. He ran a hand through my hair and turned to me. "So, uh, your boyfriend is probably going to murder me."

"You too?" Tori asked, winking at me. "What'd you do now?"

"He threw me in the lake this morning, so I pulled him in as well. But I wasn't thinking about his cell phone." His mouth went into a grim line. "It's in a bag of rice right now, but I don't have high hopes for it."

"Okay," I said. "I'll go do some damage control."

It wasn't until I had left Keane and Tori that I realized how Keane had called Adam my boyfriend and my mind hadn't automatically dinged that he was actually my *fake* boyfriend.

33

ADAM

I SHOOK THE BAG AS IF THE ACTION WOULD CAUSE THE WATER TO leech from my phone faster, but it was useless. By the time I realized that my phone had gone swimming with me, it was waterlogged and the screen wouldn't even attempt to turn on.

"Here," Navy said softly, pushing a plate of food toward me. "I gave you extra bacon."

I stared at the plate of eggs, bacon, sausage, and pancakes. My stomach growled, but the frustration lingered. I hated being unreachable for Casey. Even though Keane's mom had promised to communicate with me through her son's phone, I didn't like feeling so disconnected and out of reach. The only good thing was that I was free from Sarah's nagging texts, but I couldn't avoid her for forever, either.

"Extra bacon, huh?"

"I know it won't fix your phone, but it might make you a little bit happier."

I took a big bite of the bacon and gave her a grateful smile. "Have you seen Hollis?"

312

"She's on the deck with Keane and Tori."

"Tori?"

"She arrived while you were showering."

"I didn't know she was invited." I didn't hate Tori, but I didn't really like her either. She'd been the one to throw Hollis under the bus with her parents, had given them my name. And, at least throughout high school, she hadn't been any different than the company she kept.

"She wasn't. She just showed up. I think maybe Hollis texted her."

That made sense, since they were best friends. But the thought of sharing such small quarters with Tori did little to make me feel like this weekend was going to be as relaxing as we'd planned.

The glass door opened and Hollis came in, eyeing me like she was trying to get a handle on my mood. "Keane told me about your phone."

"I forgot it was in my pocket when he pulled me in. Fucker."

"He said you pushed him in first. Did you ask if he had his phone in his pockets?"

"Well, no."

She gave me a soft smile. "Maybe cut him some slack then?"

What, she was refereeing our disagreements now? Keane and I had endured far worse than a waterlogged cell phone since becoming friends during childhood. I didn't need her to be our Switzerland. "I'm not going to kill him," I said, digging into the eggs. "But don't be shocked if Keane goes surprise swimming a couple more times today."

Hollis slid into the chair beside me and I breathed in her delicate perfume as she leaned against me. "Maybe let's make sure he doesn't have his phone on him first?"

"I guess I can agree to that." I pushed my plate toward her. "Want some bacon?"

She looked at me with the most surprised smile on her face. "You're sharing your bacon?"

"Don't get used to it," I said. "But since you took off my clothes, I thought I kind of owed you."

"Whoa," Navy said, refilling the coffee pot. "Should I leave?"

"He was soaked," Hollis said, exchanging glances with me.

We both smiled. It was getting easier and easier to be like this with her, a fact that was infiltrating my thoughts. To think, if it hadn't been for her parents, we likely wouldn't have ended up together. Even though her dad had been an asshole by insinuating that Hollis was embarrassed by me, I paid attention to how she treated me around the people she was the most comfortable with, the people who knew that we weren't really together. If anything, she was warmer and more affectionate when we weren't trying to convince anyone.

It was natural. Like we'd never been fake together. No, it had been real from the jump.

34

HOLLIS

"PEOPLE JUST CLIMB MOUNTAINS FOR FUNSIES?" TORI ASKED, heaving a breath.

"Yeah, we do." Todd laughed at Tori and winked at me. "We also ride waves in New Zealand and dive into cenotes in Mexico."

"Speak for yourself. The only diving I do is into a bag of chips." She placed a hand over her stomach. "God, I could go for some ruffled chips right about now."

"You're always hungry," Keane said teasingly. "One night, we went to McDonald's twice."

"To be fair, the first time you rescued me from the dumpster."

I looked at Tori as we approached a switchback, spun around a tree and said, "Tell me this dumpster story."

"It's a long story, not for today." She glanced at Keane, who was bringing up the rear. "Thanks for throwing me under the bus, dick."

"'Welcome!" Keane called out cheerfully. "Hey, Adam, mind slowing down?"

Adam turned, "Maybe you could speed up?"

"I wouldn't mind if we took a rest here," Todd chimed in, smiling at me. Why was he always doing that? Smiling at me like we had some kind of telepathic connection. "Leg's bothering me a little."

"Anyone have chips?" Tori called out as we all moved to various seating positions.

Adam stayed standing for the moment, looking around and peering through the rest of the trail. My phone trilled in my pocket and I looked at it, instantly annoyed that I hadn't muted certain people's texts so that I didn't see them. Once I saw it, it was in my brain. I couldn't not think about it.

Yo, do you have time for me to run some things by you this week?

It was someone who frequently messaged me about this kind of stuff. I put my phone away, deciding I'd deal with it on Monday.

"Hot date?" Adam asked, motioning to my phone.

"No." I didn't want to explain it to him. "Tutoring stuff."

"Real tutoring stuff?" Navy asked from in front of me. "Or *do me a favor for free* stuff?"

I gave her a look.

"What? You don't need to be dealing with that crap right now. Am I wrong?"

"It's fine, Navy." I pressed harder down on my pocket, as if I could completely shove my phone from my mind. "How much longer to the top?" It was a baby mountain, more of a hill, really. None of us were prepared for a full trek, so we'd chosen the easier route so that we'd be back before nightfall.

"Are there bears in these woods?" Tori asked, smacking a mosquito from her leg.

"It's woods. So, yeah." Todd leaned against a moss-covered tree, regarding her. "And mountain lions. Maybe even some wolves."

Tori's lips flattened. "You're lying."

"We're not too far from Yellowstone, sweetheart. Which means we get wolves and bears and mountain lions."

"I'm not your sweetheart." Tori bristled. "Keane, is he right?"

"Yeah, but the bears don't really come down here unless there's food out in the open. Too much human activity."

"I guess it's good you didn't bring any chips," I reminded her with a smile.

"Tell that to my stomach." Tori patted her flat belly, making a pouting face.

"Ready to go?" Adam asked from the front of our group. "I think I hear one of the waterfalls up ahead."

"Yeah," Todd said. "You good, Hollis?"

What the heck? Why was he singling me out? "I've been good," I said, wondering what his deal was.

"Hollis, want to come up here with me? We can lead everyone else, together."

I turned, grateful, and moved past Navy and one of Keane's friends until I was standing beside Adam. He looped an arm over my shoulders and brought his head down until his lips were at my ear. "Todd is kind of a slimeball," he whispered. "Gives me some creeper vibes."

"Maybe he doesn't get that I have a boyfriend." I looped my arm around him too, proceeding around the curve of the switchback and back up the side of the trees. The positioning meant that we faced Todd for a moment and Adam squeezed tighter.

His hand moved to my pony, like he was playing with my hair, and his lips pressed to my temple. I chewed on my lip, not meeting Todd's eyes. While Adam's gesture was sweet, protective even, it felt like a performance and not real. After everything that had happened, I didn't want to keep pretending. What was the point?

Along the way, Adam pointed out different kinds of flora and told me what they were historically known for. He pointed out some markings on a thinner tree and urged me closer to look when everyone else took another water break. My blood ran cold at the markings, but Adam shook his head. "These aren't bear markings." It was as if he'd read my mind.

"How do you know?"

"Because these are rubs, not claws. See how the bark looks like it was waxed off?" With his hand on the small of my back, he moved me closer. "This." He held up tufts of hair. "This is from an elk. The bull elk prefer saplings like this one." He pointed to the roots of the tree. "See how this tree looks like it was nearly ripped from the ground? They rub their antlers against smaller trees like this one. They've got more testosterone than a heavyweight championship. September is right in the middle for the elk rut."

"What does that mean?"

"It means they're horny motherfuckers." Adam grinned, sending a spear of hot lust through me. Would that feeling ever dull? "And they're stupid too. They will walk right past you if they see a cow."

"I've never seen an elk in the wild," I told him. "Unless you count Yellowstone."

"They're all over the Tetons. This area is especially good for it." He straightened and led me back to the front of the group. "You can hear the fresh water up ahead. I bet we're near some game trails."

"How do you know so much about elk?"

"My grandfather used to take me into these woods. Taught me a couple things. Better to be prepared than not."

It was similar to my own mantra. "I like being prepared," I said with a smile. "Thank you for telling me about the horny elk."

He laughed, and the sound shook my heart. "Anytime." The buzz from my phone was deafening. Adam's attention turned to the pocket and I pulled it out. Again, the same student was reaching out to me on Facebook this time, asking if I had gotten his text. I ground my teeth and shoved the phone away.

We resumed the hike, stopping only when we got to a small waterfall. The brush and trees were cleared from the bottom of it, so we were able to stand close to the mist. It was too cold to play in the water and even too cold for the mist, but it felt nice just standing in the light fog. My hair had come mostly undone from the hike and I itched to fix it but without a mirror, it was pointless. So when the mist hit my face, it plastered every loose tendril to my skin. I wanted to wipe it away, but let the desire to be perfect go for a minute so I could just enjoy.

We ventured further, over a rocky incline, until we reached our destination: the top of the smallest mountain in the range. The top was flat from being windblown, with very sparse trees obstructing our view. People dropped their small backpacks to dig out their phones, but I just soaked it in. I had been on a few mountains around the world now, but no matter where my future took me, I knew that these jagged, shark tooth like mountains would always say home to me.

"Okay," Tori said, coming up behind me and looping an arm over my shoulder. "I guess the eight million mosquito bites were worth it after all."

"Pretty spectacular, isn't it?" With Keane's cabin behind us, you couldn't see any signs of civilization ahead. Very little of the world was as unspoiled as this, as densely populated with trees and rivers that carved their twisty way through the mountains.

"Adam, would you take our photo?" Tori asked and held her phone to him. Adam stood in front of us, posing us with the wilderness at our backs. After snapping the photo, he handed her the phone.

"How are things going?" Tori asked Adam casually as she glanced through all the photos she'd taken. "You guys seem to be hitting it off well." I elbowed her in the ribs, but she sidestepped me.

Adam glanced at me and faced her. "We're figuring things out."

"What's there to figure out? You guys sure look pretty coupled up." She tucked her phone away.

"What I meant was figuring out the mess you created."

Tori frowned. "What do you mean?"

"You were the one who gave my name to Hollis's parents, right?"

Tori glanced at me and I hoped I looked as contrite as I felt.

"Your girl was in a pickle. I thought I was helping out." She crossed her arms over her chest and shifted the weight on her back foot. She wouldn't back down from Adam.

"It might have been helpful if you'd discussed it with her first." There was no love lost between Adam and Tori, and I hated that I was the cause of it on both ends.

"It's okay, Adam." I placed my palm on his chest, hoping to thwart any frustration he might feel. But then again, where was this frustration coming from? "It all worked out. Didn't it?"

He looked down at me and I held my breath as I waited.

"It did." His arm came around my back. "I just don't want Tori thinking she can bulldoze you as other people do."

"Tori's my best friend. She would never bulldoze me." Just then, my phone rang. I should've muted it, or turned off the cellular at the very least. I shoved my hand in my pocket and silenced it.

Tori was pursing her lips, taking it all in stride. "No, you know something? He has a point. I shouldn't have said that to your parents. While my intentions were good, my delivery sucked big dick."

"It all worked out," I repeated. Because it had. "Let's get a picture together, Adam." I asked Tori if she could use her phone to take it, and then I stood next to Adam, with the same view at our back. I didn't want to use my phone for the photo because I didn't want to see the notifications from the people blowing up my phone. I could only compartmentalize so much; seeing all the missed texts and messages would send me into a tailspin I wouldn't be able to easily escape from. I didn't want anything to damper the mood.

Tori held up her phone and snapped the photo. "Okay, we've got the boring photo out of the way, let's get a real one."

I furrowed my brows and before I could ask her what she meant, Adam spun me so I faced him. I caught my breath when I faced him and before I had a second to react, he kissed me. It was the briefest of kisses, but enough to send my brain reeling when he pulled back. "Got it?" Adam asked Tori.

She whooped. "That was pretty okay. Kind of cliche if you ask me. You could do better." It was like she was challenging Adam, but I didn't want to be a part of this game. When he leaned in this time, I pressed a hand to his chest.

"I don't want a fake kiss. I want a real one."

"How can it be fake? This isn't some kind of movie magic; it's you and me."

"It's fake when it's for everyone else's benefit, to convince them that we're dating." I motioned to Tori. "This is going to go on our social media feeds and if we're going to kiss I want it to be for real. For you, and for me."

He looked thoughtful for a moment. The wind picked up, ruffling the front of his hair. The end of my ponytail whipped me in the face. As I attempted to restrain it, Adam's lips descended, capturing mine. His hands framed my face and he moved so close that our entire fronts were pressed against one another. The warmth from his body against the cold wind was welcome, so welcome that I inched closer. His lips teased and nibbled and his tongue flicked over my bottom lip. I melted into him.

When he let go, he waited to speak until I looked up at him. "*That* was for me. As every other kiss has been." His head bent so that our foreheads touched. "Trust me when I say that anytime I touch you, it's for me. Or for you. It's never been about them, not for me."

I couldn't control the smile that spread my lips. It was such an Adam thing to say, such a romantic thing. Like out of one of my books. A fantasy, really. He smiled too, the kind of smile that poured right into me, filling me up to the brim. We just grinned at each other like two lovestruck idiots.

It was on the tip of my tongue to say something that I had never said to any other guy, three words that meant so much to me—a promise and a gift.

A realization filled me. I loved Adam. Like, real love. Not puppy love, not the love I swore I had in school. This love was made from knowing him, from spending time with him. It was the kind of love that people talked about in books and movies, the love that wouldn't be easy to shake. Not that I would want to.

"I make an excellent third wheel," Tori said, pulling our attention away from each other. "Just sayin'." She tucked her phone in her windbreaker. "It's nice to see you guys swapping spit, though. Since she finally freaking admitted to it."

"What?" Adam asked, still holding onto me.

"It took a whole freaking week for her to tell me you guys had kissed."

"Me too," Navy said from a few feet away. She gave me two thumbs up.

"Did you guys just recently start dating?" Todd asked. He'd been circling us, like a shark.

"Yes," I said at the same time that Adam said "No." Todd looked between us, confused. Who could blame him.

"We've known each other a long time," Adam clarified. He turned to look at me. "But it feels like we're just really getting to know one another." He squeezed my hand in his. "And I like what I'm getting to know." He squeezed me again, but this time it pinged deeper, somewhere I couldn't reach.

"God, you two look so perfect together it makes me sick." Tori blew out a breath. "Does that mean you're going to start writing him love notes like you do for me? I'm not sure I'm ready to duke it out with anyone else for your love, Hols."

"Love notes?" Adam turned to me.

"Yeah, she writes on sticky notes and leaves them in places for people to find. I'm still finding the ones she left in my stuff after I spent the weekend at her parents' summer house."

Adam's stare was boring into me, and just as quickly as love had swept in, so did embarrassment. And it turned everything bitter.

He knew.

35

ADAM

TORI HAD JOGGED MY MEMORY OF THE STICKY NOTE I HAD FOUND in my locker senior year, and then re-found last week. I stared at Hollis, willing her to explain. But her eyes were averted, telling me everything I needed to know.

I thought of the sticky note Casey had found in her textbook, one that Hollis had left for her.

Was the note from her?

"Hollis," I said softly.

Her phone buzzed loudly and I saw the frown come across her lips. I'd had enough of her damn phone darkening her mood.

"Is that your dad?" I asked.

When she shook her head, I held my hand out for her phone. She placed it in my palm and the screen lit up, showing a dozen notifications, including a missed call.

"Who is Keith?"

"Some guy from class."

"Paying client?"

She shook her head.

I dialed.

After a minute, a man's voice picked up. "Oh good, you called me back. I missed class on Thursday. I was suuuuper hungover, so I need the notes. Do you have my email?"

Not even a hi. "Is this Keith?" I asked.

Keith's voice registered surprise at hearing another male. "Uh...yeah."

"Hollis is unavailable. If you would like to book her for tutoring, email her and she'll let you know when she's free."

"I just need her notes, man."

"And I just need you to email her instead of blowing up her phone, *man*." Hollis's eyes were going wider by the second. I shook my head, hopefully telling her that everything was fine. "Got it?"

"Who the fuck are you?"

"Her boyfriend. Who the fuck are *you*?"

"Keith. We have a couple classes together."

"Yeah? And how many of those classes do you bum off of her work?"

The ensuing silence told me everything.

"How about you stop drinking on nights when you have class and figure your own shit out? Oh, and lose this number." I hung up and handed the phone back to Hollis. "Sorry," I said sheepishly.

"No." Her face was glowing. "That was wonderful."

"Keith sounds like such a dick. He didn't even say hi," I told her.

"You never say hi to me either."

"Sure I do."

"No, you say, 'Hollis.'"

"Well, that is your name."

She smiled. "I know it is. But you've never said hi, hello, or even hey. It's always 'Hollis' like we're in the middle of a conversation and you're using my name for emphasis."

Maybe because it felt like we were always in the middle of a conversation, ever since high school. A conversation that hadn't yet finished. I would need to work on saying hi to her, though, because it seemed important to her. "Okay, well at least I don't blow off my responsibilities for booze."

"That's true. Is that what he said? That's what he did all last semester too."

"Hollis, you gotta learn how to say no. N. O. Try it on for size. I think it would fit."

"You've already taught me this word. But I'll work on it," she said, her lips curved. She tucked her phone away. And then, seeing Tori hovering a few feet away, she seemed to remember what we'd been about to talk about before we'd been interrupted.

"Tori, can we have a sec?" Hollis's voice sounded shaky and weak. When Tori was gone, Hollis sighed and walked away, so that we weren't right next to everyone else.

Her hand dipped in her pocket to mute the buzzing that was happening, again, and she looked over her shoulder at me. Her cheeks were pink, redder than what could be blamed on the wind.

"You wrote the note I found in my locker."

She nodded.

"My speech…" I tried to remember exactly which speech it'd been. "You drew a rose on the note."

"I did. I'm not an illustrator. It was just to let you know which speech I was referring to."

"The *Beauty and the Beast* speech? In the Fairytales class, right?"

"Yes."

"Were you ever going to tell me it was you?"

She lifted a shoulder. "I don't know. It's kind of

embarrassing. I told you I had a crush on you back then." I didn't think it was possible for her cheeks to redden anymore. I was wrong.

"At first, I thought that note was a prank. Like right out of some 90's teen movie."

"Why? Because the drawing was so bad?"

"It was the drawing that made me believe it to be real."

"It's real. I mean, it *was* real." She was twiddling with a long piece of grass in her hands, like she needed to occupy herself somehow.

I was struck by what she said. *It's real.* Because this—right now—was real for me too. "It is real," I said, correcting her. "Thank you for the note, Hollis." A warm tenderness swept through me, making me see her in a different light. She was a kaleidoscope of complexity, and I yearned to know more parts of her, to see her in all the ways I hadn't yet. I cupped her cheek in my palm, running my thumb along her cheekbone.

When I dipped my mouth to hers this time, I took it slow. I treated her like something I was savoring, because I was. Being with Hollis felt as natural as any other relationship I'd ever had.

My other hand moved up her spine until it met her neck. I cursed the fact that her hair was tied back and instead, dipped her back just enough in order for me to deepen the kiss.

I held her gently, so gently. But I knew she was strong.

We separated when the wind nearly blew her back. Her fingers went to her mouth, grazing across her lips. "That kiss felt like it was just for me."

I nodded, because when I had bent to kiss her, it *was for her.* But the thing was, it had turned into a kiss for me.

HOLLIS

I CHANGED INTO MY SEXY PAJAMAS. I HAD REALLY ONLY PACKED them on a whim, but when I'd been putting the day's clothes into my laundry bag, my hand had grazed the silky fabric and imagining wearing it for Adam had lit a thousand goosebumps across my skin. He was showering after spending the last hour stacking wood with Keane, and the room still smelled faintly of pine and him.

I fingered the delicate straps of the chemise. The pajamas weren't sexy in the amount of skin they revealed, but in the way you wore them, like a tease of what lay beneath. The top had a deep v-neck, the bust was maybe two tiny triangles of satiny fabric attached to a strip that barely covered my belly. They weren't the kind of pajamas that required a bra or underwear.

I never wore them. I had bought them on a whim, really, during an all too brief rebellion from practicality. The bottoms were little more than short shorts, except for the slit up each side that exposed even more leg. As far as the purposes of sleep, these pajamas wouldn't cut it, because my breasts would fall right out of the top and likely get tangled in the wispy straps.

If I made the conscious decision to put those pajamas on, I knew deep down I was telling myself exactly what I wanted from Adam. So much had changed. The day had been so revealing, so meaningful in ways I hadn't expected. He now knew I had written the note, and he didn't think me lovesick or pathetic, like I always worried. No, if anything, he'd looked… comfortable. Like the secret had given him some kind of solace.

The bedroom was dim, thanks to a lightbulb being out above the bed. It made it accidentally romantic. I didn't want to talk myself out of wearing the sexy pajamas, so I stripped until I was completely naked, conscious of the fact that Adam could step out of the bathroom and join me in the room any minute. I wouldn't be able to hear the water turn off, and for that reason I yanked the pajamas on hastily, praying that he didn't walk in as I was tugging the top over my breasts.

Every part of me tingled in acute awareness. Adam would join me in the room any minute, he'd see these pajamas and he'd know.

Catching my reflection in the mirror above the dresser, I looked so much different than I usually presented myself. My hair fell in disarray around my shoulders, and its volume almost made my top look modest. But I could see the points of both my nipples straining against the fabric, and I almost gave up then, abandoning this idea altogether. I looked wanton, unrestrained, like I had experience in seducing guys. Which I didn't.

If I wasn't so embarrassed, I might ask Tori for tips. To tell me how to shut my brain up, to tell me where to touch him so that he liked it.

Burying my face in my hands, I wondered why I'd thought this was a good idea. I should toss the pajamas back into the suitcase where they belonged, but then I'd be naked until I dug out the pajamas I'd worn the night before. And if he walked in on that, I'd be in a worse predicament.

Why was I always overthinking everything? Why couldn't I be cool, see where this took us?

I stood, resigning myself to throwing a sweater over the indecent top, when the door to the bedroom opened.

I froze and so did Adam, who wore only a towel. I watched, both of us silent, as water trailed down his chest until it reached his waist, disappearing into the towel. His dark hair looked black, bits of it spiking up. I curled my hands into fists when I felt an urge to run my hands through it.

"Hollis."

"Adam." I ran my tongue over my teeth. "You never say hi. Or hey. Just, 'Hollis.'"

"I know." He licked his lips and his eyes roamed over me briefly, almost like he was ashamed to be looking. "I like your pajamas."

I sat back on the bed, giving up the sweater completely. "I like your towel," I said.

He laughed and the bright flash of his teeth uncoiled something deep in my belly. There was no doubt in my mind that I wanted Adam, that I trusted him. I wanted whatever he wanted; I just hoped that what he wanted wasn't for me to sleep apart from him tonight.

He stepped away from the closed door, coming closer to me, close enough that I had to tip my head back to look up at him. He was still pretty wet from his shower; narrow rivulets of water traced irregular paths across his tanned chest, over the muscles of his abs. I had seen him shirtless before, and it'd rocked me a little then. But he was more than shirtless now.

"I thought you'd be out in the living room with everyone else."

"I abandoned them." I swallowed, and swore he watched the glide of my throat. "I was tired."

He reached out, brushing hair off of one of my shoulders. My chest heaved, like breathing was something I had to remember to do—not something innate to my respiratory system. "Are you?" he asked, his voice low and dark. "Tired?"

I didn't trust my voice to speak then, so I merely shook my head.

"Okay." The side of his mouth tipped up and his hand landed on the curve of my shoulder, teasing the strap of my top. I couldn't believe that such a simple touch had the effect it did. Even though I was sitting, my knees trembled. It was as if every part of my body came alive when he looked at me like that.

I wanted to touch him, but my face was right at his towel. And even though I was ready for *that*, I wasn't eager for this to accelerate at a pace that I couldn't keep up with.

The back of his hand slid down my arm, leaving a trail of goosebumps in its wake. My body was not a liar, it spoke for me when I couldn't.

His hand moved back up, not stopping until it cupped my chin, tipping it with just his fingers as his head came down. "You surprise me, all the time," he said against my lips. He wasn't kissing me, not really, more just resting his mouth on mine as his hand curled around the back of my neck, to support my head. "Are you sure?" he asked.

I swallowed again, willing my voice to be normal when I said, "I've been sure."

And then, he kissed me.

ADAM

I DIDN'T HAVE WORDS FOR WHAT SHE DID TO ME. SHE WAS PART witch and part merciful angel, pulling me in with one of her steady gazes like a spell, and relieving me when I needed relief the most. But the kind of relief I needed wasn't about the destination; it was about the journey there. I needed to take my time with her, watch her come undone under my hands, under my mouth. Because really, what I wanted was to see her completely uncontrolled, to give her what her body wanted.

I had been nursing some pretty carnal thoughts about her for the last week, at least, but seeing her body in that slip of satin, that swell of her breasts pressing against the fabric begging to be let out, had undone me in a way I couldn't articulate.

My mouth moved off of hers to glide along her jaw, testing her earlobe between my teeth, before I made my way south. Because she was sitting and I was standing, I had to brace both hands on the bed, on either side of her, to keep from falling on top of her.

My hands landed on top of hers, our fingers linking, as I squeezed and moved my kisses across her chest. The angle of her body pushed her breasts out for attention, but I neglected them for the time being, fully committed to tasting Hollis's skin in the most thorough way possible. She smelled so fucking good, like some kind of dark dessert, the kind that made your mouth water before you even knew what it tasted like. I had never known a woman like her, and I had never known this kind of deep fascination that lured me to her over and over again. I supposed that's what infatuation was.

I wanted to tell her, to give her words that would mean something. To make her feel the way I was feeling. I had never dated anyone for long, not long enough to form some kind of intangible attachment to them. But I'd be damned if someone tried to separate me from Hollis—especially at that moment, when she tasted so damn good, when her very skin vibrated under my touch.

With my head, I nudged her chin up so I could better taste the skin under it. And because I couldn't resist, I nipped the skin lightly, tugging it between my teeth as I worked my way back down.

She let out a sigh that provided a gap in her tank, allowing me to look all the way down her top.

Fuck me.

I had to calm myself down. Already, I was straining against the towel but Hollis wasn't someone I wanted just to fuck. I wanted more than that. I wouldn't spend the time analyzing the why of that, but I knew I wanted more not just for her, but me too.

I rubbed her skin with my cheek, relishing in the way it turned pink from the scruff on my face. There she was, my rose; blooming for me again.

I moved across her shoulder until I came to the top of her tank. Our hands were still clasped, the weight of my body bearing down against them. I didn't want to let go of her just yet, so I grasped the strap between my teeth and nudged it off of one shoulder and then moved to the other one.

The top clung stubbornly to her breasts, as if daring me to challenge it. Instead, I kissed a path across the heaving tops of her breasts, sucking and nibbling my way across each of them until Hollis's hands strained under mine.

I let go, half-convinced she was going to stop me, but instead she stood and the top fell, pooling at her waist.

She stood before me, naked from the waist up. A hunger I'd only been teasing became stronger, more powerful. She was cream and roses, from her breasts all the way across her body. "You're fucking perfect," I said, not caring that my voice sounded hoarse.

Her gaze dipped, landing on the full-on erection I knew I was boasting and then climbed back up to my face. "Last chance, Hollis," I said, almost afraid for her to say yes. Whatever feelings I had for Hollis rose closer and closer to the surface. It was only a matter of time before they dislodged from my throat and became words I actually spoke. I had very real, very scary feelings for her—feelings that had been planted three years ago and had been fed a hearty and steady diet the last ten days. Feelings I wouldn't be able to walk away from.

I realized it didn't matter if she said yes because those feelings weren't caused by her flesh, but by her brain, by her heart.

In the end, she didn't say yes. She stepped forward, looping her hands around my neck and pressing her chest to mine. She rose up on her tiptoes and claimed my mouth the way I wanted to claim her. I couldn't be careless with her, or with me either.

Grasping her thighs, I lifted her up until her legs wrapped around my waist and I turned so that I was seated on the bed. This gave me easier access to her skin, which I took full advantage of when my mouth closed around her nipple, tugging and laving it. Her hands curled in my hair, mimicking my pressure. The desire was sharp, hot like an iron thrust into my veins. I was impatient to taste every part of her and it was hard to force myself to slow. I pulled back to move onto her other nipple, but this time I watched what happened to her face when I closed my mouth around it, when my teeth nipped the rounded point. Her eyes were closed, her mouth open. Fucking hell, watching her gave me as much pleasure as touching her. I'd wondered how expressive her face was, and was grateful to see that she couldn't control her face when it came to desire.

I nibbled the underside of one breast and the other. She rocked against me, pressing my erection between us. It was sweet, delicious torture. The slight pressure had almost caused me to rip the towel off, to line Hollis up, and to thrust myself to the hilt. But I wanted to savor. I wanted Hollis to be so delirious from pleasure that she couldn't speak.

I flipped her over, she was flat on her back on the bed, her dark hair splayed out across the cream comforter. God, she looked like every fantasy I'd have for the rest of my life.

The movement had caused the outside edges of her shorts to flip up one side, revealing a deep slit, nearly all the way to the waist of them.

She had fucking incredible legs, and that tease of skin did little to satiate my curiosity. I played with the slit, watching her face as she watched my movements. She was a delight to witness, and when I flattened my palm on her skin and slipped it under the waistband of her shorts, her eyes went a little wide. I grazed my thumb along her exposed skin, reveling in the way she squirmed, moving so that my hand came closer and closer to her center.

With my eyes on her, I slid a finger over her skin there, in her most private place. She went wide, legs and eyes, and I marveled over the intensity in her gaze. Was she really this innocent, to be surprised by a light graze over her skin? I wanted more for her, so I didn't continue—not yet. I leaned over her, pressing my mouth to the skin below her belly button. She was so warm, her skin like velvet.

"Adam," she said, her voice the first word we'd spoken in several minutes. "I don't know what to do."

"Yes, you do." I turned my head so that I could look up at her. "You're doing it already."

"But what about you?" She gestured at my towel.

I kissed a path from her belly button, between her breasts, all the way up until I was braced over her, facing her. "I want this." I plucked at her nipple, just to watch her face change. "Trust me."

"I do."

We'd been talking about trusting her body to mine, but her reply was so automatic, so calm, I had no doubt that she trusted me more than with just her body. Sitting back so that I straddled her, I took in the sight before me. Her nipples were rosy, dark, the same color as her lips. With her hair sprawled out and her dark eyes focused, she looked like some kind of mythical creature, someone in a naughty kind of story.

I glided back down her body, my hands trailing her sides until they met the waistband of her shorts. I tugged them off and then the top that had bunched at her waist, revealing her completely to me. I wanted to treat her like fine china, but she'd proved to me she was made of titanium. I could write a dozen lyrics to the shape of her body; the way her hips curved and her hair rested around her in a dark halo. The rosy color of her lips, and the way they curved in pleasure when my mouth descended to right where she wanted me most.

38

HOLLIS

AND TO THINK, I'D THOUGHT MY SATIN LITTLE PAJAMA SET HAD been indecent. No, what Adam was currently doing in between my legs felt decadent in the most carnal of ways. I finally got it, I understood why sex was such a big deal.

But then again, was it like this with everyone? Because this felt like a Big Deal, like something that didn't happen with just anyone. I couldn't imagine letting anyone do what Adam was doing, but then again I couldn't really think beyond the hazy fog of lust that infiltrated my brain, robbing me of any deeper thought.

Strong hands gripped my thighs, spreading them wider. Adam looked up at me, and the motion rubbed his facial hair over my center, causing me to nearly buck right off the bed.

The tension inside of me was tightening, like something desperate to unravel. My body climbed a peak I wasn't familiar with, and I struggled to keep up as it happened quickly— everything happening all at once. I couldn't focus on anything, on anyone, except that uncoiling of pleasure.

Adam dipped down again, and I felt everything.

His tongue.

Inside of me.

Sweat prickled my brow as I threw my head back.

His fingers joined his mouth, stretching me and curling and I couldn't stop writhing on the bed. It was as if my body and my brain existed in two separate entities, because I lost all control. When his finger pressed firmly against my clit, my head lolled to the side and a moan left my mouth.

Later, I'd be almost embarrassed of the noises I'd made. But Adam had seemed encouraged.

When that tension snapped, when I came, everything uncoiled and my body fell back to the sheets as if I had just levitated.

He climbed back over me. "I don't have a condom," he said.

"I do."

He raised an eyebrow, and if I hadn't been totally spent, I'd have yanked him down so I could explore his face the way he'd explored my body.

"'By failing to prepare, you're preparing to fail,'" I recited.

He laughed, that dimple carving a small canyon in his cheek. I wanted to explore that canyon, to kiss him the way he'd kissed me. "Of course you have a condom."

I pointed at my bag on the back of the door. "Front pocket."

He left me for a moment and cool air rushed over my deliciously overheated body. I had never felt more relaxed, more spent. Like I had just been given a massage in places I didn't know needed it.

Adam was climbing over me seconds later, his towel discarded. I spread my legs and he settled between them. This was it, this was actually happening. I didn't think seventeen-year-old Hollis Vinke ever expected to have Adam in this way. I wanted to go back in time and leave her a message, letting her know that things would get better after Willy. I wanted to tell her how lucky she was, how Adam was even more amazing than she'd predicted.

But then half the pleasure of my time with Adam in the present was how unexpected it all was, how discovering all these little facets of him made him more than just some guy I sort of fantasized about. He was real, in the flesh, the only guy to live up to my childish dreams.

"Hollis," he said, his voice a whisper when he pressed his forehead against mine.

There was something immeasurably reverent about the way he said my name, like I had given him pleasure instead of the other way around. I was overcome with the urge to wrap my arms around him, to anchor him to me. I kissed the side of his face, his lips, his jaw, his ear. An ache bloomed from my chest. Tenderness, like a bruise I had pressed just to make sure it still ached. I closed my eyes, feeling an unexpected prick of moisture in them. Adam was still over me, but his breathing was ragged and I was overwhelmed with an emotion I wasn't able to name, an emotion that spread out from the ache in my chest.

I lifted my hips, feeling his erection immediately. I wanted to give him this, after all he'd given me, so I lifted my hips again until we made contact.

We moved in tandem, coming together over and over until that tension curled inside of me, and uncoiled once more. He was seconds behind me, his lips at my ear whispering words I couldn't make out when he met his release.

I'd never been so worn out—emotionally, physically, mentally. It was like my bones had been replaced with rubber, my brain with jelly and my heart...

Well, my heart was more tender, sore in places I couldn't soothe. And it was my heart that kept me awake with ache, long after Adam had kissed the side of my head and fallen asleep beside me.

If I thought having two orgasms and falling asleep beside the guy I had crushed on for forever would have allowed me to drift off to a deep slumber, well I was in for a surprise. Because I awoke so many times that night, glancing at the clock each time, expecting it to say a time later than it did.

I knew I was exhausted. I knew I wanted to sleep in. But I was so trapped in my mind that I simply couldn't.

It felt like I had barely drifted off to sleep when I woke to Adam's hand on my stomach, his arm draped over my waist. I probably could've ignored the press of his individual fingers and fallen back asleep because in a way it was soothing. But then I realized *why* it was so soothing. He was playing a song on my skin. Now and then, his thumb would tap lightly right by my belly button and his other fingers would take turns playing their beat. I pretended to be asleep for at least ten minutes while he created a song on my body.

"You're awake," he said, his voice hoarse.

"Yes." I was on my side, not facing him, but something about my body language had alerted him.

His fingers stilled and the bed dipped behind me as he rose up to look down. "You okay?"

I didn't know how to answer that. My body felt great, if a little sore. My brain was still as mushy as mashed potatoes. But deep down, in places that weren't in an anatomy and physiology textbook, I felt something akin to a hurricane. "I'm good," I said, as a compromise. This was not the time to tell him that I was fully falling in love with him. Because I most definitely was.

"We gotta get on the road soon," he said, and nuzzled my neck.

I closed my eyes. I wanted so desperately to give in to his touch, to fully embrace him and throw caution to the wind. I wanted that more than I could say, but when my feelings were in the turmoil they were I couldn't pretend that physical touch didn't affect me in a mental way.

"Yes, we do." I gave him a smile and sat up. There was no graceful way to walk across the room naked, I realized, but did it anyway.

"Are you sure you're okay?" Adam asked, grabbing the towel he'd left on the floor the night before. He wrapped it around his waist and approached me once I had my jeans and a bra on. I quickly yanked my sweater over the bra, feeling like I needed some kind of physical armor to cushion whatever blows he was unknowingly delivering to my heart.

But the thing was, he wasn't doing anything wrong. He was being gentle, respectful, thoughtful, and sincere. *I* was the one being weird. And I knew it, because I saw the way he looked me over like there was some kind of outward explanation to how cold I was acting.

"I'm fine," I said. "I think I have a migraine. I didn't have a soda before bed as usual."

That seemed to satisfy him somewhat, because he nodded. "Okay. Well, there should be a handful more in the fridge."

"I'll be back," I said with a smile that I knew didn't reach my eyes, ducking out of the room as soon as I could.

Frustration made my hands shake as I grabbed two cans of soda and retreated to the deck. It wasn't until I finished half of the one soda, the other cold can pressed to my forehead, before I felt like I could try to unpack my feelings.

"Hey grandma." Tori joined me, wrapped up in a robe with a cup of steaming coffee in her hands. At my look, she elaborated. "You went to bed earlier than my roommates go to bed." She took a long sip of her coffee and looked out over the fog-covered lake with me. "But then again, Adam retired early too. And neither of you left your room." One perfectly groomed eyebrow arched as she took me in. "Did you?"

I nodded and drained the rest of the can. I pulled the one I'd been holding to my forehead away and cracked the top of it.

"Uh oh," she said. "You're pretty quiet. I mean, you're often quiet, but something else is going on. Was it bad? Oh, no, honey." Instead of sounding patronizing, Tori sounded like she was actually concerned.

"I don't know how I feel. I mean, last night was great. Really great. But then when it was done, the reality sank in."

"Hollis." She brushed hair from my shoulders. "Whatever happened between you *was* the reality." She tapped my forehead. "Whatever got up in here, that's feeling. Which is very real, too, but you have to remember that last night wasn't one of your books—it was you and it was Adam and whatever feelings you've got as a result can be figured out."

I wished I had a pad of paper so I could sort through my thoughts in a more tangible way. I sighed and the frustration settled firmer in my head.

"You love him, don't you?"

It was different when it was all in my head. But when the words were said, when they were out in the open, it meant that everything *was* real. This wasn't a fantasy. My feelings weren't fleeting. They were solid. They were real.

"Yeah." Why did that make me want to cry?

"Aww, Hols. You knew this could happen. I mean, it probably happened way back in middle school."

"Maybe." I took a deep chug of my diet soda. "But even then, it was just schoolgirl feelings. They weren't from actually knowing him."

"And now you do and you like him even more than you expected to."

"Yeah."

"Is that a bad thing, though?" She leaned against me, our arms draped over the railing. "To find out the guy you have feelings for is even better than whatever fairytale you'd subscribed to in your head?"

"Maybe if my feelings weren't significantly further along than his." I dropped my head to my free hand. "He just got over the hurdle of not hating me."

"Whatever. He looks at you like you're a sandwich."

"A sandwich?"

"Guys love sandwiches." She took a long drink of her coffee. "Oh, I've got a few photos on my phone from the hike. I'm going to upload them later today and tag you guys."

"All right."

"Think your folks are going to amend your trust fund?"

"Probably not," I said, but it was moot anyway. Since my outburst, I had more or less resigned myself to the fact that the trust fund wasn't going to come through, that I'd have to do the LSAT or face the disappointment and disdain from them. And I didn't want to do the LSAT. I wanted to control where my life went after college. I certainly wasn't willing to go all the way to an engagement with Adam just to satisfy the terms of the trust. No, if anything further happened with Adam, it needed to be real, like everything else. I didn't want him to feel obligated to stay with me anymore. I only wanted him to stay if that was what he wanted to do. "It is what it is. I think I need to have a very frank talk with my parents about their expectations and mine. And," I said with a sigh, "I need to have a talk with Adam too."

"But this is why I don't do the whole relationship thing. Relationships are messy."

"But ours is fake, it shouldn't be messy."

"It's *not* fake, and that's why it's messy. You keep trying to shove it into a neat little box, pretending it's something you can stack away neatly in your mind, but you can't."

What she said made sense. I was fond of neat and orderly and expected. It was why I had chosen to move in with Navy, because she was neat and tidy but also more spontaneous and more compassionate than I was; she was someone I wanted to learn from. "We still haven't talked about high school, and what happened, and how it happened." It was the elephant in the room, that loomed over every fight we'd had—though those had been few and far between lately.

"What are you so afraid of, bringing it up?"

"That bringing it up will remind him of all the reasons he doesn't like me after all."

The back door opened, causing us both to turn. Keane stepped out, still in pajamas, his face white. He held his phone in his hands, and it shook as his entire body trembled. "We need to go back. Now."

39

ADAM

THE MOMENT YOUR WORLD FALLS APART AROUND YOU DOESN'T
happen in an instant. It happens in steps, just like the ensuing
stages of grief. The moment is a drop in the water, but it's the
ripples it creates, too.

After Hollis left the room, I checked my phone in the bag of
rice, but it was no use—it was likely permanently fucked. And as
I set it back into my bag, my scalp prickled in keen awareness
that something was wrong.

It started with the yelp across the house, loud enough to hear
in my room. And the noise from the scrambling of frantic
footsteps, the creak of the back door sliding open and the gasps
that followed whatever the muffled voices had said.

I was frozen, my shirt in my hands, when those same
footsteps made their way to my door. The anticipation that
wrapped me up was suffocating and I wanted the words one
way or another. Like a bandage being ripped off, I wanted the
bad news at once.

"Adam," Keane said. I could see it on his face, the white

cheeks and the wide eyes. His phone was in his hands, and it clattered to the floor. He didn't even look at it.

"It's Gram, isn't it?" I asked, but the words sounded underwater. My whole body shuddered in acute awareness. There was no disbelief, there was acceptance because I had already known—and it was the acceptance that hurt. I *believed* it. I knew, I fucking knew, and I could hardly swallow around the rock in my throat. It felt like my ribs were caging my lungs in, the sharp edges of my bone pricking them, because I took a deep breath in and got nothing but deep, untouchable pain.

Keane could only nod, his eyes closing briefly.

"We need to get back." Casey. Fuck. She was alone. Well, not alone. But she didn't have any family. I knew I was trying to process this, but my brain was going a hundred miles a minute. I couldn't succumb to my grief. I shoved it to the side, needing to focus on what needed to be done.

"I know. The girls are getting ready."

I nodded, trying to swallow around the lump again. I stared around the bedroom, trying to make sense of what I needed to do. "I need to call Caleb."

"I will. What's his number?"

I didn't even argue with him. Maybe I could pretend it'd be better coming from me, but how *much* better could it fucking be? "I don't know," I said, fists coming to my forehead. "I have no fucking clue. It's on my phone." I picked up the bag it was in, belatedly remembering that my phone wouldn't turn on. "Fuck!" I yelled, throwing the bag across the room. My hands shook, so I curled them into fists to keep myself together.

"Don't worry about this, Adam. I'll figure it out. Get your stuff, just get your things."

I felt rather than saw him leave the room, and in the quiet I sank to the bed, fists pressed to my eyes as the first bits of moisture stung. My jaw quivered, my body quaked, but the sound of footsteps approaching sobered me. Lifting my head, I saw from the feet alone that it was Hollis. I couldn't deal with this right now. Whatever *this* was, I couldn't fucking deal.

"Hey," she said.

I couldn't lift my head the rest of the way to actually meet her eyes. This moment was the most vulnerable of my life, and the last thing I needed was for her to see me fall apart. "We need to go," I said, grabbing my bag and zipping it up with more force than necessary. She adjusted her weight from one foot to the other, as if she was trying to decide where to move.

"I know. Can I help you with anything?"

"No." I picked up the bag and moved toward the door with my head down. At the last second, she pressed a hand to my chest, halting me.

"I'm so very sorry, Adam," she said, her voice hushed. She was sincere and gentle, and I didn't want it. I just wanted to get home, to be with Casey, and to be able to grieve without an audience.

I moved around her hand, out of the door to her car which was already running and waiting.

"I got ahold of your brother. He's going to come this week. And Casey's with my mom at the hospital," Keane said once we'd climbed in the car. I nodded and turned to gaze out of the window. Hollis and Tori were in the driveway embracing. Tori placed her hands on either side of Hollis's head and said something to her, to which Hollis nodded mutely. "Do you want to go to the hospital or home?"

"Home." It was no question. Gram wasn't at the hospital anymore, not in spirit anyway. I wasn't grieving her body, I was grieving the essence of who she was. After our mom had died, that hospital smell had lingered so long that if I concentrated hard enough, my memories would flood back and break me down with all five senses: the sight of the pink leaving her skin, the sound of her monitor giving a deafening solid tone, the touch of her hands going colder, the smell of antiseptic, and the taste of bile coming up.

I didn't want to have a breakdown in Hollis's car. I had to think about something. Anything else.

"Anyone else you want me to text?" Keane asked beside me as Hollis and Tori parted and Hollis made her way toward the car.

"Bobby."

"Lead singer Bobby?"

I gave one nod. "He's on Facebook."

"What do you want me to tell him."

Navy exited the house, meeting Hollis in the driveway. "Tell him to find a new band member."

"R-right now?"

I nodded again. Maybe it didn't make sense, but it felt easier to have Keane tell Bobby, who would tell the others. I was sure that everyone knew it anyway, but I didn't know how long I'd be wrapped in a bubble and telling Bobby and the others didn't need to wait. "Casey needs me." I turned to him. "I'm not going back." I couldn't even summon up any grief over admitting the band would need to go on without me. Gram had been my everything—my confidant, my protector, my shelter, my whole fucking heart. Everything else was just noise.

"Tell him my gram died. He'll understand. I don't want to continue to delay the inevitable."

Keane stared back at me before agreeing, his thumbs flying across the screen.

40

HOLLIS

It had been two days since we'd returned from our trip. Two days since Adam's grandmother had died. Two days since he'd last responded to my messages. I knew, from Keane, that he'd gotten a new phone. But he hadn't changed his number.

Which is why I had volunteered to bring the casserole Navy had made for Adam and Casey, over to their house.

Nerves were ever present as I pulled into the driveway, beside a car I didn't recognize. I stared up at the house for a moment, wondering if coming here was wise. We hadn't spoken since the cabin, not even a word since we'd walked out the door. I had given him his space initially, hadn't pressed him when he didn't respond to my messages. But I cared about him. I really did. I knew he was hurting and I didn't want him to be alone with that hurt.

The man that answered the door looked remarkably like Adam, but a couple years older, with more facial hair and glasses. "Who are you?" he asked.

"Uh..."

"That's Hollis." Casey appeared beside him and reached for me. I barely had a moment to adjust the casserole to my side before she'd wrapped her arms around my middle and pressed her face to my shoulder.

Crap. I wasn't accustomed to grief like this. I'd been fortunate enough to never lose anyone I was close to. Casey had lost so much—Adam too—in so few years. I wrapped my arm around her waist and held her close.

"Hollis?" The man before me lifted an eyebrow, but still hadn't stepped aside for me to enter. It had taken a minute, but I recognized him as Adam's older brother.

"She's Adam's girlfriend, Caleb."

"Then who..."

"*That* girl is just a friend. Come on, Hollis."

Which girl? The thought entered my mind before I could stop it. The living room was empty save for a dozen flower arrangements. "Where's Adam?" I asked her as I put the casserole in the fridge.

"He's out back." She looked over her shoulder and turned back to me. "He's smoking. He doesn't do that."

I looked Casey over, noting the dark circles under her eyes, the pallor of her skin. "How are you doing?" I asked, realizing I should have asked that minutes ago.

Casey lifted a shoulder, her eyes downcast. "It isn't real yet."

"I'm sure it isn't." I put my arm around her and she led me back to the living room where Caleb, who I figured was Casey and Adam's older brother, was assembling a piece of furniture. "I'm Hollis." I held a hand out in an introduction.

Caleb looked at my hand and then my face. "Yeah, Case said that."

I tucked my hand in the back pocket of my jeans. "I'm very sorry about your grandmother. I know she was well-loved."

"Right." He turned his attention back to the furniture and Casey gave me a shrug and an eye-roll. She grabbed my hand

and pulled me back out the front door. At first, I thought she was signaling for me to leave, but then she plopped down on a chair on the porch and gestured for me to take the other one.

"Adam's not doing great." She picked at the flaking paint and chanced a glance at me. "He's kind of being a dick."

"I'm sorry to hear that. I'm so sorry for all of you." I was so awkward with grief, but I wanted to be better. "Is there anything I can do to help you?"

"Make Adam stop being a dick." She leaned in, tucking her loose hair behind her ears. "He has a girl here."

The very last thing I needed to be thinking about was myself, but I couldn't help it. Those five words had the effect of a sucker punch and I leaned toward her in order to hold my stomach with my arms, to still my instant shake. "He does?" My voice sounded squeaky.

"Yeah, but I don't think she's that kind of girl. You know, like you are."

But I didn't know what she meant, and it felt like I was crossing the line having Adam's sister disclose what Adam was doing.

"Her name's Sarah."

Recognition and sadness settled together in my chest, simultaneously. This was the ex that he'd mentioned before. The one from Colorado, who knew Adam in a way I had only hoped to.

"Oh." I stared hard at the rose bush blooming off the side of the porch, focusing on the shape of the petals, the thorns along the stems. But it was like a foghorn in my brain:

Sarah is here.

Adam has avoided you because he has the person he really wants.

"I should probably go," I said, when it got too overwhelming. Casey stirred beside me, and I felt guilty for worrying about my feelings when she had so many more life-altering things happening. I closed my eyes, blinking back the burn, and turned to her. "What if I take you out for burgers later? I know you're kind of a burger fanatic." I looked back at the house. "Get you a breather."

"That sounds great." She practically vibrated in her seat. "Tonight?"

"Yep." I stood, wiped my hands on my jeans, and gave her a hug. "I'm going to say hi to your brother and then I'll take off."

"Come on," Casey said, waving to me to follow her to the back door.

I calmed my unsteady heart by telling myself to be strong. I could be strong. And then I followed her.

41

ADAM

HOW DID PEOPLE WALK AROUND JUST CARRYING THEIR GRIEF LIKE it didn't bother them? How did they smile without feeling it tug the smile, how did they laugh without acknowledging the guilt that came from the luck to be able to laugh? How did they love again, how did they trust and how did they do something as essential as sleep when there was nothing good waiting for them when they woke?

Maybe that last part was melodramatic. But the days had run together after Gram died. The first night, it had been me up late with Casey as she'd cried herself to sleep, with my head resting on her mattress so that I'd wake if she did. We didn't stray too far from each other for the first day or so, and then Caleb had shown up and, well, I had checked the fuck out. Caleb was responsible in the practical ways, so I left him to handle the funeral arrangements, to arrange a meeting with Gram's attorney.

Not once had we heard from our father. Not that it was a

surprise. But we three were an island in the center of a hurricane, and our last tether in the world was MIA. As usual.

Shortly after Caleb had arrived, so had Bobby and Sarah. Both of them uninvited. I might have been an asshole to them, but they'd stuck. We didn't talk, we just sat outside. Smoking— God, how I had missed it—and staying outside of the house in general.

Each time Caleb made a comment about how much shit he was dealing with alone, I wanted to tell him to grow the fuck up. But I was the one who'd checked out. How in the hell had I thought I could take care of my sister, when I couldn't even be present enough to handle Gram's affairs?

I flicked the cigarette in the old glass bowl and sighed.

"Ready to talk now?" Sarah asked.

"There's nothing to say."

"I thought you hated lying."

I gave her a look meant to cut her in half but she didn't take it.

"I know you're pissed at the world and upset and you've got every right to be—trust me. But maybe, if you talk about it, it'll get easier."

"I'm not going to talk to you about it." I stubbed out the cigarette and eyed the inside of the pack. I bought one pack, promising myself not to buy a second. I'd give myself enough time to polish off the cigarettes I had left, and then I'd get my life back together and figure things out. I didn't know why a pack of cigarettes was my timeline for everything, but it was the first promise I had made to myself in several days.

I fished my phone out of my pocket, knowing full well it was rude. But I didn't want to talk to Bobby or Sarah. I wanted to go back to two days ago, when I had been in the mountains with Hollis.

Fuck. Even *thinking* her name made me hurt. I wanted to be the person who could confide in their girlfriend, who could rely on her to tell me it would be okay. Even if it was a lie, it was the one lie I could do with. But something was nagging in my brain. We didn't figure things out after we'd had sex. And she'd acted so weirdly anyway—like she'd regretted it, maybe?

I hadn't finished setting up my new phone, so I had to download all my apps all over again. I had put it off since getting the phone—for obvious reasons—but with Sarah breathing down my neck, I needed the distraction. I logged into Facebook, seeing the explosion of notifications. Most of them were condolences, which I ignored for the time being. But what caught my eye were the photos I had been tagged in. I clicked on one, a portrait of my arms looped around Hollis's shoulders as we faced each other and her head tilted so she gazed up at me. Her hair was windswept and pink kissed her cheeks and nose and lips. She looked beautiful.

But this is what she'd posted? I scrolled through her feed, looking for something, anything, that mentioned me or my gram and nothing did. It was...blank. Navy had reposted Gram's obituary, but Hollis had done nothing.

"Why are you making that face?"

I glared at Sarah. She was always trying to bury her nose into my shit. "Can you mind your own business for even five minutes?"

"Nope." The chair creaked as she leaned over, looking over my shoulder at the phone. "Is that Hollis?" At my look, she held up her hands in surrender. "Dude, I've seen her all over your feed lately—she's pretty recognizable."

"I'm *not* talking to you about this."

"Why? Because I'm your ex-girlfriend?"

"No, because you're my *friend*, about to be ex-friend if you don't butt out."

"Geez." She whistled and lit another cigarette. "I get it, you're sad right now. But you've obviously got a lot of shit on your mind. You can dump it onto my lap if you want."

"If I wanted to, I'd have done it. I don't want to, so stop picking my brain, thanks." I glanced once more at Hollis's photo before closing my phone and putting it back into my pocket. I stared into the forest, watching the old pines in the back of the property sway to and fro in the light wind.

"Is it because I'm a girl? Is that why you can't talk to me?"

"It's because I don't want to talk about it, okay?"

"Man, she's got you up in knots." Sarah chuckled, ignoring every pissed off look I leveled at her. "I'd like to meet her."

"No, you wouldn't." But there was no conviction in my voice. Sarah probably would actually like Hollis. Though, personality-wise, they were polar opposites, they were both driven and steadfast.

I ground my teeth together and grabbed a second cigarette. I needed to space these out more if I wanted to have any left by tomorrow. I knew that if I burned through all my cigarettes before then, I wouldn't be able to get my shit together enough to do what needed to be done. I wanted to give myself more time to wallow, more time to sit outside alone with my thoughts. That is, if Sarah would leave me *alone.* Bobby spent most of his time at the hotel they were staying at in town so he could work remotely, leaving Sarah to bum around at my house.

I didn't want to be that asshole who compared women, but it was impossible not to. Whatever fond feelings I had held for Sarah, the timing of her visit had proved that those feelings resided firmly in the friendly category. Because when I looked at her, there was nothing. No instant fire, not even a spark.

When I looked at Hollis on the other hand, it was as if every atom of my body was fine-tuned to hers. Like every system that kept my legs moving and my heart beating and my lungs taking in oxygen worked in time just to bring me to her. It was a big feeling to have, a feeling that I couldn't escape. I had never felt anything like that with Sarah or anyone else. Hollis was big and scary feelings, and right now, and in the midst of my other feelings, the ones for her were inconvenient.

She'd texted me, asking how I was. And before I'd logged into my social media, I was tempted to reply. I wanted her here, even if just to look at her. But the fact that she hadn't posted anything remotely about my grandmother burred under my skin. And because I'd already approached that slippery slope of second-guessing everything, it was easy for me to wonder if this still wasn't real for her.

What had transpired between us over the last week had been anything but fake, for me. We'd completely failed at being fake, sliding into a groove together that felt natural and not forced. Had her dad really gotten under her skin? I remembered what her friends said on the hike. *It took a week for her to tell me you guys had kissed.*

Was she embarrassed by me? I hadn't wondered it at the time when her dad had said it, but her being silent on social media—where everyone could see—and only communicating with me privately was reminiscent of that stupid fucking high school party. I hated harping on it, but it was the only way I had known her before the last few weeks. Had this just been her pretending all over again?

The rational part of me was telling me to shut the fuck up. But when you were already hurting, it was easy to distract yourself with other ways to self-destruct.

"Jesus Christ," Sarah said, blowing smoke out of the side of her mouth. "Are you just going to keep moping or talk about things?"

"I didn't ask you to come here."

"No, you didn't. Because you don't like to lean on anyone. Adam can do it, Adam will do it. That's your attitude. It's okay to lean, you know. We can keep you standing."

"I don't need you here." If I thought about it, I might feel bad for speaking so bluntly to Sarah. But everything I said was true.

"Okay. I'm going to go on a little walk then."

"It's three-o-clock in the afternoon," I said.

"Yeah. It's three. People go on walks at three. And four. And five. Do you know what people also do from time to time? Shower. Maybe you could work on that while I'm gone."

I scoffed at her turning back. The silence would be a nice reprieve.

"Adam," Casey said from the doorway.

Fuck. I turned, the cigarette hanging out of my mouth. I knew Casey hated them. "What's up?" I tried to muster up some kind of feeling in my voice for her, because I knew what a lousy brother I'd been the last few days.

"Hollis is here. Are you going to talk to her or…"

"Seriously?" I said to no one, stubbing out the cigarette angrily.

"Hey." Her voice was soft. I didn't want to look at her, not after the bullshit on social media. I didn't want to look at her and ache, because I knew I would. I'd had enough to last me through this week, this month, hell, this lifetime.

"What's going on?" I asked, staring into the trees. I was glad Sarah wasn't here for this, because the last thing I needed was someone to yell at me for bad manners or whatever.

"I've been messaging you. But I understand if you need space to grieve. I'm so sorry. I didn't say it enough on the drive home." Her shadow loomed from behind me, casting out in front of me, getting smaller and smaller as she got closer.

I snapped the cover to my cigarette carton. "Yeah, I saw. Been busy."

"I know. And I don't want you to feel obligated to reply or anything."

"I don't."

She was silent for a moment. "Okay." It was two syllables, but the hurt in them slid through my own defenses.

Fuck. Shit. Balls.

I turned, looking at her for the first time in a few days. Taking her in, I realized that those days had felt like weeks. I resented that I had such an immediate reaction, that I wanted her more than I had the last time I saw her. She wore jeans and a sweater, looking as casual as she had up in the mountains. I liked that she hadn't fussed with her appearance.

I shook my head to rid myself of any thoughts about things I liked about her. "Why are you here, Hollis?"

Her mouth opened and her eyebrows drew together before she snapped her mouth shut again.

"Speaking of obligations," I said when she didn't answer me. "I saw you didn't feel obligated to post anything on Facebook. I mean, besides the photo of us. Nice."

"What?"

"Is this whole ruse over and done with? Is that what's going on? Did your mom and dad give in and give you what you wanted?"

"No...I..."

"And now you're done with me—at least the parts that don't fit your aesthetic."

"What are you even talking about?"

I stood, not wanting to stay seated when my body was burning up as much as it was. "You were the one so intent on getting photos up on Facebook, so everyone could see how coupled up we are. But the moment real life strikes—like Gram fucking dying—that doesn't fit into your neat and tidy life, right?"

"Whoa." She held up her hands—in surrender or to calm me down, I couldn't tell. Maybe both. "First of all, I texted you. I tried calling a couple times. But your lack of response made me believe you didn't want me to keep bugging you."

"Right, it's easy for you to talk to me in private. But it's not easy for you to post about me on your feed unless it helps you out in some way, right? Nice timing, by the way, with those photos from the weekend."

"I didn't post those. Tori did. And she tagged me."

"Oh. Tori did that? I guess that checks out. In fact, I don't think you've posted one single thing with us together. Everyone else has, though."

"I don't understand why you're so upset with me. Because I didn't post something about your grandmother on my Facebook, Adam? Really?"

"You didn't tell your friends we'd even kissed, for a week. Admit it—you're embarrassed by me."

Her mouth made an O. "Are you serious right now?"

"Dead serious." I wanted another cigarette, but my dwindling pack stopped me. "I don't know why you even came."

"Neither do I." Her eyes glistened. "We've talked about this, Adam. I don't put things that matter up for public consumption. It's just social media; it doesn't matter."

"It did when we were trying to prove we were dating."

"It was fake. None of it was real."

"So you couldn't fake care about my gram? Or me?"

"No. I couldn't. Because I *did* care. I cared about your gram. I cared about your sister. I cared about you. I still care, Adam. More than I want to."

I held up my hands. "Please, don't care about me if it inconveniences you. You just don't want your parents to see. Because they were right, you're embarrassed. Just like you were back in high school."

"I was never embarrassed by you in high school. I was *shy*. Why do you think I slipped you that note? Why do you think I never spoke to you until that party?"

Here we go. That night was coming to the surface, finally. "That fucking party. When you told me you weren't like the rest of them. But then when that asshole laid into me, you stayed silent. You didn't use your voice."

360

"You had abandoned me, while I was soaked in beer and freezing."

"I didn't abandon you. I went into the house to get Tori."

"And then got distracted by another girl on the stairs."

I squinted, remembering Kate cornering me. "I wasn't distracted by her. Not in the way you mean."

"She was showing you her rose tattoo."

"Yeah, so?"

"That's why I thought you were a bad boy. That's why it was hard for me to believe you'd ever been sincerely interested in me. Because the moment another girl snagged your attention, you'd forgotten all about me."

That's why she'd stayed silent when the dickheads started ragging on me? "You were jealous?"

"Yes. Of course I was, Adam. I liked you. A lot. You know that now. But mostly, I was freezing and wanted to go home."

"But I found Tori and Keane, sent them after you."

She blinked, those wide eyes going soft for a moment, like that was a fact she hadn't been made aware of until now. "And then you forgot about me. Or, I thought you had forgotten about me."

"I didn't forget about you. I got sidelined on my way down the stairs. And then people swarmed. When I looked up and saw you, you didn't do anything. After we'd talked about my opinion of you, and you'd tried to tell me you were your own person, not just another person in the crowd. But when it mattered, you just shrank away."

She was quiet for a moment, her hands locked together in front of her. "I should have said something. I probably wouldn't have been able to stop them, but maybe if I had stood up for you they might've let it go. But let me be clear, Adam. I have never been embarrassed by you." She hugged her middle. "When you and I started dating, I was giddy. When I say I had a crush on you, I mean just you." She looked off to the side and the light from the citronella candle glittered in her eye. "I texted you, because I am a private person. That's why I leave little sticky notes for people. I don't need people online to see my feelings for anyone else. That's why I never put up my time from Bolivia on social media. I don't care what anyone else thinks about what matters to me. I don't tell anyone what matters unless I care about them." She bit her lip. "And I care about you. I do. I'm sorry you think I don't."

I didn't know how to respond to that. She'd taken the wind out of my sails, and any bit of anger I had harbored for her evaporated.

"You told me I didn't use my voice in high school; that my silence was me being complicit in what they did to you. And you know what, you're right. I didn't do right by you at that party, or after. After high school, I spent most of my summers in other countries. Using my voice, my time, my energy to do the things that mattered to me. Social media has never mattered to me. It's for everyone else—which is why it was important to have evidence of us being together on there. But then, at least for me, I got confused where fake us ended and real us began."

Squaring her shoulders, she took a deep breath and looked back at me. Her eyes were warm, her body language was open. "I didn't tell everyone about kissing you because it was private. It meant something to me. Tori is my best friend, but I don't confide my feelings to her until I'm ready to discuss them. I'm certainly not going to confide my feelings to a social media network made up of people who view the most important moments of my life as disposable content."

She had told me this before. Her feeds contained benign posts, photos of her favorite diet soda, her favorite muffins from her favorite bakery. It was nice, but it wasn't deep enough to break the surface, to really know Hollis.

I finally realized what a petty mother fucker I was, to get

mad at her over fucking social media bullshit. I had been hurting and had decided that hurting Hollis was my only outlet.

"I don't like bringing this up, especially now. But I hope you understand that sex is something I don't do with just anyone. And if I was embarrassed by you, that night wouldn't have happened. I am going to give you the benefit of the doubt that you don't really think I'm embarrassed by you, especially after what happened. I'm not familiar with the kind of grief you're experiencing, but I imagine that it's the reason you're acting like this. I'm sorry you're hurting, Adam, I really am. But you don't get to take it out on me unless I deserve it. And I know enough to know that I don't, not right now."

I really needed that cigarette. I knew I should apologize, to admit how wrong I was. I picked up the cigarette pack and shook it. When I turned around, Hollis was gone.

42

HOLLIS

CASEY SAT ACROSS FROM ME, CHEWING A MOUTHFUL OF BURGER AS she made moaning sounds. "This is so good."

I smiled, but my burger sat before me untouched. "Here," I said, pushing it toward her. "I'm not hungry."

And I wasn't. After leaving Adam's house, I had gone home and hopped online, checking out the photos Tori had posted of Adam and me and our hike and oh, how I had ached. The photos themselves were frame-worthy, with the beautiful peaks behind us and our pink ears and noses and big, big smiles. Sincere smiles. They stood in stark contrast to any photo of myself in my parents' house—I looked free and happy in the ones Tori had taken. It felt like a lifetime ago, really, two entirely different people existed in those photos. And those photos had set Adam off. How could he doubt the sincerity of our expressions in these photos?

I tried to hide that my talk with him was bothering me. I had taken Casey out for her, not for me. And I would make sure our dinner was an Adam-less time.

"It's been casseroles or cereal and I'm super over it." She took a long sip of soda and sat back in the booth, her eyes the lightest I'd seen since I'd arrived at her house earlier that day.

"I can imagine," I said. "Day in and day out, that'd get old really fast."

"It is. Adam's not cooking and Caleb's hopeless in the kitchen. He's burnt every piece of toast he's made. Some doctor he's gonna be."

"Is that what he's going to school for?"

"I guess," she said. "He's been in school for a long time. Feels like forever." She took another bite and seemed thoughtful for a moment. "It's weird having him at the house. I mean, Adam is moody and can be a dick but Caleb is just a jerk. You met him today. He didn't even say hi to you."

Neither does Adam, I thought to myself. "Everyone grieves differently," I kindly reminded her. "Some people are angry for a long time, but you shouldn't let that affect you. They'll come around."

"I dunno. Adam's being weird. That girl has been at the house all the time, and they just sit outside smoking."

My heart twisted and I clasped my hands in my lap under the table, hating that it bothered me so much. He'd shoved me away in favor of someone else. "I think most of us have someone we rely on, to vent to. Maybe that's who she is for him."

Casey didn't look convinced. "I dunno," she said again. "I just know that he's not the same. You should talk to him again. Maybe it'll get through his thick skull."

"I should," I agreed, not wanting to tell her I couldn't. He was hurting, and I didn't want to make it worse.

"He thinks you're beautiful, you know."

The change in subject gave me whiplash. "Uh..."

"The last time we saw Gram, before you guys left for the weekend, that's what he said to her. She asked about you and he said you were beautiful." Casey's eyes were all too knowing. It was as if she'd looked inside and seen just what I needed to lighten my own heartache a little.

"Okay," I said, not knowing how to respond.

"The only thing he's said about Sarah is that she's a friend. He said it to her, too, in front of us. Adam doesn't like lying."

"Right."

"But you're beautiful," she repeated. She picked up my burger and took a big bite. After chewing for some time she looked up at me. "When I was in fifth grade, there were these girls who were super mean. Like bullies, kinda. I hated them. They made fun of me for having messy hair. But Gram's hands were pretty bad with arthritis and I never asked her to help with it."

I nodded, following along with her story.

"But something that super hurt was when I found out one of my best friends was making fun of me too. She never said it to me, but someone else told me that she started a rumor I had lice. When I asked her, she admitted it."

"That must have been hard." Poor Casey. With no mother and no other female influences in her life, she must have had a tough time the last few years.

"It was. But Gram told me that she was worthless." She took another bite and chewed for a minute. "You know what Gram said to me a bunch of the time?"

"What would she say?"

"That if you wanted to know what someone really thought of you, you'd just have to hear what they said about you when you weren't around." She sipped her soda and set the burger down. "If someone talks bad about me when I can't hear them, I don't want them as a friend anyway. Right?"

I nodded, thinking how it was such a simple but true statement.

"And when you're not around, Adam says you're beautiful.

And smart." She lifted a shoulder. "He likes you. Sarah's just a friend."

He'd said I was beautiful before the cabin trip, I knew that much. When I thought he was easing out of his hate, he'd already told his grandmother I was beautiful. I'd be lying if I said it didn't touch me. It did. And for the first time in the last two days, I felt a bit better.

When I brought Casey back home with a bag of burgers for her brothers, I stayed in the car when she got out. She motioned for me to follow her, and before I could talk myself out of it, I grabbed my purse and followed her. But I wasn't on a mission to see Adam—no, I wanted to give him some space. Instead, I pulled a few things from my purse and set to work, enlisting Casey's help.

I walked back to my car, stopping when I saw a shadow slip from the trees.

She wore all black, except a red leather jacket that had that lived-in look, worn in the shoulders and the cuffs. The red glow of her cigarette was all I could see for a minute until she approached, the floodlight illuminating her from the feet up. Her hair was blonde—ice blond—and her lips red. She had a kind of rock-and-roll vibe to her, from the multiple silver chains she wore to the dozens of bangles along one arm. As she came closer, I saw the ends of her hair looked like she'd dipped them in red coloring.

I held the handle on the door of my car, knowing exactly who she was.

"You're Hollis," she said, smoke covering her face for a minute. When the fog cleared, her bright blue eyes scrutinized me.

"You're Sarah?" I climbed in, hoping I could get out of here before it was too late.

Nodding, she stepped up to my car.

"Hey," she said, reaching a hand through the window. I

shook it, marveling at the dozens of rings on her fingers. "Wanna go for a ride?"

She lifted her chin at my car and took a final puff before rubbing the end along the concrete and tossing it in the trash that waited by the curb for the trash pickup the following day.

"Uh…" Was this even a good idea? Adam and I hadn't left things on the best note, and I wasn't sure if spending more time with Sarah would help or hinder our relationship going forward. But because *yes* was my most used word, I hit the unlock on the door.

"Cool. I need to get out of there for a minute." Her perfume was sultry and warm and filled up my car instantly. "Whatcha listening to?" She cranked up the radio.

It was so surreal, having Sarah in my car fiddling with all the controls. "Where did you want to go?"

She paused fiddling with the heater to side eye me. "I dunno. You live in this town, I don't."

"Are you hungry?" I suspected there'd be a conversation in store for the both of us and maybe having a meal would settle the unease in my stomach.

"Yeah. What do you have for diner food here that's still open?"

Half an hour later we were seated in a booth facing each other. As the silence between us grew, I tried to think about how I had ended up here, facing off against one of Adam's real girlfriends.

Ex-girlfriend, I added.

She was glamorous in a way that looked effortless. She had round sunglasses pushed up in her hair, and though it was messy, it looked like she'd just rode in after spending the day at the beach. Her skin was bronzed and glowed and her eyelashes were long and dramatic. She picked up her napkin and spat her gum in it, dropping it on the table, while I unfolded mine and laid it across my lap. I wondered why she asked to go for a ride. I shouldn't have suggested food, but I hadn't actually eaten while I was with Casey so maybe I should try to choke something down. She set the menu down and met my gaze. Her eyes were so vivid it was intimidating, and I struggled to maintain eye contact. She opened her mouth and I braced myself for whatever she was going to say.

"Whatcha gonna order?"

Well, that was much milder than I had expected. "The vegetarian skillet. You?"

"I'm debating between the burger and fries or the country fried steak." She pursed her lips. "I usually order a burger and fries because that's hard to fuck up, but a fried steak sounds good too."

I always ordered the same thing. I was boring in that way. "I haven't tried their steak but I hear their burgers are good."

"You a vegetarian?" She had an accent that I couldn't immediately place—something I didn't often hear around here.

"No. I just like the vegetarian skillet."

"How about Adam?" she asked.

So, she was just going to jump to the point then. "How about him…"

"He's miserable right now."

"I know." I knew I sounded prickly and I knew my body language echoed it, but nothing Sarah had said so far gave cause for me to be like this. "I went by earlier today and talked to him."

"You did? I've been there all day. Didn't see you."

I was trying to figure out what her game was. "Yes. This afternoon."

"Oh, I went for a walk." She dunked her straw into her glass, pushing it down and watching it rise back up to the top. "Adam has been abandoned a lot, you know."

I didn't know, so I said nothing.

"First it was his mom, though that wasn't her fault. But her death was the catalyst for everything else: his dad leaving, his brother taking off." She waved her hand like she was impatient with herself, even though she was speaking bluntly and not meandering through the conversation at all. "Yeah, his brother is technically at school, but there are good schools closer than the school he's at."

This was all mostly news to me. I mean, I knew Adam's dad hadn't been in the picture ever since his mom had died. But I didn't really know about his brother because Adam never spoke about him.

"But Adam is a good guy. He cares deeply, even if he doesn't talk about it."

The waitress interrupted us to take our orders. Sarah complimented the waitress's purple hair and they had a moment to talk about hair dye and how quickly the fun colors faded.

"So, I'm asking you not to abandon him."

"Well, you sure cut to the chase." I took a long drink of water. "I wasn't planning on it."

"Adam didn't ask Bobby or me to come, by the way. But Bobby knows about Adam—which is how I know about Adam."

I assumed she knew all of this because he'd confided in her. And, as if she read my mind, she continued.

"Adam doesn't talk about his feelings unless he's drunk, pretty much. That's how Bobby knows." She pushed her hair away from her face as she leaned across the table. "I'm telling you this because I care about Adam, but not in the same way you do. So, if you've got claws for me, why don't you retract them?"

I held my palms up. "No claws." She was giving me a lot to think about.

"Adam's signature move is to push people away when the feelings get too overwhelming. You know what Bobby told me?"

I shook my head.

"That within ten minutes of Adam finding out about his gram dying, he let the band know he wouldn't be returning. Sure, it had been a question—a big fat maybe—but in Adam's most overwhelming moment, he pushed us all away. He cut us off. So, what did Bobby and I do? We came to Idaho, to be here for him. He'll say he doesn't want us here, but as I've told him a hundred times before, we're the family he got to choose. And band or not, we'll be here for him."

I twisted the napkin in my lap. "I'm glad he has you all, then."

"He'll try to push you away too. It's easier for him to believe he pushes people away than that they abandon him. Both hurt, but if he has control then he believes he hurts less."

"I wasn't planning on giving up on him. We had a mild argument, but I don't think it's anything we can't come back from. I'm choosing to believe that he's hurting and that's why he's acting out."

I thought of how he'd tried to push me away that afternoon. Deep in my gut, I felt that he knew he was being unreasonable and irrational. I had forced myself to remain calm, to take his barbs and explain my side with care. What Sarah was saying made sense; Adam was trying to push me away before I could hurt him.

"You're a more patient woman than I was." She leaned back against the booth, regarding me. "I pushed him too hard to open up. If you haven't gathered, I'm pretty blunt. I like to think it's a strength of mine, but not everyone is as forthcoming and honest as I am. Adam needs to be eased into things. He's the most stubborn clamshell I have ever known."

But Adam *had* opened up to me about some things. Maybe he hadn't been as open as he might have been if we didn't have the history we did, but even if I didn't know everything about his past, I understood enough about his present to know that what Adam needed most from me were consistency and steadiness.

"I wasn't sure I was going to like you," I admitted. I nibbled on my lip. "But you've helped put things into perspective for me."

"I wasn't sure I was going to like you either. I wanted to meet you but Adam said no. More or less. He's barely mumbled more than a handful of words over the last few days." She sipped her water. "You're different than the other girls he's dated."

With a smile I motioned toward her. "I'm not surprised."

"What do you mean by that?"

"Oh, nothing bad," I said quickly, worried I'd offended her. "What I mean is that you have this vibe about you that I don't have. You seem more self-assured than I am."

"You look plenty confident to me."

"I am confident in who I am. I'm not confident in stepping out of the box, or getting into a stranger's car to talk about their boyfriend."

"Ah," she said, pointing a finger at me, "but you let a stranger into your car. Which is kind of the same thing."

She had me there.

"But that's not what I meant when I said that you weren't like other girls he's dated."

"Then what did you mean?"

"I mean you're the only one of them who has tied him up in knots."

"Oh, I don't think…"

"Speaking from someone on the other side, you tie him up in knots. He has ignored my texts for weeks about you. If he actually talked to me about you, then I'd know he didn't take things that seriously. Sorry," she said with a lift of her shoulder. "But that's how Adam is. If he won't talk about a girl, it's because he has Feelings with a capital F."

It was hard to believe that he had feelings for me, especially the big and scary kind like I had for him.

But I knew one thing: I could continue to travel the entire world and not ever feel for someone else the way I felt about Adam. And I knew that even if Sarah and I hadn't had this dinner, I still would have stuck around—whether he wanted me to or not. The small thing I had left for him, before talking to Sarah, said exactly that.

43

ADAM

I HAD MOVED TO THE COUCH INSIDE, BUT I WAS STILL IN A WEIRD mix of feeling sorry for myself while also loathing myself. I had been a total asshole to Hollis, undeservedly so. I knew it too. It was my curse: making people leave me before they chose it on their own.

When Sarah strolled in, I was poking a fork at a burnt edge of a cheesy casserole on my plate. Typically, I wouldn't have acknowledged her. But the cat that ate the canary curve of her lips made me narrow my eyes at her. I *knew* that look.

Still, I didn't want to give her any more attention than necessary, hoping she'd get the fucking hint and take off with Bobby.

"I know you're curious," she said. "So why don't you spare us the suspense and ask what you're really wondering?"

I bit down on the burnt cheese and nearly gagged from the bitterness. Dropping my fork onto my plate, I turned to her with a roll of my eyes. "Oh. You mean the 'when are you leaving' question?"

Her smile stretched wider, blindingly so. "Okay, you got me there. Why don't you ask me the *other* question you're wondering about?"

"I'm not wondering anything."

"Oh, fuck off, Adam. You're a terrible liar."

If it'd get her off my back, I might as well ask. "Okay, where were you?"

Sarah clapped, snapping me awake. "With Hollis. Having dinner."

It was as startling as the scratch of a record. "What?"

"You heard me." She sat back on the couch, crossing her ankles. "We had dinner. It was great."

I closed my eyes. Not a minute went by without me wanting to call Hollis and apologize. "What did she say?"

"Oh…" she said, drawing out the syllable like the word was twenty letters long. "Just that she's gonna stick around. So whatever bullshit thoughts you have about shoving her away some more, you might as well abandon them. You're just wasting your breath."

I picked my plate up and brought it into the kitchen, needing the distance to think. I hated being the topic of conversation for just about everyone except Hollis. The fact that Sarah had facilitated it gave me a little hope, because despite how annoying she was, I knew she cared. I could cut her some slack.

Sarah followed me into the kitchen.

"You know you need someone like her, someone who will put up with your bullshit."

I turned the water on, waiting for it to get hot. "My bullshit? That's exactly why we broke up."

"No, numb-nut, we broke up because you don't talk about your feelings and I have diarrhea of the mouth—we didn't jive. Oil and water, you and I." She took a deep breath. "And the other reason we broke up was because you didn't and couldn't love me. Not like the way you love Hollis."

The plate in my hands nearly cracked in half. "What?"

"Do you need to clean your ears out or something? You heard me."

"I don't think I did, because whatever you said was really off base."

"Uh huh, sure. That's why every time I say her name you look like a dog awaiting a treat."

I winced. "That's a terrible metaphor."

"It's only terrible because it's true. I love you, Adam—"

At my sharp look, she gave me a look of her own.

"Like a brother, but sometimes you behave as if you aren't very smart. The symptoms are all there."

"I don't have any symptoms."

"Tsk, tsk, what did I just say about behaving as if you aren't very smart? You are smart, Adam, and that's why it would be really great for everyone if you'd just figure your life out."

I glared at her and shoved my dish into the dishwasher. "Figure my life out? My gram just died. After the funeral, Caleb is going to head back to school and I'll—"

"Be here." She placed her hands on my shoulders, stilling me. "Because you love Casey. You'll stay here and the life you thought you had in Colorado is not going to be the same life you'll have here and that's okay because you'll make the best of it. Because deep down, you want to be here with Casey." She squeezed my shoulders. "And maybe Hollis, too."

In my mind, I had long accepted the fact that I would inevitably leave the band. And I had committed so deeply to that belief that leaving Hollis had never even been a possibility for me. Thinking now about leaving her now, after everything we'd gone through together, made me feel like I had choked down a handful of rocks that sat heavy in my gut.

"You're not arguing with me," she said slowly as if she was testing the waters.

"Because," I said, heaving a sigh, "you just might be right."

"Of course I am." She ruffled my hair. "Now, since I'm guessing you were a giant a-hole to her, how are you gonna make it up to her?"

I had nothing to give her, and I was shit at apologies. "I was working on a song about her. It wasn't really for her, it was for me."

"The fact that it's about her means it's for her." She pushed me aside, motioning for me to leave the kitchen. "Get to work. Maybe a little piano is what you need right now."

I could think half a dozen things I needed right then, all of them beginning and ending with Hollis. But Sarah was right. I needed to make it up to Hollis.

I looked out the kitchen window, my eyes catching on Gram's rosebushes. With all the uninhibited sun we'd been having lately, they bloomed so big that it seemed a crime to leave them in Gram's yard.

I needed to get to work.

So focused was I when I entered my bedroom that I almost didn't see it right away. But there, on my keyboard, was a little sticky note.

Grief is a lonely experience, but I just want you to remember you are not alone. I'm here. I'll be here still.

Underneath the note was another rose. I held the note in my hands, shaking it for a moment. I didn't believe it was actually real.

Seconds later, I unearthed the note from high school at the bottom of my dresser. I put them side by side. I knew they'd both been penned by Hollis, but seeing them side by side felt somehow full circle. Well, nearly. I'd need to complete that circle for her.

Casey knocked on my open doorway. "Hey," she said. "Hollis asked me to leave that note for you. She didn't want to violate your privacy. I told her your room stinks anyway, so I might as well do it."

I laughed despite the insult. She leaned against the doorjamb, looking way older than her age.

"My room doesn't smell bad."

"It reeks of your cologne."

Trust my sister to always bust my balls. Sarah had been at the house the last couple of days, so she had really been able to see the dynamic Casey and I had, and how we kept things running. Did I want to be a part of the band and back in Colorado? So much had changed. If I could have had the band and stayed here, I would've. But the heart of it all was that I wanted to be here, with Casey. And, yes, Hollis too. "Things are going to be a little weird around here for a while."

She nodded. "I know."

"It might just be you and me figuring things out."

"That's what we've already been doing for the last month, Adam."

I blinked. She was right.

"I know you're worried, but you don't really need to be. Gram was the smartest lady we ever knew and she knew to count on you." She gave me a smile that I didn't realize I needed from her. "Now stop being a dummy and say you're sorry to Hollis."

"Did she tell you anything?"

"No. She didn't have to. I heard you talking to her outside earlier. She's not gonna leave us. I know she won't."

"How do you know so much for only being thirteen?"

"I'm not a baby. Sometimes I think you forget that you left before I turned ten. I have a pretty good understanding of things now. Just like how I know you want Dad to stop breaking his promises to me and he never does."

Dad hadn't even tried getting a hold of us. His mother had died, and he didn't fucking care. "Maybe one day he will."

"He won't, and you know it. It's better if we stop expecting him to get better on his own."

It was surreal, having a grown-up conversation with my thirteen-year-old sister. She's seen more cruelty from the world than probably a good chunk of thirteen-year-olds, but she still maintained a happy and bubbly personality. The world wouldn't break her. Which meant I wouldn't, either. We'd be okay.

44

HOLLIS

IT WAS TIME TO COME CLEAN. I MADE SURE THAT EVERY HAIR ON my head was in place, that every wrinkle had been flattened. I was prepared to face my parents, to tell them everything.

But right at their door, I nearly chickened out. I had driven all the way to southern Utah to face them on their turf. Seven hours in each direction. I left my home at three in the morning to ensure I would make it before noon, just in case, and was banking on returning shortly after meeting with them, so I didn't miss the wake for Adam's grandmother.

It would have been a lot easier if I had just called or texted, but both would be cowardly. And if there was one thing I knew, it was that being brave was the best way to honor my feelings for Adam. And doing that meant telling my parents I had been lying to them. For two years.

My mom answered the door, the surprise on her face carefully concealed—well, nearly. I got my expressive eyes from her, and noted the way they widened. We hadn't spoken since that fateful dinner, a night that had been pivotal for me. "Hollis."

"Hi, mom. Is dad here?"

"He's just in his study."

I nodded, looking around as a way to calm my nerves. "I need to speak to you both."

"All right." She turned, heels clacking their way down the wide hallway to the living room. "I'll go get your father."

I barely managed a robotic nod as she left. I took a seat in the lone armchair, the one my father usually favored. I thought of the isolation from the sofa as a kind of armor. I would be able to face them both simultaneously. And then I'd be able to leave.

My father made me wait until he knew I'd be overcome with anxiety. It was his way. I heard every second of the clock tick, felt every beat of my heart, in the minutes that separated my arrival from my father's.

When they both finally joined me, I nearly doubled over from the stress. From the look on my father's face, he knew that he was in for something. "Hollis. This is a surprise."

"Yes." I spread my hands across my lap, smoothing whatever wrinkles had formed in my slacks. I had dressed pretty professionally for an impromptu meeting with my parents but to them, appearance was everything. They wouldn't have taken me seriously if I had worn jeans and a simple tee.

"What is this about?" He looked around the room. "I see you didn't bring your boyfriend with you."

"No." I still hadn't heard from him. It'd been a long few days and his grandmother's wake was that evening. I had waffled on whether or not to go, ultimately deciding that I needed to prove I was as solid as I had told Sarah I was. I'd be there for him whether he asked me to be or not.

"And yet you drove all this way to speak with us? It must be important."

He knew whatever I had come to say was important. I had dressed for battle. But he was a fan of gaining the upper hand

and must have sensed the anxiety that practically oozed from my pores.

"It's very important." I took a deep breath. "I've been lying to you."

My mother blinked once and my father settled in.

"For two years, give or take."

I was postponing. Like I needed full lungs in order to say each sentence.

"The truth is, I was not dating Adam when I said I was." And like a faulty dam, the truth just poured out. "He was someone I had a crush on in his school, and someone I admired from afar for a very long time. When you changed the terms of the trust, I panicked. Tori tried to help me by saying his name and in truth, the fake boyfriend I'd been telling you about had been slightly modeled after him."

They were both silent for a long moment before my mother finally piped up. "But why invent a fake boyfriend in the first place? You've been saying you have a boyfriend for the last few years."

"Because you both kept trying to set me up with sons of your colleagues or employees. I wasn't interested, and no matter how many times I expressed that to you, you were unrelenting."

My dad finally spoke. "So you lied."

I wouldn't make any more excuses for it. I nodded.

He continued. "And this Adam person just agreed to go along with everything?"

I hated how he referred to him, like he was some criminal I'd plucked up off the street in desperation. "Adam agreed, yes. And then something happened. I started to develop real feelings for him. And I think he feels those same things for me." I closed my eyes briefly, sending up a prayer to whoever was listening that what I felt in my heart was true.

"Well, I'm just shocked that you thought lying was the way to get what you wanted."

"For you to get off my back about setting me up with people you know?"

"To gain access to your trust." He leveled me with his steely gaze. "You put up this charade just for some money."

This was the part where things were going to turn. I felt it deep in my veins, the rapid race to pump blood into my heart. "Yes. It wasn't as much about the money as it was the freedom."

"Freedom?" My father stood up as if on cue in my mind, the way I'd replayed this moment a dozen times. "You come to our door. You aren't chained up or forced to be here. What freedom do you need?"

"The freedom to choose my own future." I swallowed. "Ever since I was a child, you've dangled that trust over my head with a promise that if I followed your instructions for how I led my life, I would gain access to those funds." I willed my pulse to calm, hoping to say this with as much kindness and grace as possible. "You dictated where I went while I was in high school, and what I studied in college. I'm in my senior year and you want me to go on to law school next year. And, well, that's not something I want for myself." I clasped my hands in my lap, so tight I knew my knuckles were white. "I won't take the LSAT. I'm sorry for disappointing you."

They stared at me, dumbstruck. This was my biggest act of rebellion in their eyes, nearly tied with how I'd behaved at dinner with Adam. "When were you planning on telling us this?"

"I wasn't planning on telling you at all. I was going to go to law school, because you wanted me to. I was going to figure out a way to do what I wanted while making you happy."

"What changed?"

I looked down at my hands. "Everything." When I lifted my head again, I hoped I looked strong. "I understand that this means I lose my trust. And if you don't want to pay my final semester of college, well, I suppose I will figure that out too."

My dad, who was leaning on the back of the couch where my mom sat, made a sound like he was about to speak, buy my mom's hand covered his on the couch. "We will pay for your final semester, Hollis. We paid for college for both of your sisters."

"Lot of good that did for them," my father interjected.

"But, yes, you're right. You will not receive the trust as planned."

I nodded, having already come to peace with the idea of losing it. I wouldn't be able to leave immediately after college and start making an impact in all the places around the world I wished to. But, I could start here at home until the rest of the world was a possibility.

When neither of my parents said anything, I stood on shaky legs. "Thank you," I said to them both. "I need to return to Amber Lake."

My dad looked like he'd been hit by a car. He just stared blankly, while my mom gave me a sympathetic smile. I said my goodbyes and headed out the door.

I made it to the wake right at the tail end, changing to flat shoes before dashing through the doors of the space Adam and his brother had rented out for the occasion. It was a small hotel, with one convention room, and even though the room was crowded with people it didn't feel stifling—it felt warm, cozy.

I searched out Adam's head, but I wasn't tall enough. I should have kept the heels on, I realized too late.

"Hey," Navy said, clasping my hand in hers and tugging me through a crowd until we reached a table full of refreshments. "I was hoping you'd be able to make it."

"There was traffic in Ogden, so I sped a little once I hit the border."

384

"Wooo," Navy said in a low voice. "You? Sped?"

"I know." My cheeks warmed. "I didn't want to miss it. But it looks like I'm right at the tail end."

"Yeah, there were even more people here, but it's dispersing now it's technically over."

"Hey Hollis." Keane came up behind us, putting an arm around me. There was a soft piano playing somewhere on speakers, but it could barely be heard over the conversations happening around us.

"Hey." I leaned into him, giving him a side hug. "How is he doing?"

"Better." He lifted a plastic cup to his mouth. "A lot better, actually."

It lifted my heart to hear. "I'm glad." I searched once again, hoping to see him but it was useless; there were too many people.

"Hollis," said a feminine voice from behind me. I turned, and in the crowded space I nearly bumped right into Sarah. She was standing next to a guy with shaggy blond hair.

"Hi Sarah."

"This is Bobby, my boyfriend."

Bobby's eyes were steady, focused, as he looked over my face. "You're Adam's girlfriend."

It wasn't a question, but I felt compelled to answer it anyway. But the problem was, I didn't know *what* we were. We'd both acknowledged that things had changed during our time as a fake couple. But we hadn't really figured out what that was, together. I knew, for me, it was everything. He'd gone from being a guy I'd crushed on to a guy I'd fallen in love with. Calling him my boyfriend felt so small, like it didn't articulate my feelings at all.

"Yes," Navy said for me, which was good enough.

Bobby shook my hand and introduced me to another band mate who'd made the trip for the wake. After I had shaken hands with a few other people, I was beginning to feel like a specimen under a microscope. They were all weighing and measuring me, to determine if I was worth Adam's time. And I was grateful for it. I wanted Adam to be surrounded by people who loved him, who looked after him.

I wished I had met his gram. As I moved through the crowd of people, being introduced to a number of people who had known her, my desire to know her myself just poured through me. I wanted to know the woman the way these people did. To hear them speak so reverently about her made me yearn for things that I had never know. But if I had learned anything over the last few weeks with Adam, it was that I couldn't go back and change things that had happened. I could only change what was to come.

Slowly, people began filing out, emptying the room in a slow trickle. I still hadn't seen Adam, and I was buzzing from coming clean to my parents and from not seeing him for the last few days. I couldn't wait to see him, to talk to him again. But no matter how hard I looked, I couldn't find him.

I found Casey, who launched herself at me with a hug. "You made it!"

I stroked her hair, squeezing her. "Of course I did."

"I'm so happy." She stepped back. "But Adam isn't here. He left a little bit ago."

I deflated at that. "Oh. Okay."

"You might be able to reach him on his phone."

I made a noncommittal noise. "Okay."

"Caleb is taking me back home. Want to come over for dinner?"

"Uh…"

"It's just going to be the leftovers from here. But if you come early, we can eat the good stuff and leave the hot dog salad for the boys." She stuck her tongue out in disgust.

"Hot dog salad?" I had never heard of such a thing.

"Yeah, I don't think that person likes us much." Casey shrugged and then hugged me again. "I have to go. Caleb is grumpy because he leaves tomorrow morning."

"Okay." It wasn't until after she left that I realized I hadn't told her I wouldn't come by Adam's house. Which meant I'd need to. As much as I wanted to see Adam again, I didn't want to see him if he wasn't ready to see me. A wake was bound to stir up emotions, and he might want to grieve privately. While I wanted to show him I'd be there for him, I didn't want to force my way when I wasn't welcome.

My phone buzzed in my pocket. It'd been blissfully quiet over the last week when I had started telling people no. It was still a struggle to say the word in person, but as Adam had reminded me, it was just two letters. So texts with "no" were being more liberally used.

I waited until I was outside of the doors before I pulled my phone out. I waved goodbye to Navy who climbed into Keane's car and opened my phone.

It was one word. Two letters.

But it wasn't the word Adam had taught me to use. No, it was the word I had taught him to use.

Hi.

How could one simple word have such an effect on me? It was if someone had tied a powerful balloon around my waist and just lifted me off the ground for how light I felt. I clutched my phone to my chest like it was my very lifeline.

Surprisingly, moisture pricked my eyes. I hadn't known how starved I was to hear from him until he sent me a text with two letters.

Hi, I replied.

I watched the bubbles appear, showing that he was typing a reply and closed my phone as I got into my car. I waited a full twenty seconds before starting the car, wanting to obey the law while also making sure I read his texts as they came in.

As soon as I turned the key in the ignition, my phone pinged.

I feel like we need to talk.

My car read the text to me in its robotic feminine voice and the high I had been experiencing from his first text dipped and became a low that I was ill-prepared for.

I reminded myself to calm, that a talk really was necessary at this point. So much had changed in the week we'd spent apart. There was a lot to discuss, so I had no reason to believe anything bad awaited me.

Where? It was the only word I could manage.

Deb's Pizza. I'm already there.

I drove that way, routinely taking a hand off the steering wheel to shake it. I thought I'd been nervous about facing my parents, but facing Adam when things were so uncertain between us felt wholly terrifying.

I pulled into Deb's pizza, wishing the windows weren't so tinted. Maybe if I could see Adam before entering, I'd feel calmer. But the windows were opaque. Adam would see me coming, but I wouldn't see him. I turned off my car and my phone pinged a text notification.

It was from Adam, but it was an audio file.

I hit play, expecting to hear his voice. But there were no

words to the music. It was quiet for a long moment, and then a piano began playing. I closed my eyes, knowing immediately who was playing the music. I tried to pay close attention to the melody, to see if I knew what song it was because it was so familiar. It was like the game we'd played at my parents' house, on their piano.

The melody was low and slow, starting sad with brief moments of lighter notes sprinkled in. What was the song? It was so familiar, I knew without a doubt that I had heard it before. Some of the keys were held down for long moments, and I listened to the way each note slowly dissipated, replaced by the next one.

And then it hit me. It was the song Adam had written about me.

45

ADAM

SHE WAITED IN HER CAR LONG ENOUGH TO GIVE ME PAUSE. SO I sent her the audio file I had recorded late one night, immediately after finishing the final section of the song. It was one of the easiest songs I'd ever written, mostly because it'd been so organically created. I hadn't been playing in order to create something catchy. I had just spilled all my thoughts to the piano via my fingers. There were sadder moments throughout the song, but toward the end it picked up in a thrumming beat, akin to a heartbeat. Faster and faster it went until the very end, when the lightest of notes trickled through.

I watched her dip her head as she listened, watched her concentration furrow her brows. I fucking loved how expressive she was. And that was just one of the things on the list of things I loved about her.

It was a heavy thing to say to myself. But I didn't want another few years to go by without us talking again.

When she exited the car, the moonlight hit her back,

illuminating her like a halo. I had once thought of her as half-witch and half-angel and now, I prayed she was the latter.

When she opened the door, coming into the light of the restaurant, the first thing I noticed was the light sheen across her eyes. I couldn't get to her fast enough, but I forced myself to approach her slowly. I didn't want to rush her, not after she'd been so patient with me. She wore black pants and a white shirt tucked neatly into them. Her hair was pulled back into a pretty severe ponytail, but the softness of her face balanced all of that out.

"Hello," I said, stopping an arm's reach from her.

She smiled softly, giving me a lightness in my chest. "Two hellos in one day. What's come over you?"

"Probably whatever it was that came over you the day you swore twice."

She blushed.

"You hungry?"

She looked at the menu above the counter. "Yes." She turned back to me. "You didn't want the hot dog salad leftovers, I take it?"

I shuddered, remembering the bowl of questionable contents at the wake. "No. I'll let Casey and Caleb battle it out for that."

"I looked for you at the wake, but I didn't see you."

"I ducked out early. I'm sorry."

"It's okay. I just—"

"Can I help you?" the worker at the counter asked, interrupting Hollis.

"I want a big slice of the pepperoni." I turned to Hollis. "What do you want?"

She licked her lips and it took everything in me to tell my body to calm down. I wanted to lean in, to capture her mouth in mine, to nibble right where she'd just licked.

391

"I want what you're having."

Without tearing my eyes from Hollis, I held up two fingers to the worker. "Two of those please. And two sodas. One diet and one root beer."

Hollis's cheeks bloomed that pretty pink. "I loved your song," she said.

"It's really yours. I wrote it for me, but it became yours."

She sucked her bottom lip in, like she was trying to tuck away a smile. "It was transcendent."

"Good. Because that's how I felt, writing it."

She seemed to shrink from the compliment, her eyes looking everywhere but at my face. Her shyness was so fucking endearing. I loved that she looked at me like that, like we were back in high school. Except this time, we'd have a much better ending. As long as she agreed.

"You look really nice by the way," she told me, taking in the all black suit I wore, accompanied by the black dress shirt. She reached out like she was going to touch the lapels of my jacket but pulled her hands back, unsure.

I closed my hands over hers and brought them back to her original destination. She looked right into my eyes, as her hands grazed the lines of the jacket. She flattened her hands against my chest, her fingers curling just slightly so that I felt all ten indentations of her fingertips.

Fuck.

"I don't—"

"Here's your sodas," the worker interrupted, setting the cups down on the counter hard enough to spill a little. What Deb's Pizza lacked in finesse, it made up for in pizza which is the only reason I didn't grab Hollis by the hand and run out.

"You're beautiful," I told her. "Always."

If I could live off of her blushes, I gladly would. Each time her cheeks burned pink, I just wanted to make it happen again.

"I've missed you," I told her, knowing I needed to make

amends. "I shouldn't have said those things to you. You didn't deserve it. When I pulled my head out of my ass, I realized how wrong I had been. I was reactionary. And I'm sorry."

"It's okay, Adam. I understand."

"It isn't okay, Hollis. But thank you for forgiving me." I took a deep breath and summoned up every ounce of courage I possessed. "I don't know—"

"And your pizzas," the worker said, slapping two greasy slices on the counter. I breathed in through my nose, frustrated by the constant interruptions.

I stacked the two paper plates of pizzas and tucked my soda in the same arm so that I had a hand free to hold Hollis's with. She made a move to lead me to a table, but I tugged her, angling my head to the other side of the restaurant.

"This way." I had arrived early on purpose, and the purpose awaited Hollis in the booth at the back of the restaurant.

When Hollis laid her eyes on the pile of roses on the table, her eyes went as wide as the paper plates I held.

"These are from Gram's rosebushes. She used to get mad when I was little and I had picked them for her. But I think she would approve of me picking them for you."

She set her soda down so she could scoop them up and push her face in the red blooms. Her eyes closed as she inhaled. When she opened her eyes, she looked a little overwhelmed. "These are beautiful."

"I've been looking outside the kitchen window all week at these. I can't look at them and not think of you." Her natural blush matched their shade perfectly.

"Did you get my note?"

"Yeah, I did." I played with the ends of her ponytail. "I'm glad to see your drawing skills haven't improved."

She laughed, playfully hitting me on the shoulder. "I told you I wasn't an illustrator."

"I know. And that's why I love it so much. It's the same rose I stared at the day I found it. The same rose that meant so much to me at the time. And means even more now."

"I had Casey help me."

"I know. She told me. Look," I said, sliding into the booth across from her. I set my soda down and the pizza slices too. "I don't know where this is going to take us. I know you have ambitions and those ambitions might take you to various countries far away from here. I want all of them to happen for you." I swallowed and reached across the table to hold her hand, when I was at my most vulnerable. "We will figure out the details. But I just wanted you to know."

She had been smiling shyly at me the whole time, but when I stopped she asked, "You want me to know what?"

"That I'm in love with you, Hollis."

I heard her sharp intake of breath. "Oh."

I couldn't help it, I laughed. "You and your 'oh's get me every fucking time."

She swallowed. "You caught me by surprise."

"Good. I'm going to work on doing that more often, if you're agreeable to it."

She grinned, her hand squeezing mine. "I suppose I can. It's handy, since I'm in love with you too."

I wished I hadn't just taken a bite of pizza, because I nearly choked on it. "Wow," I said, swallowing. "That is handy."

"I wish we were anywhere but here right now," she said.

"I know. Because you're so private." I gestured to the empty tables around us. "That's why I chose this dimly lit, sorta sketchy corner. No one's over here. It's just you and me." And that's how I wanted it to be. No more fake bullshit, no social media pressures. Just Hollis and me.

"Hi," I said after she took her first bite.

She laughed and covered her mouth with a napkin. "You already said that."

"I feel like I owe you a few more."

She nodded and took a sip of her soda. "Just as long as you don't say goodbye."

I rubbed my finger over the back of her hand, loving how heavy-lidded her eyes went. "Trust me, Hollis. I don't plan on it."

EPILOGUE

THREE MONTHS LATER

HOLLIS

"What are you doing?" I asked, groceries slipping off my shoulder to land on the counter. Tori was crawling on all fours on the ground of the apartment I shared with Navy—the apartment we now shared with Tori, too.

"Trying to make my cat feel comfortable."

"What?" I pulled the groceries out, one-by-one, and set them inside the fridge. "You're crawling on all fours for your cat?"

"She's hiding somewhere. She's been hiding since I brought my stuff here."

Tori had moved in the week before, sharing a bedroom with me in the meantime until she found her own place. She'd decided that living with her parents after having lived on her own wasn't the most fun she'd ever had, so she'd made the trip up to Amber Lake in order to spend time with her friends and figure out what she wanted to do next. Which, apparently, was to crawl on all fours around our apartment. When she made a meowing noise, I laughed.

"Laugh now, but it'll work. Believe in me."

"I don't *not* believe in you." I glanced at the clock. Casey would be getting off the bus soon at the edge of the apartment complex and walk the rest of the way to my apartment. That was our new routine. She'd bus to my apartment, we'd work on her homework, have dinner, and then we'd go to Adam's house until he got off of work. Technically, Casey was old enough to be home alone. But neither Adam or I wanted her to be alone. The last four months had been full of changes and we both wanted to make sure that what remained steady for Casey was that she always had someone to lean on.

Tori meowed again, shuffling across the floor in front of me. "You look ridiculous."

"Not to Margaret, I don't." She paused, sitting back on her feet. "When the hell is she going to come out?"

"Maybe when you stop scaring her more." I sat on the sofa, flipping the television on stretching my feet out on the coffee table in front of me. "I'm sure the moment you stop worrying about her will be the moment she comes out."

"Ugh." Tori crawled her way to the sofa and sank into it. "Maybe I should've left her at my parents' house."

"They're your parents now? Not your roommates?"

"You and Navy are my roommates now, so yeah, they're just the parents again." She swiped a hand over her honey-colored bangs and panted for a moment. "I probably should've changed out of my skinny jeans before crawling all over the floor."

"Probably." I heard the whistle of the bus stopping just outside of my apartment. Normally, we'd follow our routine as usual—heading to Adam's house after dinner so that Casey could be in bed before Adam got home. But Adam had worked out his schedule at his job so that he had Fridays and Saturdays off. And most of those Fridays and Saturdays, he spent doing the drive to Colorado and back. It wasn't ideal or sustainable for the long term, but it gave Adam some happiness that he'd been missing the last couple months. It was seven hours each direction, and he got very little sleep the days he traveled, but he got to do a few Friday night shows with his band and come home the following day.

He talked about doing tutoring like Navy had suggested, at her aunt's music store, but he was waiting for the winter months, when driving to Colorado every week would be more dangerous.

Christmas was one week away and because we'd had a milder winter so far, Adam hadn't stopped the travel to Colorado just yet.

The front door opened and Casey came through, bringing with her a gust of cold air and a grin. "Adam comes home tomorrow, right?"

"Yep." I patted the empty cushion between Tori and me and she slumped down to it. She was still cold from the exposure, so I tossed a throw blanket on her lap. "He left around noon."

"What kind of crap are they asking you to learn this week?" Tori asked as Casey dug into her backpack. Having Tori around to help make Casey feel more welcome had been a welcome surprise. The way Tori's mind worked fascinated me, and seeing her walk Casey through the math or English homework she brought home made me feel warm and fuzzy, like Casey's family was expanding. I settled in, watching them go through problem after problem while I looked on. Out of habit, I checked the weather conditions along the route for Adam's drive. Most of the way he was fine, until he hit Loveland, Colorado—roads were already closing for the weekend due to heavy snowfall. It made me nervous, even though Adam's car was equipped with snow tires.

I wanted to text him and ask how his drive was going but

then again, I didn't want him to look at his phone either. I felt like a mother hen sometimes and worked to suppress it.

But by the time dinner had come and gone—lasagne, thanks to Navy's cooking—I hadn't heard one peep from Adam which was unusual. He always called me when he stopped for gas at his halfway point, but it was long past the time he was due to arrive there.

Casey and I drove to her house, and worry had me chewing on my lower lip. The weather was bitingly cold in Amber Lake; cold enough to freeze the roads, but since there was no snow, we didn't have to worry about bad roads, which gave me the space to worry about Adam.

Casey unlocked the front door with my keys and bounded inside. "I'm going to take a quick shower!" she called out as she disappeared down the hall.

I sank to the couch and turned the television on, hoping to distract myself with some nonsense until I heard from him one way or another. The pipes clanked as Casey turned the water on and I abandoned the television in order to pace. He definitely would have called me. He always did.

I checked the weather again, seeing the conditions worsening shortly after where his half-way point was. I couldn't wait any longer and decided to send him a text. *Hey, how is it going?*

I stared at the screen, willing him to reply, but all I saw was that my message had been delivered.

Sinking back into the couch, I told myself that he was just focused on the drive. Maybe he wanted to keep both hands on the steering wheel the whole way.

But that did little to appease my worry, because then all I could think about was Adam getting stuck in Colorado and not being able to return home.

After Casey had changed in her pajamas, she stayed up late with me to watch a rom-com on Netflix. I braided her hair into two French braids, talking her through the process so that she would know how to do it herself.

The time with Casey had worked, sufficiently distracting me from my worry about Adam until Casey started brushing her teeth. It had been ten hours since he'd left, which was when his show was to start. Maybe he'd barely gotten to the venue and was too busy to call. I'm sure he'd call after.

I was the first to admit that I didn't love that he was gone so often. Selfishly, I wanted to spend Fridays and Saturdays with him, but I knew that we would as soon as winter really began. But the smile on his face when he came home reminded me of how much he loved it, despite all the drive time. I loved spending time with Casey anyway and we'd settled into an easy Monday-Saturday routine, just the two of us. Being at Adam's so much afforded me quiet time to study anyway.

But still, I missed him.

Casey walked back into the living room and stopped abruptly. "Who's that?"

I turned to see where she was pointing outside the windows. Headlights flashed on the glass, bouncing up and down as they came down the rocky drive. As soon as the car stopped moving, I recognized it immediately and was out the door without a second thought.

Adam had barely made it out of the car before I launched myself into him. He dropped the backpack he held and wrapped his arms solidly around me.

"You're shaking," he said, lifting me up off the ground a few inches. I never felt safer than when I was in his arms. I squeezed him, aware that my anxiety had been more pronounced than I'd originally thought.

"I was so worried when you didn't call," I replied, my lips at his ear. Despite being out in the cold, he was so warm, warm enough that I squeezed him tighter, as if his warmth could eliminate my own shaking.

"I barely made it to the halfway point and didn't get a chance. I'm sorry." He pulled back so I could face him. It had only been ten hours since I'd last seen him, but each time he returned it was like he'd been away on a long trip. I held his face in my hands, peering up into those soulful eyes I loved so.

"What are you doing back so soon?"

"Show was canceled. Whiteout conditions in Denver. And in Wyoming, for that matter." His lips looked cold, so I rubbed them with my thumb.

"Why do you look so happy about that?"

"Because that meant I got to come home." He gave me a lip-smacking kiss, and I rubbed my hands up and down his back, warming him as much as I could. "Don't get me wrong, I was looking forward to the show, but I was relieved when Bobby texted that it was canceled."

I grabbed his backpack while he reached in the back for his keyboard and we walked inside, hand in hand. Adam gave Casey hugs and sank onto the couch after she'd gone to bed. I collapsed right beside him, snuggling up against him, my legs over his outstretched ones. I didn't want to let him go. I didn't think it would be possible for us to get even closer than we were after everything, but each day there was a new layer exposed and explored, longer talks about our pasts and our futures.

"I'm sorry your show was canceled," I said as Adam put his arm around me and sighed.

"Don't be. The minute I got in the car and started the drive to Colorado, I was ready to be home again."

I leaned back so I could look into his face. "But you always look so happy when you come home. You have the biggest smile."

He smiled softly as he looked down at me. "Yeah, because I'm home. With you and Casey." His fingertip brushed the tip of my nose. "I love the band, but the band isn't everything to me."

My heart turned over in my chest. "What are you going to do in the off months?"

"Tutor, probably. Maybe even start composing music. I know a guy who knows a guy who knows a guy, and I bet I could get some easy freelance work here and there until we figure out what we want to do."

I loved the sound of that we in his sentence. Even though I was a planner by nature and ingrained habit, I loved the idea of figuring things out with Adam. He and Casey had come into my life when I was without a tether. I understood why my sisters went off and made lives of their own; why Angie had joined a commune and why Layla was swimming with sharks. They needed to build a family that fit them. And I'd needed the same.

I cozied into Adam's shoulder. "Isn't it crazy that this all started way back in high school?" I asked him.

"I know," he agreed quietly. "What if we had never shared that beer?"

"What if I hadn't been nearly drowned by beer?"

"Ah," he said. "Not my favorite memory."

"No?" I asked. "It's one of mine."

"Why?" He sounded like he couldn't believe me.

"Because if it hadn't happened, we might have kissed. And then what? I don't think we would be where we are now. Neither of us was ready for something like this back then. You had to go off to Colorado and play your music. I needed to travel the world. We might have kissed and gone our separate ways, or worse: we might have kissed and changed our plans for each other. Probably end up resenting each other."

He was quiet for a moment. "You know, I think you're right."

"I am."

"Except one thing."

"What?" I sat up straighter so I could face him.

"There is no way," he leaned in and pressed the softest kiss to my lips, "that I would have," another kiss, "kissed you," he gave me a deeper, more toe-curling kiss, "and been able to walk away from you." He cupped the back of my head, angling it as his tongue traced the seam of my lips. When he pulled back, I was breathless and my chest heaved. Somehow, we'd ended up horizontal on the couch, with him hovering over me. Every single one of my limbs turned went loose.

"Oh," was all I managed.

"Yeah," he said with a wicked grin as his head descended again. "Oh."

The end

COMING SOON

One Little Lie is the first book in a series of standalones, each featuring a different character you have already met in this novel. The next book, *One Big Mistake,* Keane's novel, releases in the fall of 2019.

If you would like to be notified as soon as the next book releases, please subscribe to Whitney Barbetti's newsletter at http://www.whitneybarbetti.com/signup/

If you are a blogger and wish to join Whitney's bloggers-only newsletter, you can sign up for that here: http://bit.ly/WB-Bloggers

To read the first chapter of *The Weight of Life* by Whitney Barbetti (a standalone), keep reading!

ACKNOWLEDGMENTS

As always, the first line in my acknowledgments belongs to my family. I spent many hours, days, weeks missing out on time with you to nurture this baby. I love you all.

To my people, the ones who were there during the process that was this book. I have so much more to say, but some things are private, and will be said to you in your signed copies. To keep it brief:

Sona Babani, for being there, always. I'm so glad you were a bitch to me a hundred years ago when we met for the first time.

Jade Eby, my beebee, for cheering me on.

Whitney Giselle Belisle, for being my eagle eye. Thanks for catching the extra nipples.

Talon Smith, for telling me what you did. I'm not sure I would have finished this book if you hadn't.

Megan Martin, for coming in and pointing out some really unfortunate typos and lifting my spirits.

Christina Harris, for lifting me up when I needed it so.

Kristen Johnson, for your memes and your snark.

Lex Martin, for everything, always. Including the blurb for this bad boy.

Debbie Snyder, for being my only friend in Idaho. You get your own pizza place in this book!

Thank you to KP! If commas were worth ten cents, my books would cost a billion dollars before you got your hands on them. Thank, you, so, much.

To the author groups who keep me sane: ST and TW. I'm so honored to be included in these groups and to have your support.

Thank you to my Barbetti Babes—I love each one of you so freaking much. If I could, I'd buy all of you tacos, and nachos. Thank you for traveling far and wide to meet me at signings, and for giving me all the feels with your love and support.

I have one million bloggers to thank, for going out of their way to pimp my books AND me! I value your support and your time, so I thank you for all the times you shared my books with your followers. I know many of you also gifted copies of my books to your friends and/or hosted giveaways for my books. I truly thank each of you. I am AWED by you. You give so much of yourself for authors like me, and I hope you know that you are so deeply appreciated.

Thank you to all my readers. One of the best things about being an author is the relationships I form with the readers who reach out. I love getting to know you on my Facebook fan page, in my reader group, on Twitter or Instagram or email and, if we're lucky, in person at a signing or at an Applebees or on a London train or wherever we both happen to be. You rock my world.

Finally, thank you to my Savior and Lord, Jesus Christ, for giving me strength when I am weak. I was weak so many times while writing this book and was lifted each time by Your grace. Psalm 34:4

THE WEIGHT OF LIFE SYNOPSIS

MILA

"Don't let go." Those were my first words to him, as I hung over the side of a London bridge. The words I would soon say again, in a moment that didn't involve bridges, but something much more fragile: my heart.

He held onto me for three weeks, in a time when I needed to be held. Needed to connect to someone who understood how loss tunneled unrepentantly through the fabric of your soul.

Although he said he'd stay, we both knew he wouldn't. I had already survived one loss—I didn't know if I'd survive another.

AMES

She spun into my life like a tornado of smiles and chatter and everything else I'd long avoided, with a persistence that I admired, albeit begrudgingly. She broke down each neat wall I'd constructed without even trying. Her presence alone caused me to remember what it felt like to smile, to look forward to what the day would bring.

But it was only supposed to last three weeks.

"Don't let go," she'd pleaded.

I'd promised her I wouldn't—but I would. I didn't have a choice.

READ CHAPTER ONE OF THE
WEIGHT OF LIFE

CHAPTER ONE

MILA

Cars passed me and I reached my arms out, letting their lights flash over my body, illuminating me in the pitch-black night, as though they could provide the warmth my arms had been missing for so long.

I tried to imagine that each pass of light had a physical effect on my limbs, like I was experiencing a life renewal on that bridge, washing me of my grief.

But when the lights stopped for a moment and all that enveloped me was silence, everything as it was before, the pain of the memories sliced through me again.

I closed my eyes, curled my fingers into fists, and pulled my arms to my center, holding myself the way he once had.

Someone brushed past me and muttered an accented, "Sorry." I was jolted from the absolute silence of that brief pause in my existence and looked out over the dark abyss in my view.

Westminster Bridge, London, was a magical place—for me, at least. From the side where I stood, legs braced against the railing, it was as if I was on the edge of the world I'd known; a world full of heartache and love and angst, and I was facing the beginning of something new.

Someone else brushed me from behind and I grabbed the straps of my backpack more firmly, reminded that the new world I had found myself in was still occupied by the same people of old, people willing to dip their hands into bags that didn't belong to them and help themselves to the contents anyway.

Below me, the dark vastness of the River Thames glided past, under the bridge, and out the other side. There were murmurs of the other people walking on the bridge, people who walked it without the intention of stopping and inhaling the atmosphere like I did. I reminded myself that while the world continued moving, I was still here—hands gripped like vices on the railing, forcing myself to stand completely still. In ten, twenty years, I wanted to remember what it felt like to stand by the side of a bridge three months after losing the man I'd loved. A bridge we'd planned to visit together, one of many plans that were now forced to be buried in the darker parts of my mind.

But I'd walked the bridge for him, for Colin. I could think of him without crying now, which was a triumph in and of itself. My chest still ached for the piece he'd unknowingly carved from me, and the regret that lived in its recesses was a near-constant reminder.

I pulled up my phone and checked the time. It was seconds from the new hour, which meant Big Ben would chime soon. I smiled at the background photo: Colin and I hanging off the edge of a cliff, safely roped. I remembered that trip—I remembered all our trips. I pressed my finger against his chest in the photo, and vowed to continue my own pursuit of happiness, despite the grief I carried.

I could hear my brother's voice now. *"Mila, you obeyed his final wishes. Don't regret giving him the last thing he asked of you."*

Big Ben punctuated the silence with his first chime and I let out a sigh and chewed on my lips. What my brother said gave me little comfort. I'd never forget that I didn't get the goodbye I wanted.

The bell chimed again and two men laughed, capturing my attention away from the water. I looked up at them, the men in dark hooded jackets, hands tucked into the pockets of running shorts as they approached. One had dark blond curls that battled against the light breeze brushing past us on the bridge. He looked like he belonged on the beaches of California, surfboard in one hand and sunscreen in the other. He had a handsome face, strong features and wide lips.

I turned my attention to his companion, a man who was attractive too—but in a different kind of way. In a way that made me unable to turn away.

His mouth was more serious than the blond man's, and his hair was dark, thick—short on the sides and longer up top. His jaw was clean-shaven, revealing his strong jaw line and full lips. His eyes were cast down, so all I saw was a set of thick lashes as he listened to the blond man talk.

They couldn't have been much older than I was, somewhere in their mid-twenties, but something about the darker haired man caught my attention so much that I didn't realize just how long I was staring at him until his head lifted and his gaze collided with mine. His mouth went slack and a wrinkle formed between his eyes as he took me in.

I should've looked away that second, but there was something about his face. The way his eyes held mine in equal measure, the way he fumbled in his steps, just barely, not enough to attract the attention of the man who walked beside him, but enough that I noticed—it pulled me in. As he moved closer, quiet enveloped me, as if the sound of traffic had been sucked up by a vacuum.

His eyes sharpened. I'd expected brown irises, but his were a light blue-green—maybe hazel. Their lightness contrasted against the dark eyelashes that framed them. He was even more attractive like this, his gaze fixed. It was as if helium had filled my belly, with how light it felt, and my hands tightened on the railing.

He and his companion paused mid-step, ten feet from me, and I didn't know what to do. Should I have averted my eyes and pretended I wasn't staring, or keep staring until he broke contact?

But I didn't get a chance to choose between the two choices, because a sound to my left jarred me, just before someone bumped painfully hard into me. The noise was back again, with a bang in my ears.

Against me, two people struggled with something—a purse or wallet, maybe. "Let go!" the woman yelled as she yanked on the strap. Each time she pulled, the man leaned back harder across my body, pinning me to the railing. He smelled sour, like he'd rolled around in fish. I winced as the scent assaulted my nostrils, and held onto the railing. The back of the railing pressed hard against my spine, leaving me biting down on my lip, leaving me without enough air to yell.

Everyone within a half dozen feet of us paused, taking in the commotion. And then of those people, half of them continued on their walk, clearly desensitized to muggings.

When no one moved to help the poor, elderly woman, I tried to yell at the mugger, but I couldn't fill my lungs to do more than squeak.

The two men I'd seen stepped in, and the struggle intensified.

The mugger tugged again as others' hands closed over his shoulders, pressing me so violently hard against the railing that the wind was knocked out of me. I chanced a glance over my shoulder at the water below, knowing I was a breath from tumbling over the side of the bridge.

The final tug was strong enough to loosen the woman's hands. Any second and he'd have the purse completely in his hands. So, I did something stupid: I pushed his shoulder, jolting him enough that he stumbled back again, and leaned far enough that I flipped right over the rail of the bridge.

I wasn't sure if I screamed. I wasn't sure if I shouted for help. I wasn't sure of anything except grasping desperately for that railing as I backflipped over it, as if my life depended on grabbing it—which it probably did.

My chest slammed against the other side of the railing, but my hands held firmly above me. It was enough to send panic like a lightning bolt through my body. My legs felt tingly then, and I waited to lose my grip and slide right into the murky water that awaited me below. Gravity weighted down my body and I felt my sweaty hands slip.

Just then, a hand closed over my wrist, and tugged it up.

I looked up at the dark-haired man I'd made eye contact with a minute before and my lips trembled open. "Don't let go," I begged.

"I won't. I promise." His other hand closed over my wrist and he pulled, maneuvering me up a few inches.

"I'm going to fall," I gasped, looking over my shoulder. The water, which had felt like a dozen feet below me when I was on top of the bridge, suddenly looked like a hundred feet away now that I dangled above it.

"You're not going to fall." He gritted his teeth, his face determined. "I need you to swing your leg up and hook your foot in this molding." He nodded at the decorative molding holding up the railing.

"I can't. My legs aren't working." Panic was setting in. My

legs were going numb from it. With a calmness I didn't completely feel, I whispered, "Just let me fall."

"What? Are you mad?" He shook his head, and a crease took up residence between his eyebrows. "I'm not letting you go," he bit out in his thick English accent.

"It'll be okay. It's not too far. I can swim."

"You *are* mad. You'll drown before you make it to the side."

"I can swim."

"You just said your legs aren't working. And a frail thing like you won't be able to paddle your way to land." He shook his head. "Why am I even arguing with you? Sam, help me."

The blond man—Sam—appeared beside him, and he reached down, wrapping around my other arm. "On three," Sam said, looking at his friend.

The three seconds they counted felt like a lifetime, but sure enough with their combined strength, they towed me up. The man with dark hair hooked an arm under my legs to haul me over the railing, but my legs collapsed as soon as my feet hit the ground.

He swore under his breath and tugged me up until he could wrap his arms around my back. With my legs loose like Jell-O, I clung to him, trembling, as he supported most of my body weight.

My face pressed against his chest, and I squeezed my lids tight, halting the tears that beckoned. It was all so overwhelming, the fear and shock and now, the safety of his hold. As I regained my bearings, I took in his scent—like apple and basil, but warm too. Perhaps the warmth was from the feel of being in his arms. But it was comforting, the first time I'd found comfort since crossing the Atlantic.

His hands, though they held me, seemed reluctant to do so. And just when I felt them start to ease up, my legs started to feel more solid and I pulled away.

Had I really just embraced a complete stranger? I backed up

a step, stumbling a little like a deer finding its legs for the first time. I looked up into his face, and he stared at me. He didn't look angry, but he didn't look entirely welcoming, either.

"Are you alright?"

I blinked at the question, which had come from Sam. Not the unhappy life raft of a man I'd held on to. I turned to look at him and swallowed before speaking. "I am. T-th-thank you." I let out a breath and pushed my hand through my hair, laughing a little at myself. "I almost went swimming."

"I think swimming is being too generous."

Sam and I turned to the dark-haired man who'd spoken. He looked between us and shrugged. "You're wearing a backpack, boots, and heavy clothing. You'd have sunk." Immediately after saying it, he looked away.

"Ah, true. Next time you want to go swimming, wear something more appropriate." Sam winked at me and put a hand on my shoulder. "Sure you're alright?"

I nodded, eyes dancing over to the other man before I looked at Sam again. "Thank you. Sam, right?"

He smiled, that movie-star smile he'd been wearing when I'd first seen him. "Yes. And this is Ames." He nudged his friend harder than necessary, which caused Ames to glare at him. "That was pretty shit luck, to be pushed over by that pickpocket."

I couldn't stop playing with my hair, thanks to my boundless nerves, the double shock of almost dying to now standing in their presence. With Ames doing his best to avoid looking directly at me and Sam smiling like I'd given *him* some kind of happiness.

"Well, you might've saved my life. Can I—"

"Then why'd you tell me to let you go?"

Ames' harsh words stopped me. He looked me up and down before settling on my face.

"Because I thought I'd fall."

417

"I said I wouldn't let go." He said it defensively, like he was angry I doubted him.

Sam pushed on Ames' shoulder, causing his expression to relax. "I think you need a beer, my friend." Sam looked at me. "And you do, too. Unless you're more of a wine drinker? And what do people call you, besides 'you'?"

Laughing, I shoved my hands into my coat pockets. "People call me Mila. And I think, right now, you could put anything alcoholic in front of me and I'd drink it."

"Then it's settled, Mila. Let's get a drink and celebrate you not sinking to the bottom of the River Thames."

Ames glared at Sam. "Really, Sam?"

"Lighten up, mate." Sam slapped him on his upper back and winked at me. "I'll buy."

"Funny joke." Ames gave him a look that Sam ignored.

"I don't get the joke?" I hadn't meant to say it aloud; I'd meant to ask Sam, but my eyes were on Ames when I asked.

"Because," Sam began, pointing the direction we were to walk to grab a taxi, "Ames runs the pub we're going to."

There was a moment, slight as it was, where I questioned climbing into a taxi with two strangers in a foreign city. But the doubt dissipated as quick as a breath when Sam all but shoved Ames into the taxi, and held the door open for me to climb in after him.

Still, I texted my brother the address Sam gave to the taxi driver. Just in case.

MORE BOOKS BY WHITNEY BARBETTI

All books are available on Amazon

STANDALONES

The Sounds of Secrets
Samson & Lotte

The Weight of Life
Ames & Mila

Hooked (dark romcom)
X & Lucy

Ten Below Zero
Everett & Parker

The Mad Love Duet
Six Feet Under (Book One)
Six & Mira

Pieces of Eight (Book Two)
Six and Mira

The Bleeding Hearts Series
Into the Tomorrows (Book One)
Jude & Trista

Back to Yesterday (Book Two)
Jude & Trista

The He Found Me Series
He Found Me (Book One)
Julian & Andra

He Saved Me (Book Two)
Julian & Andra

ABOUT THE AUTHOR

Whitney Barbetti is a mom to two and a wife to one, living in the northwest United States, where she spends her days writing full time and keeping her boys from destroying her house. She writes character-driven new adult and contemporary adult romances that are heavy on the emotional connection. You'll most likely find her curled up with a good book and a giant glass of wine, with Queen playing through her headphones.

whitneybarbetti.com

If you would like to be notified as soon as the next book releases, please subscribe to Whitney Barbetti's newsletter at http://www.whitneybarbetti.com/signup/

You can also join her Facebook reader's group for book discussions, giveaways, and sneak peeks at upcoming releases: https://www.facebook.com/groups/barbettisbabes

facebook.com/whitney.barbetti

twitter.com/barbetti

instagram.com/barbetti

Made in the USA
Middletown, DE
11 July 2019